SHADOW WARRIORS

NATHAN B. DODGE

WFP
WordFire Press

ISBN: 978-1-61475-687-3

Cover design by Rashed Al-Akroka

Cover artwork images by Rashed Al-Akroka

Kevin J. Anderson, Art Director

Published by
WordFire Press, an imprint of
WordFire, LLC
PO Box 1840
Monument CO 80132

Kevin J. Anderson & Rebecca Moesta, Publishers
WordFire Press Trade Paperback Edition 2018
Printed in the USA

Join our WordFire Press Readers Group and get free books, sneak previews, updates on new projects, and other giveaways. Sign up for free at wordfirepress.com

❀ Created with Vellum

1 CALVIN

Not even 8:00 PM and Dad already drunk. The stench of stale beer and stomach acid assaulted Cal's nose as he sat at his desk, even from the den four doors down the hall.

As if the smell weren't nauseating enough, the sounds echoing down the hall compounded Cal's misery. He could hear Dad mumbling loudly to himself and occasionally singing off-key —an ancient song from long before Mom and Dad were even married by some guy named Michael Bolton. Dad's wheezy, vodka-tainted voice whined the words: "When a ma-an loves a woman," then faded to a boozy mutter, lost in the background noise from the small TV set by Cal's bed.

Cal knew why Dad remembered the words. His mother's favorite, Dad had said. He had sung it to her the day he proposed. At her funeral barely two years ago, Cal had heard Dad humming it, tears streaming down his face, as the minister muttered what he no doubt considered words of consolation, but to Cal's ears sounded like so much static.

They still lived in the house on Radler Street in a quiet neighborhood where Cal attended the quaint, brick high school within walking distance of home. They'd be moving soon; Dad had already lost his job and the car. Moving out of the house in which he had grown up seemed too cruel to contemplate, but Cal knew that Dad hadn't made a house payment in nearly a year, and the notice tacked on the front door listed their house for foreclosure next month.

Alcohol had drowned Dad's job performance and cost them their only means of support months ago. He had sold much of the furniture in the house to buy food and liquor, as he tried, and failed, to cope with Mom's loss. Only Cal's angry protests had turned his father away from Cal's TV as he sought to convert any available possession into cash.

Like Dad's job performance, Cal's grades had gradually deteriorated. Between Dad's drinking and the looming foreclosure, school had somehow seemed to lose its importance.

The off-key singing went up an octave and sputtered into a call for his son. "Cal. Cal! I'm hungry. Can you cook us something?"

Cook something? Maybe a piece of shoe leather or a boiled pair of ancient jeans. His father was out of luck. Cal had eaten the last breakfast cereal, dry, before his father awakened from last night's bender.

Cal knelt beside his bed, reached far into the dusty hollow beneath his box spring and retrieved an old shoe box, the top taped at the rear to the body of the box to make a hinge. Lifting the top, he scanned the small pile of bills. Dad didn't know about his stash, or he would have pilfered it long since. Though mainly money received in birthday and Christmas presents over several years, Cal had added some of his earnings garnered from a year's servitude at the nearby burger joint before things had gone from bad to worse. Now, the money slowly slipped away as he used it to buy food whenever Dad ran completely out of funds. Which he usually did.

Carefully, Cal selected a ten. Enough for a couple of large burgers and maybe fries, plus one Coke. His father liked Coke. Maybe if he brought a large one back with fries and the burger, Dad would lay off the bottle for the rest of the evening.

"Hungry," the whiny voice continued, heavy with self-pity.

In a way, Cal ached for his father. In another way, he resented the self-centeredness that slowly sapped his father's life. That other part wanted to shout back, full of fury, "Just go ahead and die! What use are you to anyone, lying on the couch and drinking us into bankruptcy? Leave me alone!"

Ashamed, he stuffed the box back into a dark, far corner under his bed, well out of sight. Out of Dad's reach or knowledge. He stood, resigned, determined to try to distract his father, maybe help him for one night to forget the beckoning lure of drunken forgetfulness.

Out the west window, a sliver of new moon perched just above the rooftops across the street. He swiveled to take in the pictures by the window, the bookcase stuffed with paperbacks, the trophy for his digital clock science project, a photo of himself dressed in his uniform for the third dan black belt test in Taekwondo. By tradition, he could not progress to the fourth dan for three years, and by that time he would be out of school and probably living with his Aunt Fredene who had offered to take him in last week.

His pivot finally took him to his desk, just left of the window. His history text, open and ignored, lay illuminated by the yellow glow of the desk light. Angrily, he slapped the book closed. All that he had loved spread around him, and all of it about to be lost. He swallowed hard and turned to the bedroom door, determined to buy the burgers and try to sober Dad up for at least one night.

As he turned, he saw a flicker of movement in his right eye, as though a shadow had moved across the window.

And as he turned toward the motion, the Watcher took him.

2 LETICIA

I t had started soon after Mother came home. She breezed into Letty's room, the cloud of Rose, her favorite perfume, over-applied as usual, threatening to strangle Letty with its cloying damask fragrance. A hug, and she flitted away. Mom never bothered to stay long; she made her obligatory appearance and then continued on to more interesting diversions. Occasionally she would ask about school, but tonight she had quickly left for the kitchen, no doubt to see what Maria, their cook and housekeeper, had prepared for the evening meal.

Daddy had arrived earlier, not bothering to stop by Letty's room at all. No doubt he sat at his desk in the study, returning all the calls he had avoided during the day, awaiting Maria's announcement of dinner and enjoying an evening cocktail. Dad had a strict routine: one drink, dinner, and then he worked until ten, disappearing into bed usually about the time Mom turned on the TV or picked up a book.

Letty tried to bring herself back to the English test that loomed on tomorrow's horizon. She loved literature, spending hours reading the "modern" masters like Hemingway and

Thomas Wolfe. Not Tom Wolfe of *The Bonfire of the Vanities*, but Thomas Wolfe, giant of a man and prodigious writer. His *Look Homeward, Angel*, a sumptuous and romantic soufflé of the English language, reduced most authors before or since, in Letty's opinion, to nothing more than hacks.

She hadn't had more than half an hour study time before she heard the first argument of the night erupt. Inevitable, she thought. Daddy had gone ahead and bought the Bentley, despite Mom's objections, and she wasn't about to let him forget it.

"—not like we don't have the Mercedes and your M Four!" The sentence escalated in volume word by word.

Letty didn't want to hear it. She dived onto the pristine pink spread and buried her head beneath a pillow. Why couldn't they either learn to get along or just go ahead with a divorce? They were never happy anymore. The last time she had seen her father smile had been the day she visited him at the company main office. And Mother only displayed her plastic "happy face" at luncheons downtown with her equally rich and supercilious "friends."

Letty often wondered how friendly they'd be if Mom and Daddy were still as poor as they had been on her sixth birthday. She had received a single gift, a small baby doll with red hair ribbons and a lace nightgown, but they had smiled at her and sung "Happy Birthday" and laughed out loud when she had blown out the candles on her small cake, and it had been the happiest day of her life.

After a moment on the bed, she arose and went to the dresser, fluffing her tangled, bushy mop of dark hair back into a semblance of organization but ignoring the need for makeup. The way Mom dressed nowadays made her never want to use makeup again. She wandered back to her desk, staring down at the blank computer screen. That essay on Wolfe and the study for her next test still awaited her.

She had barely taken up her pencil when her dad's voice rose again. "You're one to complain! You spend a thousand dollars a month with that idiot trainer. He has the brain of a mouse! But then, it's his body that you want, isn't it? Are you just doing sit-ups, or is he doing push-ups on *you*?"

The last words, heavy with accusation, seared Letty's mind. Her mother screamed an epithet at her father, followed by a stream of verbal abuse. Before she realized it, Letty flew out of her chair, throwing the pencil across the room, heading for the door to confront both parents.

Before she reached the door, she stopped, seeing a hazy-edged circle in the air, poised directly in the doorway. Not simply gray, but a sparkling loop, a dark muted charcoal background filled with dazzling dots of light that gyrated and vibrated in a dizzying dance. What was that?

And the Watcher took her.

3 ANTONIO

Tony peered from behind the row of garbage cans, scanning the slice of the street visible from the alley opening. Odorous with the tang of rotting food, dried urine, and the decay of several dead rats, the alley seemed oppressive, as though the building walls to each side wanted to slide noiselessly together to crush him along with the detritus spread along their length.

Something stirred and a large spider, covered with black velvet, crawled from beneath a paper sack and paused, scanning for possible food. Tony drew back in disgust. As often as he slept in the bug-infested environs of the city's slum, he had never gotten used to spiders and the occasional scorpion. They had never bothered Mama, but she was far braver than he.

Mama. Dead now, her cold, lifeless form carried to the city morgue, where it would undoubtedly be sliced up for analysis and then buried in a pauper's grave in the city cemetery. Or, more likely now with cemetery property so precious, cremated and her ashes scattered, or the remains of her body donated to the teaching hospital in the city. Billy, the mumbling, boozing derelict who often slept near them had told him that doctors in training always needed corpses to dissect. Billy should know. He had been an EMT at one time for the city ambulance service.

Tony shivered, ashamed that he had not gone with her. When the ambulance had arrived to take her remains, the policeman had tried to persuade him to come as well, but he had run away quickly before the officer could pursue him. If the officer had gotten him in the police substation, he would never have escaped, consigned to city protective services and sent to a home. It had happened once before, and Mama had barely managed to get him out.

Shuddering again, he threw an empty can at the spider, which scuttled away. He had to move anyway—he couldn't spend the night in the alley. He considered returning to the butcher-paper tent under the bridge where he and Mama had spent their last night together. Would the policeman come back to check the spot? Perhaps, but at least Tony could feel a bit closer to Mama one last night. What tomorrow might bring he could not even imagine.

At least Tony had snagged Mama's purse and extracted the few dollars and her pitiful collection of possessions before he went to find the cop. A yellow-metal chain bracelet that she had claimed to be real gold, thin and without jewels. A tiny bottle of perfume—because it smelled like her—a scarf, a few baubles, and some change. The rest, including an empty purse, her meager stash of clothing, and her shoes, he had left.

As soon as Tony had awakened this morning, he had known, feeling the cold skin, registering the half-open eyes that saw nothing. She had waited until he fell asleep before pulling out the syringe. And it had killed her. It still protruded from her arm.

What drug had she procured on her last "errand"? It didn't

matter, she had used them all, and they had slowly wasted her body as she lost all hope, as her looks at him became less loving and more vacant. She had sold her body sometimes, he knew, to earn enough for a little food and those drugs. And it had shamed her, even though she had never done it around him, always telling him she had to "run an errand." Her body had been her only asset once his father had deserted them.

He had tried to steal as much as he could, slipping into stores and lifting a few dollars from cash bins or from a store register left open for a moment. His mother had surely known that he had become modestly proficient at stealing, but whenever he proffered a few dollars that he had "earned," she accepted them solemnly and thanked him politely. He couldn't go into most of the local stores anymore. The proprietors had grown accustomed to his antics and warned him off if he tried to enter.

His mother had been pretty once, in a wild, untamed way, her blonde hair streaming down to her shoulders, her face full of life and good humor. But beauty and verve and happiness, and eventually her life, had slowly eroded away.

He dared not stay here too much longer. The gangs would soon be roaming. Standing, he slipped out of the alley and left, along the storefronts toward the bridge. Overhead, clouds had begun to reflect the city light, their lower edges roiling in the remaining twilight. The air was heavy, stagnant, the curling cloud-bottoms hinting of rain.

Steel shutters covered darkened windows in the rows of businesses on either side of the street. No sane store owner stayed open after dark. Doors to each establishment were barred with stout iron gates. Above the ground floor, some lights showed behind window curtains, as many owners lived above their stores. The brick façades, stained with age, echoed the door and window frames, which mostly displayed peeling paint or weathered wood.

Tony's stomach felt hollow, but with dusk upon him he was afraid to walk all the way north to the closest fast food restaurant. In addition, the few bills in his mother's purse would barely purchase one meal. He needed a stash, some real money that could last him a few days.

The street held only a few remaining souls who hurried along the sidewalks, most surely headed home. Here a dowdy housewife with a sack of groceries, there a worker from that fast food restaurant back up the street a mile or so in a better neighborhood, each in a dreadful hurry to reach refuge. Nobody was brave, or stupid, enough to be out late in this neighborhood.

Directly ahead, an old lady ancient enough to be taking steps like a wounded bird, minced along, purse slung over her right shoulder. It barely clung to her, threatening to slide onto the crook in her elbow. She should know better, Tony thought, but at her age she was probably forgetful.

A warm wind sprang up, whistling down the nearly-deserted street, tousling Tony's streaked brown hair and tugging at his tattered shirt, presaging the oncoming rain. He quickened his steps as he approached the old woman, then slowed, making his steps soundless below the whistle of the breeze. Julio and Eban had showed him how to do this, and he had been successful more than once.

Close behind, he accelerated, rushing past on the outside, grabbing the purse and ignoring her strangled cry. One hand explored the bottom of the purse as he ran. He found a little change, which he pocketed, but nothing else of interest except a woman's billfold, zippered shut. Grabbing the billfold, he dropped the purse in plain sight and continued down the street at a run. Ignoring the credit cards, he latched onto the bills. A bonanza! Two tens, some fives, and a myriad of ones. More than forty dollars.

Tossing the billfold, he continued to run. Pocketing the paper money, he hurried toward the expressway and its massive, mile-long elevated roadway, under which many of the homeless spent their nights. Gangs rarely bothered the wretched humanity that collected there in the evening. No one had much money. Besides, what fun could there be in harassing people so helpless and hopeless that they rarely did anything but cower under a blanket or behind one of the massive concrete pillars?

As he approached the bridge, a group of teenagers rounded a corner just ahead. They saw him immediately. One called out, "Qué pasa, chico?" The rest hurried toward him. Impulsively, Tony turned left into another alley and accelerated, running down its length, searching for a hiding place. Too late, he recognized that the brick wall ahead meant a dead end. Few doors were placed along the alley's length. Frantically, he checked each one. All were bolted.

A large trash container stood near the rear of the alley, the kind that garbage trucks grab and lift up to empty. He slipped behind it, hoping they would think he had entered one of the doors along the alleyway. Listening, he heard them swing into the opening from the street, jabbering among themselves. One cried out, "Hey, chico, come on out. We know you're hiding."

Terrified, Tony flattened himself against the rough wall as steps approached. What could he do? If he tried to run, surely they would catch him; they blocked the alley. They might simply rob him, but if they were in a bad mood they would beat him senseless. If they didn't kill him. At sixteen, he was fairly husky even though short, and he was good with his fists, but he was no match for six gang bangers.

A flash of light accompanied by a zapping noise, as though an electric spark had sprung from a power line, turned the dark brick walls a dull red. Then the alley again became dark and quiet.

Peering from behind the garbage vessel, Tony saw the group

of bodies sprawled in a row before him, as though dead. And something else, a hazy, formless circle of black-white-gray, like TV static, that hung above the alley floor, pulsing with menace. A sharp tang, like the smell in the air after a strong thunderstorm, assaulted his nostrils.

And the Watcher took him.

4 CAL

White.

Cal's overall impression as he awoke. White ceiling above, white walls around him, a cream-colored floor. Where ceiling met wall, no seam showed, simply a neat corner. Along the edges of the ceiling, rows of long panels glowed, providing a soft light that the flat-finished, featureless walls reflected palely.

A big room, it stretched at least twelve to fifteen strides past his feet and some distance behind his head. He reclined on a bed of some sort, not much longer than his height, between white sheets, on a firm but not uncomfortable mattress. The bed had no sides or adornments, not even a pillow, simply a platform with a mattress and two sheets.

He checked under the sheet; his body bore not a stitch of clothing.

Turning to his right and propping himself on his elbow, Cal saw that he had company, although only he had regained consciousness. Four additional platforms stretched in an even row to his right. The one closest held a girl, her skin caramel, with a head of bushy dark hair. The outline of her body under the sheet made it clear that she wore no clothing either. She had a strong nose and clear features, pretty if not beautiful.

To her right lay a young man, vaguely Latino, with a wispy mustache and tan skin. Shaggy brown hair with a few sun-blond streaks adorned his head, not the typical Latino black. He looked oddly worn.

The last two beds held another girl, white with very pale skin, as though she were ill, and a young man about Cal's age with even whiter skin and white hair. Cal decided he must be an albino.

A faint aroma tingled his nostrils. He couldn't place the scent at first. He finally decided that it was a tantalizing hint of ozone. He continued his scan to the rear, behind the beds. There, in the upper wall adjacent to the ceiling light panels, a series of narrow slits spread in a row parallel to the ceiling. Cal assessed that they were some sort of ventilation apertures, as the air in the room, especially with the ozone overtones, smelled fresh and clean.

His neighbor suddenly lifted her head, making him jerk in surprise. Wide-spaced dark eyes returned his gaze. Reflexively, she clutched the top of her sheet to her breasts. Her attitude, he guessed, was because she had discovered her nudity.

"What the hell are you staring at?"

"Our surroundings," he said softly. No use waking up everyone at once. "Mainly, I'm trying to figure out where we are. The last thing I remember is being in my bedroom."

Though surprised, her belligerence persisted. "What, you think I'm the welcoming committee? Why the hell would I know anything?" She sat up suddenly, clutching the sheet and glaring at him. "Did you take my clothes off?"

As she sat up, Cal could make out a slender waist and nice bosom despite the cloth, and muscled arms that pronounced her an athlete. Her ethnic background puzzled him. She seemed to have an African heritage, but her skin was merely a deep tan. Cal revised his opinion from *pretty* to *very pretty*.

Still, her general attitude irritated him. "Yeah, I ran over and peeled off your clothes so you'd be naked like me. Wanta see?"

Those wide-spaced, hypnotic eyes widened, then the attitude came back. "So you're the local wise guy? Listen, you stay away from me or I'll call the cops."

He laughed. "Yeah, and where are they? Looks to me like we've been kidnapped and held for ransom. Except I'm not worth anything. The last thing I remember is being pissed off at my dad, and now I'm here."

She gasped, glanced around, and said, her voice creaky, "Weird. That's the last thing I remember, being furious at my dad and mom, and getting up to go yell at them."

"Were they drunk?"

The question surprised her. "Oh no, that is ... No. They just argue all the damn ..." His comment appeared to sink in. "Your father—he'd been drinking?"

He blushed, realizing he'd said more than he meant to. Finally he blurted, "As usual." He turned toward her, careful to keep the sheet in place. "So that's it? We're mad at our parents and we're sent to hell?"

She frowned. "I don't believe in hell. Or heaven. We're born, we die, that's it."

Cal steadfastly refused to get involved in a religion discussion with a girl, however pretty, that he didn't know. "So, where are we?"

Her expression hardened again. "No idea. Not hell. I was already in hell, just listening to my parents fight. Like your mom yelled at your dad for being drunk."

He shifted his legs over the edge of the platform, wrapping the sheet around his waist and legs for modesty's sake. Shaking his head, he replied. "My mom's dead, so she's not pissed off at anything anymore, I guess." He didn't want anybody's pity, least of all some girl's.

He realized, on further inspection, that the far wall behind their beds held rows of drawers, also white, set flush into the wall. He hadn't noticed at first, as the cabinets blended in almost completely with the wall surface.

The girl thought a minute, then observed. "My folks are all screwed up. They should get a divorce. But they just yell at each other. One of the joys of getting rich."

Cal stood up, wrapping the sheet around him. "Okay, I'm presentable, right? I want to inspect those drawers." He moved toward the rear wall. "Must be nice to be rich."

"Not so much. I mean, I have enough to eat and the house is nice, but my folks ... Anyway, that doesn't answer the question of how we got here."

"Got me? Kidnapped? Don't know what the heck for. My dad doesn't have two quarters to rub together. If I hadn't hidden my box of savings, I'd have starved to death weeks ago."

Cal passed the other three beds, its occupants still asleep, arriving at the back wall and the cabinets. He pulled out a drawer, finding row after row of gray shorts. Men's underwear.

"Hey, got clothing here."

That got the girl's attention. She watched as he pulled out additional drawers and inspected, taking a quick inventory.

The next drawer up had white T-shirts, and the one at chest level, the tallest, held folded slacks of various sizes that looked like the bottom half of a uniform. In the next set of drawers were what appeared to be women's underwear and bras, not fancy, but with a good variety of sizes. Another drawer held socks of all sizes, and the large bottom drawer, double-wide, contained shoes that resembled sneakers in several sizes.

Cal started pulling out underwear and T-shirts and throwing

them to the young woman. She tucked her sheet more securely under her arms and caught the items.

Cal tossed her several sizes of panties and bras. She picked, mulled, discarded. "Turn around," she told Cal.

He did, taking advantage of her activity to drop his own sheet and don shorts and a T-shirt. In a moment he heard steps and she joined him, clearly more at ease, wearing bra and panties.

"I figure you'd see this much skin if I were in a bathing suit," she told him. "Just don't stare too hard."

With a fleck of humor, he gestured at his T-shirt-and-short-clad body. "Same goes."

He had trouble not paying too much attention; up close, her looks improved. Not classically beautiful but energetic, athletic, magnetic.

His attempt at wit got a trace of a grin as she went through the drawers and picked her sizes in outer wear. He did the same, and shortly they were dressed, still standing by the set of bins.

"You're so good at finding things, could you find one thing more?"

The edge had left her voice for once. "What?" he asked.

"The bathroom facilities. I ... could really use them."

Come to think of it, so could he. Cal began to explore the back wall, headed to his right, moving slowly. He suspected that any doors to the room, including one to bathroom, if it existed, lay behind concealed panels.

At the rear corner he kept going right, moving down that wall back toward the front of the room where his bed lay. Two thirds of the way down the wall, a subtle change in texture stopped him. Yes, a tiny, almost invisible line ran up the wall; it had to be a door. He began to feel along the wall for a button or anything that would activate the panel.

It opened so suddenly that he jumped back. Inside the

revealed room he could see a sink, and to the left, an ordinary porcelain toilet.

The young woman rushed over. She looked anxious and uncomfortable. "May I?"

"Sure."

She darted inside, searched frantically, then said "Ah!" Touching a spot on the side of the door, she smiled at him as the door closed.

When she came out, he hurried in. The facilities were clean and usable, although cramped, and the tiny shower just past the toilet wasn't half the size of a decent closet.

As he left the bathroom, he saw the Latino youth in the middle bed stirring and struggling to sit up.

"Where am I?"

The girl said sarcastically, as though expecting this from each of the room's denizens as they awoke, "You've been kidnapped and are being held for a million dollars in ransom. Got it on you?"

The Latino kid's panic drained away and he managed a thin smile. Cal admired the way the girl had disarmed his potential fear and confusion. He peered under the sheet and then grinned back at her. "Ain't got anything on me. I'm nekkid."

She gestured toward the still-open drawers. "Clothes in there."

He shrugged, threw off the sheet, and moved to the clothing drawers.

"Hey, watch yourself," Cal said. "You don't need to walk around naked in front of the young lady."

"She your girlfriend?"

"I just met her, like I just met you. But I still try to be polite."

"Hey, chico, don't order me around. Tony does as he pleases."

Cal didn't have any fear of a kid at least six inches shorter than he was. He'd practiced his forms every week and kept in shape, mainly with sit-ups, push-ups, and curls, using ancient dumbbells he kept under his bed. He took a step toward the youth's bed, but the girl spoke up.

"Is that all guys are capable of, fighting over the fair lady? Listen, *chico*," she echoed Tony's words as a sort of parody, "I can take care of myself. He didn't mean anything by it. I'm Letty. So you're Tony?"

"Yeah." As Tony donned a pair of shorts and a T-shirt, he eyed her admiringly. Mainly, Cal decided, because of the tough image she projected. Both Tony and Letty stared over at him.

He cleared his throat. "Calvin. Everybody calls me Cal."

Just then the other young man bolted upright in his bed.

5 LETTY

nteresting situation, Letty thought. Alarms clanged in her mind. In a room with three naked boys and another naked girl. Well, one naked boy and two who had formerly been naked. So far, the two dressed boys seemed polite enough. The bigger one was tough and capable. She didn't kid herself that she could fight off both of them, if it came to that. And now the third one sat up, looking around in confusion.

"Is this the police station?" he asked. He stood, his sheet falling to the floor, and Letty averted her eyes. He didn't seem self-conscious, or even aware of Letty's shock.

"It's not the police station," Cal said sharply. "Get some clothes on. You're embarrassing Letty."

The albino stared vaguely at Cal, at himself, and at Tony and Letty. "It's not my fault I'm naked. I don't even know what I'm doing here. The last thing I remember is Frawley hitting me with his belt."

His reply shocked Letty and Cal into silence.

As she watched, Cal tossed the albino some clothing. He had

light blue eyes, not pink like albino rabbits she had seen, and silver hair. His skin appeared so translucent and clear that she expected to see his veins, but his skin was simply smooth and pale. The only visible color besides his blue eyes appeared to be a reddish-purple bruise across his left cheek.

As he started to dress, Letty asked Cal, "No dresses in the drawers?"

"Everything looks unisex to me."

"I don't wear 'em much anyway."

Tony said, "Too bad. It's nice to see a pretty girl in a dress. Or not in one."

"Oh, shut up, Tony." Cal tossed the words over his head. "She's in a room with boys, and she's modest like most *nice* girls."

Letty felt surprised and appreciative.

Behind him, Tony said sullenly, "I don't know any nice girls. You don't get to meet nice girls when you live under a bridge and wonder where you'll get your next meal. 'Sides, I didn't mean nekkid, just in pants like she is now."

Cal didn't reply. Letty felt a little guilty about taking the remark the wrong way. The good news: Cal sounded as if he wouldn't put up with any funny stuff. At least she didn't have to worry about the boys ganging up on her.

Letty grabbed the sheet that she had tossed on the bed when dressing and spread it out. She couldn't stand to have any mess around her, even the platform bed with its single covering. Glancing at the albino, she asked, "What's your name?"

Perched back on his bed, he said, "Alexander, but my parents called me Sasha."

"Sasha?" Tony laughed. "What kind of a nickname is that?"

"Russian," Sasha said. "My parents emigrated to the US years ago. Father worked as an engineer; Mom did programming. They worked for the government, but they died in a car accident.

Now I live—or did live—in a foster home with an asshole foster father and his fat pig wife. And their two kids. The son is meaner than a snake and the daughter is ... just weird."

"What do you remember just before you woke up here?" Letty asked.

6 SASHA

Sasha thought a moment. Odd—he remembered very clearly what was going on before he lost consciousness.

"It's funny," he told the other three. "I was starving, so I snuck down to steal some food."

"You had to steal food from your foster parents?" Cal asked.

"Yeah, they weren't real nice people. They and their kids ate dinner first, then I got any leftovers. Only there weren't usually leftovers.

"Last night—I guess it was last night—I was really hungry. I picked the lock to the attic, which is where they locked me at night, and snuck downstairs."

"Sounds like a crappy bedroom," Letty said.

"Yeah. They had just floored the attic with lengths of one-by-three lumber and left it unpainted. It was more a prison than a bedroom. Cobwebs dangled from the roof trusses, and you could see the roofing nails sticking through the wooden sub-roof. You had to be careful to duck down the nearer you got to the eaves, or you got a nail in the scalp. No walls, either, just the roof slanting to the attic floor. And it was usually stuffy.

"Frawley told me if I complained to the social worker, he'd tell her I tried to sexually harass his daughter and they'd lock me up forever. My bed was a baby bed, maybe five feet long—I had to curl up to lie on it. For clothes, they gave me whatever the son wanted to throw away."

Cal and Letty shook their heads in unison, Letty looking disgusted.

"Anyway," Sasha went on, "I picked the attic lock like I had done a hundred times before. That's odd—I remember it so clearly. Entering the kitchen, which was dark except for a little light from a streetlight through the window over the sink. Opening the refrigerator door, I remember the light spilling out around me, almost like a pool of water. Seeing all that food that Frawley and Sweety-Poo—that's what he called the Fat Pig wife —refused to share with me."

"Frawley caught me, I remember that. He had his belt, and hit me from behind, scared the crap out of me and knocked me down. He yelled at me about stealing food, then told me he was going to give me a beating I wouldn't forget. Then ..."

Sasha paused, suppressing a shiver. "I know it sounds crazy," he continued, "but a lightning bolt out of nowhere struck Frawley right in the chest. I can still see him flying backward, landing with a thump on the linoleum floor.

"That's all I remember."

"You're not crazy," Tony said. "I saw a flash of light also, and it sounded like some sort of spark."

Cal added, looking at Sasha, "I had a different experience, but like you, I remember up to a point, and then I'm here all of a sudden. It sounds like all of us were taken sort of suddenly."

Letty's face suddenly lit up as though the light had dawned. "There's a pattern here," she announced.

"What do you mean?" Tony asked.

"Our backgrounds. My parents have made my life a living

hell, arguing all day every day for two years. I can't—couldn't—even sleep anymore. Cal's mother is dead and his father's an ..." She hesitated and then said, "... an alcoholic. Tony, you told us that you're living on the street." She glanced across at Sasha. "From the bruise on your cheek, that foster father of yours—and probably, your whole foster family—treated you almost like an animal. So, every one of us has home trouble of some sort."

The others seemed to digest that. For his part, Sasha found himself in agreement.

Finally, Tony muttered, "I don't hear no trouble. All of you got a roof, all of you got food, all of you get to go to school. Trouble? You're livin' like kings, sounds to me." He stared out from under lowered lashes at Letty.

Sasha watched Cal's ears turn crimson—Cal must feel as embarrassed as he did. After a silent moment, Cal said, "Trouble comes in different packages, Tony. But yours sounds tough."

Letty agreed with a nod of her head. "But I can tell you, having two parents who yell all the time isn't fun either. You got a mom or dad?"

"Dad deserted us years ago. Mom, she worked as a whore sometimes to feed us, but she got onto drugs. She OD'ed a couple nights ago."

That quieted everybody, even Sasha, who usually just said whatever crossed his mind. Letty and Cal both appeared embarrassed. "I'm so sorry," Letty said, putting out a hand toward him. "That's really bad, Tony."

Tony had been near Letty. As she reached out, he drew back. "Don't need no pity."

After an embarrassed silence, Letty went on. "That doesn't change the fact that we all had home trouble, some worse than others, and now we're all here. Anybody want to guess why we've been abducted?"

Cal ventured, "Not sure we've been kidnapped. Given your

observation—we all had trouble back home—that doesn't sound likely. Tony and I aren't worth anything."

Letty shrugged. "My folks are rich. They'd pay a good ransom, I guess—if they ever realized I'm gone. Mom comes in my room once every other day or so, I guess to see if I'm still alive. Dad hasn't set foot in my room in months."

Tony changed the subject. "Not that it's anything new to me, but I'm hungry."

Sasha agreed. "Me, too. Whoever has us, I wish that they'd pass out sandwiches or something."

Before anyone could reply, the other girl stirred, sat up, and began to scream.

7 TONY

The screaming girl had a nice body, Tony thought, but all that hysteria made him uncomfortable. He watched as Letty rushed over to her, climbed on her bed, and began to comfort her, putting arms around her and drawing up the sheet.

Cal went to rummage in the clothing bins. Tony observed as Cal collected a pile of clothing, which he took to the bed on which both girls were now perched, depositing the assorted pieces next to Letty.

With another order to keep their eyes to themselves, Letty began to dry the other girl's tears. Shortly she had the girl dressed and guided her on a quick excursion to the bathroom.

Really, really weird. Five teenagers in a room with no obvious exit door, some clothing drawers, and a strange, pasty illumination. At least the air seemed fresh.

It had to be a jail.

The big, white kid hadn't treated Tony very well, and he seemed to have a cocky attitude. Tony thought about taking a shot at him, but as he saw nowhere to run, he decided against it. The guy projected a tough image, as though not afraid of anything in particular and he had well-developed muscles. Tony shrugged mentally. If the kid irritated him, he would bide his time, then let him have it. Rule one of the street: Don't fight without an escape plan. Rule two: If you do fight, put the guy down. You don't want him coming after you later.

Not only had his old clothes been taken, but also the money he'd stolen. It infuriated him, made him want to strike out at something or somebody, but he knew how to hide his emotions. You never showed your emotions when you were on the street. Wait, size up, scan for weaknesses. Then strike when you have the advantage. For now, he would just smile and appear not to care. He called this demeanor "Dopey Tony," as if he didn't know much, didn't care much, just sat around and smiled, sorta happy-go-lucky. Never let on. Never let on *anything.*

That Letty girl was pretty, but not his type. Smart, and not a clinger. She didn't need anybody, even parents.

What kind of jail kept men and women in the same cell? And what was with the strange, pale kid? Tony had never seen anyone like him.

When Letty started talking about how bad everybody had it, he couldn't help but laugh. Bad? They had no idea about bad. Then she'd turned those pitying eyes on him, and he wanted to strangle her. Nobody needed to offer him pity; he could take care of himself. *Should have kept my mouth shut*, he grumbled to himself.

Since Tony had instantly disliked the big kid, he turned to the silver-haired one.

"I never seen any guy with such white hair. Did your mom or dad have hair like that?"

Sasha gave a half-smile. "I'm an albino. I don't have much pigment in my skin or hair, so that makes me sort of pale white."

Tony had never heard of such a thing. "I never heard of an al—whatever."

Not put off, Sasha chuckled. "Cross my heart. It's a condition that you inherit from a parent. My dad had it. He's dead. Mom, too."

Tony had to feel a bit empathetic. "I know about foster homes. Lived in one once. The dad was pretty mean, but luckily, he ignored me, just sat around and watched TV. Least they ate pretty good, and I got a mattress to sleep on at night. And he didn't beat me. The mom actually went to collect the money. I'm not sure but what he thought I belonged to her. She needed to collect the money 'cause he didn't make much at his job."

Sasha continued to explore the wall while they talked, running his hand along the smooth edge of the storage cabinets, poking in the drawers. Just clothing, as far as Tony could tell. Certainly no food.

"How do you get in that toilet room?" he asked Letty, who was still sitting on the bed with the screamer.

Cal gestured. "There's a door there where Letty went a moment ago. You can tell a bit of difference in the texture. Stand in front and run your hand on the left side and it opens."

Tony did as directed. When he came out, Sasha quickly took his turn.

Back on his bed, Tony watched Letty comfort the wimpy girl, whispering in her ear and holding her hand. When Sasha exited the bathroom, Tony told him, "I think you're right."

Sasha stopped by Tony's bed. "About what?"

"This has to be some sort of jail or police station. But why keep us with the girls?"

Sasha shook his head. "Maybe entertainment? That would make it a mighty fine jail, but those girls aren't the type." He moved toward the far corner of the room, his hands still on the wall surface, seeming to investigate the wall carefully. "Or maybe it's a space issue? Some of the jails in town are pretty crowded."

That could be true, so far as Tony knew. "Thought LA had plenty of jail room."

"Not LA, Chicago." Sasha blinked, turned back to Tony. "Jeez—you from Los Angeles?"

"Aren't you?"

"Didn't you just hear me say Chicago?"

As Tony's brows lifted, Sasha raised his voice to the others, now that the screamer had quieted, continuing to cling to Letty and sniffling softly. "Hey, you guys. Where are you from?"

Puzzled, Cal said, "Dallas."

Letty's brows arched, looking from Sasha to Cal. "Denver." She shifted back to her companion on the bed. "And you? What's your name, by the way?"

The young girl—she was clearly the youngest of them all, sniffed and struggled to sit up. *"Estedda kah alereh,"* she muttered. At Letty's frown, she went on, *"Okah alzekah orewey, kah alereh phil eh delph."*

What language was that? Tony thought in confusion. Not Spanish, not even the Spanglish of the southwestern US. He didn't know much about languages, but it surely wasn't English.

Letty seemed to recover a bit as Tony watched with interest. "I'm sorry," Letty said. "I don't speak your language. Do you speak English?"

The younger girl pivoted between Sasha and Letty. She shook her head. "Of course I speak English."

Before Tony could stop himself, he said, "What you said a minute ago wasn't English. It was gobbledygook."

Letty shot him a warning look. "Quiet, Tony." She turned back to the other girl. "I'm glad you speak English, but what you said a moment ago didn't sound like it to me."

"But I ..." The younger girl stopped, hesitated, then said,

"Maybe I was just still too scared. Anyway, you asked where I was from, and I live in ... I did live in Philadelphia."

Letty was silent as Tony digested that answer. Then she said, "And your name?"

"Ophelia."

Tony spoke up again, following Sasha's question with one of his own. "Were you at home, or at least in your hometown, the last you knew?"

Ophelia nodded, yes. Tony repeated his question to the rest, and they also nodded, in turn.

"Holy crap," came from Cal. "We're from all over the United States. Then—why are we here?"

"Kidnapped," Sasha blurted. "I thought we were in jail, but we're from all over. Somebody doped us and hauled us here. For ransom?"

Ophelia began to tear up.

"Stop it!" Letty said sharply to Sasha, then she turned to Ophelia. "Don't listen to him. I don't know why we're here, but we weren't kidnapped for money."

Silently, Tony had to agree. Who'd kidnap a street rat for money? He didn't know anybody who'd give the price of a hamburger for him. He watched as Sasha returned to the wall, moving down from the left rear corner toward what Tony thought of as the front of the room.

"But it makes sense," Ophelia objected. "I'm worth—that is, my Mom and Dad were worth a lot. Maybe a billion. Dad remarried after Mom died, and then he passed away. Last night I heard my stepmother talking to her son about changing the will. It's supposed to be probated soon, but she's flirting with the lawyer, and she's pretty clever. Maybe she had me kidnapped. Maybe she —" Her face filled with horror. "Maybe she got someone to take me away to kill me!"

"Who are you, Cinderella?" Sasha asked, looking back from his wall exploration.

Letty turned on him furiously. "Oh, for God's sake, be sensible! Listen, Ophelia, we're all in the same boat, so I doubt any kidnapper that would want you would want us. My folks are well-off, but not in your family's class, and these guys are all poor, more or less." She threw Tony and the other guys an embarrassed glance. "I mean, no insult intended, but you said you're all broke."

Tony couldn't object to the truth. "Then why *are* we here?"

Sasha had continued to explore, reaching the next corner. "Did you notice? There's no door. At least, I can't find one."

The others looked blank. Tony had already decided the door was well-hidden, but there *had* to be one. He joined Sasha in the second corner and began to explore the adjoining wall. Just a smooth, flat coating without ... Wait. Could it be?

"Here." Tony gestured to Sasha. "Isn't this a seam?"

Sasha moved beside him. "It is. Well done! It's got to be some sort of door."

As he said that, it began to open.

8 OPHELIA

Ophelia still clung to Letty. Barely sixteen, she felt assured and comforted by Letty's mature presence. She realized that the older girl couldn't be much more than maybe seventeen, but her reassuring demeanor helped Ophelia slowly regain her own composure. The thought of her stepmother having her kidnapped terrified her, so she held onto Letty as though she were a life preserver and somehow kept from dissolving into tears again.

Then a door opened.

Ophelia couldn't help herself: she screamed. Even the two boys before the door jumped back with yells as a figure walked in. Tall and quite human-like, thinner than most men Ophelia had seen, his skin color was odd, almost grayish. The man—it had to be a male, Ophelia decided—wore a dark uniform with a pentagonal gold pin on each collar. The coat didn't have any obvious buttons or straps holding it closed. Ophelia blinked, regarded the form tall, angular form again, made a second take on the ridged face and elongated skull.

It hit Ophelia with a jolt. The figure could not possibly be human!

The alien stepped further through the door, and Tony and Sasha gave him plenty of room. Putting his hand out in a sort of greeting, he spoke.

"*Vedda elrokah evedon, rotole.*" He smiled.

Two things registered simultaneously with Ophelia. First, he wasn't speaking English. Second, she understood him.

"*Era pou vedda. Roko dinere lias?*"

She said the two sentences automatically. He had said, "Welcome to our starship." She replied in kind, "I don't feel welcome. Why have you taken us?"

"You speak his language?" Cal said sharply. "Where the hell is that spoken in the Philadelphia area?"

At first surprised and perplexed-looking, the alien seemed to catch up. "My apologies," he said in perfect English. What Ophelia considered "TV-announcer English."

"All of you have received some tutorials in my language," he continued. "It seems that the young lady remembers a bit more at this point.

"But we can discuss that later. My greetings, and those of our commander, to each of you. My name is Galigan, and I formally welcome you to the starship that we refer to as Naval Training Cruiser Five-Eight-Seven-Two-Three. You have been our guests overnight, referring to your timeframe, and I hope you all slept well."

Everyone stood in a stunned silence, until Cal blurted, "We're on a *spaceship?*"

Before Cal's question could be answered, Tony said, "Why you kidnap us, man? For slaves? For ransom? Why're we here?"

Evidently surprised by Tony's rat-a-tat questions, the tall alien surveyed him curiously, then let his focus stray to the rest, finally settling on Ophelia. She shrank against Letty, trying to somehow become invisible, only a shadow to Letty's substance.

The alien shifted to Cal. "Yes, we are in a spacecraft, thirty-six thousand kilometers above your world in a geostationary orbit. We use stealth techniques similar to some of your military aircraft, so we are not detectable from below."

Galigan stood as tall as Cal, his face narrow, with a slender, aristocratic nose, large, dark eyes, and a broad forehead. His demeanor showed intelligence, and his composure had a calming influence that gradually slowed Ophelia's pulse. He might be an alien, but somehow, his presence didn't seem ominous.

He shifted back to Tony. "We certainly want no ransom. Let me just say that we have 'borrowed' you for a while."

Before he could say more, Letty blurted, "Borrowed or whatever, why put both sexes together? Girls don't want to dress or undress around boys, and I sure don't want them even *thinking* about what I'm doing in the bathroom."

Despite her complaint, Galigan remained serene. "Have the young men bothered you?"

"Well, no. I mean, they've been gentlemen, though Tony is a bit crude."

Crude? Ophelia agreed with that.

After a moment, Galigan said, "Mr. Morales—Tony—has a rather crude background, I think you would agree. But he will not accost you. We have inserted 'suggestions' in his mind. He understands proper behavior."

"Messin' with my mind?" Tony erupted in outrage.

Galigan smiled apologetically. "Just mild suggestions, absolutely no orders placed." He turned back to Letty. "Young lady, it is extremely important that the five of you continue to live in ... proximity. Important for your future and for ours."

"But we have only one bathroom!" Letty exploded. "I don't

want to go to the toilet after a bunch of guys! Can't we have at least a second bath?"

"I'm sorry. Learning to live together, share the facilities, and become a unit is very important. I'm afraid the facilities will remain as they are."

Tony's face twisted, brow creased. "What you mean a *unit?* You want us to become buddy-buddy? Ain't gonna happen. Don't like the big dumb kid, and I'm not so damn fond of the girls."

Galigan did not so much smile as grimace. "Explanations will be forthcoming. For now, you need to follow me." With that, he turned and retreated through the door, which stayed open.

Tony didn't hesitate, but jumped through the door. Cal followed quickly, but Ophelia drew back, leaning into Letty even more earnestly, her grip tight. *They're crazy,* she thought. *They want to follow this madman from another planet to God knows where.* She clung to Letty all the more firmly.

Gently, Letty drew away from Ophelia's embrace. "Come on, Ophelia. Let's see what's going on. Think of it as an adventure."

Ophelia shook her head, frozen to the bed.

"You really are a complete wuss," Sasha observed, though he hadn't moved either. "Does everything in the world scare you?"

As Ophelia shrank back, Letty barked, "Don't be a jackass. Are you running out the door?" She held out a hand to Ophelia.

Truth to tell, Ophelia had gone far past terrified, nearly frozen in place. But Sasha's sneering countenance jarred her into motion. Darned if she would let that jerk make fun of her! Taking Letty's hand, she slid off the bed. As they passed through the door, Sasha hesitantly brought up the rear.

9 SASHA

Letty's assessment had hit very close to home; Sasha felt as scared as the Ophelia chick. Damned if he would admit it though! He followed hesitantly, a good ten steps or so behind Letty and her whiny companion.

Why could that Ophelia speak the alien's language? He had said that all of them had been subject to "tutorials." Sasha had read about "sleep learning," where recordings could be played to sleeping individuals, and they would remember what was played when they awoke. Had these aliens (and were they really aliens?) managed to do that somehow? He had admitted that "suggestions" had been inserted into their minds, so why not another language? Things were moving too fast, but he determined to bring it up with the other four when they had time.

Up ahead, the tall, gray-skinned alien had vanished around a gradual curve in the corridor. Tony, leading the way, had also vanished; Cal followed close behind.

They were traveling slowly enough to give Sasha time to glance around the corridor. To a certain extent, it reminded him of the hallways in the movies about the *USS Enterprise*. Light panels and air inlets ran along the top of walls on both sides at regular intervals. Small, screened openings dotted the walls near the floor at the same intervals, more than likely air returns. At about half that frequency, small panels at head height alternated on the left and right bulkheads. Each panel contained a small screen, several small lights arranged in neat rows, and a raised dome of shiny material pierced with tiny holes like an embedded microphone.

Yard-wide displays appeared at intersections with other walkways. Each displayed an odd, stylized symbol, a sleek spaceship partially shielded from view by a gray cloud, almost like a "system on" icon.

The main difference between this ship, if it was a ship as Galigan claimed, and the movie ship *Enterprise* was the overhead of the passageway. Unlike the sleek, smooth ceiling of the motion-picture ship, all sorts of conduits and pipes stretched across the expanse above them. Some appeared to be fluid-carrying pipes, while some had open places in their circumference that showed bundles of cables.

Small trays also occupied the upper left area of the ceiling, raceways for larger cables and groups of wires. At irregularly spaced openings, some of the pipes and cable bundles disappeared from view into vertical openings, to be replaced by others. The pipes displayed an array of pastel colors, including light yellow, pale blue, a dusty red, and emerald green. The wires and larger cables showed a brighter and much more varied array of hues—red, purple, dark blue, green, and deep blue. All the colors must be some sort of code that identified the contents of the pipes and the functions of the cables, but Sasha had no idea what they could be.

Not deserted by any means, the passageway teemed with traffic. Passersby, mostly tall and gray-skinned like their host, hurried past, concentrating on whatever task lay before them. They all looked alike to Sasha. Could they be male and female? Sasha couldn't tell, but none of them were attractive, at least by human standards. Shockingly, a few individuals looked human, both male and female. Were they aliens as well?

The gray aliens had to be from another star system, he thought, his pulse racing. No one on Earth resembled that race, although their humanoid similarities were obvious. As to the human-like specimens, they were a puzzle. Had they been kidnapped as well?

Why were he and his fellow prisoners here? To experiment on, as many science fiction movies showed, and as some people on Earth had claimed? *Then why bother to be polite?* he asked himself. *Better to just dope us up and use us as needed.*

He shook his head, and sped up after his companions, who had been drawing farther ahead. Despite his attempt to stay calm, he felt lightheaded.

The host alien waited at a large door to the left of the hallway after they had made a quarter-circle down the passage. After a moment, the door opened to a small room. The alien gestured them in and followed, the sliding door closed soundlessly.

It must be an elevator, Sasha decided, and had his hunch rewarded a second later when he felt a sudden slight increase in weight. The whiny Ophelia shrank against Letty, whimpering. Sasha started to smirk, then remembered Letty's scornful words and simply stared at the elevator control panel. Cal and Tony also examined the panel, a small screen filled with odd symbols.

The heavy feeling told Sasha that the elevator ascended, so he watched as the display showed a sequence of symbols in the upper left corner. They must be deck numbers, but Sasha had no idea what they meant.

An under-weight flicker told him that the elevator slowed. The door opened and the alien led them out. They entered a vast, high-ceilinged vault that must be the bridge of the ship.

Left and right, on upper platforms, a handful of Galigan's brethren tended various displays and controls, while at the front, on an upraised dais, three crewmen consulted a group of six displays. The displays, which resembled Earth TVs, ranged from small rectangular charts with columns of numbers to large, wide panels that depicted the Earth, schematics of what must be the orbital trajectory of the ship, and simply the background of space.

Sasha saw that they gazed out a broad, transparent port that spread fully twenty yards wide and ten high. The aliens ignored them, just as those in the corridor had.

The view through the massive window stopped Sasha in his tracks.

The familiar blue marble of Earth filled the bottom half of the field of scene, a view they had seen a thousand times in astronaut photographs. Letty gasped. Whiny Ophelia couldn't scream because Letty's hand covered her mouth. Cal and Tony had stopped as well, staring up at the view along with Sasha.

Reflexively, Sasha spun to run back to the elevator. It had closed. From behind him, Letty's sardonic contralto pierced his self-esteem. "You're good with sarcasm, but you're just as scared as Ophelia."

Slowly he turned, restraining a strong desire to smack her in the face. She was right, bad as he hated to admit it. His normally sarcastic attitude took over. After all, it had kept him sane since his parents died. "My apologies, great leader. I follow you at your command." He bowed. She frowned back, silent.

Their host stopped near the dais that protruded above them on a graceful cantilevered beam. Cal and Tony edged forward, followed by Letty and Ophelia. Sasha followed, cursing his fear, drawn to Earth's image in the window.

Although one or two of those on the bridge had looked around to see who entered, most paid no attention. Either they didn't care one way or the other about the new arrivals, or this was a familiar procedure.

Surrounding the upper curve of Earth's orb, the dark, velvet background of space glittered with a million stars. After a confused moment, Sasha recognized the brilliant, dust-scattered swath of the Milky Way, sweeping across the darkness above the white-swirled, blue globe like a sparkling tiara.

I will act brave, he thought. *I will act brave. I will be brave.*

10 CAL

Heights terrified Cal. Something of a daredevil, he had taken self-defense courses and practiced various forms of Asian combat for years. But high places scared him silly. The view of Earth, vast and dizzying, made him want to turn away and run, just like Sasha.

But Sasha's fright and Letty's sarcasm fueled his resolve. Gritting his teeth, he stepped closer to the alien and the broad, terrifying view. Yes, he wanted to run, but to where? Not much doubt now that they were sitting in a spacecraft, suspended far above the Earth, despite the fact that in their room they had not felt the slightest motion that would have betrayed their situation.

Their host smiled at Cal, seeming pleased that Cal wasn't overly afraid of him. "As I said moments ago, welcome to our ship. You have been carefully chosen. Each of you has valuable abilities that we require. Further, you have some unique genetic qualities that can be very useful to us on this ship, to my race, and ultimately to your own planet.

"We need your help in a very serious, truly life-and-death

task, an effort in which many races across our galaxy have united to preserve our civilizations."

Cal spoke up, anger kindled at the opening words. "Say 'carefully chosen' all you want—it looks to me as though we've been kidnapped. Since we were taken against our will, how can you expect us to do anything you want?"

Galigan nodded, as though prepared for the question. "Please direct your attention to the display on the bulkhead behind you and to your left."

They all turned to find a display rectangle on the curved perimeter of the room. *Like a high-definition television,* Cal thought, except larger, perhaps ten feet by five. Even as they turned, the display lit up to show a schematic of space, a spiral galaxy depicted in the center. Several smaller objects that might have been galaxies were scattered through the picture. Cal was quick to note that the resolution of the video was far superior to any Earth TV. Further, it was a full-depth 3D picture, and although it was only a schematic, he felt as though he could reach out and touch the objects shown. There was no sense of it being simply a picture at all.

Stepping near the display, Galigan said, "The depiction of the spiral galaxy in the center of this schematic is that of the Milky Way, the home galaxy to your planet Earth." He held out a pointer he had produced from a pocket, and a tiny point of bright blue light showed on the display. "Your planet is located in this particular extension, called the Orion Spur, of what your astronomers refer to as the Sagittarius Arm of the Milky Way.

"Here," the dot moved outside the Milky Way to highlight a small patch of light near and above the outer spiral, "is located the Sagittarius Dwarf Spheroidal Galaxy, a tiny companion galaxy to our own, orbiting the Milky Way in a polar orbit. Over a billion years or more, it has actually passed through the outer rim of our much larger galaxy several times. Eventually, it will be completely absorbed by our much larger galactic body. Some of your astronomers believe that the Milky Way may have achieved its spiral shape in continued encounters with the Sagittarius Dwarf and other nearby small galaxies.

"Many of the stars in this tiny galaxy are old and relatively low in most metals. However, at some point in the past, life developed in one or more solar systems. We cannot be certain, but apparently, only a few races of intelligent life developed, or perhaps a single race quickly predominated."

Galigan frowned. "Eventually, that race expanded to most of the available systems in that small galaxy. That might sound impossible to those who dwell in our own galaxy, but remember, their home galaxy is tiny by comparison, with only millions of stars, compared to the billions of stars in the Milky Way. Thus, it has correspondingly fewer habitable planets."

Cal wasn't sure how the others felt, but he was so shocked at the story that he could only watch Galigan silently. The alien continued.

"Some hundreds of years ago, that species apparently initiated a major push to settle in our galaxy. In the intervening time, it has slowly but steadily invaded the edge of the galaxy opposite the position of Earth and many other civilized planetary systems. We only discovered them about five of your decades ago.

"Tentative encounters made it quite clear that this civilization is warlike, expansion-driven, and intolerant of any other form of intelligent life. As our early exploration ships followed their movements, they have encountered a series of civilizations and summarily wiped them out, to the last living creature. In most cases, the worlds were devastated and the invaders began to remake them into the apparent image of their home planet, wherever that may be.

"This race does not negotiate, it takes no prisoners, leaves no buildings or evidence of intelligent life in existence. It encounters, attacks, destroys, remakes, settles a sizeable colony, and moves on. It brooks no opposition."

"Where is it?" Cal asked. Glad to be away from the massive window, his reasoning power had slowly returned. The Milky Way spanned a hundred thousand light-years. If these invaders were very far away, what difference did it make to Earth?

"Their home galaxy is near the very outer end of the Sagittarius Arm of the Milky Way, near the invasion point, and thousands of light-years above the galactic plane. As I said, it is across the galaxy from our position in the Orion Spur."

"Then why worry?" Cal persisted. "Even assuming their ships can travel faster than light, which has never been done, won't it take them generations to reach here?"

"Believe me," Galigan said, "faster-than-light travel is quite easy, once you know the process. But you are correct to some extent. In fact, most of their activity is far away from Earth's location or that of our own system. But about fifty years ago they began a new mission to cross a substantial part of our galaxy and establish settlements in the neighborhood of our planet and Earth. We don't know why. Perhaps there were elements of their society that broke off from the main body, or perhaps their government decided to expand even faster. In any case, they have settled on planets and destroyed numerous civilizations within ten thousand light-years, and a new invasion force is expected to move directly toward Earth and several other civilizations as well in the near future. Most of those civilizations have at least primitive star drives. Your people do not."

"Do your people and these other races have weapons as well as ships?" Cal asked. How could a bunch of teenagers help fight a galactic navy?

"Of course."

"Then why can't you just attack them now, with your allies?"

Galigan made a rueful smile. "Please follow me and you will see."

11 TONY

P assing through a hatch that opened onto the bridge of the ship, Tony found himself in a small room with several very odd-looking chairs, clustered around an oval table. They were odd in that the chairs sat on a platform base, apparently containing rollers, as they were easy to move. Even stranger, the chairs were quite narrow, much more so than any chair on Earth, and the seating surface contained nothing more than some stretchable webbing, as did the seat back. *Uncomfortable-looking,* Tony thought, as he approached one.

He managed to sit in one, which fit him satisfactorily due to his size, even before Galigan gestured. As the rest seated themselves—the girls and Sasha were okay as well, but Cal, the big guy, had to wedge himself in—Tony grinned at Cal's discomfort. Immediately, the lights dimmed and a video began to flicker on the screen directly ahead. Again, the display unit was astounding to Tony, just like the one on the bridge. The depth and—for a better word—*realness* of the picture took his breath away. In this case however, the video flickered a bit, he picture seemed to jump a frame occasionally, and the quality was occasionally a bit grainy.

Tony had been glancing around, looking for items he might steal later, but the battle scene unfurling before him caused all thoughts of theft to fly away. He was on a spaceship, for Chrissake, and he was watching a battle of epic proportions.

Galigan pointed toward the screen. "What you are about to see is a short sequence captured by one of our spy ships. It was part of a mission across our galaxy which discovered the new invasion decades ago. Please excuse the quality of the recording, as it was taken with a camera normally used to record battles and enemy kills.

"The planet shown had a population that we could not estimate directly, but it must have been at least billions. Unfortunately, it had not yet developed the leap drive that most societies with star travel utilize."

The viewpoint appeared to be thousands of miles above a planet quite like Earth. Near the spy's location, a host of ships began to dive toward the planet. No, not a host of ships, a sky full of ships, a collection of ships like clouds of mosquitoes in the summer around a muddy pool of water. *Or more likely*, Tony thought, *a buzzing, thrashing horde of flies around the carcass of a dead dog on a street near the bridge he had called home.* Cannon flashes illuminated the dark gray sky below as the ships took turns bombarding the planet in massive waves.

The scene took Tony's breath. He had never imagined that a single spaceship existed outside a movie theater or TV screen, which he had only experienced a few times in his life. Now he watched as not just a few, or a hundred, but an uncountable host of ships pummeled and pounded the helpless civilization. There must have been thousands of ships, perhaps tens of thousands. At first skeptical, he began to wonder if the awful battle might be real after all.

It didn't take long. The destruction was thorough and merciless, resulting in a blackened, smoke-wreathed planet, its life totally erased. Amid plumes of dust and smoke, towering fires raged, completing the annihilation. Eventually the screen went black.

Tony's stomach felt hollow, and not simply because he hadn't eaten for a long time.

Letty beat them all to the obvious question. "Why?"

Galigan focused on each of them solemnly. "Because they can. It is the habit this race has of expanding, their chief reason for existing. Occasionally they will swoop in and massacre only the animal life, if they think the planet's climate and vegetation meet their requirements as a starting point for their occupation. But usually they simply erase all life, let the planet lie fallow for a few years, then remake it to their own preferences.

"They can afford to be patient. Their reach is so great and their numbers so enormous that they could destroy a thousand worlds completely while they simultaneously rehabilitated another thousand."

"You say their numbers are huge," said Cal. "How huge?"

Galigan shook his head, abruptly looking older and very weary. "For those like you and me, almost uncountable. To our knowledge, they had expanded to such an extent that they had substantially populated the tiny galaxy companion of our Milky Way before they came toward us. We have sent vessels into that galaxy and explored their civilization in a very limited way. Using the data gathered, we arrived at statistical estimates about the size of their population and the number of planets that they dominate.

"Including the planets in our own galaxy that they control and the estimated habitable planets in the Dwarf Sagittarius Galaxy, we think that they have established homes in more than fifty thousand solar systems, and that their total numbers may approach a hundred trillion."

Tony saw how the others all gaped at their host. He tried to comprehend the numbers, but ... First of all, he knew that a million was a big number, and of course he'd heard the terms billions and trillions. Which were bigger?

It didn't matter, he suddenly understood. This invader had greater numbers than anything in its path.

Galigan continued. "In the video that you just viewed, the attacking force consisted of forty thousand attack ships. Since the civilization they attacked had no star drive and no real defenses, that force required far smaller numbers than had they faced a civilization with more advanced technology.

"One race, whose advancement matched or even perhaps exceeded theirs, put up a mighty opposition. The flotilla they sent to attack had more than *four hundred thousand* ships. They lost at least a quarter of their ships, perhaps half, but it didn't matter to them. They prevailed and reduced their foes' home world to a slag heap. Some years in the future, they will return and begin to reshape the planet to suit their needs.

"Thus they go on, not pillaging or plundering, but in general destroying all that they encounter. In the decades that we have shadowed their movements, they have never lost a direct confrontation. Their numbers are so incredible and their naval flotillas so prodigious that we refer to this invading race as 'The Horde.' For in fact, they truly are a horde, like the army ants on your Earth that can overwhelm anything in their path."

Letty shook her head. "How can anything, any civilization, fight such a force? If their numbers are so massive and their weapons so incredible, stopping them is impossible."

Galigan's head dipped. "You are right, at least so far as we understand at the present time. In any sort of direct confrontation, an opposing force is simply overwhelmed. No matter the level of technology, The Horde is unstoppable.

"Let me give you an example. Your own race has developed a very dangerous weapon called a thermonuclear bomb, basically the initiation of an uncontrolled micro-process similar to that on the sun. Several countries on Earth have stockpiled many of these weapons, to a total of many thousands. And to our knowledge, The Horde does not possess such weapons.

"Say that The Horde attacked Earth, and you had access to our ships to launch these weapons and direct them at the invaders. The bombs are only effective over twenty or so Kerr—pardon, twenty kilometers—at most. If a relatively modest force of fifty thousand Horde ships attacked, you could expend your entire stockpile and perhaps, if you were quite lucky, destroy half their force. Still, you would be defeated."

Tony had had enough. "So, you've kidnapped a bunch of teenagers from Earth to save the galaxy? That's the stupidest thing I ever heard of! You just told us they can't be stopped, can't be conquered."

Galigan gave Tony a patient smile, addressing the question on its merit. "You're right. In a direct confrontation, we can't possibly prevail. What then can we do?

"Remember, we have been watching this race and its progress in our own galaxy for nearly fifty of your years. They appeared unstoppable at first, and we despaired. But during the time we have observed them, we have discovered several weaknesses in their battle plans and technology that can be exploited. Also, apparently due to the nature of their society, they are not nearly so flexible in their planning and deployment of forces as most of the races they encounter.

"They are like a bully, who dominates because of his size and imposing power, and so he becomes lax, believing that he cannot be defeated. We have never seen a member of their race. If we attempt to capture a ship, they will fight until resistance is no longer practical, and then they will self-destruct.

"Some of our scientists speculate that the race is insect-like in terms of its physiology, as their societal structure is somewhat like bees or ants. That is, they establish central bases or hives, and sub-hives, and there is a very rigid structure to their military and planet-settlement functions. But no one knows for sure.

"Their star drive is quite primitive, and their weaponry far less effective than our own. They ignore those deficiencies, plodding ahead at a steady pace, destroying all in their path."

"So you're saying that they're not flashy and swift, just slow and sure," Cal said sarcastically. "They take their time killing you, but they *will* kill you."

Tony hated to agree with the big kid, but he did. "So you kidnap people from other planets to fight for your civilization? Sacrifice us instead of your own soldiers?"

Galigan gave him another tired, patient smile. "No, we kidnapped—or rather, borrowed—you to fight for *your* civilization. You see, The Horde is moving toward Earth rapidly, at least rapidly for them. Unstopped, they should arrive in between ten and thirty years, perhaps even less. We have a plan to stop them, or at least divert them, but we need your help. If you will give it to us, you and the others here that we have invited aboard"— Tony laughed out loud at that—"we believe that you can help save the Earth and other civilizations, including our own."

Ophelia wailed, "I just want to go home!"

As Letty reached toward her, Sasha, on her right, turned and slapped her.

12 OPHELIA

Ophelia turned tear-filled eyes on Sasha as he said, "Get a grip, for God's sake! Do you have to cry about everything?"

Across the table from her, Cal stood, turning as though to come around the table to confront Sasha. Sasha stood his ground, appearing unafraid of Cal.

Before Cal could move, their host produced a small wand and waved it at Sasha, who collapsed in a heap on the floor. He lay staring vacantly up at the ceiling, arms and legs jerking.

Ophelia rubbed her face, trying to feel happy that the jerk had gotten what he deserved, but that didn't stop her from shaking. As Letty patted her shoulder, she tried to keep from crying again.

Cal swung toward Galigan. "What did you do?"

The wand vanished into a slit on the right side of the alien's coat. "Nothing permanent, I assure you. Merely a few signals scrambled, enough to keep him subdued. He should be fine in a few minutes." Galigan bent over and scooped Sasha back into his chair.

"Please let me finish. I expect all of you are hungry by now, and surely the amount of information you have absorbed is very wearying.

"First of all, you are correct. At present we know of absolutely no method by which we can defeat The Horde. Their navies are far too large, and their population provides them with as many soldiers as they require. Further, their hive mentality assures that, unlike my race and yours, there are no strong individuals. There is simply a group mentality with a powerful desire to advance the goals of their society.

"But as I said, they have weaknesses. There is little individuality, so there is no incentive for change. Over the fifty years we have monitored them, their technology has not advanced, and their stodgy command-and-control mentality has kept them exploring doggedly through the near arm of our galaxy. We have no idea for certain, but they may have other exploration fleets in different locations across the Milky Way.

"Although we cannot confront them directly, we have learned to nip at them, irritate them, to slow or stall their advance. When distracted enough, they fall back a bit to consider. Sometimes they change direction slightly, to avoid a concentrated area of irritation.

"By experimentation, we have learned to make surgical strikes, brief assaults that cripple small elements of their forces. When these attacks occur frequently enough—not frontal, but to the side, on the flank, near the rear of their force—they can be nudged into changing course a degree or two, turning to address the brief attacks. Over time we have vectored their forces away from a few civilized systems that lay in their path."

Sasha stirred.

Ophelia whimpered and moved away.

"Don't worry," Galigan assured her. "He will be quite docile for some time."

"So you expect some teenagers from Earth to help you win a war?" Tony repeated. "A war you just told us can't be really won? Sounds to old Tony like you want *sacrifices*, not soldiers."

Somehow, Cal made Ophelia feel warm and safe. He cast a hostile glance at Sasha, an irritated gaze toward Tony. "We're not stupid. At least I'm not, and Letty surely isn't. I can't speak for a street rat." When Tony bristled, Cal said, "You called yourself that, Mex." Turning to Galigan he continued, "Smart or not, we don't understand your technology and it would probably take years to learn. Besides, as advanced as you are, you probably have droids that could do a better job than we can."

"Droids? Ah, robotic machines. Yes, we do have very intelligent robots, even androids, as you say. That is, robots made in our image. However, our experience is that very young members of a number of races, including yours, make the best fighters. Not alone, but with implants that we can provide. That is a major reason you were selected, your genetic tolerance for the devices we will interface to your brains."

Ophelia stood up, pulling away from Letty. Her tolerance for the frights of the day had been exceeded. "I don't want anything in my brain. I just want to go home." She burst into tears and ran for the door.

Before she reached it, bright stars filled her vision. Even though she could feel herself falling, she couldn't stop. As the floor rushed up to meet her, consciousness fled.

13 SASHA

A dull, pulsing ache at the back of his head awoke Sasha. When he tried to sit up, lightning struck. Blinded, he slipped to a horizontal position, groaning in the blackness.

"So. Our brave Sasha who administers slap therapy is just as much a whiner as the one he slapped."

Sasha's eyes popped open. Turning his head cautiously, he made out Letty staring at him across Tony's recumbent form. Her expression reminded him of his foster mother, the Fat Pig. He started to reply, the most acid, insulting words he could conjure up, and it struck him. His behavior. He had lived in the midst of such insulting, punishing words and actions from those around him that he had slipped into the same despicable behavior. The thought shocked him so thoroughly that he began to shake, so hard that his bed actually vibrated.

Letty came beside him in an instant, immediately showing concern. Her about-face astounded him until he realized that such behavior defined Letty's personality. A genuinely empathic person by nature, she demonstrated concern for everyone. Her anger had been at his act of slapping Ophelia; it wasn't aimed directly at him as a person.

"I'm fine," he said gruffly, unable as yet to return any politeness for the bit of sympathy she had shown.

He stirred, rolled toward the left side of the bed away from Letty, and sat up. The back of his head still pulsed with pain as though he had fractured his skull.

A glance around showed that they were back in the featureless white room. He tried to make his reply at least neutral, not hostile. "I don't remember how we got here."

She stepped back from him. "When you behaved like a total jackass and slapped Ophelia, that Galigan guy pulled out a small metal wand and waved it toward you. You fell in a heap, and when you came to, you were Mr. Plastic Man, doing whatever we liked." She paused as if waiting for his reaction to that, but he still felt too dull to reply.

"Ophelia got the same treatment when she got all hysterical," Letty went on. "We were all brought back here, and those of us who were still conscious were fed some sort of glop that Galigan insisted had nutritional value. Then he gave us each a tall drink of something that tasted a bit like diluted lemonade. The next thing I knew, I woke up a few moments ago, with everyone else out cold on their beds. And I have a little cap stuck to the back of my head. I think he drugged us."

Warily, Sasha reached to touch his head, and encountered a small lump at the very back of his skull. Experimentally, he tried to move it and lightning struck again.

Letty gave him an evil grin. "So it smarts when you touch it, just like mine does."

"You could have warned me," he growled.

"And miss a chance to watch you suffer? No way." As she started back to her bed, she said over her shoulder, "If you touch Ophelia again, I will hurt you severely. Got it?"

Sasha didn't see how she could possibly injure him unless she caught him asleep again, but maybe she could. He didn't like her, and he couldn't stand the whiny, crybaby Ophelia, but at this point he didn't want to make an enemy of Letty. "I won't touch her. I promise." After a moment, he offered, "I didn't want to hurt her. I just wanted her to quit behaving like a baby."

"So you think we should just stand by and let these kidnappers make us into involuntary soldiers?"

Truth to tell, Sasha really didn't have any strong opinion yet. He mainly felt more than happy to be away from the Frawleys.

In a way, he suspected that he felt a good deal like Tony. His situation, bad as it had been, didn't resemble the hopelessness of Tony's, but it had been very uncomfortable.

One part of his mind told him to resist as hard as he could against any agency that had taken him hostage against his will. But a second suggestion, whispered subtly from his subconscious, reminded him that this new situation might be better than his former one. What if Galigan had told the truth? What if an alien race was bearing down, hell-for-leather, on Earth's solar system? Might it not be better to explore their new situation, see what it offered, before he refused to play ball with their captors?

"I'll say this," he made a measured response. "If—*if*—this Galigan has told the truth, maybe I can do more good here than where I came from. In that foster home I was as much as a captive as I am here. And if Galigan's not the biggest liar on Earth—uh, in the solar system—I might be able to help."

Letty seemed surprised at his thoughtful reply. Saying nothing, she returned to her platform.

The other three roommates were quiet. It occurred to him that he needed to urinate again rather badly. Ignoring the pounding in his head, he stood. "I assume the door to that bathroom still works?"

Letty roused from her reverie. "Yeah, I just used it."

As he headed to the bathroom, Letty said, "Did you notice we're not dressed the same? We have on sort of uniforms now, though without any markings."

Glancing down, he realized that he no longer wore the khaki-colored pants and shirt of the day before. The dark gray, two-piece uniform, as though made of linen or smooth cotton, had a row of silver buttons down the front, and even though Sasha had slept in it, it held not a single wrinkle. "Nice material," he commented, moving on to the door in the corner.

Bathroom functions taken care of, he exited to find Letty still awake, the others still unconscious. He grinned at Letty. "You won't believe me, but I opened the door with a thought."

She hopped off the bed and came toward him. As she did, he thought, *Close.* Silently, the almost invisible door did just that.

Joining him, she said, "I just pressed the button like we did before. Show me."

He paused. "Okay, think about the door opening. That is, tell it to open, only don't speak."

She blinked. "You're kidding."

"Told you that you wouldn't believe me."

"Hmmph." She took a step forward, regarded the door carefully, blinked again, and appeared to concentrate. Again, the door slid aside. "I'll be jiggered."

"Huh?" Sasha had never heard that particular expression.

She waved away his confusion with her left hand. "Something my grandmother used to say—I'm probably the only teenager on Earth that still says it. At least, that was true when I was on Earth. It's sort of like saying, 'I'll be darned.' Okay, when I go in, how do I lock the door?"

Sasha showed her to think "locked" to be sure no one walked in on her, which seemed to make her more comfortable.

Before closing it again, he took one last look inside. Though the same off-white color as their bedroom, the bathroom walls had an enamel texture. The toilet and small shower looked ordinary. In addition, a nook at one side held a pile of soft, white towels, a bottle of what must be liquid soap, along with yellow sponges, or maybe they were loofahs. To his right, a lavatory projected out of the wall, taking up less space. The facilities were tight but adequate.

Returning to his bed, he wondered, as Ophelia began to stir, just what the day held in store.

Anything can happen, he thought. But so what? *This is the best living I've had in years.* Short of sudden death, just about anything would be an improvement on the Frawley home.

Oddly, he realized that he was no longer neutral, but actually happy in his new situation. He found himself beginning to look forward to whatever the day's activities brought.

14 OPHELIA

Cal and Tony were sitting on the side of their beds, holding their heads as Ophelia finally sat up. As she watched Tony rub his head and cringe, she was glad that she was not the only with an awful headache.

Letty came to sit beside her. "Are you okay?"

Ophelia nodded. "I have a headache, but it looks to me like Cal and Tony do as well. What happened to me?"

"I guess I'll tell you what I told Sasha," Letty said. She told Ophelia how Galigan had used the wand on her when she panicked, how he had fed them and returned them to their room.

As she finished up, Letty told Ophelia, "Each one of us has a background where we had trouble at home, then we showed up here. Do you remember what happened before you ended up here?"

Ophelia blinked. They all had problems at home? "You bet I do. I had just discovered that my stepmother was making plans to cut me out of my dad's will."

"Really," Cal interjected. He came to stand beside Letty. "Tell us about it."

Stumbling at first, Ophelia told of the last minutes before she blacked out, to awaken in the white room. How her stepmother had been cordial and friendly at first, and then, once her father died, had grown ever colder and more remote.

"She hired new servants," Ophelia told them. "And I was convinced they were spying on me. Then one night, I was about to go downstairs, when I saw them talking in the entry. I hid and listened."

Ophelia could still see her stepmother and stepbrother beneath the enormous chandelier, its many-faceted crystals spreading bright dots of light over the vaulted ceiling, around the circular walls, and onto the white marble floor.

"SHE'S UPSTAIRS?" Margaret had muttered.

"In her room." Jason's voice, equally low.

"I talked to Liston today," she told her son. "The delay in filing the will, because Harold's death was so *untimely*, is finally past. Under current provisions, I get ten percent, she gets the rest." Ophelia had not wondered who *she* might be.

Jason's voice went up a few decibels. "What can we do?"

"Shh. I fawned all over him today. He's single, and he knows Harold's finances intimately. I suggested my fondness for him, and that I would personally be very grateful if the terms of the will could be made more favorable."

Ophelia could almost hear Jason's grimace of disgust. "Surely you wouldn't sleep with the man, Mother. He's a decade or more older than you are."

Margaret's voice was complacent, almost satisfied. "Certainly not without marrying him. But think positively, son. Having a lawyer in the family could confer many advantages."

He remained silent for several moments, as if digesting that. "Maybe," he said at last. "How did he react?"

"Positively, though he tried very hard to conceal his real feelings. With a bit of encouragement, he could cut Ophelia out of all but a few million, maybe even make me her guardian. If we play this well, she'll be powerless to attack our position."

AS SHE FINISHED, Letty had an expression of horror on her face, Cal appeared troubled, and even Sasha showed a bit of concern. Only Tony looked simply puzzled.

"Don't know much about rich folks and the law," he commented. "Could that old woman take your money even though it was your dad's?"

Ophelia had no idea, and she said so. "Margaret really sounded confident," Ophelia concluded. "Maybe she could—will —be able to, I don't know much about the law and wills and so forth."

Before she could say more, the outer door opened and Galigan walked in. He said cheerfully, "I see you are still suffering slightly from the incisions made to place your implants. You no doubt have rather piercing headaches. Don't be alarmed; your discomfort will go away very soon."

"Ophelia," Galigan addressed her, "I hope you feel better today, perhaps a bit less anxious."

She nodded slowly. "Yes. My head hurts, like the rest of us, but I don't feel so scared now."

"Your pain will diminish," he repeated. He stepped back a bit and addressed all five. "More activities today, I'm afraid. Each of you must undergo a battery of tests to determine whether you are suited for our purposes."

The term "implants" finally seemed to worm its way into

Sasha's mind. "Wait a minute," he said sharply. "You implanted even more things in our brains?"

"Of course. It is fundamentally the reason we chose you. You have a natural ability to make maximal use of them. But the process is now complete."

Tony looked as angry to Ophelia as Sasha did. "Why should we do anything for you when you just jammed our brains full of more mind-control devices?" His words were almost yelled. He started toward Galigan menacingly, anger showing on his flushed features.

Galigan plucked the small wand from beneath his jacket. "Please, Tony. You saw what this is capable of."

Tony stopped moving but continued to grumble to himself.

Ophelia almost had to grin. She didn't like the idea of some sort of devices stuck in her brain either, but at least she wasn't the only one worried and concerned.

Finally Sasha's frown faded. He moved toward the door. "You can test me all you like."

"Thank you. By the way, Ophelia, the rest of your friends all have nicknames. Do you have one as well, or do you usually go by your full name?"

She hesitated. "D—Daddy always called me Opi."

"Opi. Delightful. All right, Opi, if you and your friends will follow me, we can proceed with the testing."

Sasha moved promptly out the door following Galigan, Tony close behind. Opi glommed onto Letty's arm and walked out beside her. Glancing back, she saw that Cal brought up the rear.

What now?

15 CAL

Cal lingered behind the others, deeply suspicious of all of it. Dad needed his help. Every day he remained by himself, he drank more. Cal had to get back!

Maybe he believed, a little, what the alien said. But so what? At the rate the dangerous alien race moved, ponderously, by Galigan's own admission, it might take them hundreds of years to get close enough to Earth to be a threat, much longer than Galigan had suggested. By that time, Earth's science and technology might be advanced enough to destroy the invaders no matter how great their numbers.

He sympathized with the predicament of Galigan's race. Perhaps the oncoming Horde already endangered it. If so, Cal could understand Galigan's feelings of urgency. But that didn't concern Cal. His priority had to be staying close to Dad and trying to keep him alive, even if he had to put up with Dad's drunken self-pity.

Galigan and Tony and Opi and Letty and Sasha could do without him.

He felt a little guilty, seeing Letty's expression sharply in his mind, remembering her quick defense of Opi and her assertiveness as she stared him down when she first awoke. Somehow, he liked being around her, knew he would like staying near her if he could.

Angrily, he concentrated on Galigan, not looking in Letty's direction.

Again they boarded an elevator. Galigan spoke a single word, which sounded like "*roleska*." The elevator began to descend this time, rather than rise.

"There are many young people like yourselves on this ship," he told them. "For that reason, we have adjusted our normal waking and sleeping periods to the twenty-four-hour day of Earth. You will see many more in the gathering room we are approaching. Please refrain from speaking to the others for now. There will be time for greetings later."

The elevator opened onto a broad hall that held several dozen teenagers like themselves, diverse in racial heritage, including African, Asian, Latino, and white, probably European. Through the hubbub Cal caught various conversations, mostly in English, but a few in other languages. He noted that the groups stood in areas of the floor marked with clear blue circles. Galigan gestured them to one side, into a vacant circle.

"Please remain here," he told them.

For the first time, Cal registered that Galigan wore a darker outfit with more gold decorations, resembling a military dress uniform.

Tony began to gravitate toward a group of Latino youths. Galigan put a hand to his shoulder. "There will be time for meeting some of your peers a bit later, Tony. For now, your tests will start shortly."

Galigan pulled out a handful of packages from his invisible pocket and gave one to each of them. "These are nutrition bars, which will provide all the sustenance you will need today."

With that, he left them. Cal could hear Tony muttering to himself, but he stayed within their blue circle.

Opening the package, Cal found an oblong bar that looked like nothing so much as a large Snickers bar.

Feeling starved, Cal wolfed it down. It tasted like a chocolate bar also, quite satisfying, and he no longer felt hungry.

The hall, Cal saw as he gazed around, displayed the same color as their room, an off-white that covered the bulkheads and overhead. A balcony ran around the bulkhead about halfway up, the protruding walkway and its attached railing a deep magenta. Light panels and air inlets dotted the overhead.

Cal saw that the young people were divided mainly into groups of five, although he saw a few groups nearby with six, and one with only three. He could see nine groups, probably between forty-five and fifty youths.

No one appeared to be more than seventeen or eighteen. His group drew a few curious glances, but they were quickly ignored and the overall murmur of conversations continued. Most were definitely in English.

Letty sidled up beside him. "What's the problem?"

So she had noticed his expression. After an awkward pause he said, "I'm worried about my dad."

She nodded. "Probably for some of the same reasons I'm worried about my folks."

He swung around. "It's not the same! You've got two parents, and the worst that can happen is their divorce. My dad is all I've got, and he's drunk eighty percent of the time and suicidal the rest. Without me there, I'm afraid he'll kill himself."

After a moment she put a hand on his arm. "He *is* killing himself," she said softly, eyes filled with sadness. "Whether he uses a gun or a bottle, the result will be the same. The bottle just takes longer and is a whole lot more painful to you."

Cal tried to be angry, tried to develop enough hatred at her soft truths that he could yell at her, contradict her, defend the drunkard his father had become. But he couldn't. She hadn't spoken in anger or pity or even with some idea of hurting him. Just the truth, something he didn't want to consider.

"I just want to help him," he said, hearing his own despair.

The hand on his arm tightened. "I know."

Just then one of the ship's crew stepped up to him. Apparently an officer, he stood even taller than Galigan and wore a uniform similar to their host's, though it bore different decorations. "Calvin Adam McGregor?"

Cal turned, regarding the tall figure with surprise. It had been a long time since anyone had spoken his entire name. "Yes."

"Please come with me." The man, with his odd accent, stumbled over some words, unlike Galigan with his impeccable English. At least he made himself clear. Cal followed him through a nearby doorway, noting that several others had been picked out as well, leaving by additional hatches scattered along the bulkhead.

Cal followed his guide down a long, narrow passage. Sparse light panels created dim illumination along its length. At the end of the hallway, two doors were set to the left and another two to the right, plus one directly ahead. The officer led him to the one at the end, into a room not much larger than a closet. A helmet, rather similar to one for riding a motorcycle, except a bright yellow and a bit rounder, sat on the top of a high-back chair, and the man gestured for him to put it on.

Having become fairly used to Galigan, Cal passively let the man help him sit down and strap on the helmet. No wires connected it to anything. Apparently any communications to or from the helmet were handled wirelessly.

"Pay attention to the display," the man told him. "There will be instructions in your language which you are to follow very closely. This device will test your basic knowledge, your intellectual capacity, your judgment, and your ability to make quick, accurate decisions. Continue until you are told to stop. You will be given specific opportunities to take brief breaks."

As the officer left, the display before Cal came to life. He had no expectations about the upcoming test, but he still felt surprise as simple mathematical problems popped onto the screen. The instructions told him to either think about the mathematical process and its answer, or type in the answer on the keyboard.

After a bit of experimentation, he found that typing on the standard "qwerty" keyboard helped him marshal his thoughts more than trying to communicate mentally. The test proceeded through algebra problems and on to calculus. He had completed only one semester of advanced math, so quite quickly the tests approached a level that left him clueless.

He felt that he had acquitted himself well up to the higher levels of mathematics when the questions shifted abruptly to language and grammar. This time the instructions directed him to visualize the answers rather than use the keyboard.

The new implants worked, although Cal still refused to think about electronic *things* now residing in his brain. He had only to see the solution in his mind and the machine understood.

By the time the second set of tests ended, he felt more at ease with the process, if not the fact of mental communication.

Just when he had become comfortable with the mental Q and A, the format changed once more. Following detailed instructions, he found himself playing a very advanced video game which involved combat against bulbous, silver-gray space craft that begin to attack him rapidly and savagely. The ships resembled those of The Horde he had seen in Galigan's video.

With only a few seconds to become accustomed to the flight controls and weapons-launching lever that resembled the control stick he had seen in pictures of fighter jets, Cal was thrown into the midst of a frantic, confusing battle between himself and the silver ships.

Frantically he fought, learning the complex control mechanisms and at the same time defending himself. Initially, he lost every encounter, and a side display began to show unhappy results in large red numbers.

Gradually, he achieved a bit of proficiency, and a list of green numbers began to increase. The combat continued to be frenetic, the special effects frightening in their realism. Huge ship-mounted energy cannons pummeled his imaginary ship, explosions constantly flashed around him, and a new ship replaced every one he destroyed.

When the exercise ended very suddenly, he sat back, exhausted, uniform soaked with sweat and arms so heavy that he doubted he could lift them back to the control mechanisms.

The opening of the door surprised him, as the same alien stepped inside and motioned him to leave. He rose unsteadily, realizing that only once had he taken advantage of a restroom break. As he followed the man he asked, "How long have I been in there?"

The man took a moment to puzzle out his meaning. "Nearly twelve of your hours."

Astonished, Cal felt his jaw drop.

Back in the large gathering room, a few youths still congregated. His own team, except for Letty, stood where he had left them. Even as he joined them, Letty came through the door adjoining his, looking as tired as he felt.

A young soldier returned them to their room. Cal entered first, and before anyone else could pass him, he took fresh underwear from the storage drawers and slipped into the shower.

16 LETTY

Letty sat bolt upright, suddenly awake. Her imprisonment, marooned in space, wasn't a dream. If she could believe her own senses, she remained closeted with four other teenagers, most of whom she would rather have avoided.

Cal—well, he wasn't so bad. Rather handsome in fact. But the rest ranged from supremely irritating like Sasha, to whiny like Opi, to simply crude and socially awkward like Tony.

Opi. She was sweet but really a wimp. Still, Letty had quickly defended her.

She'd found Sasha to be rude and antisocial, although he had at least learned to respect her. Thoughtful, and perhaps not as much of an idiot as she'd first assumed, but that didn't make her want to spend any time with him.

Tony was just what he had claimed to be, a street person, though she refused to use the term "rat," with little civilized behavior or knowledge of the niceties of polite human interaction. The sort that, if Letty had noticed him on the street back home, she'd have crossed to the other side.

How, she thought to herself, *could she get out of here?* Chances didn't look good. With exotic devices planted in their brains, she didn't see their hosts just letting them run home.

At the thought of the implants, her hand strayed reflexively to her head. Nothing—no lump, no cap. Experimentally, she pressed on her skull at the former location of the cap, but it felt firm and healed. *Great, not only do I have some electronic gadgets stuck in my brain, but the entry hole is sealed.*

She sat up on the edge of her bed. The others still slept or were drugged. She still wore the uniform from the previous day. Either that or someone had re-dressed her and the rest of them as they slept. On impulse, she left her bed to lift the edge of Cal's sheet. He wore an identical outfit.

Odd, she decided, that none of them had protested the installation of whatever now resided in their brains. But what could they have done? Sasha had been a bit rebellious, and Galigan had used that slender wand to reduce him to a slobbering moron. Then he had cowed Tony with the threat of the same device.

Galigan might murmur that they were simply "guests," borrowed for their services for some unspecified time, but in fact they were prisoners, just as Sasha had suspected at first. Their room might not be called a jail, but effectively it served the same purpose.

Could it be a different room, in fact? For all she knew, dozens of identical rooms lay scattered around the ship.

Looking about, she scanned the walls for clues about her location. The door. Still in the corner to her right? Sasha had pointed out the faint crack, the fine line that divided door edge from wall.

It struck her like a thunderbolt. She could now see that faint line from where she sat! She left her bed to approach the door. The line showed clearly from a distance, and something else. Simply a flat off-white before, the wall now had a visible texture, faint whorls once invisible but now glaringly apparent.

I can see better. A great deal better.

Turning, she saw Tony rousing, trying to sit up, rolling sleepily toward her. She dragged him out of bed.

"What the hell? What's goin' on?"

"Do you feel that little, plastic bump on your skull?"

His hand strayed to his dark hair, moved back and forth. Puzzled, he muttered, "It's gone," almost to himself. His attention came back to her. "Why does it matter?"

"Listen. In the corner, where you found that tiny line on the wall that marked the edge of the door. Can you see it now?"

"Of course not." His gaze followed hers to the wall. "It's too —" His voice went up half an octave. "I *can* see it! And ... what did they do to the wall?"

Triumphantly, she went back to her bed. "They didn't do anything. We can just see a whole lot better."

He scratched his head, retreated to his platform, climbed on. "Is it those things in our brain?"

"No idea. Maybe it's them *and* some other things they did to us. Whatever, I can see about ten times better than before. Wake up the others."

He hesitated, getting off the bed. "I gotta pee."

She considered. "So do I. You go first, then wake them while I finish up in there."

He nodded, the door to their bath opening long before he came close to it. "It's more sensitive."

"Or our brains are sending out stronger signals. Hurry up!"

When she left the bathroom, all were awake. She found Sasha inspecting the line in the door as though he had a microscope. As she joined the others, an amused Opi compared her vision with Cal's. Tony simply sat on his bed, watching.

Sasha abruptly backed up from the door, apparently focusing on it, and it opened immediately.

"We can command this door with our minds, too."

As she joined them, Cal said. "You're right. I had to wear reading glasses, but now I won't need them." He motioned to the fabric of his uniform. "I can make out the interweaving of the threads in our clothing as if I had a magnifying glass."

"So can I," Letty said. She motioned them to gather at her bed. "Clearly, our bodies have been improved. I had a bad cold a couple of weeks ago, and I still felt raspy yesterday. Now, I feel perfect. I'll bet the rest of you do, too."

She sat on her bed as the rest made a circle around her. "There are more important questions to consider. Let's talk about our tests yesterday. Cal, you first."

As Cal began to describe the various series of tests, Letty noted frequent nods among the others, often joined by her own.

When he finished, Opi and Sasha said that theirs were identical, and Letty found that theirs matched hers as well.

Tony's had been somewhat different. The video game war exercises were identical, but many of the math and grammar exercises had been replaced with logical problems and reasoning tests.

After a moment Letty said, "Tony, how many years total have you been in school?"

He frowned, and Letty could imagine him trying to work out whether she had insulted him. "It's an honest question," she assured him. "How many years, your best estimate."

His face twisted in concentration. "I went real regular through the sixth grade. Not a lot after that."

She nodded. "The rest of us have been in school at least through the tenth or eleventh grade, so we've learned stuff you haven't. That doesn't make us smarter than you, it just makes us recipients of more information. Do you see? They were testing your native intelligence, not your knowledge."

Cal frowned. "So they were searching for the same qualities? Why? What do they mean?"

As he spoke, Galigan strode in.

17 SASHA

Galigan greeted them with a hearty, "Good morning." He beamed at each one in turn and said, "My sincere congratulations. All of you have passed the strenuous and exhausting test sequence that we require of candidates. You will be entered into the program immediately to become a full-time Shadow Warrior team. You should be very proud."

Sasha found himself trying to come to grips with all Galigan had said.

Not Letty. She said, loudly, "So, we passed a test that makes us cannon fodder for your navy? We're supposed to be happy because we could be good fighters in this hopeless cause of yours? By the way, what the hell are Shadow Warriors? Whatever they are, I don't think I want to be one."

As if troubled by her outburst, Galigan shifted his feet and surveyed them all again, his smile fading. "The ... Shadow Warriors are our elite defense force. They are the only reason we have successfully fought The Horde over the past few Earth decades.

"Shadow Warriors feint and strike, nipping at the heels of the invaders of our galaxy. Their ghostlike appearances confuse our enemy, keep them off-balance, enabling us to alter the direction of their movements, as I told you before. What little control we have over The Horde is due to the success of our Shadow Warriors."

He summoned his smile again. "You can be such a team. You five were chosen as a potential Shadow Warrior crew, and the testing has verified your potential. Our evaluators are confident that you will make an exceptional team.

"You, Cal," Galigan turned to him, "have demonstrated outstanding potential as a commander. You have many skills of the accomplished soldier: aggressiveness, initiative, strategic thinking, leadership abilities. You will be the designated commander.

"Letty," he turned to her, "you have fine strategic planning potential. Although lower in aggressiveness and initiative, you have the ability to be assistant commander, the person behind the captain, advising him and assuring that his battle plans are well thought out. You will serve initially as Cal's sub-commander and co-pilot.

"Opi, Tony, and Sasha, all of you demonstrated any number of the traits of Shadow Warriors, but you must have further training to validate your specific assignments. Opi, you have fascinating possibilities, and I will follow your progress with great curiosity."

Sasha watched Opi blink in confusion, raising her eyebrows, as Galigan backed up so he nearly stood in the open doorway. Outside, groups of teenagers marched past, each with a different guide.

One group, Latino in appearance, stared through the door as curiously as Sasha gazed out. He deduced that they would soon be going to some sort of assembly. *Wonder what my good qualities are?*

Galigan verified Sasha's guess by saying, "Please follow me. We need to provide you with food before our next meeting of candidates."

They followed, Cal showing irritation with each step he took, Letty appearing concerned as well, and Opi looking fearful, as usual. Sasha brought up the rear this time, interested and curious, and he could see that Tony felt the same.

Again, the elevator, crowded this time with other teenagers that gave his team a thorough going-over but remained equally silent.

The elevator door opened onto a large, low-ceilinged room that proved to be a cafeteria, with a long food-line and real "Earth food," not the gray glop that Letty had said they'd been fed the first time.

The main feature turned out to be fruit, enormous piles of melon slices, bananas, bright red strawberries, and dark blueberries, as well as large bowls of several varieties of apples and oranges. Sasha gratefully gathered a huge mound of the various fruits on a small tray, stacks of which sat at the front of the line.

There were also platters of breadstuffs like muffins, rolls, even cinnamon buns.

The choice of drinks included fresh milk from a dispenser. Grabbing a plastic glass from a stack beside it, Sasha filled it to the brim.

There were no plates provided, so Sasha piled the tray high with food. He joined his "teammates" at a table beside which Galigan stood, motioning to them.

Sasha didn't find any meat, but the abundance of food meant that nobody would go hungry. He hadn't experienced anything like it in the months he had spent with the Frawleys. He relished every bite, cramming in mouthful after mouthful and chewing as though at any moment, their hosts would come and snatch away their trays. Tony, he noticed, did the same. Conversation didn't exist.

The room itself, perhaps a hundred feet square, had an expanse interrupted only by a few large pillars that more than likely were part of the basic ship structure. Walls and ceiling were the regulation, nondescript off-white, lit by the same scattered panels. The floor consisted of tile or linoleum like that in their quarters.

Sasha couldn't detect any odor of baking, so the prepared breads must have been cooked elsewhere. Could they even have been acquired on Earth? *Possible*, he thought. The buns and rolls reminded him of deli food.

Hundreds of humans his age, with only a few of the aliens, congregated in the area. Everyone ate and drank as silently as Sasha and his group. Equally intimidated, in all probability.

A loud, harsh word issued from what must be several speakers embedded in the ceiling: *"Velax."* After a moment, Sasha recognized the word as "Assembly," although his discovery didn't register at first. Galigan immediately motioned them to take their trays to one of several square openings on the periphery of the room. When Sasha dawdled for a moment, Galigan's wand appeared in his hand, and Sasha raced to the tray drop as though on fire. The departure from the lunchroom, a mass movement, took seconds. *Other candidates must have seen the wand work,* Sasha thought. Plus, he had seen several other of their captors produce the thin rods.

A plain stairway led down one deck. Very low tech for a space cruiser, Sasha thought. They emerged into the same massive room where they had waited for their tests.

This time, metal chairs filled the room, attached securely to the floor. As he sat down beside Tony, Sasha wondered how the aliens had changed the room so dramatically in a day. Even as he puzzled over it, his casual stare upward revealed that the railed balcony about halfway up the walls, vacant yesterday, held rows of soldiers who watched the groups below with particular scrutiny. With a shock, he recognized humans clad in the same uniforms among Galigan's race.

Before he could question what that might mean, an officer ascended a raised dais at the front of the room. Taller than Galigan and quite distinguished, with sparse silver hair, a few facial lines accentuated his age. There was no bright trim, such as Earth-style military ribbons, but the lapels of his uniform jacket each held a single gold diamond. Sasha thought they must signify both his rank and a variety of awards.

"Greeting to new warrior candidates," the officer began, his voice booming through the room. He wore no obvious microphone, but his voice sounded amplified.

Puzzling on where a microphone might be hidden, Sasha got his biggest surprise of the day so far. The man wasn't speaking English! Was it the native language of the aliens? It must be, and Sasha understood it all, just as he had the word *"velax"* a few moments before.

So we learned this while we were out, just like Opi did, he thought—and shivered despite himself.

"I am happy to say that those in this meeting have scored well on their aptitude tests and are now full candidates to become Shadow Warriors. Congratulations on your accomplishments.

"With the next breath, I warn you that your upcoming training will be rigorous and exacting. Some of you will not succeed. My hope is that many of you will qualify, becoming new Shadow Warriors."

A buzz of whispers and a few outright conversations flitted across the room. Sasha exchanged glances with Tony and with his other roommates who had settled one row behind them.

The officer continued, "I am Captain Alitan and I am in charge of this training vessel. My race formed the first Shadow

Warriors units. Our home planet is named Molethan, and we are Molethians. We founded the Shadow Warrior organization to combat the invasion force we call The Horde.

"You notice that you understand our native tongue. That is due to a combination of implants that expand your mental and some of your physical abilities, and additional training that took place while you slept. If all went as planned, you now understand me perfectly. If so, please raise your right hand."

He scanned the room carefully, apparently seeing if anyone failed to poke their hand into the air. "Very good. I believe everyone has learned our language successfully.

"Now, it is my responsibility, and that of the dedicated group of teachers who work beside me, to see that you successfully become fighters against the great threat to your civilization and ours in this galaxy you know as the Milky Way.

"Our task is serious, even desperate, but our duty is an honorable calling. We represent the last hope of your Earth and dozens of other intelligent species in this arm of the galaxy. If we do not succeed, we will all fail together, and our civilizations and races will be destroyed.

"I know these last few days have been perplexing and frightening. I freely concede that we have snatched you from your homes and interrupted your daily lives. However, our need and yours is so great that we deemed our actions necessary to the survival of all intelligent life within a ten-thousand-light-year radius.

"Now I ask you to wholeheartedly join us in this venture. With your cooperation, our training, and the technology we will provide, there is an excellent chance that we can stop our mutual enemy from its continued excursion toward Earth."

He looked to and fro over the assemblage. "Before we adjourn, I will be happy to answer your questions."

18 TONY

Tony became increasingly edgy as he listened. Not like Cal or Letty. He had no great desire to go home; he didn't have a home. But he did have questions, and he itched to ask some of them.

Before he could respond to the captain's invitation, a young man popped up near the front of the hall and began to ask a question in a language that sounded like babble to Tony.

Captain Alitan interrupted him. "As you confirmed a few moments ago, you now understand my native language. Though all warrior candidates on this ship come from North America, there are several languages spoken on your continent. Because of that, your new language is common to everyone in this room."

Showing surprise, bemusement, and finally comprehension, the young man considered a moment, and then said in the captain's tongue, "How convenient that we all can understand each other. Very well. You have indicated that not all of us will successfully continue training. If we fail, what then? Will we simply be tossed out the nearest airlock?"

Alitan frowned, then said, "As of this moment, all candidates in this room have qualified for training. You need to concentrate on success and worry less about failure."

"But what if—" the young man tried to continue.

"You understand what your duty is here," Alitan said sternly. "Follow my advice, and perhaps you will not need to be concerned about shortcomings."

The young man sat down slowly.

Across the room, another arose. "Sir, we have had items implanted in our brains, yet the incision seems healed already. I have two questions. First, how long have we been here? And second, how can you be certain that the implants will not harm us?"

Alitan nodded. "I will address your second question first. I have had implants for more than thirty of your years. They have improved both my well-being and my physical performance. You needn't worry about them. As to your stay aboard, it depends on exactly when you arrived, but for most of you, it has been several weeks."

Several weeks! Tony gasped in unison with the congregation around him. He thought he had been aboard for only two days. They must have been kept under sedation for a long while.

Next to him, his team muttered and looked at each other, and Cal seemed about to explode.

Most were so taken aback at the revelation that the murmur in the room died away to a hushed silence.

Before anyone else could speak, Opi stood, and Tony rolled his eyes.

The captain nodded. "Yes?"

"I don't want to be here!" Opi blurted. "I just want to be home, to be with my family, on solid ground and not up here, far away from everything I know, far away from everything that's familiar." As she spoke, her voice elevated to a wail.

Galigan stood at the side of the room, near the front. He

stepped forward to get the captain's attention. "Sir, if I may ... I am familiar with the young woman's circumstances."

"Proceed."

Galigan turned to Opi across the sea of heads. "Opi, I know your situation well. Who do you suppose determined that you were a good candidate for this demanding position?

"In fact, Opi, you have no family. Your mother and father are dead and your stepmother and her son are plotting to cheat you out of your fortune."

"But you could help me!" she protested. "You know so much, you could prevent this from happening."

"Not without giving away our existence, which we are not prepared to do at this time." He motioned, returning the floor to his captain.

Alitan raised his voice. "This applies to all of you. We have watched you for years and have chosen you, a few thousand, from your entire population.

"First we determined your eligibility to join this program based upon certain genetic traits. Then we filtered your numbers, picking only those whose personal situations were dire. We have said that we 'borrowed' you, but I freely admit that you were abducted. Effectively, you were taken against your will.

"Here, your situations will be much improved. You will be treated better here than you would have been in your own homes. For those of you who make it to full combat status, it is true that some will die. But if you work hard and succeed in your training, you will be honored in this service, both in life and, if necessary, in death.

"You, and many others like you on other ships around this world, and countless hundreds more orbiting other worlds like yours, are the only hope against The Horde. You have a profound opportunity to affect the future of billions of lives in this arm of our galaxy."

"I don't care!" Opi's scream shocked those near her enough to make some jerk in their chairs. "I'd rather die at my stepmother's hands than live in this awful place! I won't fight! I won't train! I won't! I won't!" She dissolved into tears, and Letty managed to pull her down onto her chair.

The captain frowned momentarily, then brushed Opi's outburst aside. "Other questions?" he asked smoothly.

A young woman of Chinese extraction, stood up. "She's unstable," she said with a disgusted expression. "Best to get rid of her. But what about malingerers? What if someone purposely fails the training?"

Captain Alitan grew more severe, his mouth firm. "I assure you that you cannot fool your trainers; they are very good at their jobs. Most have been teaching aboard this vessel for a long time. Should the consensus be that you are malingering, you will be put in a group with fellow shirkers. You will continue to train, as well or badly as you choose. When the time comes, you will be sent together into battle, ill-prepared though you may be. If you are not prepared, you will surely die."

The young woman sat down, shaking her head.

Another young man stood, tall and blond, with a rough beard. He muttered a few words in his native tongue, then changed self-consciously to the new universal language. "What if we pass?" he asked. "When we go to war, do we fight until we die, or do we have a chance to survive?"

The captain actually smiled. "A reasonable question. We will treat your service in much the same way it is done in the armed forces of many countries on Earth. You will be assigned a minimum of twenty-five missions. You may be assigned more. Upon completion of your assignment, you will be allowed to retire.

"Some of you will die. Those who survive will have the option of returning to their families on Earth. You may also be given the opportunity to train future Shadow Warriors as well. That will be up to you.

"If you choose to go home, synthetic memories will be implanted so that you will have no memory of your service. Then your life will go on, assuming The Horde has been deflected from your arm of the galaxy."

Cal stood up. "What if we simply refuse to serve? You've admitted that we were kidnapped and brought here against our will. Your goals sound laudable, assuming you're telling us the truth.

"Even if you are, you have no right to snatch us into military service. You took me away from my father who's in bad health and desperately needs me. I don't have any reason to cooperate with you. So now what? Will you just kill me, or let me go home to my father?"

Dead silence reigned at first. Then a second youth across the hall stood as well. "Back home, I had a bad situation, too. My mother and father are dead, and my little sister and I were scheduled for a foster home. She's not here, so that means she's alone somewhere without me, without *anybody*. She needs me, and I'm not there for her. How can you justify this?"

Another quiet spell. It seemed to Tony that the alien captain wasn't sorry about their situation at all, didn't particularly care what the other kid or Cal felt. When Alitan spoke at last, his voice carried not one iota of sympathy.

"I will tell you this: All of you come from negative situations which you could not resolve nor contribute to in any positive way. Had any of you stayed there, those situations would have become progressively worse. You may think you are owed an explanation; you may *think* you are needed in whatever environment you called home.

"You are wrong. Your presence here may lead to the salvation of multiple worlds where billions of people dwell. Your world needs you; my world needs you.

"What you think or wish to do in this situation is of no import to me or to any member of my crew. You are here to be trained to do a job and be deployed to that end.

"You may choose to train and become a member of an elite team, or you may choose to malinger, or you may refuse to train at all. In the last two cases, as I have already stated, you will be classed with other misfits, positioned as cannon fodder in our first attacks, and you will die. It is your choice. I repeat: the only ways you may go home are to legitimately fail your training or to complete your assigned missions. You will train as a team, and if you do not do well, you will die as a team. It is as simple as that. This assembly is dismissed."

With that declaration, he turned and left the room.

Galigan came to collect them. Angry and frustrated, both at Opi for being such a sissy and at Cal for being a noble idiot, Tony followed the group back to their room.

19 LETTY

As he left them at their quarters, a sober Galigan told them that they should "assess your position" and be ready to start training the next day.

All were silent. Cal sat, obviously fuming, on his bed. Opi crouched, sniffling and weepy, on the floor in one corner of the room. Letty seethed inside but she held herself in, feeling that if she said anything she would get in a fight, probably with Cal.

Both Opi and Cal didn't get it. They were willing to throw away their lives, Cal on principle and Opi just because she was the biggest weenie in the known universe. Letty was so angry that she wanted to smack Cal right in the face to get his attention, then smack him a few more times.

So furious that she wasn't sure she could control herself, Letty went to her bed, lay down, and refused to look at her roommates, let alone talk to them.

After an hour or so, Tony flopped onto his back on his mattress and said out of the corner of his mouth, "That alien captain's pretty scary, but y'know, this is a good opportunity to me. I ain't got any family left." He threw it back to Sasha. "What about you? Your deal back home is about as bad as mine."

"Sounds good to me," Sasha said. "Plenty of food, a chance to learn some kick-ass technology, and become a respected member of a combat team. I'd thought about joining the army when I turned eighteen anyway, because it's a good way to get ahead if you work hard. This is a better offer. If you die, you go out in a blast. If you live, you're a pretty special guy. Sort of a win-win."

Letty wanted to cheer. Tony and Sasha had said the first sensible things she had heard from her teammates all day. She sat up on her bed.

"Well said, Sasha. You too, Tony. Maybe you guys are not as dumb as I thought."

Tony and Sasha both grinned at her.

Sasha went on. "But the thing is, since our designated team captain is a complete idiot who's going to refuse to train, what does that mean for the rest of us?"

Cal's head swiveled, his glare taking aim at Sasha. "Kidnapped and forced to fight, and I'm an idiot? What about resisting? Why not make it hard on them? We'll probably die anyway, so why cooperate?"

"You might win big by goin' along," Tony pointed out. "Doesn't buy you anything to resist."

"Except satisfaction," Cal said, and Letty stood up, trying to decide whether to let him have one in the chops.

"Seems to me," Tony gave him a sly grin, "it'd be more satisfyin' to kick that Horde bunch around. And it could make you pretty important here."

Sniffling, Opi got up and returned to her bed. "If they're telling the truth. How do we even know what they're saying is true?"

"Have to see." Tony grinned again. "So far, they don't sound like liars to me."

"I understand your position, Mex," Cal said with a grimace, standing up. He eyed Letty warily, and Letty could tell he knew how angry she was. He didn't pay any attention to Tony as he continued, "A street rat has nothing to lose, Tony said it himself. And Sasha—hell, this is an improvement for him too. But the rest of us—"

He stopped because Tony had slid off his bed.

"Gettin' just a little tired of that street rat stuff."

"You called yourself that, Mex. Better be careful or you might find out what a street rat feels like to get stepped on."

"Don't like Mex much either, gringo. You don't shut up, you might find out how a street rat fights."

Cal moved toward Tony, scowling, "So you think—"

Tony didn't say another word. His fist flashed out, so fast that Letty barely saw a blur. It connected—hard—with Cal's jaw.

Cal flew backward, landing on the floor with a *thunk*. Shaking his head as though to clear cobwebs, he tried to scramble up, until Letty jumped beside him and shoved him roughly down.

"What the—?" Before Cal could say anything else, she stepped astride his body, twisting to give Tony a searing stare. "That's enough, Tony. Back up or you'll get hell from me."

Tony's sly grin flickered, and he retreated to his cot.

Swiveling back to Cal, she said, "Don't you move a single damn muscle!"

The wrath that had been building for hours had finally exploded. As Letty had listened to Galigan, then to Commander Alitan, she'd finally begun to make a few deductions about her own situation. And further, her deductions had piled on top of her resentment at Cal and Opi for being—as Sasha said—idiots.

Now she vented all her vitriol, as Cal stared up at her in shock. "You listen, and you listen real good, you dumbass. You got what you deserved just now, bad-mouthing Tony with that 'Mex' business. Maybe you can get away with crap like that in Texas, but where I come from, we treat people as equals until proven differently."

"But I just—"

Letty bent over until she and Cal were nearly nose-to-nose. "Didn't I tell you to shut up? You just lie there and listen for a change!" She straightened enough to swing her glower around the room. "That goes for the rest of you, too. Got it?"

The other three watched her with surprise, Opi tremulous as usual, Tony and Sasha with obvious new respect.

"I figured out some things today." She raised her voice enough to stifle any competition. "The only reason it took so long is that we've all been in shock. That's over for me. After what we've seen the last two days—maybe it's been weeks but it seems like only a couple days to us—is anybody dumb enough to think this is some sort of reality show? Do you still think this is an elaborate con on TV?"

Nobody said anything. "Good," she said, "'cause if you said yes I'd have to pop you one. Good shot, by the way, Tony. You finally shut Cal up, which he needed."

She turned to stare down at Cal again, her voice still raised. "Okay, so here's the way it is. This is real. It's not a dream, not a drunken nightmare, not due to an OD. I don't do that stuff, but in case any of you happen to, you are sober now.

"Galigan lied to us at first, probably to make it less scary, but Cal got it right in the assembly. We've been waylaid, kidnapped, abducted, shanghaied, whatever you want to call it. And they aren't going to let us go home.

"I believe these aliens. They have no reason to lie because we're a captive audience. It sounds like these Shadow Warriors are like the soldiers in the American Revolution who hid behind trees and took potshots at the lines of British soldiers to keep them off-balance."

"Galigan said something like that," Opi sniffed. "How does that help us?"

"Opi, you dear, sweet little wuss, it doesn't help us at all except in one way. It makes our course clear."

Opi looked outraged, but Letty paid her no attention. On a roll now, she wasn't letting anyone deflect her from having her say.

"You haven't figured it out either," Letty said, turning back to Cal. "Opi has an excuse, she's probably been timid and overly protected all her life. But you certainly haven't—and yet you stood up there this morning and made a fool of yourself—and us, your teammates as well. You certainly aren't an idiot, but you're *acting* like an idiot. Captain Alitan doesn't care what you think and he doesn't care what you feel. He just wants soldiers who will fight and do what damage they can to turn The Horde before we all die.

"Here's the way it is, Cal, and you too, Opi. They need us, and they will have us. We will fight, or we are no use to them. So we *must* train, and we *must* excel, and we *must* become a top team. I believe them, that if we get well-qualified and fight and survive the missions we're assigned, we'll be free.

"Tony is already for it," she said. "Sasha is too, right?"

Sasha nodded. "No worse than home. A chance to be a hero."

"Exactly." Letty's curly bush of hair swished as she rounded on Cal again. "You've got a single chance to get home, Cal, and you too, Opi. That's to do as our new commanders wish, to get to be so damn good, *so superior* at this Shadow Warrior business that we always win, and then survive to go home. It's the only way we'll ever see our homes again."

Behind her, Opi sighed. "What if they're lying? What if they put us into battle, and keep doing it until we all die? What if we have no chance at all?"

"Then we die." Letty said flatly. "But I'd rather die trying to get home than just sit here sulking and whining about how bad my lot is."

"You can say what you want," Cal sputtered. "Dad needs me and I have to get back to him. I will not help these people, no matter how noble their goals are if it keeps me from my father."

Letty laughed. Cal's words had been burning in her stomach for an hour now, and her anger surged as she confronted him.

"That's what I thought yesterday. And then, as I listened today to that other kid talking about his precious sister, I begin to think, what if our being here is the greatest thing that could have happened to those we love?

"That kid with the sister—what if he's sheltered her and mothered her ever since they lost their parents? What if she desperately needs some independence? His being taken may be the break she's been waiting for."

She swung toward Opi. "And you. Hell, your evil stepmother is probably plotting ways not only to get your money but to eliminate you completely. Think what your disappearance will do. She's going to have to explain what happened to you, and whatever she says, it's going to look extremely suspicious. First your father dies, then you disappear. She may spend the next ten years in court trying to get even a smell of your money, and may get indicted for murder to boot.

"Tony and Sasha, I don't need to do any persuading there. Tony, nobody will even notice you're gone. Sasha, if your foster father is only half as bad as you say, I'll bet he won't tell anyone you're gone just to keep the money rolling in."

She turned back to Cal, stepping aside to allow him to stand up. She even gave him a hand, although she pointedly stood between him and Tony. "And you, our brave and stupid leader. What if leaving your dad by himself is for the best? Maybe your being gone will force him to stand on his own. At worst, he drinks himself to death—but he was doing that anyway. At best, if he's worried about finding you, maybe he'll clean up his life. Either way, his life will play itself out without any help from you.

"As for me, I've been worrying about not being there to 'help' Mom and Dad with their problems. But their problems don't have anything to do with me. They struggled and struggled with their little business, and then, all of a sudden, they were rich beyond their fondest dreams, and they haven't been able to handle it.

"Whatever their problems, they need to fix them on their own. I can't help them, and how I ever thought I could is beyond me. Maybe they'll reunite to search for me, and maybe the search will bring them back together.

"Or maybe it will completely split them up." She shrugged. "If so, it was probably beyond their abilities, and certainly mine, to right the ship. Either way, they don't need me."

Letty pushed Cal toward his bed. He didn't resist a great deal. When he had perched atop it, she retreated to hers and, like Captain Alitan, let her eyes sweep the room. "There's one more thing. Even Tony and Sasha have a bit of nostalgia for our home world. Opi, you and Cal and I have stronger feelings.

"Let me repeat myself. The only way we get home is to do the job they brought us here for. Maybe they're lying through their teeth, but if they're seriously laying it on the line, then the only way we get home is to become so damn good that we survive. It's our only chance. Maybe not a good one, but it's the only one.

"I suggest that tomorrow, we set the goal of being number one at everything we do," she said. "Can we be that good? I have no idea, but that ought to be our goal. Cal, give up the idea that you can save your father. Opi, quit sniveling and be a team member. Tony and Sasha, you're in my corner, but you have to get the chips off your shoulders and pull with the rest of us."

Tony said, "I can do it, I s'pose. Does that mean I got to love gringo?"

"His name's Cal, not 'gringo.'" She swiveled to face Cal and gestured at Tony. "And his name is Tony, not 'Mex.' I don't give a rat's ass whether you love each other or not, but you have to work with and tolerate each other or we don't have a chance."

"Okay, I'm in," Tony said. "Why don't you be our commander?"

"Because it's not my choice, Tony. The tests show what we're best at. Let's get a good night's sleep tonight and be ready to go tomorrow." Letty swiveled back to Cal. "Can you do that?"

His gaze didn't waver. "I don't know." But his demeanor said that she had given him food for thought.

"Tell you what." Letty sat back on her bed. "I'll come knocking early in the morning, before Galigan shows up. You let me know then. If you don't want to play ball—and you, too," she waved a hand toward Opi, "Tony and Sasha and I will request replacements. We'll tell him that you two won't cooperate. From there forward you're on your own, and God help you." She nodded toward the other two young men. "That okay with you two?"

They returned her nod, both enthusiastic.

"Good."

For the rest of the afternoon, Cal sat silently on his bed. Opi remained muted as well. Letty, Tony, and Sasha held lively discussions about training, the war with The Horde, and what tomorrow might bring. Letty had no idea what tomorrow would have in store, but she felt better about it than she had since she awakened in the white room.

20 CAL

"Cal ... Cal."

As promised, Letty stood over his bed, shaking his shoulder, her hoarse whisper calculated to let the others sleep.

Rousing, he mumbled, "Wish I had a clock."

"You do—me. It's roughly five-thirty my local time. That would be six-thirty your time. I never could sleep late."

Cal stared up at her, aware again of the very feminine aura she projected. The two girls had no perfume or cosmetics, but when freshly washed, Letty's natural aroma up close fascinated him. Some guys might say that Letty wasn't as beautiful as Opi, but her pleasant features and her dark eyes, with their thick lashes, commanded attention.

Seeing his sudden assessment, she stepped back, flushing. "I need your answer. We have to make decisions today, and we're doing it, with or without you."

"It's yes."

She searched his face. "That sounded too easy."

He shook his head. "It wasn't. I wrestled with it half the night. You had one thing on your side—impeccable logic."

"Impeccable, huh? Well, I was on the debate team."

A tiny smile tugged at the corner of his mouth. "So that's where it came from. Your analysis of us, at least those of us who thought we had a real stake back home, was thought provoking, as well as your summary of our situation. It doesn't really matter what we want. We're here and we don't have a choice. What I wanted to do was suicidal. If I can't help this race, whoever they are, they can't use me. By helping them I become valuable. You're right. Whether or not they're lying about letting us go after our service is up, it's our only chance.

"So I'm with you. But I think Tony's right. You grasped the situation, you analyzed our choices, you laid it out. You ought to be the commander. You have what it takes. I think you'd be great."

Letty moved back from his bed. "No. If we trust them, we trust their tests, and those tests say you're the best fit. We can't second guess what we don't understand. If you're with us now, you're the commander, and that's it." Letty let her gaze stray toward Opi's bed. "That's one down and one to go. I hope I persuaded her too, but I don't know ..."

She turned back to Cal. "If you want a free shot at the bathroom, go now, especially if you want to shower."

He nodded and made his way to the door.

As usual, the shower made Cal glad he wasn't claustrophobic. On the other hand, water temperature was easily adjustable, which made it easier to shift to a colder setting—which he preferred. His close encounter with Letty had left him with an increased pulse rate and a few miscellaneous thoughts that he needed the chilly water to wash away.

Clean and refreshed as he emerged, he noticed that Sasha and Tony were up, Tony wondering aloud if breakfast would soon be available. Only Opi continued to sleep, and Letty, clearly dreading her answer, didn't wake her.

Tony and Sasha took their turns in the bath, and Letty and Cal sat on their beds silently, Cal admiring Letty's take-charge attitude and keen analytical skills.

He let his mind drift to the upcoming day. Would they indeed start training today? How long would it take them to begin to function as a team? He felt ashamed that he had taken so long to figure things out. *Just put it behind you*, he told himself.

Opi finally roused, sat up, blinked, and silently moved to the bath. She came out once, wrapped in a long towel, to get new underwear and then retreated again. When she left the bath at last, dressed and somber but not weepy, she went to her bed, and Letty joined her.

"What's it going to be?" Letty asked.

Opi turned to her, still troubled. "You were right last night, I guess. We aren't going home, we're too valuable. But Letty"—she grabbed the older girl's arm, pulling her closer—"what do I do? I'm scared all the time, worried about everything!" She spoke softly, but Cal could still make out her anxious words. "You're right, I'm the biggest wuss ever. I was scared of the dark as a child, and I still am! I'm scared of creepy things like spiders, and I hate scary movies, and I don't make friends easily. How can I ever fit in here?"

Letty smiled and put her arm around Opi, and Cal could guess her thoughts. Getting Opi to ask the right questions was half the battle. "We'll figure it out," Letty told her. "Galigan said you were special, so we just have to figure out how."

Before Letty or Opi could say anything else, the outer door opened, and in walked another member of the crew in uniform. Except he was human, not a Molethian. Someone born in India, Cal judged.

"Good morning," he said, in the slightly sing-song English

that those from India often speak. Cal felt relieved that at least part of their instruction would be in their native tongue. "I am your training officer. You will refer to me as Lieutenant Raj, or sir. Now, stand at attention."

Letty hopped up and stood straight and rigid by her bed. Cal followed her example at once. Tony stood, a little uncertain. He finally straightened, letting his arms drop to his sides, just as Opi did the same.

Sasha moved too slowly. Staring at their training officer doubtfully, he sat for a moment on his bed as though he didn't quite understand. Not as though he'd attempted to defy or ignore the lieutenant, he just didn't move quickly enough.

In three long steps, the lieutenant stood beside him. "Up!" he said. Just one word, not even very loud, but Sasha sprang up as though his life were at stake.

The office stood toe-to-toe with him. "The first thing you *will* learn is that orders will be obeyed promptly and accurately. When I call you to attention, I expect *immediate* compliance. Is that clear?"

They all nodded, including Sasha. Somewhat breathless, he wheezed, "I'm not sure what that means."

The lieutenant smiled. He was at least four inches shorter than Cal, and his uniform completely concealed his arms and legs, but his whole demeanor projected energy and strength. His smooth, dark face, with a razor-sharp mustache, radiated power, and also a commanding intelligence. "Never seen an old war movie on TV? Never mind; let me give you a quick tutorial. The rest of you watch. I'm only going to demonstrate once."

He turned his back to them, spreading his legs into a narrow, vertical V, straightening his back and bending his legs very slightly, so that his knees weren't locked. He placed his arms behind him, holding them so that each hand grasped the opposite wrist. Turning, he looked them over, making sure they had copied the stance. "This is the official, formal position of 'attention.' If you are familiar with the term from any of Earth's military services, you will see that it is slightly different, but we are following the Molethian custom, as this is a Molethian ship."

Cautiously, the rest altered their postures to copy Raj's position.

Glancing back at Sasha, Raj said, "Unlock your knees! You are not a statue. Do you want to pass out like a wimp in front the ladies?

"We have found that this posture is more comfortable for long periods—it is somewhat similar to the 'parade rest' position of many military organizations on Earth." By now well intimidated, Sasha relaxed just a bit. "That's better. I assume you are ready for the day. Please follow me."

"Sir?" Cal interrupted nervously.

Raj turned to him and nodded. "Sir, you're not one of the aliens, the Molethanians, or however they pronounce it. How did you get into *their* military?"

Raj laughed out loud. "It's *Mo-le-thi-ans*. Because, Cal, this is not the first time the Molethians have 'harvested' teenagers from Earth."

"Have you served your twenty-five missions?" Cal asked. As Raj scowled, he added, "Sir."

"I've served seventy-two missions."

Cal joined the shocked chorus of gasps.

Raj went on. "Once you've fought The Horde, once you've seen them advancing implacably, destroying all intelligent life in their path, with no pause, no attempt to negotiate, no hesitation, and no mercy, you begin to get a real sense of mission. You want to stop them, kill them, do anything you can to eliminate them. They're coming, and our home is in their path."

"So—sir—" Sasha put in, "do you fight anymore?"

"Not now. Molethian command persuaded me that I could

be more valuable training. If you train hard, I can make you as effective as my first team."

"Sir?" Letty clearly had figured out the proper question procedure.

"Yes."

"Sir, what happened to Galigan?"

"Galigan has completed his service and transferred to another ship. He is a psychologist and he has gone to a new assignment. I am taking his place. You don't need a psychologist anymore; you need somebody who can teach you to fight and survive. Now follow me."

He strode purposefully out the door, all five scrambling to follow. Almost trotting to keep up, Cal tried to grapple with all Raj had just said. At the very least, he decided, everyone understood who was boss.

21 TONY

Tony trailed Letty as they followed Lieutenant Raj
down the hall. A glance back showed Sasha stumbling
after them, still mentally, as well as physically behind
the rest. Cal brought up the rear, walking fast and urging
Sasha on.

This Raj was a pretty tough guy. They would all be wise to
snap to it when he gave an order. Tony made a vow to move as
fast as Letty in responding to their trainer.

Their first stop was the dining hall, crowded with trainees
their age, all eating furiously. "You have fifteen minutes," Raj
announced. He pointed to one of three exit doors from the cafeteria. "You will meet me there at zero-seven-thirty." He pointed to
the digital clock on the bulkhead, labeled with bright, white
letters just below the display. "On this ship, we use Earth Standard Time, so we have a twenty-four-hour clock, like many military organizations on Earth."

The clock read 07:15 at the moment.

Breakfast consisted essentially of the same fruits and baked
goods as before, with milk as necessary. Keeping careful track of

the time, Tony made it through the lines quickly and stuffed down an enormous amount of food in less than the requisite time. He made it to the exit with a minute to spare, but Letty already stood there. He would have to hustle to stay up with her.

Cal and Opi also beat Raj, but Sasha hustled across the room between crowded tables and throngs of diners, to arrive maybe ten seconds late, but Raj sounded surprisingly sympathetic. "Hard to quit feeding when one has had as little food as you have the last months. It's okay this time, but don't be late again." Sasha hung his head, still chewing, his pale face bright red with embarrassment.

They followed Lieutenant Raj out, down two flights, and into a narrow tunnel leading to an entire hive of what must be training rooms. Raj led them past a right turn to the end of the passage and into a small control center of some type.

It must be one from a warship, Tony thought, or at least a model of the cockpit. Perhaps a Shadow Warrior ship?

He didn't have time to speculate, as Raj ordered them into a semi-circle around him. The room didn't span more than ten feet or so, the front wall curving into the two side walls. Each wall was crammed with displays that showed everything from a partial view of the Milky Way (very large, centered on the front console) to various kinds of charts, mostly black and white, to small rectangles that appeared to be tactical displays, each surrounded by groups of touch panels.

To the front were two seats, one placed slightly forward and centered, the second to the left, both fixed to the cabin floor. To left and right sat additional seats, each also placed before a separate group of displays and controls.

A fifth station sat at a small auxiliary console to the left rear. A larger chair stood in the middle of the room, beside which Raj stood. "This is my supervisory chair, where I will observe some, but not all, of your training exercises and tests. You see, I am responsible for several teams, and I must see to all of you each day."

He gestured to the clusters of displays and controls. "Behind me are positions for the pilot-captain and co-pilot-scenario controller. They are responsible for the overall mission and for making sure that all team members carry out their assignments. The pilot is in charge of the mission and the co-pilot assures that the steps of the mission are carried out in proper sequence.

"To the left is the navigator position. The navigator is responsible for placing the ship at the correct spatial coordinates for each step in the mission scenario. At right is the weapons console. The weapons systems officer is responsible for the attack on the target, and the assessment of the damage and success of the mission.

"Finally, this last chair is for the auxiliary member, who may be required to serve as a substitute for the other positions. That person's primary duty is mission planner, also called the strategy consultant. This individual works with the co-pilot on the attack plan after a mission is assigned. After approval by the co-pilot, the strategy consultant presents the scenario to the pilot for approval. Normally, the strategy consultant also grades the mission and the performance of the other four crew members, and makes suggestions to improve team performance.

"Any questions so far?"

Tony felt at sea, barely comprehending all Raj's sentences.

Letty immediately piped up. "How are we assigned?"

Tony noted how Raj's gaze took them all in. "The pilot and co-pilot are set, as you know. As for the rest, we will decide that as you progress in your training."

With that, Raj began to explain the display units. They were labeled in Molethian, which were easily comprehensible to Tony. It dawned on him that he should not be learning the complex functions of the bridge equipment with such ease.

"Sir, we've already learned this in our sleep," he blurted.

Raj smiled. "So you have, Tony. Pardon me. You will often be referred to by your last names, but the training environment is a good deal more relaxed, because of the mores and customs of the Molethian society. Were this an Earth military unit, I am sure the training environment would be more rigorous and rigid. I will often call you by your nicknames. I am just learning both those nicknames and your full names, which we have on record."

He focused on Cal. "Calvin Adam McGregor—Cal." He proceeded on to Letty. "Leticia Elizabeth Washington—Letty." Shifting to Tony, he said, "Antonio Morales, no middle name—Tony." Moving to Opi, he went on. "Ophelia Nathalie Adrienne Prefontaine—Opi." Opi's names were clearly French, the last pronounced *"Pruhfohntahn."* The lieutenant finally settled on Sasha. "And, finally, Alexander Anatoly Valentin Sharapov —Sasha."

Sasha's brows shot up. "Really? Anatoly? Valentin? I thought I had only two names."

Raj dipped his head. "Our research is thorough." Returning to Tony he said, "You are correct, Mr. Morales. Both with some sleep-induced learning, and also due to some of the data files now resident inside your skulls, you are quite familiar with the controls on the bridge of a Shadow Warrior cruiser. However, I must discuss them so you begin to bring that information to the fore."

He continued to cover each set of controls and information displays. As he turned to his left, facing a panel with a maze of display grids, odd, display-based slide switches, and stacks of numeric indicators, he asked Tony, "And now, Mr. Morales, what would you say that this position is meant for?"

Tony grinned. "Navigation. You have attitude controls on the left, propulsion overrides to the right, and tactical and visual displays ahead." He motioned to the largest panel, four feet wide by thirty inches high. "Outer perimeter display, normally the ship's forward view. I think ... Yeah, it can switch to a tactical, forward, aft, orthogonal, and plan. Also full three-D in all views, including tactical."

"Right you are."

Tony couldn't keep from grinning. For the first time in years he felt that here, at this moment, he truly *belonged* somewhere.

Their tutor said, "Mr. McGregor, take the center seat. Ms. Washington, take the co-pilot's position. For now, Mr. Morales, take the navigator slot."

Tony slipped into the seat as though afraid someone might steal it.

Raj turned to the others. "As for you, Mr. Sharapov, take the weapons chair, and Ms. Prefontaine, take the auxiliary chair. Mr. Sharapov, as you can see ..."

Tony tuned out the others as he stared at the displays and devices in the navigation console. The more closely he scrutinized the controls, the more information seemed to emerge from his mental vaults.

Summoning up a piece of the inner library, which felt surprisingly easy, he recognized that an array of microphones scattered over the area before him meant he could give many commands verbally. Every function activated from his position had a corresponding manual activation capability. Based on his experience with the doors in their quarters, he inferred that at least some commands could be issued mentally.

The switches to the sides of the large display were small, flat surfaces that activated navigation functions by moving a finger over them.

Internally, he checked off the functions: Sensor arrays, including radar and ladar, as well as visual, infrared, ultraviolet, and X-ray detectors. A projection unit could display star charts not only of the entire galaxy, but those of many inhabited solar systems, of which there seemed to be a great many. All the information emerged from somewhere in the labyrinth of his new memory as he needed it.

The main display could depict each view as revealed by any of the sensors. It could also show a tactical view or map, or it could overlay a visual or radar scene with the appropriate tactical charts. In all, a navigator's dream, and one that Tony glommed onto with glee.

To his right he could hear Cal and Letty chatting about their setup as Lieutenant Raj interjected comments. Behind him, Opi and Sasha talked about the weapons controls and the variety of devices at the station's beck and call.

Although Tony had figured out that some console functions could be activated mentally, like the doors in their living area, something else told him, maybe data from the implants, that many functions needed voice or physical activation. Why?

Again, the answer came immediately. In the heat of battle, with a thousand thoughts flying through each crew member's head, confused mental transmissions might activate incorrect ship functions. Physical and voice-initiated functions protected crew members from inadvertent mistakes in ship operation.

He started when Lieutenant Raj appeared beside him and pressed a button marked Example Flight just off the edge of the console.

The console came alive instantly, showing a forward view as the simulated ship moved into a solar system, past a gas giant and toward the inner planetary orbits, moving rapidly.

"Play with it, Mr. Morales," said Lieutenant Raj.

Tony began to switch sensor arrays, viewing the system and its star in the various frequency ranges. Nearing an inner planetary orbit, he switched to a tactical overlay, which immediately displayed all planets in the inner orbits, orbit radii, plus revolution and rotation information.

"You can use the manual override controls in this mode to take control of the ship trajectory," Raj said.

Tony did, taking the ship inside the orbit of that star system's equivalent of Mercury, close enough that the sun became a large, yellow disk on the display. His console warned of impending dangerous temperatures. Pulling away, he rocketed to the outer planetary orbits of the system as the simulation came to a close.

Sitting back, Tony wiped perspiration from his brow. With some surprise, he found his shirt damp with sweat. He had become totally involved in the exercise, navigating the ship and interacting with the console. Turning, he saw that the rest were watching him, including the lieutenant.

"Congratulations, Mr. Morales," Raj said. "You completed the scenario by yourself, one of the first in your trainee class to do so. You were born to that chair. Make it your own."

Seeing how Cal regarded Raj skeptically, Tony almost laughed. *Ha,* he thought, *didn't think a street rat had it in him, did you?* He still held the smile when Lieutenant Raj announced a lunch break.

22 CAL

Cal managed to get a seat across from Letty in the dining room, while Tony, Sasha, and Opi sat at the next table. The lieutenant had announced, to their delight, that they would have an entire thirty minutes for lunch. With their meal nearly consumed, they had a handful of minutes left before returning to the simulated cockpit.

Surprised with a variety of new foods, including some sort of fish as well as the usual baked goods and fruit, Cal had eaten well for perhaps the first time. *No fun fast food*, he lamented silently, but at least he was eating healthily.

"You still mad at me?" he asked Letty.

She finished off a bite of banana. "Not mad. Frustrated that you'd get thrown out with the dregs when you had such potential."

"Thanks for that."

"You're welcome. The thing is, if you're going to be the commander, you have to be the commander of the whole crew, not just the ones you think are 'worthy.'"

Cal started to object and then dropped it. He really didn't

consider himself prejudiced. Tony just irritated him. He didn't like Tony, but that had nothing to do with working beside him. "I promise," he said, "I'll love everyone equally."

They were talking quietly enough that the other three, engaged in their own conversation at the next table, didn't hear. Letty smiled.

"Look around," she said. "What comes to mind?"

He twisted to survey the dining room. They were seated to one side of the dining hall at one of dozens of tables, all with groups of two to five young people eating frantically. Although he saw diverse races, including Asians, American Indians, those of African descent and Hispanics, most of the conversations he heard were American English. He had to assume that all were from North America, as Galigan had said.

As his attention returned to Letty, he said, "Just a bunch of teenagers like us."

"Assuming we're from North America, and I think we are, then we're from all over. These Molethians must have a heck of a worldwide network if they could spy on us, check our DNA, and determine that we were better off fighting with them."

Cal stuffed the last half of a cinnamon roll in his mouth. Lowering his voice, he said, "Still wonder if they're telling us the whole truth."

"Does it matter?"

"Like you said, not really."

Cal let his view drift to the next table, where a group of five males were talking loudly and guffawing at one guy's remarks as he stole several looks at Letty. Cal frowned just as the guy glanced their way again. He saw Cal's frown and stood to move toward their table.

"Whatcha looking at?" the guy demanded.

The typical lame-brain bully taunt, Cal thought with irritation. There always seemed to be at least one bully in a crowd;

even the Molethians had managed to draft one. Cal hesitated to stand. The guy was big, but Cal doubted the oaf could stay with him for thirty seconds. He continued to stare back, trying to appear neither challenging nor retiring, simply neutral.

"Thought so," the bully grinned. "You're that coward that got up yesterday and whined about going home. What a sissy! Should I call you Mary Sue?"

He stood between the two tables where Cal's team sat. To Cal's surprise, Tony stood up very suddenly, right beside him. "Don' particularly like folks talking about my teammates."

"Sit down, greaser. I'd hate to have to send you back to Juarez in a box."

Tony smiled that easy smile. "Greaser, huh? Ain't that funny, a big glob of lard like you callin' me a greaser?"

"Why you—" The bully barely managed to pull back his fist before Tony kicked him squarely in the groin. As he bent over in agony, Tony calmly hit him twice in the face, one-two, his arms such a blur that Cal could only think, *Glad that's not me this time.*

Immediately, the other four young men arose and started toward them. Cal got up as well, coming around the table.

Raj stood quite suddenly in their midst. The four on the other team knew the drill. They snapped to attention, as their friend rolled and cried on the floor. Cal and his team quickly stood in the prescribed position.

"What were you four doing?" Raj demanded. He ignored the writhing figure on the floor.

"He hit our friend," one said. "We were coming to help."

Lieutenant Raj seemed to compare Tony's victim to Tony himself. "He outweighs Mr. Morales two-to-one. You thought he couldn't protect himself?"

The dining hall had gotten extremely quiet, a hundred-plus

youths watching Cal and the other team closely. After an embarrassed pause, one guy said, "He blindsided Jess. He hit first."

"Ah, yes. Just after he threatened Mr. Morales and insulted Mr. McGregor, am I correct?"

Their mouths gaped.

"Yes, I was over there." Lieutenant Raj nodded to the opposite side of the lunchroom. "But I can read lips, did you know that?" Face as hard as granite, his eyes were laser cannons. "Go to your quarters—I will deal with you later." He motioned, and two crewmen quickly arrived to lift the groaning bully and carry him off.

Raj turned to Cal and his team. "You're due back in the pod in five minutes." Without another word, he turned and followed the two crewmen and Tony's target.

A bit grudgingly, Cal muttered, "Nice going. Thanks."

Tony grinned. "Tol' you we street-rats're pretty tough."

He went to the exit, and the others, appetites gone, followed. All the other diners watched them go in silence.

23 LETTY

Letty's internal clock had her up long before whatever constituted morning on the ship. Taking advantage of her early start, she slipped into the bathroom for a pleasantly warm shower. The claustrophobia-inducing stall had a footprint perhaps thirty inches square, but the mix between hot and cold adjusted easily. Although it sprayed a fine mist, clearly designed to conserve water, she could take as long as she liked. The Molethians were so advanced technologically that she guessed they reused every drop of water repeatedly. *Probably recycle the sewage too,* she thought with a twist of her mouth.

In fresh underwear and regulation training uniform of slacks and a crisp shirt that resembled army khaki, she left the cubicle as Cal quickly entered. Lieutenant Raj hadn't mentioned it, but she made her bed carefully, pulling the sheet tight and centering the pillow.

When the lieutenant appeared, he lectured them on making their beds and keeping their personal areas clean, pausing to compliment Letty. He reminded them that they were allowed fifteen minutes to eat before exercises began. Letty grinned all the way to the dining hall.

Cal sat by Letty again, saying little. She really didn't mind. Despite his faults, he wasn't a bad sort, and he was handsome. *Dressed in decent clothing, he would be quite appealing*, Letty thought. She laughed to herself. He could say the same thing about her, she thought ruefully. She hadn't had the luxury of any makeup or perfume in several days. At least she had been able to stay clean.

In the training pod, Letty thought it even smaller and more oppressive than she'd found it the previous day. Not as bad as the shower by any means, but with the minimum amount of space for five people plus the instructor. When she asked Raj how it compared to the cockpit of an actual Shadow Warrior ship, he told her with a flash of humor, "Identical."

Standing beside the pilot's console, Raj said, "You familiarized yourselves with the controls yesterday morning, and during the afternoon you had ample opportunities to fly your simulated craft, even changing positions a good deal. Today will be your first mission. In the future, you will exchange positions, giving each of you a chance to learn the commander's role. Today, however, we will start out with Cal in the command seat, Letty in the co-pilot's, Tony as navigator, and Sasha at the weapons console. Opi, please take the auxiliary chair. You may move at some point to navigation. Any questions?"

They were silent, and Letty reflected wryly that they didn't know enough yet to ask for clarifications.

"Your mission scenario is coming up on the console main screen," Raj told them, as a series of paragraphs and diagrams flashed onto the screen.

Thankfully, they were in English, which made Letty feel better, as she still had trouble with Molethian number symbols.

Raj repeated the description. "You are starting from planet

Grizzeldo, a fictional planet some fifteen hundred light-years from here, close to the outer fringes of a fictional advancing Horde flotilla. A Horde expeditionary force has been spotted moving toward the Antszi System, about twenty light-years away. It is a small force of one hundred ships, with about twelve refueling ships, which also carry ammunition.

"Your assignment is to destroy one or more of the supply vessels and force the sortie to retreat prematurely, as they have only enough fuel to complete the mission. Each fuel ship destroyed will force the mission to be terminated earlier."

"This is a typical Shadow Warrior scenario," Raj said. "Do the maximum damage, risk the minimum losses, and quickly retreat. Remember, our numbers are few compared to our enemy, so an unspoken part of every mission is to survive for the *next* mission. Ready?"

They all nodded, but Letty observed uncertainty on every other team member's face. *Probably on mine too,* she thought.

Raj retreated, closing the door into the pod. After a moment's hesitation, Cal ordered Tony to plot the course to their destination. After considering a moment, he added, "We'll go in at maximum speed. I'd like to get there quick. We're supposed to beat them getting into the system, but I'd like to find a good hiding place."

Letty didn't say anything, but she fully approved.

Tony's fingers danced over the touch-sensitive controls. "Course locked in, sir."

Cal pressed the launch button, and there was a jerk as their simulated ship left the carrier.

The rear visuals showed them blasting away from their command ship, a very long, silver cylinder. Wondering briefly how much it resembled a real carrier ship, Letty abruptly realized that she could feel the acceleration in her chair. The realism remained a constant wonder for her.

Glancing toward navigation, she grinned at Tony. "You're enjoying yourself."

"Yeah." He radiated sheer joy. "I *actually* *understand* this stuff."

Another few moments and they leaped away from their base orbiting Grizzeldo. Letty had no comprehension of the physics behind the leap drive. Somewhere, probably in her implants, she had acquired vague knowledge about higher dimensions, adjustment of coordinate groups, and so forth, but it was still magic to her. One moment they were *here*, near their mother ship, and an instant later they were *there*, twenty light-years away from their origin, staring at the small disk of a planet on the forward display.

Tony sang out, "We have entered the Antszi solar system. Straight ahead is Isoldo fourth planet from the sun. It's very Earth-like, and is the target of The Horde exploratory group. Isoldo has no intelligent life. It has two moons, both somewhat smaller than our own."

Sasha followed, "No detected activity around the planet; we have beaten The Horde sortie to the system."

Tony's clipped, precise English sounded absolutely nothing like his normal speech. While she could only guess, Letty had to believe that tapping into that enormous database snuggled inside his skull called up language appropriate to Tony's station as well as navigation knowledge. It was very weird.

As Cal scanned his instruments, Letty peered over his shoulder at the main display. It had tremendous resolution, not quite as good as staring out a glass portal onto space, but still impressive, and the view staggered her. Their simulated voyage had brought them into the densest part of the galactic arm, meaning that stars were closer together in general. What lay before them took her breath. A massive star cluster just a few light-years away provided the backdrop for the solar system they had entered, the light so intense that details of the planet were hard to discern. She knew that it was a simulated picture, but it was still hard to pull her eyes away from the scene.

"My goodness," Opi said behind Letty. "At night, it must be so bright." Her voice faded.

"In this solar system, there really isn't any night," Letty finished for her. "Is this system part of that cluster?"

Tony consulted the charts. "It's on the fringe, but it's so close you could make an argument either way. You're right. Night here would be a real star-gazing experience."

Cal shifted his gaze to Tony. "Plot a course to hide behind the smaller moon. It's not very big, but then, neither are we. I want to be able to survey the whole group of ships as it arrives."

Cal's all-business attitude pulled Letty away from her fascination with the starry background. Obediently, Tony plotted the course, and Cal steered their ship into a holding pattern near the smaller moon, near enough to the rim of the orb that they would be hard to detect by incoming vessels.

In the aux chair, Opi spoke up. "Why so few of the enemy ships? I thought they sent thousands."

Letty had been studying the scenario carefully as Cal guided them to their holding position. She concentrated on the display. "It's not inhabited, one of the rare planets that they can simply settle without a battle. They're probably disappointed that they don't have to blast its surface to bits."

Opi nodded.

In the weapons chair, Sasha appeared immersed in study of the gun controls and weapons-launching mechanisms. Letty touched his arm and asked, "Got it figured out?"

"I did that yesterday." He indicated the control devices, two enormous gloves that fit over the hands of the weapons officer. "Just studying the array of guns. Know what the most effective weapon is?"

"It's probably stuck in my head somewhere, but tell me."

Sasha grinned. "It's a roughly forty-millimeter explosive bullet-launcher. Has multiple barrels. Sort of a Gatling cannon, like it came straight out of our own Air Force weaponry."

Her brow crinkled. "Really? You'd think as advanced as they are, they'd have all sorts of high-tech energy weapons."

"They do," he said. "This laser cannon is pretty neat. It's really a powerful laser beam combined with a high-velocity particle beam. It'll do some damage all right, but turns out that it's fairly easy to build a good shield against particle beams and lasers, particularly on a large ship like a battle cruiser.

"But the projectile gun," he went on with enthusiasm, "is a beauty! It fires those huge bullets—and they are huge, an inch and a half in diameter—at an amazing velocity, nearly three miles per second, much faster than the speed of sound through air. At that speed they have enormous momentum, and there's no energy shield in the galaxy, at least that the Molethians have encountered, that can stop such a weapon, especially one that explodes on impact. Fire these at an oncoming space cruiser that masses at several kilotons, and even it doesn't have the armament to stop such a bullet.

"That old baloney about death rays in science fiction stories is so much crap," he concluded. "A hail of these bullets could take down the biggest Horde ship in existence. The only problem with it is that the shells are so large that the ammo storage is limited. But it's the most effective weapon on the ship."

Interesting point. *Surprising, and maybe disappointing in a way*, Letty thought. The beautiful, sleek Molethian Shadow Warrior ships fired plain old bullets, just like fighter planes on Earth had in the last dozen wars or so.

Sasha glanced at his display and announced, "Detecting incoming vessels, about four million kilometers away. They are slowing, approaching the target planet. It's definitely The Horde expeditionary force."

Letty understood that the real measure Sasha used was actually the Kerr, the Molethian measure of distance. However, it approximated the kilometer in length, so her implants interpreted the length as kilometer, something with which she had some familiarity.

Cal concentrated on Tactical and Letty followed suit. Only a tiny group of dots showed, far out past the orbit of the moon that hid them.

"How many?" Cal asked. "Hard for me to tell."

As if in answer, the console spoke. "Approaching ship convoy verified as Horde design, ten cruiser-class formations of ten ships, plus twelve supply ships with refueling platforms. Current vector will bring all ships into high-radius orbit around target planet in eighteen minutes."

Cal grinned at Letty. "Ask and ye shall receive."

"Is that from the Bible?"

"I think so. Sasha, when will they be within strike range?"

Sasha's hands flew over keys and across slide switches. "Still figuring some of this out. Give me a sec."

Letty reviewed weapons options as Sasha worked. She was familiar with the controls, their functions and how to use them. She found that she understood the basic ability of Horde ships as well. No doubt a combination of the massive storage chips they had acquired, plus additional knowledge embedded in their minds as they slept over what had apparently been two or three weeks. The same way they had learned Molethian.

They didn't know any sort of attack strategy. They had to learn that on their own. Oh, they had examples on some of those chips they could call on, but they needed actual experience to cement their understanding. The reason, Letty thought, behind the exercise they now undertook.

Cal interrupted her thoughts. "My knowledge base says we

can do very small leaps, so-called 'micro-leaps.' How accurate are they? I can't seem to access that data."

Tony answered before she could. "For anything over a hundred thousand kilometers, say seventy-thousand miles, pretty good, I think. We can micro-leap down to maybe ten thousand kilometers, but the accuracy is a bit iffy. Their measures are converted into metric values, and I automatically speak metric in this chair. Letty?"

"Me, too," Letty answered. "And now I'm thinking in metric. Probably the subconscious learning. Okay, Cal, what now?"

"What I want to do," Cal said, "is leap right into their midst, blast a couple of the fuel ships, and leap away. While they're trying to figure out what happened maybe we can make another pass and get two or three more. I doubt that we can get all twelve, but we may bag enough to shorten their mission."

Sasha spoke up. "Can't they call for help?"

"No," Letty said. "Search your data files. All galactic civilizations communicate via electromagnetic waves. The only way to send a message faster than light is with a small leap-drone. Horde ships don't have them. Their leap drive hasn't been miniaturized like the Molethian drive."

Tony was glued to the forward view. They weren't scanning The Horde ships with any energy beams, visible or millimeter. They simply watched from just at the rim of the moon, where their presence would be hard to detect. "They're fairly spread out, so hitting more than two fueling barges will be hard. Inter-group distance is on the order of a dozen kilometers."

"Damn." Cal studied the display. "Micro-leaps?" he prodded.

Letty shrugged. "You heard Tony. We can leap as little as about one nano-light-year, or about ten thousand kilometers. The accuracy is about a pico-light-year, or ten kilometers, for longer leaps, but is less accurate on ultra-short leaps. But that's still pretty darn accurate."

Cal said, "Thanks. Tony, take a sighting. Don't scan them, just a visual estimate. How far will they be from us when they go into orbit?"

Tony continued to grapple with the instrumentation. "This moon we're behind has an eccentric orbit. Our current position is about two hundred thousand klicks from the planet."

"What's a klick?" Letty had never heard the term.

Tony glanced up, confused. "Huh?"

"What's a klick?"

"Geez, it just popped out." He scrunched his brow in concentration. "Oh, it's another term for kilometers. Two hundred thousand kilometers, give or take. Two hundred thousand klicks," he repeated, savoring the term.

"Okay," Cal said. "Tony, plot a course as follows. When I give the word, I want to micro-leap into the middle of one group, fire, let momentum carry us to the second, and maybe we get two groups. That'd be four fuelers. Sasha, you've been bragging about that cannon. Make sure you know how to use it and we can give it a try."

Letty felt odd, listening to Cal giving orders just like some sort of navy officer. Then she thought, *That's what he's training to be.* No one objected to the terse commands, and Tony didn't even say anything rude.

Another twelve anxious minutes, then Horde ships began to go into orbit around the planet.

Cal gave instructions. "In just a few minutes, all the ships should be on our side of the planet. I'll bring us just outside and tangent to their orbit as the first two fueler groups approach the planet. If Tony's plotted the micro-leap accurately, we'll be very near both. Sasha, you'll have about two seconds to line up and fire before we're past, then three or so seconds to get in position to blast the second. We can't risk greater exposure. I assume the warships will respond quickly."

Sasha's said, voice strained, "Give me warning as we leap."

Tony had everything set after a brief conversation with the nav computing unit. He waved a hand at Cal, and Letty wondered if a prayer to the Molethian God, if there were one, would be appropriate. Instead, she said, "Good luck."

Cal called out, "Attacking now!"

24 CAL

The planet appeared beneath them on the display, a string of Horde ships stretching from directly ahead into the distance. Tony had plotted their course to bring them in behind the column. Surely Horde sensors would activate, but that gave them a few seconds' edge.

They approached The Horde ships at about ten kilometers per second. Cal said, "Fire control to weapons console."

There came an odd *"Brrr"* sound, and the pod shook as they flashed past the first group of fuelers. Three seconds, and their ship approached the second group of two ships. Sasha fired again. They leaped, bringing them back behind the small moon.

Tony, glued to the nav console, announced, "All four fuel carriers destroyed. We got away clean."

Letty turned to Cal. "They can't stay here long with only eight fuelers. They'll have to return to base in a short time."

Cal grinned. "They'll have to turn tail and run pretty quick. Tony, plot another micro-leap right behind those last two groups of barges. If we get three or four more, they have no choice."

At his side, Letty frowned. "It's the captain's call, but we've done a solid amount of damage. Going back in for another encounter is a lot riskier, as Horde ships will be on full alert. Are you sure? We've hurt them pretty bad."

"Why not hurt them worse? Tony, you ready?"

"Got it done. Captain, they won't be surprised this time."

"We'll be in and out so fast they won't even know what hit them. Be sure you get behind the fuelers. All the cruisers are ahead of them."

"Uh, Cal ..." Opi began.

"Save it, Opi," Cal said. "Ready, Tony?"

Tony muttered something, adjusted his calculations. "Okay."

"Sasha, I'll leap in and out in about three seconds. Hit 'em with all you've got right off. Those cannons do the job."

Cal triggered the leap, and directly ahead they spied the two fuel ships.

"Preparing to fire," Sasha yelled.

The ship shook violently, as a splash of red light filled the forward screen. At the edge of the display, two Horde ships soared up from beneath them. They had been hidden in the shadow of the two fuelers, invisible to Cal's scanners.

"Ship destroyed," an emotionless female voice said from the console. "Mission failed."

Tony twisted in his seat to face Cal. "Couldn't leave well enough alone, could you? We did damage, probably screwed up their mission. But you just had to go back like the heroic captain and risk your ship again."

Sasha joined in the chorus. "Pretty dumb, *Captain*." He emphasized the word. "You just got us all killed because you wanted to be a hero. Didn't Galigan tell us that they have about ten thousand ships for every one we have? Dumb, dumb, dumb!"

Cal didn't rise to the criticism. "I just wanted—" he said.

Cabin lights came on and the outer door opened. Cal felt as sick as Letty looked as they swung around to see Raj entering.

"Well, things went pretty badly there at the end, huh?" He smiled broadly, surprising Letty, who thought he would be ready with even harsher words that her teammates.

"I want a report from each of you first thing tomorrow, what went right, what went wrong. Opi, collect the reports as Mission Critique Manager and summarize them. Everyone, at least two or three pages. Study desks and workstations have been delivered to your quarters, plus five mobile personal systems. I want these well-written and thorough. Exchange your reports with each other on your mobiles. Sasha, you have responsibility for assessing each mission with Opi. We will have a debrief meeting later."

"Won't be hard to write," Tony said with a straight face. "Got a pretty good idea what went wrong."

Raj turned to Cal. "Mr. McGregor, in a real battle, there are *no* second chances."

With that, he dismissed them to their room. They found it quite crowded, with five small desks to the left side, a computer on each one, and a tablet resembling an iPad, and a printer.

Cal avoided everyone's glances, his hands sweaty. He dreaded reading their summaries.

25 CAL

Other than leaving for meals, they stayed in their quarters, engaged in writing the summary reports. Opi collected and read each, returning Tony's twice for grammar and spelling. She and Sasha then re-read them, discussed them quietly in the limited privacy of a corner, then called the others together.

They presented their findings to the team as all five sat in their desk chairs in a circle. Cal looked at his folded hands the entire time. Nobody talked to him except Letty, and he barely answered her.

After breakfast the next morning, they met Raj at the same simulator that they had used the previous day. Tony still had nothing to say to Cal, nor did Sasha. Opi, speechless also, stayed glued to Letty's side.

In the cockpit simulator, Raj's cheerful expression puzzled Cal, given their performance—neither upset nor overly unhappy. "Today's exercise," Raj said, "is a variation on yesterday's. In this case, The Horde is attacking a planet and they have run into some fierce defense. As usually happens, they have sent for reinforcements, so twenty attack ships and ten refueling vessels are approaching in a convoy, the attack ships mainly to protect the very valuable fuel. This time, you must intercept the ships, destroy all the refueling and supply vessels, then damage as many of the remaining warships as you can.

"Letty, you take the command seat today. Before you start the exercise, review all information provided, which includes some suggestions as to how you might accomplish the maximum damage. Cal, take second seat. Opi, you take the navigation seat, and Tony, you're in the weapons chair."

Raj moved Sasha into the observer chair, telling him, "Take notes and be prepared to critique the exercise to me and your teammates after it is completed. Opi will assist you."

They all nodded, although Tony had gone several shades redder and Sasha scowled.

"What do I do?" Opi asked after Raj departed, her face red with embarrassment.

Tony snorted, but after a moment he seemed to remember that they were being judged as a team. "Think 'navigation,'" he told her. "Things will start to pop into your head. Then access the info on navigation to a target."

As Cal watched, she nodded skeptically and concentrated.

Letty read the scenario, Cal peering over her shoulder, still silent. She finished quickly, so he read alone for the last few minutes. As he finished, she asked, "Any problems?"

"Seems straightforward," he said cautiously. "Except ..."

After a long pause, Letty prodded, "Except what?"

Behind him, Cal heard Tony say, "No, no! You can't let your mind wander!"

Cal huffed an irritated breath. *Opi's completely useless! The quicker we can ditch her and get a capable person in the fifth seat, the better. After all, the fifth person might have to replace anybody else on the team. Opi couldn't take the place of a floor mat!*

"What?" Letty poked his arm.

Cal drew himself back into context. "I don't get it. I tried to lead the team to do this exact maneuver yesterday, and we got blasted, and everybody was on my ass. Today, we're supposed to do what I tried to do yesterday! None of us really had a clue yesterday, but it was all my fault!"

Letty remained silent long enough that Cal felt sure he had offended her, that he'd sounded like a little child complaining that nobody loved him. She surprised him with her reply. "First of all, everybody was *not* on your ass. I certainly wasn't, and neither was Opi. That leaves Sasha and Tony, and you guys have *never* gotten along.

"But that's a good thought. Yesterday you took a chance, but it wasn't practical because we'd already made one pass and they knew we were there. Today we have a lot bigger risk, doing exactly what you tried to do yesterday, but at least we still have the element of surprise.

"Let's delay this exercise as long as we can." Letty sat back in the captain's chair. "The more we study, the more we learn, right?"

The outer hatch opened. "Ready to go?" Raj asked. "We have just enough time before your lunch break."

Letty's head pivoted from Raj to the team and back. "Are we on any sort of timetable, so that we have to do an exercise this morning?"

Once again, Raj surprised Cal, and apparently everyone else, by their widened eyes. "You're scheduled for two exercises today, each about two hours. However, if you decide that the next scenario takes a bit more study and analysis, you can delay both exercises until after lunch."

"Great!" Letty said. "Could we go to the lunchroom now? I'd like to have a team discussion before we start the exercises."

Raj nodded gravely. "Very well."

As they started down the corridor, Cal just ahead of Letty, he heard Tony say under his breath, "You should be the captain, for sure."

He almost stumbled when he heard her reply. "Tony, don't be an idiot."

26 SASHA

The lunchroom was deserted, as most teams were in their first exercise. Why would Raj put off their exercise without much thought?

As he puzzled on Raj's behavior, Sasha also studied each of his teammates. *Mine for better or worse.*

Tony: like Sasha, he kept watch, cautious and defensive. Sasha and Tony were alike in that way. Both just wanted to survive.

Letty and Opi. They were rich. Even though they weren't very happy, Sasha could see that Letty was determined to do her best, lining herself up with him and Tony.

As for Cal, he sounded just like a daddy's boy. Maybe he really did want to care for his father, but he sounded weak, effeminate, whiny. Sasha didn't like him, didn't like his attitude or the chip he carried on his shoulder. Tony had delighted Sasha when he punched Cal. Cal might make a good captain, his aggressiveness might pay off in battle, but he had to forget his father.

As far as he was concerned, their situation appeared far from hopeless if they could become a real team. Was that possible? He wasn't sure. Opi might be a lost cause, and he had doubts about his own usefulness. But as Letty said, they only had one chance.

Sasha took a chair on Letty's left, as Cal sat on her right and Tony went to the opposite side of their table. Opi hesitated, sidled up on Tony's left, and sat.

"I think I had an epiphany a minute ago," Letty told them.

Tony frowned. "A what?"

Opi spoke up. "Like a brainstorm. Something that had been cloudy in her understanding just got a lot clearer."

Letty smiled. "Thanks, Opi. Cal said something to me that made so much sense I asked myself, 'What's going on?' Think about our next exercise. Not only do we have to destroy *all* the fuel barges, but also some of the attack ships. And yet, when Cal tried that yesterday, we got massacred! What does that tell you?"

Nobody spoke. Letty smiled and added only, "I'll let you chew on that a while."

An uneasy ten minutes went by. Twice Tony tried to ask a question, and once Sasha thought about it. But Letty shushed Tony, and Sasha decided he'd get the same treatment.

Suddenly, Cal's brows lifted. "Of course!"

Tony frowned. "Okay, smart guy, what is it?"

Cal refused the bait. "I'm not sure what we're supposed to know, but I know what Letty figured out. We were supposed to *learn something* from yesterday's disaster. Yes, I won't argue, it was my fault. But what did we learn?"

"That's easy," Tony said. "Don't let you lead the team."

Sasha killed his laugh as Letty rounded on Tony. "Oh, shut up, Tony. You're a smart kid, but your mouth is too loose. Cal's right.

"Our assignment is exactly what he led us into yesterday when we got blasted. Today Raj wants us to do even more. Granted the force is smaller, but he expects us to attack, attack,

attack, then stick around and attack again. We must have learned *something* yesterday that will give us an edge today."

Cal sat back in his chair. "Nothing obvious to me."

Sasha, for his part, couldn't think of a single thing either. And yet ... what Cal said made sense. He and Letty were onto something.

Opi raised her hand timidly, like a child in a classroom, leaving it about halfway up, and Letty let out an exasperated breath. "Just speak up, Opi. This isn't grade school."

"Well ..." Opi hesitated, and Sasha had to think that at home she must have been the most browbeaten stepchild since Cinderella. Just as he had pointed out.

"I mean," Opi continued, "I saw something that I thought ... It probably doesn't mean anything."

Letty smiled and said, "It's okay, let me be the judge of that. What did you think?"

Opi hesitated once more, and Sasha clasped his hands together to keep from slapping her again. Reflexively, he wiped them along the pants of his uniform. *Be patient*, he thought. *Be like Letty, be patient. It works for her.*

"During the exercise," Opi blurted out, "you know, I'm supposed to observe what everyone is doing. After the first attack, as we were pulling away, I happened to see the small display to the right at Tony's station."

Tony interrupted, "What display?"

"It's one of about four small displays at the lower right on your console, maybe eight by twelve inches, that displays tactical view. You didn't notice because you were setting up the second attack."

Tony scratched his head. "I saw those little displays earlier. Didn't think they could be very important 'cause I can get tactical, or any other view, on the big display."

Sasha felt totally embarrassed. He hadn't even seen the stupid screen in question.

Opi went on. "Yes, it is tactical. It *always* shows tactical. I like it because it always shows the big picture. And I like to see the overall picture.

"As we blasted away, just before we used the leap engines, The Horde ships began to move, in unison. Each in a specific direction. Before I could see any more, we leaped."

"What direction? Doing what?" Cal asked, voice elevated.

Opi shrank back in her chair.

"Cal!" Letty raised her voice.

Cal checked himself, sat back. "Sorry, Opi. I just want to know how I screwed up."

"You didn't screw up," Opi said quickly. "It was a setup, I think." She turned to Letty. "I tried to mention this just before we attacked again, but Cal told me to wait until later."

Letty nodded, giving Cal a particularly hard eye. "Proceed." It amazed Sasha how her calm and supportive voice provided Opi encouragement.

"As we leaped again and started a second attack, Tony had his concentration on—what do you call it—the attack vector, with Sasha getting ready to fire, and you and Cal were focused on the enemy ships. I watched the tactical display again. And it showed, just for an instant, that The Horde ships had re-positioned into a sort of distorted globe arrangement surrounding the fuel ships, with the larger number to the rear.

"My guess is that what Cal did yesterday, instinctively, is what Shadow Warrior forces often do, come in hard and fast, attack, then leap, come for a second attack, and so forth. The Horde has figured that out, so I think they go into a standard defensive formation when their supply ships are attacked. I think that was what the simulation showed us. There are probably more defensive formations that The Horde uses, but the exercise showed us that one.

"Cal decided to be aggressive, and we were set up. But by being aggressive we found out something that teams who might not have attacked again had no chance to see. So, Cal, the better teams, the teams that decided to try to do the most damage, would have all been destroyed, because only they would have taken the chance to attack again. By losing you won!"

Her teammates' expressions varied from perplexed to dumbfounded, even Cal's. Sasha couldn't believe that whiny little mouse Opi had seen something the rest of them had all missed.

"Let me get this straight," Tony said. "By getting us all scragged, Cal won the exercise?"

Opi smiled at him, and Sasha realized he had never seen her smile before. "No, Tony, we lost. But by losing yesterday we have a better chance to win a lot more in the future."

Letty grinned ear to ear. "Yes, we will. Keep watching, Opi, and try to catch something else. Now, how do we use this information to win two exercises this afternoon?"

By lunchtime they had a plan. Grabbing a quick meal, they split up, males and females. Letty and Opi sat alone in the very far corner of the lunchroom, near the doors to the training rooms. Sasha didn't want any company, so he sat alone; Cal and Tony ended together at a third table. From what Sasha could see, they ate in silence, methodically cleaning up several plate-loads of food.

As Sasha ate, he reviewed the exercise from yesterday, including Cal's aggressive move that had cost them a victory and what Opi had discovered from it. He grunted in disgust. What Opi had seen earlier was suddenly and blatantly obvious. Finishing his food, he dropped by the girls' table for a moment.

"One thing," he said to Letty. "I know there is a controversy about who is the best captain. I admit I had the wrong idea here, but I've figured it out, finally."

"So what did you figure out?"

"There are a lot of leadership qualities in you," Sasha said. "You're careful, deliberate, sure of your footing. I think you'll be a great planner, and a great second-in-command. But that won't make you the best team captain. Cal is a natural leader, and he'll be a good one when he learns a little a bit more about command. Sometimes a leader has to be aggressive, or the team will fail. I think when Cal learns to control himself, he'll be a really good captain for us."

Into the silence Opi added, "I think so, too." Quickly, she continued. "I really like you, Letty. You're kind and supportive, and you are really helping make us a better team. Like Sasha says, you are going to be a great co-pilot. You'll be a good brake on Cal when he gets too aggressive. But Cal should be the captain."

Standing up, Letty beamed. "You're finally using your heads," she said, patting their shoulders. "You're absolutely right." Quickly, she led them back to the simulator.

27 LETTY

As Letty slid into the command chair, Cal took a deep breath. "I hope this works."

"It will." She turned to Tony and Opi. "Need to rehearse it again?"

They exchanged glances.

"Think I got it," Tony said.

"Me too," Sasha echoed.

"Good." Letty signaled Raj, who keyed in a code on the console to start the exercise. This time, he sat in the instructor chair, raising Letty's pulse and perspiration level. *What the hell,* she thought, *if I screw this up, it won't matter whether Raj is here or not.*

"Initiate launch," she directed the console, and immediately the now-familiar bump and jerk signaled the simulated launch.

As vibration shook her seat, the forward display flickered, then came alive with the Milky Way backdrop above.

Opi called out, "We will use thrusters for approximately five minutes, then leap to the Corvison system."

Minutes later they orbited the Corvison sun, some forty thousand kilometers from the destination planet. On the magnified display, they saw the vast battle taking place, thousands of ships in mortal combat.

"Odd that the convoy's only bringing twenty more attack ships," Sasha said from the observer seat.

"Maybe that's a trap, too," Tony muttered from the weapons console. "It's a lot fewer attack ships than yesterday."

Letty gave him an over-the-shoulder glance. "Let's stick to the plan. I think we've learned a principle here that we need to apply. Opi, where's the convoy?"

Opi had been searching the scanner arrays. She switched to tactical. "Directly behind us and maybe a quarter million klicks out. One micro-leap and we'll be on top of them."

"What part of the fuel convoy is most vulnerable?"

Opi blew up magnification on the visual scanners. Even at maximum, the ships were merely a group of dots. She switched to tactical. "To the left and about halfway down the column. One ship is a bit out of place. It'll be an easy kill."

"Going in," Letty said, voice tense, and she triggered the micro-leap.

Their ship lay no more than a few hundred kilometers from the convoy, approaching so fast that they crossed the remaining distance in a flash. The familiar rattle of the Gatling cannon shook their pod as Tony tried his hands at the guns, and Letty leaped again.

Turning their simulated ship about to face the enemy, some two light-seconds removed from the action, Letty quickly analyzed as Cal counted and Opi plotted their second attack.

"Got the stray fueler," Cal said.

Letty saw that Opi had never taken her eyes off the small tactical display rectangle. "It's forming," Opi said. She leaned over and activated a slide switch, bringing the tactical view to the main display. "See? A modified globe, with two extra ships now concentrated opposite where we attacked. Just like before. Whatever direction we come from, they load up on the other direction, assuming we will come back from that angle and try to catch them off guard."

Cal pointed, and a red dot formed on the tactical picture. "Notice, at the top of the globe they created a weak spot, only one ship positioned directly on point."

Opi bent over the console. "Plotting vector."

Letty gave her the thumbs up. "Let's do this."

The leap brought them to the exact top of the convoy (top being a relative position only), just a hundred kilometers, two seconds, from the lead attack ship. Tony opened up with the Gatling gun as they approached and shot past the ship. He adjusted the weapon and sent a hail of shrapnel flying ahead of them through the remaining vessels.

They leaped again, circling about three hundred thousand kilometers out.

"Status?" Letty barked.

Opi and Cal, she noticed, were frantically assessing both visual and tactical displays. She felt a warm glow; they had done some serious damage to the enemy.

Tony grinned triumphantly as Cal yelled, "We got 'em all! Every fueler is destroyed."

Opi spoke up from the nav console, still timid but louder than her normal whisper. "There's a nice opportunity here. The Horde ships are confused and their pattern has sagged. Some ships are out of position."

"Perfect," Letty said. "Opi, pick some isolated ships and let's hit them hard again, make them pay."

They made three more passes, each from a different heading, totaling eight ships destroyed and four others with various degrees of damage.

Eventually The Horde ships reorganized into a small,

outward-facing, defensive globe that Letty judged would be much harder to pierce. "Take us home," she told Opi with glee.

Over her shoulder, Lieutenant Raj said nothing, but he wore a thoughtful expression.

Cal got the command seat back for their second exercise, and Sasha and Tony resumed their original seats. By that time, their expertise had begun to make itself apparent. After a quick analysis, they attacked a still-larger convoy and cut it to pieces.

As they trooped triumphantly to dinner, Tony said, "Way to go, Letty! You're a good one, girl."

"Hey," Cal said, finally cheerier, "I did well, too."

Tony nodded. "Yeah, well, you may not be as dumb as I first thought."

Everybody laughed, even Cal.

Damn, Letty thought. *Maybe we took a little step today toward being a real team.*

28 LETTY

The days begin to fly by. The following day, Letty and Cal alternated at pilot at first, but Tony was assigned exclusively to navigation and Sasha to gunnery. Opi became permanent fifth chair, which meant at first that she simply observed a lot and occasionally whispered to Letty.

By the third full day of training, their trainer no longer simply threw them into unusual situations, but began to give them detailed mission briefings the evening before each set of exercises. Letty and Opi huddled together much more often, while Tony and Sasha, responsible for route and attack planning, hung out regularly, eating together and often conferring in their quarters to discuss the day's exercise or to discuss the briefing and make suggestions to Letty and Cal.

Letty, for her part, felt a definite decrease in tension. She wouldn't have said that her fellow team members loved each other by any means, but at least they had become consistently civil—even to Opi.

A week into their training, Lieutenant Raj announced after the day's exercises that they were allowed free access to most of the ship, though not the weapons or duty areas. In addition, they could go to the cafeteria, a gymnasium, and a break area that resembled a coffee shop, whenever they were off duty. Letty and Cal began to frequent the refreshment bar, sometimes with Opi and occasionally with Tony and Sasha as well. There were enough tables that any number of teams began to congregate there, and they began to make a few friends among the other groups. Letty had met people from several other teams, two from Canada. To those teams, she was able to talk in English, but another team from south Texas, whose primary language was Spanish, she spoke with in their new common language, Molethian.

Letty began to form an early morning habit of catching a quick breakfast with Opi and reviewing the mission plan that they had constructed the night before. More and more, she became dependent on Opi's critique and her razor-sharp analysis of the upcoming exercise. Opi seemed to have an uncanny eye for Horde tactics, and more often than not, her remarks had helped Letty formulate the mission plan for each exercise.

For their noon meal in the lunchroom, they were all eating together more often than not at the same table, perhaps splitting up occasionally to eat with casual friends they had made. Letty had kept a lookout each day for the overweight bully who had tried to provoke Cal, only to be put out of action by Tony. She never saw him again. They did continue to see the other members of that team, who occasionally cast dark glances their way, but didn't seem to want to provoke another confrontation.

By the two-week mark, Tony started to interact with Cal regularly without the chip on his shoulder, and Sasha slowly become pleasant to everyone, even Opi. As for Opi, she mainly spoke in low tones to Letty, but at least she didn't seem like a nervous wreck around the others.

By the fourth week, Cal was permanently installed as pilot.

He had quit mentioning his father, losing some of that drawn, depressed face that he had hung onto the first days. He was even polite to Tony, and even laughed once or twice at Tony's wisecracks.

Letty settled into the co-pilot position securely, happy to plan the missions and relying more heavily every exercise on Opi's insight and singular talent for detecting details of Horde battle strategy. Further, the worry and burden of her parents' constant fighting had disappeared.

As she prepared for bed at the end of the sixth week, she reflected that for a kidnappee forced to train for galactic war against an evil empire, she was about as happy as she could be. The problem was that the structure and discipline of training would not last forever. The training was all about war, and in the back of her mind she knew that real battles, not simulated ones, were coming. Resolutely, she decided to ignore the future and simply plan on excelling tomorrow in their activities. Past that, it was out of her hands.

29 LETTY

As she slipped off her sleeping platform, just seven weeks since that first victory, some patterns remained the same, Letty observed. Sasha arose from sleep like a zombie, and Opi still spoke very quietly. Cal got up as early as Letty, and Tony stayed horizontal to the last possible moment.

She looked up from her desk computer as Lieutenant Raj walked in, leaping to her feet and calling the room to attention. Around her, the others sprang up, too.

"As you were," Raj said, and everyone relaxed.

Yesterday had been another good day, with three successful missions. They had won all but two of sixty-plus flown since they'd begun training, including their first-day loss.

One issue pricked her generally improved feelings, something that had bothered her for a long time, which she had discussed only once before, with Galigan. She knew that it probably only mattered to her and Opi, not the guys, and of course Opi would never mention anything that bothered her.

Determined to bring her concern up once again, she waited until Raj had said, "Congratulations on your fine performance yesterday. Before we proceed to the regular team meeting, are there any questions or concerns that you want to discuss?"

Of course, he meant related to training, Letty knew, but that didn't deter her. "Yes, I do, sir. May I speak to you privately?"

Raj grinned. "It couldn't be about yesterday, with three successes. If you still have concerns about that loss three days ago, I've already given you a full critique. Whatever you have to say, I believe that you should all speak freely before each other. No secrets."

"It's not the loss, sir," Letty said, noticing the brittle tension in her voice. "It's personal."

Lieutenant Raj remained silent, as did her teammates remained, watching her. Afraid she would sound as wussy as Opi, Letty went on doggedly. "I, uh ... It's our living conditions. When we'd been here a couple of days I discussed it with Galigan, but ..."

Raj nodded, and she plowed on. "I mean, sir, we're three ..." she started to say "boys" but realized it would sound demeaning, and besides, none of them, she and Opi included, were children. "We're three young men and two young women, all sleeping in one room and sharing a bath. I didn't say anything at first because I was scared and confused and worried, and I just wanted to go home and have my mom tell me it would be all right.

"Now we know that won't happen. We're here to stay, and we have to make the best of it. I've accepted that, and as I have become more or less acclimated to our training routine, those concerns have come back up. The guys have been perfect gentlemen, but I mean, at our age sex is a really big deal, and let's face it, people say our hormones are going crazy. What if, living this close together, some of us get interested in ... romance?

"Another thing. We share the same bath. I mean, when I go in there, I don't want anyone else even *thinking* about what I'm doing. It's just too embarrassing. You have taken pains to provide for … for feminine hygiene issues, and I really appreciate that the necessary … supplies are available. But I'm very self-conscious about time-of-the-month issues, and I expect that Opi is, too. Isn't there some way that we can have two bathrooms?"

Raj had continued to nod, registering her comments, neither upset, amused, nor anything else, simply listening to her concerns. When she finished, he said, "Thank you for honestly expressing your worries. I appreciate your candid exposition, and I am sure that your teammates do as well."

Letty glanced around, nervously. The three guys' faces glowed red, and Tony couldn't quite suppress a smirk. Opi looked very relieved, as though Letty had expressed all her unspoken anxieties.

Raj went on. "I am very familiar with your issues. However, we have found that it is imperative for teams to live together. Bathing and toilet facilities are always limited on space cruisers, so the only practical solution is one per team. Indeed, on older ships, there is only one for several teams!

"Letty, your bodily functions are no mystery to your teammates. In fact, the Molethians have the same basic life functions as do humans.

"I realize that a female raised in your American culture may be concerned about propriety. While you must make some sacrifices in terms of your cultural sensibilities, I assure you that those sacrifices can be made without compromising your basic privacy."

Raj gazed around the room at Letty's comrades. They had remained rooted in place since Raj entered. "There are lessons to be learned in this close and admittedly intimate existence," he said. "Tolerance for each other's quirks, patience in waiting for those bathroom facilities, an understanding of the strengths and weaknesses that each member brings to the team. Our commanders believe that day-to-day closeness, despite its disadvantages in terms of privacy, are crucial for welding your group into a unified, smoothly operating team.

"It is what we bring to the conflict that makes us far superior to The Horde. We are not a mindless mass that plods forward without thinking, doing a single job, forfeiting any semblance of creativity and originality. It is the reason that we will ultimately vanquish our enemy.

"With respect to your concern about sexual activity, we have managed it to a certain extent. Your implants include some suggestions that deter both sexes from overt advances."

Tony twisted around, suddenly angry, and both Cal and Sasha visibly tensed.

"Galigan said you really couldn't control our minds! Did he lie to us?" Tony demanded.

Raj held up a hand, and Tony stopped. Letty almost had to chuckle, despite her concern. That training had been effective. The Tony of their first day together had been nearly unstoppable, short of Galigan's wand.

"No, Tony, you are not being controlled. We dare not do anything to affect your native abilities to fight and to learn. However, our implants do make available certain standards of behavior and examples. That doesn't mean that Cal couldn't, for example, decide to kiss Letty." She involuntarily inhaled, and she saw Cal stiffen, suddenly alert. "But he would be made to understand that such behavior would impair the team's cohesiveness and ability to implement its duties. For any moves beyond that, Cal would be reminded that sexual advances might repel Letty and certainly would anger his other team members.

"Further, about those time-of-the-month issues. Molethan medical technicians did not want to interrupt cycles already in their course, but an additional implant has halted them. It is similar to the birth control chemicals that are available on Earth. So you no longer need to worry about that."

The lieutenant interrupted himself. "We are about to be late for an important meeting. Letty, I hope I answered all of your questions."

Letty ducked her head, embarrassed. "Yes, sir."

"Good. Now, double-time to the conference room."

They did so, marching swiftly down the hallway, Letty still discomfited. Despite that, curiosity tugged at her mind. What was up?

30 TONY

Entering the usual meeting area, Tony watched the assembly hall fill rapidly, and noticed that there were more chairs than ever. Although not as big as the cafeteria, it held plenty of room for more than two hundred chairs. As he scanned the growing assemblage, he began to inventory the other teams. Most cadets, as he had noted from the first, were about the same age, from fifteen to seventeen or eighteen at most, and all dressed identically in the tan uniforms.

Past that, the differences were subtle. There were dark-chocolate-skinned, and also lighter-skinned teenagers of African heritage like Letty, but most spoke English or Molethian. Some primarily Latino teams were present, plus a large number of Caucasian teams, and a scattering of teams with diverse racial backgrounds. He could also make out what he thought of as "American Spanish."

As Captain Alitan took to a platform in the front, a voice rang out. "Room, atten-*tion!*"

The young warriors, jammed wall to wall, shot erect, and

Tony estimated that more than two hundred people were crowded together. What was about to happen? It had to be a big deal.

The amplified voice of the Commander quieted the room. "Please be seated. If you can't find a chair, stand along the walls."

Amid some rustling and a brief babble, most of the recruits settled into seats and the few left standing moved obediently to the edges of the room.

"Thank you," the captain said. "I have good news today. You have completed your initial training and are now members of a full-fledged team. Those that did not qualify have been returned to Earth with new memories. Everyone in this room has met, and in most cases exceeded, the standards that we set for Shadow Warriors.

"I now declare that individual team training is ended. You have had a very strenuous few weeks of learning and adaptation. You will now be allowed two days of shipboard Rest-and-Relaxation to get to know each other better and enjoy yourselves."

A murmur of pleased voices met his declaration.

Alitan exhibited the first smile Tony could remember. "Further, now that you have officially completed the first round of training, you receive a salary as a Shadow Warrior. This does not mean that in every case, your teams will finally make the grade to become a fighting crew. However, as is the case with the armed services you are familiar with, now that you are in the final qualification process, you have earned the right to a training salary.

"This salary will be credited to you each standard month, and when your service is finished, you will be able to obtain it when you return to Earth. Even those who do not finally qualify will be able to claim their earnings up to their discharge when they are returned to Earth."

Commander Alitan paused as a ripple of sound swept the

room again, first bubbling appreciation, and finally a ragged cheer. He allowed himself a second brief smile and continued.

"I am happy you are pleased. You have earned both your leave and your salary. Granted, it will not be a fortune, but you will have some savings when your service is completed.

"Now, let me announce your next level of training. Beginning three days hence, the forty-eight remaining warrior teams on this vessel will begin an intra-ship competition. The training will be a double-elimination, to determine the top teams. Six elite teams will compete against teams from the other sixty-three ships orbiting Earth, all in geostationary orbits, as is this ship. From this competition will come a unit of thirty crews to be immediately deployed as Shadow Warriors.

"You and your teammates were all recruited from the United States and Canada. Other ships contain teams from Central and South America, China, Southeast Asia, Europe, India, and Australia, so Earth is well represented. However, you must not think of yourselves as representing a geographical area but as the very best warriors to counter the great threat of The Horde.

"Teams disqualified along the way will retrain for five days and then compete once more. In the second competition, six more teams will qualify and begin inter-ship contests. After additional training, competitions will qualify the next twelve teams. Competitions will continue until all but the bottom twenty percent have qualified. That lowest group will receive additional training and be deployed for fleet duties other than combat. However, they may have an opportunity to join Shadow Warrior units later on. Thus, everyone present will serve our forces in some way."

The captain's gray eyes swept the attendees. "I urge you to do your best to prevail in the coming contests. In that way, even the teams which do not initially qualify will gain experience and ultimately have the opportunity to join our struggle. Now, my congratulations for your efforts so far. You are dismissed to your holiday."

He stepped down to tumultuous applause. Even Tony found himself clapping and cheering. *Odd,* he thought. Abducted and forced to live with four other people, none of whom he had liked very well at first, except maybe Letty, then told that he would be fighting in a war, and he was happy.

Better than living in the streets, he concluded.

Letty managed to catch his eye with a wave, although the noise level made conversation impossible. He followed her back to the room, and before long Sasha, Cal, and Opi returned as well.

Letty surveyed the group, motioning them to gather around. "Sasha and Tony, you okay with the speech?"

Sasha nodded, and Tony said with a grin, "Yeah, kidnapped and all, I'm happy."

She singled out Opi and Cal. "We three had more at stake back home, but we agreed before to throw in together and do this, come what may. I assume we're still together, but I want to verify it. So, here's what I declare: I am one hundred percent devoted to competing, to winning the competition, and to becoming a member of the Shadow Warrior corps. That is," she thrust her right fist into the circle they had made, "I am *in.*"

Tony promptly grabbed her hand. "In." It felt good.

Sasha topped Tony's hand. "In."

Opi hesitated a fraction, then she put her smaller hand on Tony's wrist. "In."

Last of all, Cal shook his head and put in both hands, one above the group's outstretched hands, one below, clasping all of theirs in his. "I'm in."

"Hot damn." Letty released her hands and grabbed Tony,

hugging him fiercely. Then she did the same in turn to Sasha, Opi, and last of all Cal. That hug lasted a fraction longer.

When she released him, Tony cracked, "Hey, Cal, if you want to kiss her, I won't tell."

Embarrassed, Cal managed to grin.

31 CAL

Ready for physical exercise now that they had access to a gym, Cal rose even earlier than Letty. As Raj had promised, shorts, T-shirts, white athletic socks, and running shoes had been placed in what had previously been an empty drawer.

Raj had also shown him a running track, one that circled the perimeter of the ship, rotating slowly to create an effective pull like the ship's artificial gravity. Following directions, he made his way to a door near the outer hull, opened it, and stepped onto a meter-wide, rapidly moving metal belt. He nearly stumbled, but caught himself and began to jog against the rotation.

He slowly increased his speed until he ran at a solid six to seven minutes per mile. Thinking about his running rate made him chuckle. They might talk all they wanted to during a training exercise about distances in kilometers, but his mind naturally reverted to miles whenever he was on his own.

Though the track tube was quite cool, he was soon perspiring heavily, but he increased the pace until he began to feel the burn in his leg muscles, telling him that they were truly stressed. Gradually he slowed to a brisk walk, until he cooled a bit. With that, he returned to the center of the ship to the gymnasium. It was crowded for the early hour, with dozens of Shadow Warrior cadets working to improve their physical shape. Although the Molethian training command did not mandate exercising, it was encouraged and Cal guessed that most of the teenagers on the ship were getting with the program.

Managing to find a barbell rack with a variety of unused equipment, he started with curls of twenty, twenty-five, and thirty pounds, taking it easy after his time off. He alternated seated presses with a pretty blonde who batted her eyes at him and flirted mildly, taking the time to talk a bit before he moved on, though he didn't ask her name. He found Sasha doing triceps exercises and worked with him the rest of the way, moving on to lats, abs, and deltoid exercises. The gym was well supplied with modern machines, some of which had logos of companies he was familiar with from his school gym.

They talked little, concentrating on the reps. After half an hour, they left, Sasha for a shower, and Cal detouring to the cafeteria for breakfast, ravenous after his first heavy workout in weeks. Feeling guilty, he knew he had pushed too hard. *I'll regret this tomorrow*, he thought.

Filling a plate with scrambled eggs, steak, and a variety of fruits, he spied Letty alone and joined her. She smiled as he came up.

"Want to join me?" she asked.

"Are you sure? I probably smell pretty ripe about now."

"I've smelled worse. There was a kid in one of my classes ... but that's a story for another day. Exercising, huh?"

He sat across from her, staying back a bit. "Yeah. Haven't lifted a finger for weeks. Tomorrow I'll wake you with soft crying and maybe a whine or two."

"Aw, you're in such good shape, you'll be fine. I used to do a little cardio, but not much else, and nothing here at all."

He leaned forward a bit, swallowing eggs. Maybe enthusiasm, maybe anticipation, he wasn't sure. "Come work out with me tomorrow." He managed a grin. "I may need to lean on you to get back to our room."

Surprised for a moment her features morphed into a pleased expression. "Okay. If you won't run off and leave me."

"I promise."

"Good. Now, we need to talk."

The frown and wrinkled brow made him nervous. Had he done something to offend her? No, she wouldn't have agreed to go running if he had. Still a bit worried, he joked feebly, "Hope I'm not in trouble."

"Trouble? No, silly. This is serious."

He plowed, full speed, into the pastries. "What?"

"It's Opi. She's so timid, and she still hardly says anything. But I've been working with her, and she has real talent. You know these great mission plans I've been coming up with?"

"Great is correct. You're a genius."

"No, I'm not. She is. It's like that first day, when she figured out that Horde formation. I get her alone early and we talk. Sometimes I've had to push her, she's so reticent about saying anything. But she's getting better, beginning to show initiative and actually speaking up.

"I think it's time to formally anoint her."

"Anoint?"

"Give her a title. She still feels like a nothing, a cipher, a hanger-on. But she's not. She's a genius at spotting trends and evolving what she sees into strategic plans. Cal, if we can keep bringing her along, I think she's our secret weapon. I think we can win it all with her."

His brows had risen. He tried to sound neutral, hoping she

didn't take his attitude for outright disbelief. "That's a pretty dramatic call." *In fact*, he thought, *it was outrageously positive, almost unbelievable.*

Still, he reminded himself that Letty had made the statements, and he had come to believe that her opinions merited special consideration. *Down-to-earth*, he thought, and laughed inwardly at the description.

After consideration, he said, "How can I help?"

"No argument?"

"I've learned to trust your judgment."

She smiled, the slight flush on her cheeks showing her pleasure. "Thanks. Okay, mainly give her your support. Encourage her, tell her you appreciate her contribution. Make damn sure Sasha and Tony hear you."

He smiled. "I will, although I think Tony is changing his tune. He might have his eye on her a bit."

"Noticed that too, eh?" She grinned. "Here I am, only one of two girls in the team, and the other one is the knockout."

He stood, deciding to say what was on his mind. "I think both our girls are beauties."

As she pushed back her chair, her mouth shifted into a softer smile for a moment. Then the sassy grin returned. "Go take a shower, you stinker." She turned and headed back to their quarters.

32 LETTY

Letty fretted, nervously twisting her hands together behind her back as Raj explained their first competition. Could Cal make an impact with the speech he had prepared? Could she still bring Opi along, developing her slowly, making her understand her value to the team, giving her a sense of belonging and importance? She thought so. But sly doubts remained to bedevil her as Raj summarized the competition ground rules.

"—will be as follows," Raj was saying. "All teams will compete in a double-elimination for positions as the top representatives of Ship Twenty-Two, as Commander Alitan told you. The rules for inter-ship competition are a bit different, and I will cover them should this team advance as a contender in that competition.

"In the intra-ship competition, you are competing for one of three undefeated spots. Winners enter the undefeated bracket. Losers of one exercise enter a bracket in which they continue to remain in that group so long as they win. Those with a second loss in the one-loss bracket retire to the sidelines.

"When inter-ship contests begin, a new round of competitions on this ship will begin, as remaining teams compete. Competitions continue until all but the bottom twenty percent of teams qualify. Teams qualifying in later rounds will be added to new squadrons, or replace Shadow Warrior losses.

"By remaining in training and competition, most teams will eventually be battle-ready, although some teams may take substantially longer to qualify. I assure you, no matter how long it may take this team, you will get your chance to battle The Horde."

"Won't matter to us," Tony said. "We're going to qualify first time."

"Absolutely," Sasha joined in.

Letty almost glowed at their enthusiasm.

"Good for you. Now, your first test will begin in about ten minutes, once I am notified that your opposing team is ready. I will brief you on the mission scenario, and you will have thirty minutes to complete an attack plan, which you will then present to me. Any questions?"

Satisfied, Letty remained silent. Apparently her teammates felt the same.

"Good. Back in a few minutes." Raj departed, leaving Letty with feelings of anticipation and apprehension. She signaled Cal with a sharp glance.

Before they could desert the circle they had formed around Raj, Cal said, "Guys, I have an announcement."

Everyone but Letty looked puzzled. *Here goes*, she thought.

"All of us, I'm sure, think we have helped to complete so many of our training exercises successfully," Cal said. "All but one, maybe." He put his hand on Opi's shoulder, causing her to jump, and Tony to chuckle. "More than once, we've congratulated Letty on our battle plans, our successes.

"In fact, Opi is responsible as much as Letty, maybe more.

Because of that, I am giving Opi the permanent assignment of Strategy Officer, responsible for operation planning with our team executive officer and co-pilot, Letty.

"Opi, your excellent plans and insight have helped to make us successful in our training. Now we ask you to be a major part of our push to represent Ship Twenty-Two in the inter-ship competition. Congratulations!"

Suddenly pale, Opi managed to nod, although nothing came from her mouth.

Tony jumped across the circle and said, "Way to go, Opi!" He took her hand and squeezed it.

Sasha hesitated, then managed to pat her shoulder. "Congratulations, Opi. I guess maybe I underestimated you."

"Yes, you certainly did," Letty said firmly. As Sasha blinked, she continued, "Opi, we all underestimated you. You're an important part of the team." She addressed them at large. "Okay, you got maybe five minutes. Take a bathroom break, whatever, but get ready. And I mean mentally, too."

Raj returned in less time than he had stated. "All right, here's the assignment." He handed Letty a small data tablet. "You have thirty minutes."

The rest looked over her shoulder as she and Opi scanned the scenario.

"Simple," Tony said. "Half a dozen Horde ships are attacking. All we do is knock most or all of them out. We've done this several times." He turned to Opi this time, not Letty. "Pretty simple, right? We get an easy one for our first test."

Even before he finished, both Letty and Opi had begun to shake their heads. Letty motioned them to her bed, where she placed the tablet so that everyone could see the screen. "It can't be that simple," she said. "This is a *competition*. From now on, we don't get easy exercises. There has to be a catch."

Everybody remained silent, Opi shifting uncomfortably as the group focused on her.

Cal spoke to her in an encouraging voice. "Take your time, Opi. Think about it. Is there anything that really catches your attention?"

For more than a minute she didn't move a muscle. Letty had begun to wonder if Opi were paralyzed with worry when Opi said, very casually, "You know, I noticed something in Exercise Thirty-two. It wasn't of any consequence then because we had decided that a frontal attack contained the most surprise if we hit them slightly off-center. I noticed that after the encounter there were two ships trailing the convoy, a few thousand kilometers back. If we had made our normal rear quarter or side attack we would have been mincemeat. In that exercise, those ships were never involved due to our frontal attack, as they were far to the rear of the formation. I wonder ... Could this be a setup?"

Letty hugged Opi. "Definitely a possibility! Opi, you're a genius!"

"And what do we do?" Sasha asked. "One thing to know there might be a swindle going on. How do we react?"

Cal grinned. "I got that. Sasha, grease up those Gatling guns. So far as we know, Horde ships can't do any sort of micro-leaps like our ships. We're going to come in behind them, blast both trailing ships, then micro-leap right into their middle, give them a spray from your guns, and leap out before they even know what hit them."

Sasha grinned. Tony grinned. Cal kept grinning.

Letty smiled as broadly as she ever did, "I think we've got this one!"

Opi, suddenly brimming with confidence, clapped her hands.

33 SASHA

Leading them back from the first exercise, Raj's comment wiped the grins off their faces. "I'm glad you're so amused, but that's just one win. I will admit that you weren't caught flat footed like your opposition, but still, don't let a little dumb luck go to your head."

Sasha grinned. No dumb luck. Who would have thought that timid mouse Opi would be so good at seeing little things that could spell the difference between defeat and victory?

Entering their quarters, Raj told them, "You can have two hours to enjoy your victory and take your lunch. As you know, you have another exercise this afternoon, and two a day until the first three champions are determined." He left them to bask in their win and worry about the next match.

They grabbed quick lunches, Opi eating very little, Sasha, Cal and Tony consuming enormous meals, and Letty appearing to force herself to down a full plate because she knew food was fuel and she would need plenty in the afternoon. Back in their room, they relieved their nerves in different ways. Cal paced back and forth, Letty went to the bathroom four times, Tony alternated push-ups with sitting on his bed, and Sasha and Opi sat on her bunk and talked for the first time Sasha could remember. Their conversation was mainly nervous chatter, but Sasha congratulated Opi on her well-planned mission scenario, and she seemed pleased at what must be his first ever words to her that weren't critical.

When Raj finally returned, Sasha felt a surge of relief. Now they could get back to action!

"Your mission is somewhat different this time," Raj told them. "A large Horde installation is being built, one that intelligence suggests will become a major sub-capital and supply center. This is a chance to badly hurt the enemy, but the installation is far into Horde territory.

"Military intelligence is by its very nature sketchy at times. Your best information is that the installation is defended by only a very small force, as its location has been a heavily guarded Horde secret. You must go in, destroy the site with our most powerful supernuclear bombs, and get away quickly, in case Horde reinforcements are closer than anticipated. The rest of the details are on this tablet as usual. You have thirty minutes. Questions?"

None.

Raj left, and Opi began to study the mission scenario, seated on Letty's bed, as they all tried to read over her shoulder. The description consisted of only a few paragraphs plus some coordinate groups.

Opi, still puzzling over the exercise, remained deep in thought.

"Important target, not a lot of defense," Sasha remarked, more to himself than Opi and the rest. "Maybe a test to do the most damage in the shortest time and get away safely?"

Cal zeroed in on Opi. "Is there a problem?"

She looked up vaguely, as though surveying that remote

system with some internal telescope. "It's too simple. Yes, Sasha, it's a test to do as much damage as possible, but I think there's more ..." She trailed off, still light-years-away.

Tony said, "It's another trap."

"Not a trap," Letty said. "A hitch. The mission is as well-defined as possible with the available intel, but there are things we haven't been told. That perhaps Command doesn't know."

"That's it!" Opi came back from her mental sortie to the enemy planet. "I was doing some reading in the library—"

"We have a *library*?" Sasha interjected. Where had he been when they announced access to a library?

"They didn't announce that publicly," Opi said. "I asked Raj, and he showed it to me. It's small; no real books. Just electronic data storage and data viewers. I've been reviewing old battle summaries. We have almost no time. Here's what you do." She quickly listed several steps to take during the exercise. "That's a plain vanilla approach, but it takes in the chance of some sort of ambush. In the meantime, let me go back to the library and research a couple of ideas. I'll meet you in the simulator."

She didn't wait for approval, jumping off her bed and flitting out the door.

Letty grinned. "Opi has caught fire. Guys, we've got an edge that's something special."

When Raj entered some time later, they were rehearsing the steps that Opi had left them. Tony was in the middle of a hand-flailing example. "If we don't come in from above, but sneak over the horizon, we can gain a few more seconds' advantage!"

As they stood to attention, Raj said, "Opi?"

"Sir, she went to do a little research," Cal said. "She'll meet us in the cockpit."

Raj frowned. "Start time is in fifteen minutes. I hope you understand that short of illness, a team member who doesn't arrive before the start of the exercise results in automatic disqualification, which counts as a loss."

"What?" Cal relaxed for a moment, swinging toward Raj, then snapping back to attention as he realized his breach of conduct. "Sir, I'm sure she will meet us on time. But ... if a team member doesn't show up, can the other four just continue the exercise?"

"If a teammate is truly incapacitated—that is, ill or injured—that is an option." Raj's concern began to be reflected by the team. "But unauthorized absence by a member disqualifies the team and might even place you on reserve status, at the bottom of the competition ladder.

"She's not missing," Letty spoke up.

Raj gave her a stern look. "What?"

"She's not missing, sir," Letty corrected herself.

The lieutenant directed his hard expression at each team member in turn. "Your recent success does not excuse you from normal military discipline. Is that clear?"

They shouted crisply, "Yes, sir!"

"Good. The exercise begins in ..." he glanced at the station clock, "thirteen minutes. If Opi is not present at that time, your mission will be scrubbed. See you in the Assembly Area A."

He left them staring at each other with sudden concern. Sasha didn't hesitate a second. He headed toward the door. "I'll get her," he yelled back to them.

"Wait!" came from Cal. "Do you even know where the library is?"

Sasha didn't care. For the first time, he realized Opi's importance. One way or the other, he'd find her.

34 OPI

She almost had it. The browsing application in the Molethians' data storage bank did not approach the efficiency of the internet browsers back home. It took longer to produce an accurate query that would return the information she desired.

A very nice droid, looking like nothing so much as a miniature Molethan, had gotten her started, but after that she had had to wend her way through a great deal of irrelevant information. Time was growing short; she had to hurry.

She knew Raj would be upset if she were even seconds late, but what she was looking for could make the difference between victory and defeat. *Only a few more minutes,* she thought frantically. *I'm so close!*

The next file hit the target. This had to be it. Hastily dictating notes to her tablet, she had written up most of her ideas when Sasha blew through the hatch to the library.

"Come on!" he said frantically. "We're almost out of time. If you aren't back in time for the exercise, we forfeit!"

"Forfeit?" Opi sprang up, grabbing the tablet. "Let's go."

They ran out of the data storage room, through several passages, and down two flights of stairs, as Sasha didn't want to wait on an elevator. Opi silently agreed.

They piled into the meeting room as Cal, Letty, and Tony stood anxiously by the red door where they always gathered. Raj stood there, too, glowering.

"Finally!" Cal blurted out. "Just a minute or so to go. Did you find what you were searching for?"

Opi stopped in front of Raj and came to attention, as did Sasha. "Sorry, sir!"

"You made it, barely," Raj said sharply. "Don't let it happen again."

"Yes, sir," she gasped, panting.

Raj turned and they followed him into the warren of test modules. As they hurried down the narrow hall, she whispered to Cal and Letty, "I got most of what I wanted. I could have gotten more, with some additional time. But ... I think I got enough."

In the simulator, Raj wished them luck sat in his supervisory chair.

Cal grabbed Opi by a shoulder. "Is there a catch?"

"I think so. Letty," she pulled out her tablet from a pocket and showed her a quick summary.

Letty's brows arched. "Really?"

"Really." Opi turned to Cal, about to explode with anticipation. "Set in the destination coordinates. I can tell you what to do on the way." She turned to Raj. "Sir, do you wish a formal report?"

Raj shook his head and they took positions.

Shortly, Tony said, "Ship's vectors laid in. Departure at your direction, Captain."

"Launching," said Cal.

There came the familiar bump and sudden feeling of motion as they left the mother ship in the simulation. As they rocketed away, moving far enough from the big ship so that they could leap successfully, Cal said, "Okay, what's going on?"

For a moment, Opi felt that rush of excitement again. "I've been scanning old historical files on Horde settlements, how they colonize once a planet has been restored, how they sprinkle their sub-centers of government into regions as they settle and begin to populate that region.

"As you know, the area we are to attack today is a development that is slated to become a new regional capital. Destroying it could be a huge blow to their empire, and they know it, just as we do. So, before they establish a new center, *they construct an enormous defense base*, capable of housing thousands of fighters, and they make it *fully operational* before they even start to build the new capital on top of the subterranean base."

Tone gulped. "You mean—?"

"Yes, Tony," Opi interrupted. "That's not a vulnerable construction project. It's a new city being built on top of a dome that has tens of thousands of Horde ships on full alert."

Cal blinked. "Wait a minute. We can't destroy a base like that, and we surely won't make a scratch on the new city."

"Check your weapons stores," Opi told him.

Cal did so. "Standard surface bombs, Gatling gun, beam weapons, and the supernuclear bombs to be launched against the city. I guess we could get close, make a micro-jump, and try to drop the bomb on the city before they launch a counterattack. We might get away."

Letty lit up. "I see where you're going." She swung around to Cal. "Forget the damn city; it's peanuts. Consider that underground fortress. To construct it and fully populate it with fighters and support crews could cost a king's ransom, probably a hundred times the cost of building the city. That's what the super bombs are for. We have to go for the military base. It will set them back further than anything else we could do."

"And how do we do that?" Cal scratched his head.

"That's my department," Letty told him. "Tony, when we leap, bring us in pretty far out. Does the planet have a moon?"

"Three, including a little one that is only a couple thousand kilometers above the planet. It has a really fast orbit."

"Maybe too fast, but okay. Where is it now?"

"Behind the planet from the installation."

"Excellent. Plot us a vector in behind the planet so Cal can land us on the baby moon. We need to be situated just so the base is barely visible as we go past. Considering it's so small, the gravity will be less than nothing, so be prepared to use the grappling hooks when we touch down." She glanced at Tony. "A tiny moon like that orbits the planet quickly, right?"

Tony consulted his screens. "Every two hours."

"When we land on the moon, I want to let it carry us over the base, hidden well enough so that we can survey Horde movement without giving ourselves away."

"Good idea," Cal said, and gripped the steering yoke.

When the planet appeared, Cal brought them in on the far side of the planet, close to the tiny satellite. It resembled nothing more than a big, oblong rock, about the size and shape of Mars' small moon Phobos, at not much more than twenty kilometers along its major diameter. He managed to touch down, barely clinging to the surface due to the miniscule gravitational field, until the grappling hooks dug in.

Shortly, Opi could see traces of the city under construction, becoming visible at the horizon.

The tiny moon skimmed so close to the surface of the planet that the horizon made a flat line across the forward viewscreen. They studied its brownish-green surface, freckled with blue splashes of water. One enormous ocean made a blue rim to the right.

High-magnification scans revealed thousands of machines,

working tirelessly to build a new regional capital for The Horde empire.

Nearer to them, only a few dozen kilometers from being below their observation post, a lengthy crack in the soil on the planet abruptly appeared and then widened to make a large rectangular opening. Several Horde ships zipped through. Moving briskly away from the planet, they disappeared on a vector out of the solar system, as the opening shrank and closed. As Opi watched, the city fled beneath them as the tiny moor hurtled on in its orbit.

Cal gave Opi a high five. "Hail to our brilliant strategic planner. The base is there, just as she predicted."

Tony said, "I assume that you want to launch our attack at the last minute, using the moon as concealment. That means we have to go around again, which takes two hours."

"Two extra hours. Can we afford the time?" Cal asked.

"We have ten hours in terms of ship time," Opi said.

"But," Tony said, "what if we go around a couple or three times, four to six hours, and the door doesn't open again? We might never get in."

"Got a better idea," Cal said. "Tony, when we saw The Horde ships launching from below ground, did you get a good location on that hangar door with respect to the surrounding topography?"

Tony nodded. "Pretty close. Within a few meters."

Cal turned to Letty, "The usual number of conventional rocket-powered bombs?"

"Yes, four."

"And the supernukes. Also self-propelled, right?"

Letty nodded.

Cal simply vibrated with excitement. "Here's what we'll do," he said.

They waited, impatient, for the revolution of the tiny simulated moon.

Now that the team increasingly depended on her, Opi felt a mountain of pressure to succeed. What if she were wrong? What if somehow she had miscalculated or missed some key detail? She found her palms becoming moist and wiped beads of perspiration from her brow.

After what felt like eons, Tony announced, "Target coming up. You sure this will work?"

Cal grinned again. "No. But if I'm right, we'd better not be seen. If we are, about a thousand ships are going to boil out of that hangar door, and then we have exactly two choices. We can do the bombing run and die, with little chance of success, or jump away and forfeit our advantage, as The Horde will know their new base has been discovered. In that case they'll begin to attack the nearby worlds and decimate them. Either way, we lose the exercise."

Cal turned to Sasha, as Opi crossed her fingers. "How are the calculations coming?"

"Are you kidding?" Sasha said sourly. "Our velocity calculations are based on sensors that are partially blocked by the moon we're hanging onto. Tony's going to give me vectors based on guesswork, and I'm going to toss four medium bombs and one huge one at a hundred-meter-square hole that's a few thousand kilometers away and hardly in sight when I launch. That's all."

"I thought the console computer did all the calculations."

"Sure, but I have to feed it a pile of data, and if any of it happens to be incorrect, that screws the whole calculation."

"So can you do it or not?"

"Hell yes. Now let me alone so I can work my magic." He didn't sound angry, just testy.

To Opi, it seemed as though a few centuries passed.

Abruptly, Sasha said, "Launch data set."

"Launch!" Cal ordered.

Hands in the weapon control gloves, Sasha squeezed off the five launches.

They caught a flicker of motion in the forward viewscreen as the rocket-propelled weapons launched, suddenly dropping from view beneath the satellite.

Cal released the belly hooks and launched, thrusters on full, braking them slightly so that the moon sped quickly ahead, giving them a clear view of the upcoming construction. Directly in the foreground lay the countryside beneath which The Horde base lurked.

Nothing yet. The weapons were tiny compared to a Shadow Warrior ship, and stealth-configured as well. Almost before they expected it, the first bomb struck the soil-covered hangar door to the underground base.

One, two puffs of smoke, then a third, as bombs detonated one after another on the same spot. The third didn't cause just smoke, but an irregular hole in the underground hangar door, into which the fourth disappeared. Two seconds later, a plume of fire erupted, tearing the entire door loose. It flew up, then plummeted, as a ship tried to take off from below, crashed into it, and was carried down in the debris.

Into that dark, smoky hole, the supernuke disappeared.

"Leaping now!" Cal cried, and slammed the leap throttle.

In a heartbeat, the planet appeared hundreds of thousands of kilometers away on the forward display.

Cal fired braking thrusters to decelerate, and they waited several tense seconds as light from the planet raced toward them. Then a golden spot of light erupted in the center of the display. They glanced at each other, grinning.

Cal leaped again, and they hovered a few thousand kilometers above the planet. Tongues of fire and plumes of dust and smoke roiled kilometers above the surface, not a single Horde ship or sign of life evident.

Just a simulation, Opi told herself. Not really all that destruction, nothing but a video animation demonstrating what such a weapon could do to a Horde base, or a Horde city, or a planet, for God's sake. She knew The Horde deserved it, knew they were not owed the slightest iota of pity. She remembered the videos Galigan had showed them, showing the result of their depredations. Still, considering how real bombs, especially the supernuke, could cause such destruction made her hands shake.

As they left the simulator cockpit, Raj said, "Well done. You were the only team that properly diagnosed the situation and were successful. How did you do it?"

Cal put his arm around Opi. "We had a secret weapon."

None of them said anything else. They went to their evening meal leaving Raj scratching his head behind them. He didn't even lecture them about getting swelled heads.

35 TONY

At dinner, the chow hall presented a contrast in team spirits. Some of the teams chatted excitedly, their animation proclaiming that they had been victorious today and their prospects were looking up.

In contrast, the majority of teams sat quietly, talking among themselves, their moods announcing that they had experienced at least one loss.

Sitting beside Opi and staring about, Tony felt a deep satisfaction. They had been doubly successful now, and he had contributed. All in all, he thought, he could have done a lot worse in teammates.

As for Letty and Opi, well, Letty reminded him a lot of his favorite teacher in third grade. That sweet, nurturing lady hadn't cared that he came from a poor family, wore old clothes, and never had a penny for lunch. Letty had the same supportive way about her, like an older sister he'd never had.

And Opi was amazing! She saw things Tony would never have noticed. Could she even like him a little? Their interaction had mostly been within the operation of the team, but sometimes now she even smiled at him. He almost whistled out loud. Life in general had gotten better than he could have imagined scant months ago.

Lost in daydream, he almost didn't see Lieutenant Raj approaching their table. As he started to hop up, Raj said, "Keep your seats."

Half risen, the team settled back uneasily. Raj normally didn't drop by their table, so something must be up,

He bent over their table, allowing his mouth to stretch into a wide grin. "Don't worry; you're not in trouble. Just wanted to let you know. You are now one of twelve undefeated teams. If you win a third match, you will be one of the six teams qualifying for the finals. At that point, you will be allowed a team name, other than just Thirty-Six.

"Just thought you might like to be thinking about that name. But no name if you don't win."

As he left, Cal said, "A name! How cool is that?" He glanced around at them. "Do I hear any nominations?"

"It ought to be something significant." Opi's brow puckered. "Maybe some great fighting ship from our history."

"Sounds good to me," Tony was always more than happy to go along with Opi these days. "Like what?"

She studied the tabletop. "Maybe the Enterprise?"

Sasha grimaced. "Really? Name us after a Star Trek ship?"

Letty skewered him with a withering glance. "Not from a TV show, you dummy. Right?" She nodded at Opi.

"Yes. Really, Sasha, do you think I'm that big an idiot?" Opi matched Letty's look. "I meant the World War Two naval ship or the NASA space shuttle. If not that, maybe Nimitz, or a later one like the George Bush."

Cal appeared to be thinking it over. Tony, for his part, didn't know much about Star Trek, but taking the name of a famous war vessel sounded okay to him.

Before he could add anything, Cal chimed in. "Opi, I don't think we're naming a ship. I think the name is supposed to be for our team. If that's true, maybe we should use a person's name, like Admiral Nimitz, who was a famous naval officer, or George Bush, a president. Actually, two presidents. What other person's name could we use?"

Tony didn't have the slightest notion. He had studied little history and had no idea how far World War II lay in the past. He knew the United States had fought many wars, but their chronology in history remained a mystery to him.

"We could name ourselves after a famous general like, for instance, Napoleon. Or Alexander the Great. Or even U.S. Grant from the Civil War," Letty said.

Cal frowned. "Not Napoleon, we're all from the United States. And besides, he lost his last battles. Alexander the Great conquered a lot of land, but he didn't live long, and his successors carved up his empire soon after he died."

"And Grant," Sasha said. "Wasn't he supposed to be a drunk?"

"I don't think that's so," Letty said. "But it's beside the point. And why does our name have to be American? I think it should be one that shocks other teams, scares them."

"One way to scare them is to keep winning," Sasha said.

"You're right about that," Cal agreed.

"Well, if I'm right, and if Letty wants a scary name, what about Genghis Khan?" Sasha suggested.

"Huh?" came from Tony.

"Listen," Sasha continued, leaning forward in his chair. "You talked about great generals. Genghis Khan might have been the greatest general in history. He founded the largest empire that ever existed, so big that at one time it stretched from Korea to Europe. Something like half the people in the civilized world were his subjects."

Cal frowned. "But the Mongols were barbarians."

"No, they weren't. They had tough laws, and they executed those that broke the law. But they were very lenient with most of their subjects, and their laws were well spelled out and very fair for their time in history. They established trade routes and set up highways.

"No kidding," Sasha insisted. "I've read about this guy. He was a good general, and good at picking subordinates, and at negotiating among the powerful forces in his empire. His very name struck fear into the entire world outside his empire. I think that would be a great name, one nobody will forget."

Tony, for his part, liked this Khan guy better the more he heard. A leader, a tough guy, but someone willing to argue and not simply kill anybody that disagreed. "Sure, why not?"

Letty, first surprised and then thoughtful, said, "Not perfect, but it has a ring."

"Fine with me," Opi said. She poked Sasha's arm, "Even if dumb old Sasha suggested it."

Instead of acting shocked, he shrugged. "Had that coming, I guess. What about you?" he asked Cal.

"Like Tony says, why not? If too many people make fun of us, we can reconsider."

"Win all your matches, and nobody's gonna say anything," Tony said slyly. "I'm with Sasha on that."

With dinner finished, Tony decided to go back to their room and sack out. Halfway to the mess hall door, three youths intercepted him. As they stepped in front of him, he recognized three teammates of the guy he had cold-cocked a few weeks ago.

"Remember us?" the first asked. Shorter than his teammates, his puffy cheeks and dull eyes gave him a vacuous demeanor.

Inspecting all three, Tony said, "Sure. Hard to forget anybody as ugly as you."

The youth started forward, but the second, taller youth,

equally dim-looking, grabbed his arm and said, "Glad you remember us, greaser. We owe you payback, for us and for Jess."

"Jess?" Tony consulted the ceiling. "Ah, I remember him. Did he heal okay?"

When the fat member of the team made another move, the tall one stepped in front, blocking Fatty's path. "We're not crazy. We ain't startin' anything in front of everybody. We're not about to get kicked out. We got a chance to be somebody."

Tony looked left and right. His teammates and most of the other trainees had left. "So do I. Why not let it drop? Your pal picked a fight with the wrong guy. Don't be stupid like him. Let's forget it, and go kill the bad guys."

"We can't," the tallest one said. "Jess and Sam are brothers, so Sam's got to settle it. Are you a coward? Just a coward that got in a lucky punch?"

Nobody called Tony a coward. He might be smart enough to run when it made sense, but damned if he would back down. "Come on, man. Show me what you got."

The tallest held up a hand. "Not here, not here. We settle it, but we do it alone, nobody but us, no witnesses."

Steamed enough to throw caution to the winds, Tony said, "Name the place."

The third guy, middling tall, whom Tony thought of as Mr. In-Between, said, "Later, in the gym, after everyone's in bed. There's a small room behind the big gym. Maybe for storage, but it's empty now. At midnight."

"Midnight."

Tony turned and walked away.

Now I gotta whip three of 'em, he thought. *When am I going to learn to walk away* before *I take a challenge?*

36 TONY

Near midnight, sure his friends were asleep, Tony rose and dressed in gym shorts and a T-shirt, his normal workout attire. Hoping the auto-door wouldn't arouse anyone, he made his way along the hallway, down three flights of stairs, and into the gym. A lone team member, female, pumped iron on a weight machine in the far corner of the large room. Otherwise, the space was deserted, except for the rows of exercise equipment.

Several exercise bikes displayed a Nautilus logo, while two weight machines said Body Craft in silver letters with a red "t" at the end. Tony wondered how on Earth, or how in space, the Molethians had slipped into a fitness store somewhere below, purchased the equipment, and managed to ship it into orbit. He'd heard somewhere that NASA did that for the space station, so he supposed it wasn't out of the realm of possibility.

The hatch at the back of the gym led to the small room his enemies had described. Opening it, he found they were already in residence. All three. Dressed in uniforms—uniforms from one of the Asian combat disciplines, he supposed. He wondered how they had come by those. Maybe you just had to ask your trainer. The upcoming contest suddenly assumed a more sinister complexion.

Tony cleared his throat. "Okay, who wants it first?"

The taller one smiled, not a very nice smile. "Why, we just thought we'd take you all at once. You're such a big, brave boy, that shouldn't be a problem for you, right?"

More difficulties. He swallowed. "I guess if you're too chicken to take me one-on-one, you gotta do whatever you gotta do."

"Nobody's chicken, greaser," the tall one said. He started forward again with a nasty expression. "Come on, guys—"

The outer door opened and in walked Cal.

"What you doin' here?" Tony asked in surprise.

"Just wandering around. Heard there might be a physical contest in here. Thought I might be your cheering section."

Tony frowned. "I don't need any help." He did, but damned if he'd say so.

The edges of Cal's mouth lifted. "Hell, I know that."

The tall youth turned. "You heard him. Get the hell outta here."

Cal shook his head, as though he were lecturing a small child. "Now see, you don't understand. I'm just here to make sure everybody obeys the rules."

The short, fat one stepped forward. "What rules? There ain't no rules!"

Cal *tsked*. "That's where you'd be wrong, pal. Here's the way it goes down. Tony's going to take you on, one at a time. If one of you beats him up, I won't interfere. But when he can't get up, we're done. On the other hand, if he finishes one of you off, the next in line gets a shot. Fair enough?"

"Fair? There ain't no fair!" The fat one rushed Cal, head down.

Had he bothered to keep Cal in view, he would have seen Cal launch himself. His head came up as Cal's foot made solid contact with his knee. It popped and dislocated with a sharp crack. He might have screamed, if he'd had time, but a millisecond later Cal's straight jab caught his nose. It broke, spewing blood in a halo around them both.

Tony noticed with interest that the fat kid went straight down without a sound, other than the thud when his head met the floor.

Cal straightened up. The two remaining teammates paled. Cal smiled again. "Everybody understand the rules?"

Slowly, they nodded.

Tony yelled, "You cowards gonna fight or just stand there?"

Mouth contorted, the big one charged.

WALKING BACK TO THE ROOM, Cal said abruptly, "Tell me something."

Tony considered, then said, "Maybe."

"I don't mean this as insulting, I'm just curious. Your name is Latino, and you look sort of Latino, but your hair is light brown, and you sure don't talk Latino. How come?"

Tony thought a moment. "Mom was Anglo. Really pretty when I was a little kid. She had blonde hair. My father, he ran off before I started to school. He came from Mexico, might have been illegal. After he left, Mom spent a lot of time with her relatives, before the drugs ... Anyway, didn't have many friends in the barrio. Guess I picked up some of her words, and lingo on the street. That okay with you?"

"Sure. You need to know your teammates, right?"

"I guess." Tony massaged skinned knuckles. "Didn't need your help."

"Yeah, you did," Cal said. He hesitated. "But not much."

After a moment, a grin eased onto Tony's mouth. "You know, you were pretty good back there."

Cal grinned. "Hey, I been saying."

As he opened the stairwell hatch, Tony said, "Five bucks says I could have taken both of them together."

"You haven't got five bucks, or any money yet. Anyway, no bet. You probably could've."

"Probably? What the hell you mean probably?"

He and Cal continued to argue good-naturedly all the way to their room.

Nobody ever said anything to Cal or Tony about their encounter, or the subsequent disappearance of the other three crew members. Tony wasn't sure, but he suspected that the small storage room contained concealed cameras.

37 CAL

Cal suppressed a yawn as he and Letty took a table in the mess hall. Letty had awakened Cal far earlier than usual, completed their exercises, and dragged him to the table, at which he pulled up a chair. The serving line hadn't opened, as the service droids behind the counter were still stocking the line with food. *Only a handful of early risers, as waking early certainly didn't qualify as a characteristic of people his age,* Cal thought.

"So what's up?" he asked, still foggy.

"I'll tell everyone later, but you're the captain, after all, so you ought to know first."

Settling back in the chair and striving mightily not to rub his eyes, Cal frowned. "Effectively, you're the captain. I just sit in the center chair and yell commands. You and Opi put together the plan."

"Not so. You accept and approve our plan. You *are* the leader, make no mistake. I am a very good planner, and Opi is a budding strategic genius, but you provide the impetus."

"So, again, what's—?"

"Up, I know, I'm getting to that. It's become clear to all of us how essential Opi is to our success. We can't risk her being late to the start of an exercise. Too much danger in her losing us a match."

"Agreed."

"I asked her to start spending any free time possible in the library, reading over old Horde battle scenarios and reviewing records of old exercises. I suggested it to her after our second mission yesterday, and she jumped on it like a cat on catnip.

"She was there all night, she woke me up when she came in this morning. She's found a treasure of historical files, and after four hours of sleep she's back at it this morning. I made her promise to come to breakfast. She will, even if I have to go down there and drag her back.

"The point is, I want her to find out as much as she can ahead of time. I think it makes more sense than a frantic trip to the library at the last minute."

"It sounds good to me," Cal said, a little doubtful. "Except ..."

"Problem?"

"Just don't want her totally exhausting herself before our next match. I mean, she's always seemed ... fragile, and I don't want her unfit to help us during the exercise."

"She won't be. She's promised to get a good night's sleep this evening. Aha, here she comes now."

Opi had entered the dining area looking about as sleepy as Cal felt. She brightened when she saw them, and rushed over.

"I got some terrific info." Opi sounded triumphant, and as confident as Cal had ever heard her. She didn't bother to sit down. "I think we'll be in a lot better shape today."

Cal glanced at the clock over the main hatch into the mess hall. "It's still early. Why not go back and catch forty winks? Then you can get breakfast."

"Uh-uh. If I go to sleep now, I'll be drugged the whole morn-

ing. I'm going to take a shower and see you guys back here in thirty." She waved and trotted off.

"God, what a change." Cal almost had to pinch himself to
make sure he wasn't dreaming. "Opi's become an entirely
different person over the last few weeks. That's your doing, Letty.
It's amazing."

"If our team gets to the top three, I'll strut all over the place.
Now let's get back to the room. I need a shower too."

Cal circled the table, determined to be the gentleman and
help Letty out of her chair. As he bent over to slide the chair
back, she turned and started to rise, and their faces, and lips,
brushed. She sat down abruptly and he stared at her, reddening.
The rush of emotion had him asking, *Am I falling in love?*

"Sorry," Letty muttered. "Sorry. Sorry. I didn't mean ... That
is, it was just an accident."

"I know," Cal assured her. Standing back, he let her rise, then
said in a tone that he hoped sounded lighthearted, "Not a terrible
accident for me. Sort of a fun accident."

Letty grabbed his arm, her grip almost painful. "We can't let
anything, even something that happened inadvertently, divert us
even for a second. And the rest of the team, we can't even let
them *imagine* that our interest is in anything but the whole
team." Her grip tightened until Cal was sure it would leave a
bruise. "Right?"

Cal studied the floor. Finally, he got around to returning that
piercing gaze. "Of course. Just an accident, that's all."

He pulled back. Noted that the breakfast line had been
opened. "Listen, go ahead and take your shower. I'll eat first, then
catch the shower while you guys have breakfast."

"Uh. Okay. Good idea." She turned to the exit. "See you."

"Yeah."

But he continued to watch as her slender, lithe body moved
out of the room. Only then did he get a tray.

38 LETTY

Lieutenant Raj joined them in their quarters after breakfast. After inspecting their beds and the clothing drawers, he told them that they were getting sloppy, lectured them on the importance of neatness and cleanliness to team discipline—except Letty, whom he complimented—then put them at ease to discuss the new exercise.

It would be a relatively straightforward mission. They must attack a group of six Horde ships, one of which was a flagship, or Horde command ship, do as much damage as possible, and return to base. Emphasis would be put not only on inflicting maximum damage, but on getting safely away and preserving their own ship.

"Today's competition has a new twist," Raj announced. "The team you are competing against is going to be in on the mission with you. You will meet beforehand, discuss the mission, and come up with a joint plan. Both teams will be judged on the level of strategy, cooperation, and success of the mission.

"I am going to give you the usual half hour to discuss the

mission, then you will meet with the other team and put together your joint attack."

"Weird to be cooperating with your rival," Sasha muttered.

Raj shook his head. "Not at all. Think about it." Before he left, he gave them a white placard, labeled EXERCISE C23. "Just hold that up in the meeting room," he told them. "Your partners will have a similar card."

After he left, Sasha muttered, "Still think it's weird. How do you cooperate with your opponents? Makes no sense."

"Come on," Letty huffed. "It makes *perfect* sense." She punched Sasha on the shoulder. "Don't you get it? Our normal inclination is not to cooperate, 'cause we're in a competition. But Shadow Warriors don't attack individually, they attack as units, in coordination. By doing the best job of fighting along with another team now, we begin to learn how to cooperate. That way, we don't just win, we gain experience at the same time." She tossed a glance to Opi, who'd been scanning the scenario. "What's your opinion?"

Opi shook her head, unsure. "It's not some sort of trap, like the last two. I didn't see any summaries of similar exercises in the library. It could be a straightforward assignment, and the real trap is not undertaking the mission in the spirit of cooperation with the other team."

"In other words," Cal chimed in, "the best way to lose is to not be a good team member."

She smiled gratefully. "Yeah, maybe that's it. I think the best way to win is to be a good team player."

"I agree. Let's go down to the meeting room and meet the other half of our unit."

Following Cal, Letty reflected that although she had disagreed with Sasha, she still felt as uneasy as Cal and the rest. Tony in particular, she noticed, was silent and brooding.

Teams had begun to gather as usual in the large conference

room. Cal spotted the identical sign at once, and they pushed their way across the room to their opposites. Assuming that their captain held the sign, Cal held out his hand. "Hi. We're Team Thirty-Six, and I'm—"

The other team leader stopped him. "We know exactly who you are. You're the jerks that got our friends on Team Forty-Four thrown out of the program."

His angry words stopped Cal and the others cold.

"What are you talking about?" Sasha demanded.

Cal and Tony exchanged a glance that Letty caught. She wondered what Cal and Tony had been up to that the others had never been told.

Another member of the opposite team answered. Tall, rangy, and haughty, the only girl among four young men, she looked barely fourteen, despite her crisp uniform and close-cropped black hair. "Jess Briggs. Your skinny Latino kid, yeah, him right there," she said, pointing at Tony, "caught him off guard and hurt him. Then you guys ambushed the others and beat them up."

Before Letty could say anything, Cal said softly, his voice lethal, "I've got a fat news flash for you, *girl*. Jess threatened Tony, and Tony didn't put up with it. Later on, three of 'em, count 'em, *three*, tried to gang up on Tony. It didn't work out so well for them. That was the only gang-up."

Startled by this revelation, Letty kept enough presence of mind to insert herself into the conversation. "That's beside the point. We have to cooperate and do our best together to succeed in this exercise. If teams do not cooperate, they lose."

The tallest of the young men, the one with the card, laughed. "I don't see a single damn reason why we should work together. It's a competition. A *competition*. We don't like you guys anyway, and if we can screw you up, we will. Got it?"

Afraid that Cal was about to explode, Letty talked fast. "Listen," she said, "could you and our planning officer just have a private meeting, for a moment? I think you'll find it worth your while."

"We don't need any ideas from your planning officer! We have a mission plan already, and it's all we need."

Letty began to think that she might be the one to explode. "Okay, let me just say this. Shadow Warriors work together to achieve mission goals. Why do you think we're assigned to work together on this exercise? If we don't cooperate, we'll *both* lose."

The team captain sneered. "Somebody's got to win."

"Says who? We're not training to play games the rest of our lives! We're training to *fight*, real battles where people will die if they aren't the best and haven't made the most of their training. When a unit of Shadow Warriors is attacking Horde forces, do you think cooperation and coordination are important?"

He scowled. "Sure. But that's—"

"There aren't any 'buts.' This isn't just about learning to use the equipment; it's about learning to fight as we'll have to in combat. This exercise is designed to make sure we understand that."

The team leader scratched his head. Even his teammates, including the sexy air-head girl, had begun to listen up. After he thought about it—surprising Letty—he said, "So we cooperate. What does that mean?"

Letty gestured to a nearby group of chairs. "Sit down and let me explain."

39 OPI

Shifting his focus back and forth between the display and status screens at his station, Tony announced, "Coming up on secondary leap point. Distance to last known coordinates of The Horde force, five hundred thousand kilometers."

It still tickled Opi at how formal and intelligent Tony sounded when he sat at the navigation station. Once he had the helmet on and was connected with his console, proper English, or occasionally Molethian, replaced his careless vocabulary and street slang.

She wondered if her personality changed that much when she put on her helmet and got busy coordinating with Letty and Tony during an exercise. Probably not, she concluded. She did all her communicating verbally, not via mental links.

"Remember," she cautioned Letty, "micro-leaps from this distance aren't accurate enough. We have to be within about forty thousand kilometers, then do the precise micro-leap."

Letty turned to give Opi a confident smile. "Don't worry. We've got this figured out. Right, Tony?"

"Absolutely." He turned around, gave her a thumbs-up.

"Relax, Opi," Cal said. "We'll do a leap to about ten thousand kilometers from the enemy, take a reading to make the final leap, and we'll land right beside those mothers. Sasha, you open up on the command ship from our side while Alpha Team does the same. Then get as many shots as you can at the guardian ships, and we'll get outta there."

Alpha Team. The term irritated Opi. The other team had insisting on being the Alpha Team. Cal had grudgingly agreed, at Letty's urging. So they were Beta Team.

Actually, it thrilled Opi that Cal listened closely to Letty, because Letty listened to Opi. Cal had even begun to consult Opi independently.

The two-way comm crackled in her earphones. "Beta Team, we are preparing last two leaps. Follow our lead."

Opi snorted. Their lead? It was her plan! She stifled indignant feelings; now they didn't have to worry about *two* enemies—just The Horde.

"Leap sequence ready," Tony informed Cal.

"Leaping now," Cal said.

A blink, and the star field changed slightly. A tiny hesitation, and the forward screen showed ships all around them. The Horde flagship lay dead ahead, a hundred kilometers away. Compared to normal Horde attack ships, visible as small ovals on the screen, the flagship filled the display, a silver disk five hundred meters in diameter, maybe fifty thick. Cannon bubbles dotted its exterior, all the ones Opi could see turning toward their ship. Both Shadow Warrior ships were coming in from dead astern, their partners' ship to their right and below.

The bumpety-whirr of Sasha's guns opened up. To the right on the screen, Opi saw the other team's weapons firing. She held her breath as that ship slipped off the screen and Sasha poured fire into an escort ship beside them.

Behind them, the flagship turrets must have opened up. Opi

felt a shock in the deck as the projectile cannon consumed the rest of his ammunition. Pieces of The Horde escort ship hull flew in all directions as they flashed past the disintegrating ship.

"Team Beta, return to base," Opi heard through her earphones. "Team Alpha breaking off attack."

"Roger that!" Cal barked. Opi saw his hand close on the controls.

After a moment's awkward hesitation, he said, "I can't initiate the leap engines. We've got damage to the power supply in three places. Only thrusters are available."

"Only thrusters? What the hell—?"

Before Cal could say anything else, their earphones came to life again. "Team Beta, enemy ships coming in. Initiate leap *now*."

"Can't go to FTL drive," Cal radioed back. "Give us a hand, Alpha. We need help to get the other three ships, then we can transfer to your ship for return."

One of The Horde ships neared, and Sasha busied himself at the weapons console. "We've still got beam weapons; cannons are out of ammo."

The voice on the earphones sounded concerned. "Sorry, Beta. Our weapons are depleted. We're initiating return to base."

On Tony's tactical display, Opi saw the tiny triangle that represented the Alpha ship turning away.

"Really? Just leaving us behind?" Cal realized that instead of talking to himself, he had yelled those last words. He brought the ship around. "Status of flagship?"

Monitoring the forward status displays, Letty said, "Damaged but not destroyed. It's heavily armored."

Turning the ship directly toward the flagship, Cal advanced thrusters to maximum. "Sasha, everything you have aimed at the flagship."

It approached rapidly, still some kilometers distant.

Deciphering his intent, two of The Horde defense ships banked around from pursuing the Alpha ship toward theirs. On the flagship, multiple weapons turrets swung toward them.

"Bombs?" he asked Sasha tensely.

"Four surface bombs left," Sasha replied. "No cannon shells; still have beam weapons."

"Arm bombs for contact ignition," Cal directed, "then fire on flagship. Beam weapons, maximum intensity."

The vibration of the Gatling cannon was absent, but Opi felt other bounces and thumps. They were taking hits. She could see multiple flashes from the flagship's weaponry. Their own shielding couldn't possibly hold for long.

"Sorry, guys," Cal said, as the flagship loomed on the forward screen. "It's the best I can do."

The flagship filled the screen. Then the display went blank as the simulator bucked one last time.

The overhead lights came on.

"Simulation ended," the impassive female voice announced. "Attack ship destroyed. Horde flagship destroyed, two defense vessels destroyed."

"With leap off-line, we had no way home," Cal said. "Best to inflict as much damage as we could and cover our other ship's getaway."

A moment of silence. Opi saw Cal cringe, no doubt expecting his teammates to let him have it. "What are you sorry about?" she asked, her voice louder than her normal just-above-whisper level. "We destroyed their command ship. That's what we were tasked to do. You made the right decision."

Sasha turned from the weapons control console. "The other team left us to die, didn't even try to help. You covered their ass and completed the mission to boot. Way to go, I say."

"Me, too," Tony nodded. Opi was shocked to see him smile at Cal.

Cal stood, ditching the helmet and starting toward the simulator door, his face grim. "Yeah, but we still lost."

One by one, they followed him out the hatch, up the tunnel to the meeting room, to an empty table and chairs, awaiting the inevitable meeting with Raj. There were a few other trainees there at the moment, but their conversations stayed muted. *Maybe they were losers as well*, Opi thought sadly.

Alpha Team showed up in a few minutes. The lanky team leader gave Cal the thumbs up. "Nice shot at the end. The summary report said you got the flagship."

"Why didn't you hang back, help us, complete the mission and give us a ride home?" Sasha asked angrily.

"Hey," the pretty air-head team member spoke up. "One of us needed to make it back. Nothing we could do for you."

Cal simply glared at them, while Letty gave him and Sasha wordless "don't say a thing" stares that felt very loud to Opi.

"Congratulations," Letty told the other team. "You made it back safely. Best of luck in the next round."

Cal remained silent, his fury obvious.

They didn't see Lieutenant Raj coming across the room until he stopped beside both teams. Opi and the others sprang to their feet.

"Yes," Raj told the Alpha Team captain, "best of luck in the one-loss competition. You still have a chance to qualify."

"What, sir?" The Alpha Team commander turned in fury. "What do you mean, 'one-loss competition?' We just won! Your *pet team* got blown to pieces!"

Raj stiffened. "You will come to attention when you speak to me, Mr. Scott."

He moved until he stood nose-to-nose with the opposing team captain. Though shorter by several inches, Raj nonetheless gave Opi the impression that he stared down a long distance at the Alpha Team captain.

"First, let me remind you that team members will show proper respect to officers at all times. Is that clear?"

"Yes, sir, but—"

"Is that *clear*?"

"Uh, yes. Yes, sir."

"Second, you are expected to demonstrate courtesy and respect not only to your officers but toward other teams as well. Do you have any argument with that?"

The captain lowered his head. "No, sir."

"Good." Raj stepped back. "Now, with respect to your status, you lost, repeat *lost*, the contest. In the heat of battle, with your companion ship damaged but continuing to fight, you turned and ran instead of rejoining them. You not only sacrificed your fellow warriors but left the mission a failure.

"On the other hand, upon recognizing their hopeless position your companions turned and made a suicide attack on the primary target, destroying it and several of its escort vessels. They died in the simulation, but they completed the mission. Their sacrifice cost The Horde dearly. Command ships of that class are few and far between, typically one or two to every ten thousand attack ships. Team Thirty-Six completed the exercise successfully."

"But, but ..." The Alpha Team captain nearly wrung his hands in frustration. "We saved our ship! We didn't lose it in battle!"

"Had you turned to fight with your companion ship," Raj continued, "you might have completed the mission and saved both crews. You have a good deal to think about, Captain. This is not a game. It's preparation for war, something you apparently have not fully realized. If this kind of poor performance continues, you will be relegated to reserve status, or brain-wiped and returned to Earth. I'm not sure you have the stuff of which Shadow Warriors are made. Dismissed!"

The other team fled, bolting through the hatch.

As they listened, Opi noticed her teammates beginning to brighten. Lieutenant Raj turned back to a row of grins.

"As you were," he said first. As they all relaxed, he said, "So, you won again. You have made the quarter-finals, which means you may announce your team name." They clustered around him, and he continued, "Congratulations are in order. You did not forget your mission, and you were prepared to sacrifice the ship and your lives to assure its success. Well done."

His smile faded into a thin-lipped, stern expression. "As I told your opponents, these exercises are not games. What you did in this exercise, in which you were in no actual danger, you may someday have to do in a real battle. In the conflicts you are preparing for, lives are at stake, not training points."

Each of them nodded thoughtfully, Opi considering that in all her wildest dreams, she had never had the slightest notion that someday she would train to be a warrior.

"By the way." Raj had turned to leave, then stopped. "What will your team name be?"

Cal gestured to Sasha. "Your idea, you tell him."

Sasha puffed up his chest. "Genghis Khan."

Raj chewed that over a moment. He gave them a sanguine nod. "It has a ring to it, I'll say that."

He left them hugging, patting each other's shoulders, and talking excitedly at the table.

40 SASHA

As Raj left the simulator the next morning, Letty told the team, "Opi and I think we have a handle on the exercise. It's by far our toughest, but we can survive. Sasha, you're the key."

"Me?" Sasha touched his chest. His mouth formed the word but no sound came forth.

Letty laughed. "Yeah, Sasha, feel the pressure! Just kidding. The thing is, this is our riskiest mission. I don't think they ever get easier, but we have a chance to survive."

Tony spoke up. "As we found out last time, the point of some of these exercises is *not* to survive."

Letty nodded as though such a consideration seemed obvious. "And this could be it. But we do have a chance."

Opi took up the summary. "According to the scenario Raj just gave me, the mission is to destroy a major Horde regional headquarters. There aren't a lot of those, a few dozen at most, and you can bet they're well-guarded—basically, each is a military base. Let's review it. Our command has managed to capture a Horde vessel, a supply ship. Usually those ships self-destruct. In this case, The Horde crew abandoned the ship, but the self-destruct didn't work. Our attack ship is in the hold of the supply ship. From inside our ship, we can operate The Horde ship controls.

"The idea is to slip into The Horde settlement and right up to the operations center of The Horde headquarters. Then we shed our disguise and blow up the headquarters, blasting as many additional ships as we can on the way out.

"If we get lucky, we may escape in all the confusion. You can imagine that there are tens of thousands of ships near the headquarters location, including a major supply depot. The main point is to knock out The Horde headquarters. Given their rigid command structure, knocking out the center deals even more damage than simply destroying property. Got it?"

Everybody nodded. Sasha wondered if he could possibly do everything that he needed to in just seconds. *We'll soon see*, he thought.

"Here's our plan," Opi said, transmitting data to their personals. They reviewed it, back and forth, Sasha in particular asking specific questions. After an hour, they notified Lieutenant Raj that they were ready, and Cal called for them to get to stations.

They left the carrier, their simulated ship entombed in the hold of The Horde supply craft.

"As we approach the Ops center," Tony said over helmet comm, "what do we do if special entry codes are required?"

"According to the mission statement, The Horde supply ship will automatically answer identity queries without our intervention," Cal said. "We'll move in as close as we can. If there's any indication that we've been detected, we can open the cargo doors of the supply ship and blast out, hoping to avoid direct battle for the few seconds it'll take us to do our job. After that, we try our best to escape."

Sasha felt an unfamiliar case of the jitters. He kept thinking of how Letty had said their success depended on him, and the pressure had begun to build up. He hadn't thought much about pressure when Letty and Opi had their abilities on the line. He found his respect for both Letty and Opi growing. It terrified him to think that if he didn't do his job correctly, he could doom the whole team.

"Whose leap engines are we using, ours or The Horde ship's?" Tony asked.

"The Horde ship's," Letty answered. "It's a relatively short distance, about ten light-years. That's a standard leap for a Horde ship."

Sasha almost laughed. Just months ago, a short distance to him had been a couple of city blocks. Now, Letty blithely mentioned—and everyone agreed without much thought—that ten *light-years* was "a short distance." It almost made his head spin.

Shortly they leaped, and in moments they were approaching The Horde headquarters installation. Only a simulation, of course, but Sasha could almost feel the confinement of their battle cruiser hiding inside The Horde transport.

"We are being queried by The Horde central control," Cal announced. "Sasha, get ready. Tony, shift Sasha's secondary screen to tactical, give him an overall layout of the base."

Tony did so.

The small display to Sasha's left lit up to depict the planet they approached. The large installation sprawled for square kilometers beneath them, and ahead a hundred kilometers or so. Above the base were dozens, hundreds of Horde battle cruisers, moving in low orbits, either guarding the site, preparing to land, or moving out of the system on some mission of their own.

Several of the battle cruisers circled an enormous refueling platform. It hovered no more than twenty kilometers directly above the surface installation.

The ships, standard Horde fighter-bombers, were ominous

and intimidating up close. Shaped like bulbous torpedoes, their noses bristled with beam cannons. Near the front of each, a large, dark blister designated the crew cockpit. Shadow Warrior ships always targeted the pod containing the crew.

The platform itself stretched more than a kilometer in diameter, oval-shaped, either a dark-colored metal or dark paint. Beam cannon blisters dotted its circumference as well, and a central dome undoubtedly served as its command pod.

The platform had less armament than The Horde ships, probably because it depended on the fleet for its defense. The cluster of ships around the fuel-depot platform, Sasha decided, ensured a reciprocal relationship of fuel and ammunition to all the ships guarding the operations center, and stout defense for the platform. A kernel of a plan began to form in Sasha's head.

He turned to Opi. "Can you spare me a moment?"

"Absolutely. A question about the strategy?"

He finished his internal calculation. "No, I've got an idea. I would like to hear your analysis." He beckoned her closer, and took off his helmet. She joined him, and he rushed through the description.

When he finished, she nodded. She patted his shoulder. "I like it. If we have a chance to get out, that's it."

He noted his satisfaction level at her approval with curiosity. "Thanks," he whispered, and went back to his console.

Quickly, she beckoned to the rest of the crew and they huddled as he continued his preparations.

Cal's voice came over the comm. "Deploy point coming up."

After a tiny hesitation, Sasha said, "I'm going with the change in plans, as Opi told you, if you approve.

"Do it," Cal's voice came back over his headphones.

Sasha made a change in the supernuclear device programming. The Horde ship weapons handling hardware did the rest.

Turning to Cal, he said, "Since you control the supply ship

maneuvering, set it into a landing pattern for the base below, and start it transmitting landing codes. Okay?"

A short hesitation. "Transmitting codes," Cal said. "Provisioning platform coming up. Ready to deploy, Sasha?"

"Ready."

The belly doors of the supply ship opened and they slid out, with no more than a whisper of sound, a low grinding noise. Immediately, the doors closed, and the supply ship moved down in a tight loop toward the operations headquarters below.

Transfixed, Sasha stared in wonder at the enormous supply platform, now no more than a kilometer away. The amount of traffic had effectively obscured their appearance, he realized. They were moving with a dense convoy in the process of passing over the platform. Their attack ship, among the multitude of larger Horde ships, went completely unnoticed. The Horde fleet had allowed a viper into its bosom, and didn't even realize it.

I hope this works, Sasha thought as he initiated the weapons sequence. Cal spun the ship, facing the platform, and Sasha emptied the Gatling cannons onto a specific twenty-square-meter section on the hull, the command pod.

Even as the stream of projectiles reached their target, the four rocket-propelled bombs followed. With weapons clear, Cal triggered the micro-leap. Their viewpoint changed to two hundred thousand kilometers above the surface of the planet.

One second. Two. Three ...

A bright beacon shone in their viewer, a brilliant dot a few millimeters in diameter, but impressive at that distance.

Cal sounded confounded. "Did our bombs do all that?"

"No, just started it. That platform was filled with fuel and ammunition. If we got lucky, that blast took a lot of ships with it. But keep watching." Sasha tried not to sound too puffed up.

A much bigger, brighter star almost filled the screen.

"The nuke?" Cal asked.

"If it really landed, we destroyed the whole installation. If it even got close it still destroyed the whole installation. Either way, we're done. Let's go home."

Before they could begin the return maneuver, the lights went up and the outer hatch opened. Raj walked in, frowning.

"Get to the gathering room. Now," he told them, and walked out.

They didn't stir at first. After an uncomfortable moment, Sasha said, "I guess I screwed up. Sorry."

Casting concerned and worried glances around, they left their cockpit positions and headed up the tunnel after Raj.

41 LETTY

Sasha managed to catch up with Letty on the way. "I guess I cost us the win."

Letty shook her head. "We don't know that. Besides, he didn't look mad, exactly."

"Concerned, but not angry," Cal said over his shoulder. "Sasha, don't worry. We're in this together. If we lost a competition, we'll still be in the running, and we'll keep trying to win."

As they gathered around the table Raj stood by, Opi said, "My fault, not Sasha's. If it lost the exercise, I take the blame."

Raj, listening to them as they approached, asked abruptly, "What did you do in the exercise?"

"Let me tell it," Letty said.

Cal interrupted. "No. I'm team captain, so it's my fault, regardless. I'll tell it." Firmly, he related their actions.

Raj listened, seeming to absorb all the details. Finally, he couldn't hold the smile any longer. "Amazing. No one has ever done that. Whose idea was it to hide the bomb in the supply ship? Doing that, then diverting The Horde defenders from noticing the supply ship by hitting the service platform and destroying it with its own munitions was genius."

"Sasha," Cal said. "He changed our mission plan on the fly."

"In all the simulations and competitions I've witnessed, that's a first," Raj said.

"Opi's been studying lots of Horde technology and operations center configurations," Sasha said quickly. "She told me where I needed to concentrate fire."

"But Sasha did it," Opi interjected. "It worked so well that after we came out of the supply ship's belly, I don't think any of The Horde ships detected us until we started firing. And then we were gone."

"Quite a show," Raj continued. "You have the highest score on that exercise that has ever been earned. *Ever.* That's four victories in a row.

"You are only one of two undefeated teams to have completed four matches. You know what that means?"

Letty did. She had studied the contest rules, studied the standings after each competition, and followed their progress with painstaking care. "We're in," she crowed. She slapped Cal on the back, hugged Opi and Sasha. "We did it!"

"Right you are," Raj said after a moment, as the impact of Letty's words sank in. "You have finished the primary competition and qualified as a representative for our ship to the inter-ship competition, which begins in less than forty-eight hours. You, Team Forty-Four and Team Seventeen are fully qualified. In the one-loss competitions, there are still two contests to determine the other three one-loss contestants. Congratulations.

"You get an entire day off tomorrow. Spend it wisely."

Some of the other teams had heard their excited talk. As Raj shook hands with each member of their team, other young people began to gravitate to their table to shake their hands and offer congratulations as well.

Finally extracting themselves, they returned to their room, bubbling with excitement and still congratulating Sasha and Opi.

As they entered their quarters, talking excitedly about how they would spend their day of leave, Sasha had a terrifying thought. His four teammates were becoming family to him, something he had experienced only as a very small child. Furthermore, he had actually begun to like them, Letty and Tony most of all.

42 OPI

Still blinking sleep out of her eyes, Opi opened the library's hatch and crossed to a desk with a data reader. *Sure could use a little breakfast*, she thought. Unfortunately, the breakfast line wouldn't open for nearly two hours.

On the other hand, that was why she had risen before dawn, taken a quick shower, and hurried to the library. Nobody would be there for hours, she knew, giving her blessed peace to study.

Inputting the code Lieutenant Raj had provided, she opened the file "Key Battles with The Horde, 41517-41536."

The numbers stood for a span in Molethian history. The current Molethian annum, according to Raj, was 41551, Molethian years being a bit shorter than Earth years. The origin of the dating system, year one, had never been explained so far as Opi knew.

When the file opened, she said in Molethian, "Save comments and annotations to Opi File Three." Then she selected the record she had last been reading and continued her study.

Opi still had trouble understanding the Molethian attitude toward history. They were absolute demons at recording it, she'd found. So far as she could ascertain, every single Horde battle had been recorded. That included archives that stretched over the intervening decades since The Horde's entry into the Milky Way had first been discovered.

She puzzled over the second item. So far as she could discover, no one on their ship had ever accessed the records for study. All these wonderful, detailed histories of the decades-long conflict with The Horde had never been used to increase understanding of their battle practices.

Perhaps a separate archive held the analysis and categorization of the battles that had been fought. So far she had found no scholarly treatises, no learned tomes that summarized how their enemies fought, describing their strategies, strengths, weaknesses, and so forth.

This wonderful data mine, Opi thought, *never even used.* At least not on the training ship.

As she read, she dictated her comments on Horde strategies and possible ways to counteract their forces. One thing became clear. The Horde had several weaknesses, which they overcame with the simple expedient of massive forces.

"Crazy," she said out loud. "If I had twenty percent of their ships, I'd wipe them out in less than a year."

"Guess we need to get to buildin' more ships," a voice behind her piped up.

Opi levitated from the chair, turning to find Tony standing at the door.

"Dammit, Tony, you almost stopped my heart! What are you doing, sneaking up on me like that?"

He grinned, embarrassed. "Just came to see what you're doin'. Letty said you'd be here. Didn't mean to scare you."

She relented, wiping away the scowl. "Okay. Sit down, I guess."

43 TONY

Tony sat with a relief. He had begun to enjoy being with Opi. She was so pretty, and as he had listened to her in her briefings and as she interpreted her plans, he had found her to be intelligent, clever, even possessing a wry sense of humor.

As he'd entered the library, it hadn't occurred to him how deeply she concentrated, so he could understand how his sudden voice could have been startling.

"Sorry," he said again. "Letty said you might be studyin', and it occurred to me that now we're gettin' into the big leagues, a navigator might need to do a little studyin' also."

His second apology and explanation seemed to mollify her. She sat back in the chair. "I'd say that's a good observation. The more you know about Horde tactics and strategy, the better you can do your part to fight them."

"Thing is," he told her, "I never studied much at all. Not sure I know how, matter of fact. Don't even read very good. Least I didn't. I'm better at it now, since the Molethians shoved all that stuff into my head."

She nodded. "Yeah. Whatever they did to us, I read a lot faster than I used to."

"You think I could study better now, too?"

Opi considered. "Yeah, you could, I'm sure. You really want to learn all this Horde battle history and philosophy?"

"Why I'm here." Suddenly he blurted out, "'Course, it doesn't hurt that maybe I can do it with a really pretty girl."

For a moment he wondered if saying that might make her angry. Instead, her hand involuntarily went to her hair, touching, tucking, arranging. Just a quick movement or two.

"You really think I'm pretty?"

"Are you kidding?"

"Well, I mean, after all, Letty is so energetic, and she has such a great personality. I figured all you guys would spend your time buzzing around her."

He nodded. "She's pretty, no doubt. And I like her. But for my money, you're the prettiest girl I've ever met."

She blushed, hand straying to her hair again. "Oh, Tony, I'll bet you flatter all the girls."

"Haven't known that many, but I say what I mean." He felt a sudden rush of concern. "But, listen, I'm not trying to flirt or anything. I mean, you're a teammate. I told you my opinion, but I would never do anything to hurt you or the team."

Face sobering, she nodded. "Of course you wouldn't. That's the kind of guy you are."

Pleased and embarrassed, he smiled, and she gestured to the table next to his chair, which held another viewer like the one she studied. "Here. You can use this screen. And sometimes I like to talk through things that I've read. Would you listen and discuss them with me?"

"Yeah. Not sure I'll understand it all, but I'll listen."

"Hey, I didn't understand it at first. You'll be up to speed in no time. Come on, let's get back to work. We have only a day or so before we have to be back into competition."

Tony sat, realizing that at that moment not only did Opi like him but she trusted him. It seemed, as he took his seat, that a whole new world of possibilities had opened up before him.

44 CAL

The next morning, Raj called Cal to his small office in the command area, the first time Cal had been so directed. As he entered at the lieutenant's invitation, he found Raj consulting a pair of video screens and perusing a paper document, or what passed as paper for the Molethians, although it had the texture of thin plastic. The desk was more of a platform for electronic devices, but he did have a small storage cabinet to his right. The whole office measured barely ten feet square, but Cal suspected that having one's own office on the cramped training ship had to be a special honor.

Cal stood at attention. "Sir."

Raj nodded. "At ease. I have news. Good news first. Due to some scheduling issues, the teams on Ship Forty-Seven, which will be our first competitors, will not be finalized until this evening. Thus you get another day of leave. I'm sure you're crushed to hear that."

Responding in kind to Raj's lighthearted comment, Cal said, "Terrible, sir, just terrible. Somehow we'll struggle through."

"I'm sure you will. Use that day wisely. Now, some details

about the upcoming competition. You and the other undefeated teams from this ship, plus the top three one-defeat teams, will compete with the top six teams of Ship Forty-Seven. There will be two rounds of competition. In the first round, there will be six individual competitions, team against team, with a single winner in each competition. The one-loss teams on each ship will compete with the no-loss teams of the other ship. The six winning teams compete for three final spots. Those three teams move on.

"So the first round of competition involves two combat missions. After that, all competitions are one mission against another competition's winners, with the three winning teams from the first competition taking on the three winning teams of one of the other two-ship contests.

"This means that all six of our teams may move on, or four, or two, or one, or none. The winners move on, without regard to the parent ship. The winners of our first double competition will meet winners of the contests between Ships Sixty-Three and Forty-One. Past that, winners compete until the undefeated teams are reduced to twenty-four, who become members of the new elite battle group. The contest is also double-elimination. From the one-loss group, another six teams will be chosen, to make up the thirty teams which will immediately join active battle groups. The next competition will produce thirty more teams to report to battle groups or replace losses—and losses will occur, I am sorry to say.

"Any questions?"

Raj had just told Cal that Genghis Khan had to win four straight inter-ship matches, and they would qualify for the elite group. That was all he needed to know. "No, sir."

"Good." Raj held up a data tablet and Cal stepped forward to take it. "The tablet includes your first mission description. I will meet you in the assembly area at the usual time day after tomorrow. You are dismissed. Enjoy your additional day of leave."

"Yes, sir." Cal nodded crisply and returned to quarters. He knew, and he bet that Raj understood, that there would be little leisure the following day. With their mission scenario in hand, the team would be doing a lot of study and analysis.

45 LETTY

One more day off. Letty woke early and met Opi and Tony in the mess hall.

Letty couldn't see that Tony had gained an ounce since she had known him, but he still ate like a man consuming his last meal—a plate of eggs and meat that looked like ham, plates of fruit, at least six sweet rolls, four glasses of milk and several pieces of cheese. Why he wasn't as big as a blimp completely mystified Letty. She'd been eating more herself lately, and her middle showed the accumulation of at least two or three pounds, if not more. Opi had probably gained a little, though not so much. It was enough to make Letty scream in frustration.

"If you can possibly stand to quit eating," she said, although her tone wasn't exactly cutting, "we need to get to work. Have you finished the summary of the scenario?"

Opi promptly said "Yes." Trust Opi to be ready. But Tony's nod surprised her.

"I can eat and talk," he assured her.

"Maybe so, but I don't want to see you talking with your mouth full of food. It's disgusting."

His face fell. "Sorry."

Opi seemed a bit annoyed about Letty's criticism, but Tony shoved his plate aside and said, "Ready, boss." He grinned as he said "boss," and Letty still found it hard to fathom how greatly he had changed. *In fact,* she thought, *we all have.*

"I've never seen anything like this exercise," she continued. "It's not even a battle assignment. Just trail a friendly supply convoy and watch for Horde ships. So far, our experience indicates that The Horde rarely goes in for ambushes or surprise attacks. Matter of fact, I don't get the point of this whole scenario. Shadow Warriors are about attack, attack, attack. Here we're a bunch of glorified babysitters for supply ships, which The Horde almost never attacks unless they're right on the battle line. What gives?"

Opi frowned. "I really haven't studied convoy movements. You're right, guarding supply ships isn't normal Shadow Warrior duty. It's like a reserve ship assignment. Tony?"

Opi's deference to Tony surprised Letty even more. He had become a very talented navigator, but other than spending extra hours in the simulator, as time would allow, she hadn't thought of him as a student of Horde battle strategy.

Tony matched Opi's thoughtful expression. "I might have an idea about that. Be right back." He sprang up and ran out of the mess hall.

Letty cocked an eye at Opi.

Opi laughed. "He's not off his rocker. We worked together yesterday, and he's a quick study. Although, his running off is unusual even for Tony." She managed a gesture of puzzlement. "I don't know either, but he's very serious. He really wants to be the best."

Sasha joined the table, his tray piled as high as Tony's, and plopped down by Letty. "Where'd Tony run off to?" he asked.

Opi replied as though she could read Tony's mind. "To get some additional data. He'll be back."

Letty had eaten two bites of melon when Tony suddenly reappeared, data tab in hand. "I knew it!" he said triumphantly as he sat beside them at the table.

"Knew what?" Opi and Letty said in unison.

"Shadow Warriors are rarely used as escorts. I read about an incident from maybe forty years ago, when the allied civilizations first started fighting The Horde. At least, I think so. It's hard to understand exactly how the history is laid out."

"The chronology," Opi added. "Every battle ever fought against The Horde has been summarized. Trouble is, the battle descriptions aren't always set down in historical order. These Molethians are the greatest data storers in history but they don't do much with it."

"Exactly!" Tony agreed, his motions so agitated that Letty had to stifle a laugh. She had never seen Tony so excited about anything. "Anyway, what happened was an accident," he said. "The supply ships were plodding along, and the Shadow Warrior escorts were probably bored out of their minds, thinkin' they were totally wastin' their time."

"Oh my gosh, you're right! I read about that," Opi said.

After a moment Tony said, "You tell them. You're better at this than I am." He patted her shoulder.

"Okay. You're sure?"

"Yeah."

"Well, apparently—"

Just then Cal sat down by Sasha. Letty explained what Tony had found, and after a moment, Opi went on.

"The Horde had begun a new initiative," she said. "The invasion force had been encountered, but its whereabouts were still unclear. The supply convoy approached a planetary system where the Alliance thought that the invasion might occur. Turns out that the system wasn't suitable to The Horde for some reason, and the invasion force had already passed it up.

"A group of Horde reconnaissance ships accidentally discovered the supply convoy, tracked it, pursued it, and ambushed it before it got to the system. Several hundred supply ships were attacked, with maybe a few dozen Shadow Warrior escorts. Only a couple of the warrior ships survived, and none of the supply ships."

Tony blurted, "It's a trap. Everybody will be suspectin' somethin'. After all, it's a test. But the size of the attack force, nobody will expect that! If you aren't prepared, you'll be blasted to dust. Either that, or you withdraw and lose the contest that way."

All heads turned to Cal. "Interesting," he said. "Problem is, how do we know that our scenario is *that* scenario? I mean, it may be, but there could be a hundred different escort-ship missions. Would they really spring that on a warrior team?"

Letty finally put her thoughts into words. "First, as we established before you came in, there haven't been many escort missions assigned to active Shadow Warrior units that we can identify, so this is a fairly unusual situation. On the other hand, the scenario may be unusual, but almost all our tests are different somehow. Maybe in this case it's not whether we win, but how we react to an impossible situation. Maybe it's how much damage we do, how quick we react, how we die, and how we fail."

That silenced them all for a moment. Then Tony said, "Bullcrap! It's about winnin', first and last. If we know more, if we learn more, and if we're better prepared, we have a chance to win. Isn't that what it's about?"

Sasha said, into the next silence, "You know, some might say if we know more than the other guy, we have an unfair advantage. But somebody else once said something like, 'Those who do not remember the past are doomed to repeat it.'"

"Santayana," Letty put in.

"Santa-who?" Tony asked.

"A philosopher," Letty said. "He's been dead a long time. But it's beside the point, and by the way, Sasha, what is your point?"

Sasha said, "I think Tony is saying that well-read is well-armed. Historically speaking, anyway. If we know more because we study more, I don't think that's cheating. We know more, so let's not decide that we'll see how well we can die, at least in a simulation. Let's figure out a way to save the day, just like James Bond in one of those spy movies."

Tony clearly approved the sentiment. "Hell, yes."

Opi beamed. "You know, I wondered why, on this mission, we got to specify some of the munitions. Why don't we do this ...?"

In three minutes they were all beaming just like Opi.

They met with Raj in the gathering room, along with the team from Ship Forty-Seven. Other teams were scattered about the room, most reviewing training material or quietly discussing previous results.

Genghis Khan's opponents, crisp and sharp-looking, consisted of two guys and three girls. Their captain was a tall, red-haired young woman, very pretty. Glancing left and right, Opi tightened her lips. The three guys of Genghis Khan looked like cats given large bowls of cream.

Opi did appreciate that the opposing captain let their ogles roll right off. Her goals and instincts matched Cal's, and she came across as just as ruthless as she was beautiful. "Captain," she said as she shook his hand.

"Captain." He did the same.

"We are Team Clean Sweep. I'm Rheena." She pivoted to point out her team members. "Co-pilot James"—equally tall, dark-haired, serious—"gunner Michael"—short and slight, a vague smile—"navigator Phyllis"—shorter, blonde, also a showstopper—"reserve Tanya"—skinny, plain as a board, and obviously seething not to be the pilot.

Cal reciprocated, as Opi decided that their opponents were capable, intelligent, and tightly wound. Rheena bound the two guys with sexual tension, she felt sure. Phyllis appeared to be a talented but timid yes-woman, as Opi had been until a few weeks ago, and Tanya's narrowed eyes said that she would kill Rheena instantly if she thought she could get away with it.

"—and Ophelia, our Strategic Planning Manager," Cal concluded.

Rheena adopted an odd, sardonic smile. "Strategic Planning Manager? That's an odd name for your bench reserve."

Cal's brow wrinkled, and Opi almost laughed. In a first, she decided to poke a little and stir up the opposition.

"She means the useless fifth member, Cal," she said, with as beatific a smile as she could manage. "Sort of like Tanya, right?" Opi gestured to the plain-faced girl.

The murderous look from Tanya caused her no surprise, but the captain's pleased expression shocked even Opi.

"Please," Rheena said more softly, "I'm sure you're an excellent backup."

"Actually, I'm pretty bad at backing up any of the other positions." Opi's smile stayed pasted on her mouth as she thought that she might be willing to help Tanya if needed. "But I have other talents."

"I'm sure you do," Rheena's smile widened further. "And I'm sure all the guys on your team appreciate those talents."

Well, Opi thought, grin still pasted, *maybe I'll let Tanya watch while I kill Rheena.*

To the side she glimpsed Raj about to move, and Cal's dismayed alarm. She had to say it quickly.

"Actually, my *talent* is planning our mission strategy."

"Really?" James, the tall, dark-haired co-captain blurted the word out, but Rheena silenced him with a glance.

"I plan all our exercises," she said, her smile superior. "Isn't your captain capable of that sort of thing?"

Raj stepped forward. "That's enough conversation for now. We need to be getting to our—"

"Sir!" Opi cut him off. His shocked look at her was a first. "Sir, may I please respond?"

Opi almost laughed at the stern demeanors on her team-mates' faces. Yes, now they were a real team, a real *family*.

At first she thought Raj would hurry them to the simulator, but he paused. "Why yes, Opi, you may."

Opi turned back to Rheena, Cal looking as surprised as Raj.

"Sure, our captain can plan, but he respects my talent, which is *not* the one you suggested."

Before she could say anything else, Cal stepped forward. "Let me take this, Opi."

He turned to Raj. "Sir, I believe that Rheena has insulted both our team and our planner." Opi was pleased to note that he did not refer to her as team captain. "With your permission, I would like to challenge Team Clean Sweep to a wager."

As Cal finished, the training officer of Clean Sweep, a Molethian, moved into the group. Before Raj could reply, the Molethian interrupted to say, "Wagering money such as a trainee's earnings is not permissible."

The look Raj gave him was hard enough to stifle another word. Raj turned back to Cal, his gaze including Opi. "What would you suggest, Cal? Instructor Melkan is correct about bets for money."

Cal managed a grin, and Opi had to choke down a laugh as he said, "Oh, nothing so crude as betting money, sir. I was thinking that the losing captain should come to the other team's quarters and make a sincere apology. And ask, please, for forgiveness for doubting the other team's ability."

Opi noted that Raj seemed to be trying to suppress a smile as well. He turned to his opposite.

"What about it, Melkan? Would a wager for team's honor only be appropriate? It appears to me that your team is quite confident."

The Molethian trainer, first puzzled then caught between the normal Molethian reserve and a sense of outrage, seemed within an inch of eruption. Finally, he managed, "I'm not sure that's appropriate, Raj."

Raj nodded. "I understand. Our team is very good."

The Molethian stiffened, and Rheena appeared ready to attack Genghis Khan. Finally, Clean Sweep's instructor said, "Very well—a wager based on an apology only. If you insist."

"We do," Cal volunteered, then apologized to Raj. "Sorry, sir. Your call."

Raj nodded. "Agreed."

"Better go practice your apologies," Tony wisecracked, and the whole Clean Sweep team surged toward him.

Instantly, both instructors called their teams to attention. Raj turned sternly to Tony, his voice a whiplash. "Enough, Tony. Double-time to the test cockpit—*now*." Opi and her teammates knew better than to hesitate. They vacated the assembly room in seconds.

As they entered the training pod, Opi said to Raj, "I didn't get a reply from you on the special requests. Did we get approved for the decoy supply ship and the supernukes?"

"Yes. A bit unusual, but you're allowed to specify what you want. Do you suspect what the exercise is about?"

"Watch and see, sir," she said, as they entered the cockpit simulator.

THEY HAD ALL the simulated supply ships but the decoy primed to leap when Cal tagged the slide switch, and every ship had leap engines warm and primed to go. Then five hundred Horde ships sprang into existence all around them.

"Launch ordnance!" Cal ordered Sasha.

With a flick of the leap control, all but the decoy leaped two million kilometers away. With their sensors trained on the ambush site, they clustered around the forward view screen. Six seconds later, the fusion blasts lit up cubic kilometers at the spot they had occupied moments before.

The simulation ended abruptly. The lights came up as the console announced, "Four hundred Horde ships destroyed with supernuclear cluster bombs. No Shadow Warrior ships lost. Team victorious."

They had won in thirty-five minutes.

Two hours later, Captain Rheena, strained and exhausted, visited their quarters to make her formal apology, through clenched teeth.

Opi wondered with an inner grin what that team thought of their captain's planning abilities now. Clean Sweep had been swept.

47 SASHA

"Let me get this straight," Raj said. "Opi and Tony found a Horde battle summary that paralleled your last mission scenario?"

Sasha said, "Yes, sir. She said you gave her access to the library, and Tony started working with her. I mean, reading about The Horde isn't against the rules, right?"

"No. Of course not." Raj sounded pleased to Sasha, whom he had found practicing in the simulator gunnery station.

"Opi's really amazing," Sasha said with a grin. "Cal's a good leader, but Opi's the reason we keep winning."

"Glad to hear your attitude toward her is now sensible. But that's not why I came by."

"Oh? A new assignment, sir?" Sasha waited expectantly.

"Yes. I wanted to see if you were all hard at work this morning on your leave day, and you are. You're all demons at doing your homework, and it's working.

"I need you to take a message back to the rest for me."

"Yes, sir." Sasha waited expectantly.

Raj handed him a data tablet. "Your first set of matches are six-against-six, facing teams from the other ship. Our ship didn't do so well in the first round; only two of our teams won.

"Tomorrow you will take on one of the winning teams from Ship Forty-Seven. There will be a drawing later in the day to determine your opponent. I will let you know as soon as I find out."

"Sorry we had only two winners."

Raj shrugged. "Breaks of the game. Your team had by far the highest overall score in the last contest. Team Seventeen also scored high, so our two winners did extremely well.

"Team Seventeen is the Street Fighters. They've heard about your excellent planning, and their team leader asked if you would help them prepare for the next round. Please inform your teammates of their request."

"Okay, sir." Sasha considered a moment. "How do you feel about us working with another team?"

"I encourage you to work with them," Raj said. "Word is getting around that you're one of the best-prepared teams. As you progress, I expect other teams will be interested in some joint preparation. All of you ultimately will be fighting the same enemy, after all. What you can teach the others will keep more of our warriors alive."

"Yes, sir. I'll tell the team, and I'll say you have no objection. But I think we should vote on it."

"Fair enough." Raj left.

Instructing the console to power off, Sasha went to find Cal.

After his conversation with Sasha, Cal called a team meeting. He didn't know the Street Fighters by sight. Really, he hadn't met that many other trainees on the ship. Why meet them, after all? Essentially, until the intra-ship trials were over, they were your enemy. Now, however, they were no longer competitors, so Cal had no problems with helping.

Despite his positive feelings, Cal agreed with Sasha that it should be a team decision. However, he didn't want other teams, especially the Street Fighters, to overhear their discussion, so as they ate he told everyone to return to quarters for a talk.

Together in their room, he explained briefly.

Tony jumped in immediately. "Really? Another team wants us to spend our time helpin' them try to win? We're bustin' our butts trying to stay ahead of the game, and they want our help?"

Cal understood. Most teams, he felt, were probably filled with teens just like theirs, still trying to make sense out of their situation. He said as much.

Letty agreed emphatically. "All the other teams, even those

we competed against, will be our allies against The Horde. They're not our enemies."

Opi spoke up. "When I do my team briefing, after Tony and I do our research, I can brief two teams as easily as one. Besides, I like that we can meet some others our age. I'll be happy to do it."

"Raj was very encouraging," Sasha said. "I think he wants this to happen, wants us to start to making friends. After all, assuming we become an elite team—"

"Which we will," Opi said firmly.

"Of course. As an elite team, we're going to have twenty-nine other teams as allies. Hopefully, the Street Fighters are one of them."

"That settles it," Tony managed a grin. "If even Sasha goes for it, I'm in."

After a unanimous positive vote, Cal said, "I'll tell Lieutenant Raj when we meet to get the exercise outlines. And I'll ask the captain of the Street Fighters to meet us tomorrow when you brief us prior to heading to the simulator."

They had gathered their desk chairs in a circle at the rear of the room. As Cal started to push back and get up, Opi said, "Cal, as long as you called a meeting ..."

He sat. By now he knew that any time Opi wanted to tell them something, they should listen. Intently. "Sure. What you got?"

"I've studied so many major wars against The Horde that I ..." Opi's expression showed she was deciding how to phrase her thoughts.

After a moment, she went on. "I've begun to see repetitive themes, things that happen in battle over and over in similar situations. I'm starting to see patterns, predictable tendencies, in Horde strategies and overall fighting tactics.

"There's something else. I don't think the Molethians make up the simulations that test us. I think they come from battle records, that whoever it is that makes up the simulations bases every exercise on some historical conflict. Of course, they have to program in enough intelligence to react to what we do in the exercise, but I think everything we've seen, from our early exercises to the current inter-ship competitions, is based on the records I've been researching."

Letty said, "You're saying that you may very well have read about today's test."

"Yes and no. It's more than that. There are so many records of Horde conflicts that it'd take me a lot longer, at least a few weeks, to review all of them. But I don't have to, that's my big discovery."

Everyone else remained silent. They were probably waiting, Cal thought, for Opi to pull another metaphorical rabbit from her hat.

He had the same hope, he had to admit. It shocked him how dependent they had become on the young woman. *Letty and I may be the leaders*, he thought, *but she's the power behind the throne.* Aloud, he encouraged, "You don't have to see a specific battle description. Why not?"

"It's the patterns. They're predictable. As I begin to read the summary of a new battle, a record I haven't studied yet, I sometimes get to a point in the narrative where I don't have to read anymore. Even though the description may be new to me, Horde tendencies, habits, procedures, whatever you want to call them, are not. At some point, I say to myself, 'Oh yes, The Horde did that in such-and-such, and I know what they'll do next and how this will end.' And further, I'll realize, 'I could win that battle against The Horde using such-and-such a strategy.'

"Of course, the archives contain accounts of a lot of victories, but a lot of defeats also. And even in the victorious conclusions, I often think that had I been in control, my win would have been cleaner and come a lot sooner.

"The point is, from now on, even if I haven't encountered a

specific situation, I think I can make up a good briefing based on typical Horde battle plans. Really, they're very predictable, and they aren't very imaginative or innovative. They don't have to be. They simply overwhelm an enemy with numbers.

"But now," she beamed, "we don't have to worry about numbers or ambushes, or new tactics, or any of that. I think I am putting together enough information to give us an edge in just about any situation."

"Galigan was dead-on," Letty said, grinning. "He said you have some really interesting qualities and he wanted to see where they took us. I think they'll take us to elite status."

She reached across to pat Opi's hand, just as Raj opened the door to their room. They all hopped up, and he said, "As you were, GK. I bear information about the second competition of round one."

They gathered around to hear his summary as he handed Cal another data tablet.

49 LETTY

Ten minutes after Raj left Opi said, "This is a common Horde attack scenario. There are several ways we can counter their tactics."

"Explain." Cal always pushed for details.

"We're supposed to aid a planet that has come under Horde attack. The Alliance normally doesn't get involved with what they call 'suicide scenarios.' That is, straight-on confrontations with overwhelming Horde superiority.

"However, in this case the inhabitants have quite a respectable defensive prowess and The Horde is being held in check. Due to the stalemate, the idea is that a swift Shadow Warrior offensive might tilt the balance and cause a Horde defeat. 'Course, that usually leads to an overwhelming Horde response that assures they don't lose a second time. But any time you can defeat The Horde, that's a major victory."

"We've never fought a direct, slug-it-out battle with a Horde flotilla," Cal said. "There has to be a catch, right?"

"Right. It's something that most of the competitors won't

know, having never fought a major war, so nobody will be prepared. Except us, and maybe the Street Fighters."

Tony managed a quick grin. "Those Street Fighters are some lucky suckers."

"Don't kid yourself," Cal said. "They didn't get this far by being incompetent. We may help them, but they're pretty good. All our competitors are at this level."

"Good thing," Tony came right back. "Don't want to go fighting no Horde 'longside a bunch of amateurs."

Opi and Sasha laughed, and his remark even got a smile from Cal.

"Mission at eight in the morning," Opi said. "Tell them we brief at six. Now I've got work to do. Tony, come on." She headed for the library, and Tony started after her.

As they left, Sasha grumbled, "Opi and her pet."

"Jealous?" Letty asked.

"Not really. I just can't believe that's the same Opi and that Tony would follow anybody around like an old hound dog."

"Yeah, it is hard to believe," Letty said. "But hey, Sasha, even you're civil nowadays."

He gave her a grin and said, "Back to gunnery practice."

UP AT FIVE the next morning, Letty made sure that everyone else rose early, too. At six they met in the gathering room, and the Street Fighter captain introduced everyone.

Named Cirilio, he had a short, stocky body and a demeanor as intense as Rheena's, though more polite. Mary, his second, willowy and a full three inches taller, appeared easygoing and casual, complimenting her captain, as Letty did Cal, she thought. Carlo, their navigator, had unmemorable features, average height, and a quiet demeanor, while Weapons Specialist Delilah, chocolate-skinned and quite attractive, reminded Letty of the mythical Amazons. Their fifth member, Romey, impressed Letty as a thinker, and she assumed that Romey had the same assignment on her team that Opi did on GK.

As the briefing terminated, Romey came forward to Opi. "That was terrific. The way you are familiar with Horde tendencies and tactics is amazing."

Letty watched as Opi blushed. She still wasn't used to such flowery compliments.

Romey went on. "I've had a few of the same ideas. Your presentation was really organized and thorough. When you have time, I'd like to get together and discuss your methods." Opi looked pleased, and both teams went their ways with friendly good-byes.

Cal caught Letty's eye. "Breakfast?"

"See you there in twenty." Letty checked the wall chrono and saw that she had twenty minutes for her new routine. Waving to him, she headed to the hatch leading to their simulator. Since the beginning of the inter-ship competitions, she had decided to make an early inspection of their training pod, to be sure that everything was in order. There hadn't been any problems for their first mission, but still, Letty liked to be thorough.

They would be in a different simulator for this exercise, one of the few times that Genghis Khan had not been in the same cockpit where they had trained. Letty quickly located the one that Raj had designated. She entered the cockpit, and pulled up in surprise.

Another teen, someone she didn't know, examined the main display unit. "Hello," she said, rather more loudly than necessary.

The young man turned, startled. "Wow, you scared me! What are you doing in our simulator?"

"*Your* simulator?"

"This is where they told us to come," he said. Tall and dark, he had an athletic build and curly hair, and Letty found him quite handsome. "Are you one of the teams we're up against?" he asked.

"I don't know. What team are you?"

"We're the Rebels, one of the winning teams."

Letty nodded. For some reason the young man made her uneasy. "I'm pretty sure this is our simulator for today," she told him. "If you want to come with me, we can check."

"No, that won't be necessary," he said cheerfully. "I'm new to your ship, so I probably screwed up. I'll go check."

He quickly left the cockpit.

For a moment, Letty poked around the various stations. Had he been trying to learn something about their plans? It wouldn't have done him any good. Opi never loaded their flight plan until they entered the simulator, just before the start of the contest.

After a few minutes, her check complete, she went back to their quarters. Back in their room, she told Cal that she had scoped out the new simulator.

"One thing," she added. "Somebody was in there when I went in, one of the members of a winning team from Ship Forty-Seven. He thought he was checking out his team's simulator, so maybe I went to the wrong one. We need to make sure where we're supposed to go."

Cal shrugged. "Their team is still new to the ship. He probably just made a mistake. Listen, I have some more thoughts on today's exercise."

"Okay. You know I always get hungry before a match. Let's go catch breakfast and talk about it."

Soon the entire team was stuffing food down their throats as hurriedly as when they were in training. For once, they had a reasonable amount of time for breakfast but, Letty reflected, old habits were hard to break.

When Raj dropped by their table, he verified their simulator designation and volunteered to make sure that the Rebels got to the right one.

"I don't know if they are your opposite. Assignments have been made, but I haven't checked yet, so I don't know the matchups."

In the cockpit, with their mission well-analyzed, they began the simulation, leaving their mother ship and readying to travel to the battle site.

As they prepared for the leap, Opi said, "I've had Tony plot a course to come in several hundred thousand kilometers from the planet, but not in the plane of the solar system. It will give us a good view of the battle, but from far enough away that we won't be detected immediately.

"The planet has a couple of moons, but as we know the Horde reserves sometimes hide out on or behind satellites, just as we do, I'm keeping us in open space. As we diagnose the situation, we can start the attack strategy Tony and I have worked up.

"Remember, we're one of over a hundred ships in this simulation, so we have to concentrate on the small sector above the planet that is our responsibility, and let the rest of our attack force handle the other attack points."

"Ready to leap," Tony announced.

Cal paused a moment, twisting to see each team member. "Everyone ready. Leaping now."

With the usual silence, the distant orb of their destination appeared on the screen. They were too far away to see individual ships, but smears of smoke and fire dotted the planet's surface.

"Okay, Tony, time to move us in. We'll take a—"

The simulator vibrated, and bright lights flashed across all their main screens. The captain's forward viewer turned totally red.

Abruptly, the lights came up, the console power died, and the dispassionate female voice of the console responder said, "Ship destroyed by Horde attack. Simulation over."

"Holy crap," Sasha said, as Letty's heart sank to her ankles. "We just lost."

50 CAL

Their debrief with Raj in the assembly area was short and sweet. He had little criticism, telling them that their mission analysis had been precise, but a group of attacking Horde ships had blindsided them. He encouraged them to keep an optimistic outlook, continue preparations, and recall that they were still in the competition and eligible to become a first-tier Shadow Warrior crew.

"Remember," he told them. "Even with the best preparation, sometimes in a battle you can lose without doing anything wrong. Take a few hours off and then get back to your studies."

In their quarters, all but Cal retreated to his or her own space, stunned and silent. Opi wore a desolate expression, Tony sat on his bed saying nothing, while Sasha faced the wall at his desk. Cal stopped at the door and studied the others. Letty eyed him from where she sat on the edge of her bed.

A silent two minutes passed. Cal never moved during that time. Finally, Letty stood and came over to take his hand and squeezed it.

"It'll be okay," she whispered.

Cal roused, shook his head, released her hand. "You're damn right it will be," he said softly. Raising his voice, he said, "Conference by the back desks. Everybody grab your chair."

Tony and Sasha looked up in surprise.

Opi responded lethargically. "Now?" she said.

"The commander should only have to say something once, Opi. Get your butt back there." Cal strode toward the back of the room.

"Now, wait," Tony said. "No reason to get on Opi. Not like it's her fault—"

Passing Tony's bunk, Cal rounded on him, his voice climbing a dozen decibels as they stood nose-to-nose. "Did you hear me say anything about fault? Did you?"

"Well, no, but—"

"Then get back there as well. *Now.*"

Gradually, they all joined Cal. *Like a bunch of beaten children,* he thought. *Like the first day we were here, I bet. Like I looked the day Tony popped me one.* He gazed at each, in turn, holding their eyes for a moment.

"Okay, we lost. I'm not sure how, but we did. My only guess is that we happened to leap into an area covered by a Horde patrol in the simulation, and they detected us before we saw them. It was an accident, a freak of the competition. But listen, I've read a little about wars, and a lot of battles are won and lost because of accidents and freak mistakes.

"Opi, look at me."

Opi had been sitting as still as a statue. Slowly, she looked at him. Not tearful but devastated.

"Opi, I don't know how we lost, but this is not, repeat *not,* your fault. And no one thinks so on this team. Right?" His eyes swept them one more time.

Tony nodded vigorously. "Hell no."

Letty said, "No."

"Absolutely not." That came from Sasha.

"Okay then. So we had a bit of bad luck. The chance of that happening again is as near zero as we could probably calculate. That being the case, we need to move on, keep our concentration, win our next few matches, and get back to elite status. Anybody in here disagree with that?"

Not a head moved; nobody said a word.

"Good, that's settled. Now, Opi, we need you and Tony to get back to your studies. We should have another match in a day or two. I still think we're the best team in the competition, and bad luck or not, we're going to prove it. Questions?"

Shocked, Opi said, "Then you still want me—"

"What a silly question. You think I can do what you do? No chance! You're the key, Opi. We've won with you before, a lot of times. Today we lost with you, but ultimately we'll win with you a lot more. Get your rear in gear and prepare for the next match. Got that?"

She hesitated, glancing from Tony to Cal and back. "Tony?"

"Damn straight, I'm ready."

Cal managed his first smile. "Glad that's settled."

As they started to break up, Sasha said, "Opi."

Rising, she said, "Yes?"

Sasha went and stood in front of her. "I want you to do something for me, okay?"

Cal could see her struggling to look positive. "Okay."

"I want you to slap me as hard as you can."

She drew back. After a moment she said, "I can't do that."

He moved directly before her again. "Yeah, you can. Imagine I just slapped you, like I did when we first met. Better yet, imagine I'm Rheena. Does that make it easier?"

The name caused her brow to crinkle. "But I—"

Sasha grabbed her hand. "Think of me as Rheena, imagine me as that big, red-headed witch with a 'b.' Even better," Sasha jerked on her arm, "imagine that I'm her and I just said you're Genghis Khan's slut."

With an explosive grunt, Opi back-handed him with all her strength, her right hand smashing into his face.

Sasha staggered, blood showing at the edge of his mouth, the red imprint of Opi's knuckles on his right cheek. Clearly horrified at her action, Opi said, "Oh my, oh my goodness, Sasha, I'm so sorry!" She came toward him, trembling. As she did, he held out his arms and wrapped her up. "Thanks, friend. Don't be sorry."

When he finally let go and she drew back, she said, "Sasha, just because we disagreed once, you didn't owe me anything."

He wiped blood off the corner of his mouth and grinned. "Yes, I did. Or I believe I did. So we're more or less even.

"But that's not the reason I egged you into taking a shot at me. I want you to remember how you felt when you hit me, when you heard the terrible things Rheena said. I want you to be mad, stay mad, from now on. Only concentrate that anger at The Horde.

"We need to keep that anger inside and focus it, let it help us as we prepare. Because in the end all of us, if we make the cut, will be going out to fight The Horde. And we need that anger to fuel us and give us the energy to follow through on every mission."

Before he could say anything else, Captain Cirilio of the Street Fighters appeared in their door. Seeing them huddled together, he quickly said, "Sorry, if I'm disturbing a meeting, I can come back."

"No, please, come on in," Cal told him.

Relieved, Cirilio took a pair of steps past the threshold. "Won't take but a minute. Just wanted to say thanks. We won easily. Opi, your briefing was right on the money. Can we continue to share your research?"

Flabbergasted didn't even come close to describing Cal's feelings—and he could see his teammates felt the same. "You won?"

"Absolutely. Can we still come to your briefings?"

Cal said, "Sorry. We'd love to, but we lost. We'll be in the other bracket. Congratulations."

Cirilio appeared baffled. "Lost? How? We followed your plan and it was a snap to win."

"Well, we lost," Cal repeated. "Luck of the game and all that. Anyway, best wishes for your continued success."

Cirilio thanked him and left quickly, face somber. When he had disappeared, the members of Genghis Khan stared at each other.

"How could they win and we lose?" Sasha asked.

Cal shook his head. He had no idea, but he did voice an opinion. "I know all the match scenarios are close to the same. I don't have any idea if they are identical, and they may not be. For example, Opi picked a particular leap point in the simulation. Maybe they picked another spot as their initial leap point." He directed his attention back to Opi. "Let's accept our loss and move on. I'm willing to bet that we don't lose again."

Cal took Opi's arm, pulled her into the center of their circle. "You're the one, Opi, you'll help us get there. I agree with Sasha. You're my friend and I'm proud of you. I have faith in you. We *all* have faith in you, and don't you forget it."

Of course, they had to coalesce into a group hug. As they did so, Cal thought, *Maybe we didn't lose today. Maybe we won the biggest victory of all.*

51 OPI

When Tony came into the simulator cockpit, Opi was bent over the console, concentrating as usual. Hearing him, she looked up. "Oh, good. You can help me." She cocked her head as he sidled up next to her. "How in the world did you find me?"

"You weren't in the library or the gathering room or the mess hall. This was the only other place I could think of." Tony sat at his usual station. "How can I help?"

"I want to run the simulation again, just like we did it during the competition. I want to find that minute when we performed the simulated leap. There's just something ..." she trailed off.

"Hey, it's okay that we had a little bad luck. It's like Cal said, luck, that's all. Nobody blames you; you heard what Sasha said."

She managed a reflective smile. "Sasha, yes, very sweet and clever, egging me into whacking him. You know, it made me feel better. Maybe he had it right. I need to stay mad.

"But that's not for now. You're right, Tony. Nobody blames me. Even me. Something happened in that simulation that wasn't right, I know it. Cal says the matches aren't necessarily identical, but I think they are. So if the Street Fighters won, we should have won. But we didn't.

"Either a computer malfunction or something else went wrong. I want to run the whole simulation again."

Tony's frown reflected his doubt about the process. "Are you sure? I mean, can we do that? I'll bet we need some sort of permission at least."

"I got it. I already talked to Raj."

Still doubtful, he said, "Okay. What now?"

"Our scenario is still in there. Just start it as we leave the mother ship."

Tony did so, not terribly enthusiastic. When he got to the leap point in the scenario, he said, "Ready for leap."

"Do it."

He did. On the main display, the target planet popped into view as a tiny disk in the distance and Opi waited, breathless, for the flash of red light and the declaration that they had lost. Instead, they simply hung in space.

Then, momentarily, the display blanked, flickered, and the planet abruptly appeared again. As they watched, their scanner began picking up ships near the planet and readying the attack parameters.

Just as they started to engage the enemy, Opi said in a raised voice, "End simulation."

The lights came up as the screens died.

"Didn't know you could do that," Tony said.

"I couldn't have done it the first time. When Raj set it back up, he gave me monitor control, that is, his control. What just happened?"

"Don't know. Except the attack on us didn't happen, and it sort of felt like the simulation hiccupped."

"Yeah, it did. Do me a favor, go get Raj."

Tony considered. "Okay, but I'll have to dig him up. You know he's all over the place when he's not with us."

"Then dig him up."

He saluted and gave her his devilish grin. "Yes, ma'am."

It took nearly half an hour. When Tony finally returned with Raj in tow, she blurted, "Sir, I don't think we really lost. I think there's something wrong with the simulator or the program."

Eyebrows up, he said, "Now, Opi, I said you could rerun the exercise, but you know there's nothing we can do about the outcome."

"Just watch, sir."

At her bidding, Tony started the scenario again from the navigation chair. At least he tried, but the simulation wouldn't initialize.

"Simulation software removed," the console announced. "New exercise to be downloaded shortly."

"What's that?" Opi jumped over to the captain's chair in alarm.

Tony echoed her. "What's going on?"

Raj shrugged. "Sorry, Opi, it appears the maintenance crew is ready to prime the cockpit simulators with new exercises for the next round. Which means we need to leave. When they start to load, this is a restricted area, for obvious reasons."

"But that's crazy!" Opi yelled. "When we reran it a moment ago, the attack on us didn't occur! There's something wrong with the exercise! I know it. I know it!"

Raj frowned, and Opi knew she had gone too far. "I'm sorry, sir," she apologized, coming to attention.

Instead of dressing her down, however, he pointed her back to the gathering room. As she and Tony walked behind him up the corridor, he said, "Opi, I know you're very disappointed. You have real talent, as does your team. But even the best teams sometimes lose. Don't let it get you down. Remember, six once-defeated teams will qualify for top status. You can still get there, and I believe you will."

They passed through the doors, and Opi said fiercely, "I *know* that there's something wrong, sir. Our previous contests didn't go like this one did. You always get a chance to orient yourself. We leaped, and we died, just that quick."

He shook his head. "Opi, these exercises are carefully monitored, and the programs have been meticulously checked. Believe me, there wasn't a problem. Now, go and lick your wounds, and then get ready for your next match."

"But ..." Tony tried to take up the plaint.

"No more," Raj said. "The only way defeat can get you down is if you let it. Now, climb back on that horse and ride it to victory." He turned, and walked away.

"I never rode a horse," Tony said wryly, "but I think the last one we tried to get on threw us off."

"Hmmph." Opi still seethed with anger that Raj wasn't going to investigate her concern. Which was impossible now, with the evidence vaporized, up in smoke.

"Damn!" She stamped her foot.

"His ignorin' us sorta reminds me of the way homeless get treated. Most folks don't have much time for our type."

Her head whipped around. "Your 'type' are now the best navigators in the fleet."

He grinned, and she changed the subject. "Listen, you saw that display jerk and glitch right at the point where we got blasted during the competition, right?"

"Sure did. Like a DVD with a bad scratch." After a moment he said brightly. "Once, before Dad left, we had a TV and a DVD player."

"Good analogy. Tell you what. Let's go find Letty. I've got an idea."

52 LETTY

Letty had been trying unsuccessfully to relax. Sitting on her bed, she had been going through some of the yoga exercises she had learned in gym some two years ago when Opi and Tony rushed in. Cal had gone off to exercise, but Letty had slept in.

"What's up?" Seeing Opi's face, she knew something had the younger girl in a lather.

"We were robbed. I'm convinced."

Tony nodded vigorously, punctuating Opi's words.

Letty digested for a moment. "You mean our loss. How could we have been robbed? It's a computer simulation."

As though she couldn't trust herself to speak, Opi said, "Tony, tell her."

He shrugged and started, "Opi got permission to rerun our match. I set it up and we ran it, just like yesterday. When we got to the leap, just as we showed up by the planet, the video went off. Then we got a bunch of static, and the scene came back, and no Horde ships attacked us. It was like somethin' had been cut out of the simulation.

"So we brought Raj in, and when we tried to run the match again, nothin' happened. The simulation wouldn't even run. Then a voice over the speakers announced that the new match was being set up."

Opi took up the story. "So Lieutenant Raj never saw what we saw. He fed us the same old BS, how anyone can lose, we need to go forward with a positive attitude, and all that crap."

Letty held up her hands, thinking that Opi had to get past their defeat. "What else can we do?"

"We can find out how we were screwed, dammit! We did not, not, *not* lose that match! I've gone over all our test scenarios, and none of them allow a sudden ambush before the team can get oriented. Sure, it's theoretically possible, but chances are so remote you'd never test for such a thing. After all, what's the outcome? You leap, you get blasted, test over. How does that help you train, or eliminate a less-capable team?"

Letty shook her head. "Opi, we got defeated and that's it. I don't see there's any recourse."

"Then why didn't the Street Fighters get knocked off the same way?"

"I don't know. Like Cal says, maybe the scenarios aren't identical, just similar."

Abruptly, Opi changed the subject. "Tell me about your encounter."

"What encounter?"

"The guy in our cockpit. Cal said you found somebody in our simulator. Give me every detail, what you saw as you entered the cockpit, where the guy stood, what he said. Everything."

Struggling to recollect details, Letty told Opi and Tony exactly what had occurred, from the time she entered the simulator until the young man left.

Opi's demeanor, Letty decided, was scary.

"Things are beginning to make sense," Opi said. "Before I

went to the cockpit to rerun our exercise, I talked to Raj about how test scenarios are set up. Here's how it works: Normally, the software is downloaded shortly before the competition. A droid technician goes to each cockpit and checks to make sure that there are no problems.

"Because test sequences may need a bit of tweaking, there's a socket on the console that allows a chip to be inserted. The chip has special diagnostics and the ability to change the program if there's a problem. It's like a flash drive on a PC, but I don't know anything about how the Molethian technology works, if it's like ours or not.

"Anyway, Raj told me when I first asked him that the tests are identical. But then he told me technicians sometimes alter a download slightly if things aren't working correctly. So maybe the tests are not identical, but they're pretty close.

"When a technician adjusts the simulation program, it's just like the situation with a programmer finding a bug in his software and performing a fix. They plug in their memory cube, initiate some sort of monitor program, and make the revision."

"You mean our alien friends don't write perfect programs either?" Letty had to laugh.

"Exactly. But here's the point: *Anybody* could enter the cockpit after a new exercise is loaded into the simulator and use the diagnostic to alter the program. If the guy you found in our cockpit messed with our download, we might have had a different simulation in which a Horde ship ambushed us."

As she thought that over, Letty got up and walked around her bed. "Of course! The guy I found in the cockpit." She slapped her forehead. "Geez, I guess I'm too darn honest. It never occurred to me that anyone ..."

Tony said. "Didn't our defeat bother you? The fact that we never got a chance to get our bearin's, and we're dead? Like Opi says—that's not a logical test."

"Of course it bothered me! It's just, I wasn't brought up like that. I went to a private school—there was an honor system. I just couldn't imagine ..." Letty huffed to a stop.

"Okay, let's assume you're right. We're still down to the same question: what can we do? According to the rules, we lost. I don't think the military staff would even consider an appeal."

Opi mused. "I don't either, Letty. I don't know what to do. But we were cheated by that other team. I had suspected something like that, but now I know it. I *know* it."

"I'll think it over," Letty said, her outlook on the day ruined.

Opi grinned. "Okay, it's your problem now. I'm going to keep studying. C'mon, Tony."

Like a switch clicked off in Opi's mind, Letty thought. She'd investigated, and she understood she could do no more.

Tony and Opi left, and Letty, her day of relaxation ruined, begin to consider alternatives.

53 CAL

ONLY ONE WIN AWAY.

The first thing Cal thought as he awakened. *Close. We're getting very close.*

Two more weeks had flown by.

Opi continued to study, becoming even more of an expert on Horde strategies and battle tactics.

Tony studied with her, following her around, as Sasha had said, like a faithful dog. Whatever his motives, his performance continued to accelerate. Cal bet himself that Tony could take on every other navigator in the fleet and show them a few things, and that included experienced pilots like Raj.

They had participated in two one-loser-bracket matches and won both with absurd ease. The time had stretched out, as inter-ship matches took longer, and more time was given to teams to recover from the intense competition.

Their continued successes made that single loss increasingly improbable. Cal had asked Letty to retell him about her encounter with the Rebel team member. Increasingly, he found himself inclined to believe Opi's theory, and he knew that Letty had joined Opi's camp as well.

The two matches in the one-loser bracket had been on other training ships. They had taken a shuttle to the tests, a small spaceship that Raj had informed them resembled a Shadow Warrior fighter, but without all the consoles for team members.

The experience had been exciting and exhilarating for everyone except Cal. He had sat, wet-palmed, jittery, and frozen to his seat, as they dropped from the bay of their training ship.

The sensation had been nothing like the simulated drop of a Shadow Warrior fighter in their exercises. The transition from the training ship's artificial gravity to the much more problematical grav unit on the shuttle had make his stomach do several flips.

The view through the small, side portals was a shocking reminder that they had been aboard a large ship, as they slipped away from the nearly-invisible training ship. Simulated views of space in their trainer cockpit didn't come close to the real thing, either.

The bright, dust-strewn slice of the Milky Way, along with bright nebulas, glistening star clusters, and the bright beacon of Venus, all directly outside Cal's viewport, jolted him with the reality of a true orbital voyage to another ship.

At least he hadn't wet his pants or lost his lunch. He was thankful for that. Their first trip to another training ship had been far worse than the sensations during the matches. The only good thing was that returning from the second match, the flight had seemed more routine and less harrowing.

Their quarters were currently deserted. No doubt Opi and Tony were already in the library, Sasha had gone to gunnery practice, and Letty pored over the battle records of their two recent victories, probably in the assembly area. Cal had allowed himself to sleep in, as he had a mid-morning meeting with Lieutenant Raj to discuss the next match.

Glancing at the wall chrono, he saw that he had only forty-five minutes. Quickly showered and dressed, he made a breakfast pass through the mess hall, to arrive at Raj's office a full minute early, standing at attention until Raj beckoned him in through the open door. Before he could assume the attention pose, Raj gestured to the lone chair before his desk.

He sat. "Good morning, sir."

"It is a good morning for you, Captain. You have had two easy victories, solidifying your reputation as one of the best-prepared teams. That has puzzled the whole command staff about how you could lose a match so decisively. Which is why I called you in.

"I received the information on your next opponent in the one-loss competition bracket." An odd expression flickered across Raj's face. *Almost,* Cal thought, *like well-controlled anger.*

"I'm new on the training staff," Raj said. "You and the two other teams under my responsibility right now are only my second training class."

Into the pause, Cal ventured, "You don't seem like a new training officer, sir."

"Thank you. I do have the advantage of being an experienced combat pilot. I told you I had exceeded by a fairly wide margin the usual Shadow Warrior mission count. That makes me, I believe, a more proficient training officer, but I'll leave that conclusion to you and my superiors.

"The fact is, although you haven't had any contact with my other teams, they did not do well initially. One team managed to lose the first match, and then the third one-loss bracket match, so it is destined for the reserves.

"The second team won twice, then twice more among the one-loss teams, but lost their last match a few days ago. Frankly, from the start, I knew that both those teams were not top material.

"Your team, on the other hand, had an ... an aura, a feel. You didn't start out as a cohesive group, but you came together rather quickly, and now I think you are the best on this ship. Maybe the best in the fleet.

"I must admit to outsize pride in your team, because I feel that I've had some part in your success. And as yours is my only team still standing, so to speak, it makes my stake in your success even more important.

"It also makes your single loss all the more confounding. I admit to skepticism at first. I thought originally that Opi was simply upset and obsessing over an unlucky loss. But I've had time to consider, and over time, I've begun to wonder about your loss as well.

"Which brings me to the subject of our meeting. Your next scheduled opponents are the Rebels, the team that caused your only defeat. I thought your team would want to know as soon as possible, Opi particularly."

"I didn't know the Rebels had lost a competition."

"They were undefeated initially. They won both of their first-round competitions on this ship, the second being the one with your team," Raj said. "They also won in the round of sixteen, but lost in the round of eight to our Team Seventeen, which is now qualified in the elite group. Then they won a match in the one-loss group to come to this round.

"A close examination of their victories revealed another win in which their opponents were eliminated almost immediately, just as happened to you."

"What are the chances of us catching them for a second match?" Cal wondered aloud.

"Normally, fairly small. Competition rules don't prohibit a rematch, but the randomness of assignments would make the chances small. However, in this case I nudged the odds."

Cal couldn't avoid gawking. "Really, sir?"

"Yes. Because of my extensive warfare experience, I have solid credibility with the top officers in the training command. I went to Captain Alitan with our suspicions. Given your record, he agreed to this rematch. He also agreed to empower me to assure the validity of the outcome, and he further agreed to strict privacy, telling only his executive officer of our plan."

Heartening news, Cal thought, but he had to ask, "What does this mean for us?"

"First, the matches for this round of the one-loss bracket will be held here on our ship, also a change I was able to gain. Second, you will undergo the competition in a new cockpit, one specially set up for videos of the participants during an exercise. We normally use it only for teams who are having trouble in training."

Raj paused, and asked, "You getting all this?"

"Yes, sir. So you believe Opi?"

"Officially, I can't believe or disbelieve. A top-notch member of a high-performing team has brought a very specific allegation that an unusual event happened in your simulator. This caused a malfunction that precipitated your loss. We have the unprecedented opportunity to investigate one aspect of that allegation, so we are."

"May I suggest one additional step, sir?" Cal asked.

"Of course. I don't guarantee to follow it."

"Yes, sir. There are storage lockers in the cockpit simulators. I assume they match the real Shadow Warrior ships. I don't have any idea what's kept there. Every time I've checked, they've been empty. I'd like to have somebody secreted there, to watch and hear what happens."

"The video and audio record should cover that."

"Not as well as someone in the simulator, sir," Cal said stubbornly. "An observer can get a first-hand view, if you'll allow some peep-holes in the cabinet. If a Rebel team member shows up and tries to change the simulation program, confronting them in the act might tell us even more."

"I see." Raj nodded. "But I think we can do better than that. I can hook up the monitors to the cockpit next door. That way, if one or more members of the Rebels show up and try to change the simulation, we won't give them a chance to try to overpower your spy and get away.

"By the way, who do you want in there? Yourself?"

"Maybe Tony," Cal said. "He's smaller, and he can hide easily in that cabinet, which would be a tough fit for me. And I know from personal experience that he can take care of himself. But I'd like to be in the simulator next door, sir."

"That'll work." Raj stood, indicating that the interview was over. "Brief your team, Captain. I don't know if we'll catch anyone, but at least this should give your team some closure."

On the way back to quarters, Cal felt as though he were walking about two inches off the floor. A nasty smile crossed his face. "Come on, Rebels," he said under his breath. "We're ready for you this time!"

54 TONY

Tony concentrated on breathing in and out, counting breaths, expelling as much air as possible through the small breathing holes near his head to keep the air in his hiding place as fresh as possible. Only one thought crossed his mind. He was bored, bored, bored.

Tony had never owned a watch or personal adviser, but since he'd last seen the chronometer at his workstation in the new cockpit, he felt it had been years, maybe decades, since he had closed the door on the locker.

At first he had killed a little time by examining the dimly lit cabin, trying to discern the differences between this cockpit and the one in which they had trained and conducted many of their exercises. Eventually he had given up, trying to relax with no success.

"Please hurry and show up," he said through his teeth. Glad to be doing the assignment and proud that Cal had specifically asked him to keep watch, he had come to the conclusion that he might be in his cramped, stuffy post all night long. "It's for Opi," he repeated. "It's for Opi."

Opi had become his dream girl. Even thinking about her in the stuffy storage compartment made his pulse quicken, his hands perspire. As well as his developing feelings, he trusted her thoroughly. Opi had to be right about their loss, and here was the chance to vindicate her, to show that her planning abilities were beyond reproach.

"For God's sake, Tony, stay awake," he muttered.

What a difference a few months made! Tony had not despised Opi as Sasha had at first, but he had thought her hopeless as a team member. A whimpering mass of jelly, with no apparent talent and a tendency to go to pieces whenever anything out of the ordinary happened. Like Sasha, and maybe Cal, he had mistaken sensitivity and a sheltered life for weakness and incompetence.

Now, he admired Opi as he had few people in his short, rough-and-tumble life, and he had gradually come to like the other members of the team as well.

Cal, blunt and occasionally obnoxious but a decisive leader who would never let a team member down—even if he had not yet grown to like him.

Letty, thoughtful, competent, sure, the steadying influence to Cal's advance, advance, advance attitude. The "big sister" of the team.

Sasha, the quiet observer, who practiced continually until no one, Tony felt sure, had mastered weapons as he did.

And, finally, Opi—the thoughtful spectator, who caught patterns none of the rest of them saw, who reviewed and categorized and catalogued, who understood Horde armies better than most of the Molethians, though she had never been in a single live battle.

In a way, the team had evolved into the family he had never had, a feeling he knew Sasha shared. The others—well, they might not feel exactly like that, but even Cal, Letty, and Opi were beginning to gravitate increasingly to each other, and to him and Sasha. *Very odd,* he thought, *that any sort of bonding could occur between those with such oddly different backgrounds. How in the world had this weird collection of personalities come together?*

He shrugged mentally and refused to let the mechanics worry him. They had come together, despite their best efforts, and now they represented the epitome of Molethian training. Even the three team members with better former lives might now concede that their abduction had been for the best.

A sharp *click* interrupted his thoughts. The simulator hatch opened and two forms entered, hard to distinguish in the pale light emanating from the displays.

"Lights, thirty percent," the first shadowy form said. As the interior lights brightened, they revealed a tall, dark-haired youth. He addressed his shorter companion, also male. "Plug in the cable and activate override."

The second nodded, produced a cable and plugged it into the console. He stood back as the taller youth extracted a small cube from his pocket. Attaching it to the cable, the tall one addressed the console. "Download modification B, full."

He grinned at his colleague. "Once this is in, our opponents get clobbered again."

The shorter teen laughed. "We'd never have lost if we hadn't been locked out of that one simulator."

Carefully, Tony toggled the inner door opener and edged out, so quietly that the two youths bending over the console didn't notice. As the other console displays came to life, he stepped up a couple of paces and said conversationally, "So, what's goin' on, guys?"

Both jerked as though electric current passed through them. The taller one whirled and yelled, "Who the hell are you?"

"I'm the guard," Tony said. "This is our simulator for the next competition, and I just wanted to make sure no rats got in to chew any wires."

"Rats? Why you son of—"

As the taller teen brought up his hands, Tony thought he might have to defend himself. Before either intruder could move, the door burst open. Raj and a Security Forces officer charged in. The security man gripped the first Molethian hand weapon Tony had seen. It rather resembled a ray gun from an old science fiction movie, a dark gray, elongated oval with a fat grip.

"Don't move," the officer snapped.

As the two guys shrank back in terror, Raj said, "Freeze download, per Rajasekaran-four authorization."

"Download halted," the console responded.

"What are you doing in here?" the security officer asked sharply.

"W-Wh ... We're just going over our strategy for the next exercise," the taller kid said. "This is our assigned simulator, and we wanted to check our strategy out—"

"This is *not* your assigned cockpit." Raj's voice went up a level. "The Rebels are assigned to Simulator D-Nine. This is C-Six, not even close to yours." He indicated the cable and cube. "What's that?"

The short kid reached to extract the cable. "We were just—"

The SF officer stopped him again. "Don't touch it. Back up."

The young men did, brows damp. As they did so, Raj said to Tony, "Did you see these two install the cable?"

"Yes. And I heard them discuss it." Tony repeated the short conversation.

The taller Rebel started toward him. "That's a lie, you miserable—"

Tony backed up a step and shifted his gaze momentarily to Raj. "Sir, may I?"

"No," Raj snapped. He addressed the two Rebels. "We heard the same conversation. You're the liar."

The security officer motioned with his weapon, said to the taller kid, "That's far enough, son. Unless you want to be hurt."

The teen pivoted toward Raj. "Sir, this is all a misunderstanding! We meant no harm. We were just doing our duty, getting ready for the next competition."

"If that's all there is to it, you won't mind if we load your program onto an analysis system and examine it." said the security man.

The punk paused, then made a dive for the cable.

This time Tony didn't ask. He took one long step and grabbed the Rebel's arm, jerking him around. As the kid pivoted, Tony let him have a short jab directly to the midsection. With a *"whoof,"* the Rebel team member collapsed to the deck.

Raj gave him a warning stare. "Enough, Tony."

The shorter punk backed up against a bulkhead, fear contorting his features.

"Sorry, sir," Tony said. "But that was for Opi." He came to attention. "Sir?"

Busy picking the tall kid off the floor, Raj said, "Yes?"

"Sir, I think my work here is done. May I be dismissed?"

Raj was having trouble with his face, and it suddenly occurred to Tony that he might be hiding a smile. He finally said, "Yes. Return to quarters until you are called."

"Yes, sir!" Tony brushed past Raj and the security officer and went to find Cal in the other cockpit and then tell the team.

55 SASHA

Sasha ran, full out, down a dark street that went nowhere, with Frawley in hot pursuit, holding a large, fiery baseball bat that grew larger and burned hotter at each step. His foster father was closing in when—

The swish of the door to the team's quarters woke him. He sat bolt upright in his bed, Frawley dissolving into gray wisps of fog.

A glance at the chrono showed the hour: 0503.

Lieutenant Raj stood in the doorway. Sasha scrambled off his bed and to confused attention as his teammates did the same.

"Good morning, Genghis Khan," Raj said. Bright and shiny as a new coin, Raj's uniform showed not a wrinkle, hair neat and mustache trimmed, despite the hour.

"Good morning, sir," They responded in unison, by now an ingrained routine.

"Your attendance is required at a mandatory meeting," he said. "Dress and come to my office immediately."

"Yes, sir." Their unison replies were reflexive also.

As Raj left, they scrambled for clothing. Sasha noted with amusement that even the girls were a lot less self-conscious now.

Opi still ran to the bath to change, but Letty simply turned her back to don bra and blouse, and slipped pants over her sleep shorts. Sasha avoided a glimpse of her bare back as she started to change. Letty had trained him well.

In a handful of minutes, they jogged together down the passages and up the stairwells to the command deck of the ship.

Raj's office door was closed, but they waited patiently, lining up against the opposite bulkhead at attention to avoid blocking the passage. In a short time, he opened it and joined them, motioning them to follow without speaking.

Raj led their team down two different passages and up another deck. They followed him into an amphitheater about a third the size of the team gathering room, with rows of seats in tiers above a sunken deck. The deck area resembled a courtroom, with three rows of metal chairs with brown cloth seats, an open space, and what resembled a judge's bench.

The arena-style room had begun to fill. In the half-circle row of seats, on several different levels, cadets and training officers were taking their places or just entering. Curiosity aroused, Sasha joined his teammates. He wasn't certain why they were present, but he had a guess.

Eventually, thirty or forty trainees and officers, both human and Molethian, had gathered.

Sasha had just decided to ask Raj to confirm his guess when a number of Molethians began to file in through a door at the rear of the deck area. They were followed by two trainers, one of them human, and finally the five members of the Rebel team. The team's appearance answered any of Sasha's remaining questions.

Captain Alitan entered last, ascended the bench ponderously, and sat, at which point the others on the deck area seated themselves. Except for the five Rebel team members and their apparent trainer, who was Molethian. He was staring stoically ahead.

The defendants, Sasha thought.

Captain Alitan looked very unhappy.

He first addressed the observers at large. "This hearing concerns a cheating incident in which two trainees were caught in the act of sabotaging a test simulation for one of our fleet competitions.

"This is not, for those of you who are natives of Earth, a trial of any sort. We have verified proof of wrongdoing, and this hearing is concerned only with statements from the wrongdoers and determining their punishment. Is that clear?"

The Rebel team nodded, clearly miserable and terrified, and Sasha discovered that he felt a strong sympathy for these children —for they were scarcely more than that. They had been abducted, forced into training and now faced penalties for actions that could scarcely be attributed solely to them. Commander Alitan's severe posture made Sasha fear for their lives.

Alitan began to call the Rebel roll. "Carina Alioto, how do you plead?"

Apparently she had been coached, for the dark, diminutive young woman stepped forward and said, "Not guilty, sir. I had no knowledge concerning the actions of three of our team."

"Very well. Samuel Dorney, how do you plead?"

The young man, who resembled Cal, seconded his teammate. "Not guilty, sir. I was also not aware of any illicit activities."

"All right. Marian Bralee, your plea?"

A slender, black girl ducked her head. "Guilty, sir."

"Tirth Bhutian, your plea."

That was the short kid that Tony had told Sasha about. "Not guilty, sir. I only followed orders, with no idea of any cheating."

"According to the taped evidence, you knew exactly what you were doing. Do you wish to change your plea?"

"No, sir."

"Very well. Carlton Maxwell, how do you plead?"

He was the tall young man both Letty and Tony had described. "Guilty, I guess, sir. But our trainer made us do it."

Alitan frowned. "You are a liar as well as a cheat. Your trainer, Upper Lieutenant Galver, has submitted to a truth verification procedure at his own insistence.

"That procedure proved he had no knowledge of your true purpose," Alitan said, "although he made a highly questionable decision to lend you the console editing kit. He believed your assurances that you only wanted to work on your mission plans. Your statement is rejected, and your status is entered as guilty."

Alitan scanned those in front of him. "Now to the punishment. Upper Lieutenant Galver, you are guilty of no crime, but doubly guilty of malfeasance in practice and neglect of duties. A competent officer would certainly have uncovered this series of transgressions by your team. You are hereby reduced two grades to Under Lieutenant, stripped of all training responsibilities, and you will be assigned to clerical duties for the remainder of this training cycle. Your future will be determined when this ship's current mission is completed."

The officer dipped his head, embarrassed and upset, and Sasha couldn't blame him. The officer's career had effectively been terminated with his condemnation to clerical duties. Sasha expected that, if it were possible on Molethan, the officer would soon resign.

Alitan directed his stern demeanor to the team. "Alioto and Dorney, you requested verification also, and our analysis agrees with your plea. Your dishonest teammates did not bring you into their conspiracy. Your acceptance of the others' claims of working on new battle plans, while a bit naïve, is reasonable, and you are found innocent of charges. You will be returned to reserve status and may yet join a Shadow Warrior team. Please be seated."

Obviously relieved, the two backed into empty chairs.

Alitan returned his attention to the conspirators. "You three represent all the worst to which civilized minds can aspire. Your acts of cheating not only prevented more deserving teams from qualifying, but also damaged your own training, making your team far less effective. Your punishment will more than likely be extreme, and I will remark that in our regular fleet service, such transgressions are automatically punishable by quite severe penalties."

The black girl fell straight back, fainted away. With a Molethian oath unfamiliar to Sasha, her disgraced trainer rushed to her side. Shortly, he helped her into a chair.

Satisfied that the young woman had not sustained any serious injury, Alitan addressed the gathering again. "The determination of punishment will be made over the next few days, and we will reconvene at that time. If there is no other discussion, the spectators are dismissed."

"Captain?" Sasha realized he had stood and spoken.

Alitan looked up in surprise. "When I referred to discussion, I did not include the spectators, young man. However, what is it you wish?"

Sasha gulped. Well, as his father had said long ago, "In for a penny, in for a pound."

"Sir, pardon my interruption. But I'm one of the teammates wronged by the three members of the Rebel team. May I speak freely, sir?" In the corner of his eye, Sasha could see Raj, mouth in a firm line. *Going to catch hell for this*, he thought.

Oddly, Alitan didn't act offended. Perhaps he expected Sasha to deliver a scathing indictment of the three team members. He said, "Proceed, but be quick."

Sasha nodded. "Sir, I'm proud to be training to be a Shadow Warrior. I was taken away from a bad situation and given a chance to make something of myself. I'll fight The Horde as long as I can, and so will my team—and we've got a great team."

Alitan didn't smile, but he dipped his head a bit, his demeanor a fraction less stern.

"But let's face it, probably not everybody feels that way. And besides, there are a lot of trainees, and with that many people, there's bound to be a few bad apples, people my age that just aren't right for training. Whether they washed out or just cheated, these guys couldn't cut it.

"They're miserable humans who would have probably not done very well at anything they tried to accomplish back on Earth. But remember, they were kidnapped, brought here against their will. They did wrong, cheated us—but on the other hand, they were made to do what they were doing.

"Please do the right thing, sir. Wipe their memories, send them back to Earth. But don't imprison them or punish them harshly because they failed—because your training failed as well.

"One last thing, sir. I have learned to greatly appreciate the kindness and professionalism of your training officers. I've tried to be candid, so let me also say that I have great respect for you and your team."

Sasha sat, fully expecting a savage outburst from the bench.

Instead, after a pause Alitan said to Raj, "Upper Lieutenant Rajasekaran, your team is not only talented but outspoken. I will take this criticism in the spirit that it is offered—as a respectful request to consider all aspects of this situation when assessing punishment.

"This assembly is dismissed."

Sasha didn't wait a second, scooting out the door of the chamber. If he moved fast, maybe Raj wouldn't catch him.

Later in the day, Raj summoned the team back to the gathering room for a meeting. Cal noticed that Sasha kept his head down. Raj had cornered him earlier, and Cal imagined that there were still echoes of Raj's tirade bouncing around inside his head.

When they were seated around a conference table, Raj told them, "As you can imagine, this cheating business has really fouled up the competition process, but we've come up with a solution.

"The three teams that were defeated by the Rebels for a first loss are again classified as undefeated. The first two undefeated teams will compete based on a lottery, and the third will be matched with the winner. Thus the undefeated teams will have to play one or two extra matches, but we see no other fair solution.

"Does everyone understand this?"

An extra match? Trivial! They were back in the competition and undefeated as well! "Sir, that's fine with us," Cal said. "We just wanted a fair chance. Right?"

Everyone nodded.

Raj said, "I'm glad to hear it. Our competition is now far behind schedule, but we plan to catch up quickly. We will have the drawing here in the gathering room in an hour. Lieutenant, you are assigned to attend."

"Yes, sir."

"The winner of the drawing sits out the first match, then plays the winner of the first match tomorrow afternoon, while the loser joins the once-defeated bracket to continue competition. The winner of the second match of undefeateds automatically qualifies. It's a tough schedule, but at least, you have another chance. Questions?"

Not a peep. Cal figured that everyone would wait until they were alone, then go into a riot of screaming and hugging.

As he passed Sasha on the way out, Raj said, "You're pretty quiet, now. No other learned pronouncements?"

Cal noticed how Sasha hunched his shoulders. "No, sir. None at all."

"Next time you make a speech to the captain," Raj said, "I suggest you have a large number of successful missions under your belt first."

"Yes, sir."

"Now, get out of here and go study. Go on, git!"

"Yes, sir!" Everyone said it in unison.

As Raj departed, the team scattered. Cal figured the yelling and screaming could happen a little later.

I can't believe it." Tony muttered to himself as he read the summary of a drawn-out, interesting battle with The Horde that had taken place more than two Molethian decades ago. The account read like the basic pattern for most of the battle scenarios they had experienced. Tony shook his head. He had an immediate hunch that many of their exercises had originated from the summary he had just read.

"I'm working," Opi told him. "Quit talking to yourself; it's irritating."

Seated side by side in the library before data viewers, they rapidly scanned as many records as they could before evening.

Tomorrow would be stressful. Cal had lost the drawing, so they had one competition in the morning, and a second in the afternoon. Not much time to plan mission scenarios, for sure.

"Stop what you're doin'," Tony said. "You've got to see this, at least for a minute."

Opi huffed, paused the data viewer, and turned impatiently. "Okay, what?"

"It's this summary I've been readin'. It's crazy! It's like most of the exercises we've been through came from this one long battle. Call it up on your reader."

"I've got mine paused. Why don't you just move over?"

"Sure," Tony said. No problem. Sitting close to Opi didn't appear on his list of undesirable duties.

She took control of the scanner and ratcheted it back to the beginning of the summary. She could read ten times faster than Tony, so in minutes she had scanned the entire article. Then she sat back, deep in thought, and Tony waited as patiently as he could.

Finally she stirred. "Okay, you're right, I needed to read this. It follows like a string of the tests we've taken. Oh, there are variations, but by and large the conflicts represent eighty percent of the exercises we've seen. That's remarkable."

After wallowing in her approval for a few seconds, Tony said, "I got to thinkin'. Once when we were talking, Sasha told me he's done programmin' before. Could we use this report as the basic form for any battle and have him concoct a program for us? It needs to evaluate a scenario accordin' to the rules you've developed to respond to basic Horde tactics. It might make your job easier."

She shifted from the display to Tony. "Yeah, it might. Tony, that's a great suggestion—building a program that sets up a sort of template for any mission. Problem is, I don't think we have enough time to get him to do anything by morning."

"Sasha told me that he had asked Raj about data analysis tools on their systems. I don't know what that means exactly, but I think he could make up something to analyze data pretty fast. He was really excited about it before he started doing all the extra gunnery practice. He said somethin' about, you don't have to know any sort of compiler language to program, you just tell the console what you want and it writes the program. Never done any programmin' myself, so

I'm not sure what all he meant, but he was pretty impressed."

Opi shook her head. "I still don't see how—"

"One thing," Tony interrupted. "You said that we need to get so familiar with Horde battle scenarios that we can figure out how to counteract any given situation.

"Whether we do or don't use it right away, this is a pretty important thing to make up now, before we're fightin' for real. Even if it doesn't help us right now, it might be important when we enter the Shadow Warrior force."

She studied the display. "Yeah, I've been thinking about how to generalize the knowledge we've been collecting. You're right, go get Sasha. He probably can't help us for our competition in the morning, but at least we can get started improving our planning abilities for the future."

"Exactly." Tony sprang up and went to find Sasha.

58 SASHA

I can do it, I guess" Sasha said. He felt dubious about the whole idea, and he could tell by Opi's expression that his doubt showed. "Yeah, I did ask Raj about doing some programming. I learned a bit of C and C-Plus-Plus in school, and assembly language programming on a couple of microprocessors. We may be talking about a lot a time to do what you want, though."

Opi pursed her lips. "You mean you can't finish tonight?" After a moment she giggled. One of her few remaining faults, in Sasha's opinion. "I'm kidding. I know you can't do much tonight, but maybe you can start working on some sort of tool that will help us when we're Shadow Warriors for real."

The future. That sounded reasonable. If he could come up with something that could sift through scenarios, evaluate Horde tactics and options ...

"Maybe," Sasha said. "Raj told me a little about this voice-activated programming and how to call it up. It's like you tell the operating system what you want and it puts together a string of code that does it."

"What's an operating system?" Tony asked. "And why do you need to make up codes? Do we need to keep it secret?"

"No, no." *Easy to fall into computer jargon,* Sasha thought. He had loved working with computers and programming in school, and his teacher in science had said he had real talent, but of course the Frawleys would never let him use their computer or their son's laptop.

"An operating system is the main program that operates every computer," Sasha told Tony. "Different computers have different operating systems, but they all do basically the same thing—control how the computer operates."

Opi nodded in understanding, but Tony looked lost. "Think of an operating system as simply the boss computer program," Sasha said. "And as to code, that's just another name for a program, or part of a program. Nothing to do with secret code."

Tony finally nodded, so Opi said, "I know it sounds crazy, but is there anything you could do for tomorrow? If I'm being an idiot to ask that, tell me."

"You're no idiot, 'cause you know how hard that would be," Sasha told her. "If I were using some standard compiler language it would take a lot more time. In this case, I'll have to see how it goes."

"Give it a try, and we'll cross our fingers," Tony said.

"I have a question first," Opi said. "Why don't the Molethians have any sort of data analysis tool like this? It would make my work so much easier."

"No idea. Have you asked?"

Opi said blankly, "Well, no, but I would think if they had such a thing, they'd offer it to me. Raj knows what I'm doing."

Sasha shrugged. "Don't ask me, ask him. Okay, let's see what I can do with this. I asked Raj about it weeks ago. I wanted to write a video game for my entertainment, and for you guys as well. Then I started spending more time in the simulator practicing and I sort of let it go."

He pulled up a third chair, pushed Tony and Opi aside, and addressed the terminal. "Algorithm construction, data examination and analysis. File under Sasha Program One."

"Ready," the console replied.

Sasha grinned at his friends and rolled up imaginary sleeves. "Everybody stand back," he said grandly and dug in.

59 OPI

Even with the auto-programing capability, Sasha could only get a limited amount accomplished, though they worked until after midnight.

He did manage to finish an initial program, one that, he claimed, would search for certain standard patterns that he had specified, and perhaps reduce Opi's effort five or ten percent. Past that, he needed more time, although he commented as he, Tony, and Opi were wrapping up, "This compiler is really pretty neat. With some more time to get used to it, I think I can really speed up software development."

Up early, the team had washed, dressed, and eaten a bit when Raj joined them in the mess hall. He handed them a tablet. "Just like the first test. Thirty minutes to study and plan, then straight to the simulator. You are facing a major invasion force and you must do as much damage as possible."

They all followed Tony and Opi to the library. Sasha initiated his program, Opi loaded the scenario from the tablet. Most of the team watched the screen as Sasha's program ground away while Opi read the pertinent exercise details on the tab.

When the results showed up, Opi examined the summary. "Sasha, your program works!" she exclaimed. "At least, pretty well for a first-pass. I recognized a basic Horde battle plan, and the program results pretty well agree with my thoughts."

"What's the plan?" Cal asked.

"Hold on, cowboy, I just figured out what we're facing."

Which got a grin from Cal, as she had never been that informal with him before.

"Let's go to the cockpit now," she continued, "and Tony and I can start loading in some navigational info."

Cal sent Letty to Raj's office for permission to go to the simulator. This time he insisted on going with them and watching carefully as they went about preparing their plan.

The cheating scandal, Opi thought, *has forever changed the way the training staff view working with cadets.* There would be less freedom from now on, and the assumption had changed from, "Nobody would ever cheat," to "We have to assume everyone cheats until proven otherwise." Sad, but probably realistic.

Breathless from her frantic efforts, Opi turned to Cal only moments before the scheduled start of their exercise. "That's all I can do on short notice. The good news is that unless I totally don't get it, the scenario is familiar and easy to plan around. If we haven't won in less than half an hour, I'll hand in my planning badge."

"No chance of that," Cal said. He turned to Raj. "Sir, would you like to make a bet? Of course, we don't have any money, but maybe you could guarantee us another couple of days off when we qualify for Shadow Warrior deployment."

"So, you're certain you'll qualify?" Raj's normally skeptical attitude reasserted itself.

"Absolutely. I'll bet on that also, if you wish. Double or nothing."

"No deal. You get several days off if you qualify, so that should keep you happy. Tell you what. I'm going to sit here and watch you crazy people do your magic. Does that scare you?"

Opi realized, as everyone paused, that having Raj around made absolutely no difference to her. "No sir. Not as long as you stay out of the way."

Tony laughed, and even Raj let his lips turn up a fraction.

"Very well, Opi, go get your victory."

As the simulation started and they left the mother ship with the usual thump and jarring vibration of the deck, Opi said, "This is a very standard scenario. What makes it difficult and dangerous is that we are attacking a flotilla of about a thousand Horde ships, and we are alone."

"Really?" Sasha gaped. "Raj mentioned 'a large invasion force' in the briefing, but a thousand? We've never even taken on a hundred."

"That's our job, Sasha," Opi said.

He shook his head. "You're the boss."

"No," Opi contradicted, "Cal's the boss." She turned to Cal. "How about it, Sir? Ready to do some damage?"

"Yes. Looks like a solid plan," Cal said. "First, a quick attack on the scout ships they always send out. Deprive them of intelligence. Then hit the supply ships, to reduce their operational capabilities."

Opi grinned. "Exactly."

"Let's go," Cal said. "Leaping now."

They approached the flotilla. The scout ships were hundreds of thousands of kilometers ahead, and focusing on the targeted solar system.

"Still undetected," Letty announced, monitoring the scanners.

"Micro-leap," Cal directed, "just past the lead ships. Sasha, cannon salvo for the ships we first encounter and beam weapons for those farther on. As soon as Sasha finishes, Tony, plot us a course at least a light-year away."

It went off like clockwork. Cal triggered the leap, placing them in the midst of the six scout ships. Sasha fired cannon and beam weapons in sequence, and Cal leaped again without having to give any additional orders. Tony plotted three more turns and leaps as they approached the initial attack position.

"Three scout ships destroyed," Letty announced, concentrating on the co-pilot displays.

Abruptly, Cal said, "I may want to change the plan."

Opi said, far more calmly than she felt, "Yes, Sir?"

She saw Raj lean toward the pilot's chair as Cal answered her.

"We've done enough exercises by now that I know the routine," he said. "We attack a few peripheral ships, then make a run at the fuel and ammunition supply ships.

"But Opi, this is a huge chunk of a flotilla, by far the largest we've ever attacked. With a thousand ships, they probably have a hundred or more ships carrying fuel and munitions. If we were leading a larger force, twenty or thirty ships, I'd say 'go for it,' but we're alone. There doesn't seem to be any way for us to do enough damage with our available cannon ammunition and remaining bombs."

Opi surprised herself with her calmness. What had she overlooked?

Cal asked his question to Raj. "What's the one thing that might cause a thousand ships to retreat?"

Raj paused. "The loss of their flagship, their command ship. The flagship is the very center of their rigid command-and-control hierarchy. As best as we have been able to determine, every single transmission goes to the command ship.

"The flagship usually commands several tens of thousands of ships. If there is one in this fleet, there's no way to take it out. It's heavily armored and there will be hundreds of defenders around it."

Cal glanced at Tony. "Does this fleet include a flagship?"

Surprised, Tony checked tactical. "Yes, sir."

Opi turned on Cal, but before she spoke, he asked her, "You're big on Horde tendencies in certain situations. What happens when Shadow Warriors attack the fuelers in a convoy?"

Opi took a breath. "You know as well as I do. They take up a standard defense posture. A globe is formed around the fuelers. In this case, with so many ships, it would probably be two globes, a smaller one inside the larger, making the fuel tanker section of the fleet virtually impregnable."

"Exactly. And if they shift a lot of ships into those globes, how would the flagship be defended?"

Opi gulped. Good question. She ransacked her brain. This wasn't anything that Sasha's new software would find in its current primitive state.

"They might shift up to fifteen percent of the defenses to the fuel section, and redistribute the remaining ships. It might leave a gap or three around the command ship, but they would be few and tiny."

Cal spun around to Tony. "Find that gap, Tony. Find it, and plot a course to it, when the time comes.

"First things first. While they're confused by the damage to their scouts, I want you to plot a micro-jump right into the midst of the fuel ships.

"Sasha, don't use the cannon. Use the beam weapons and spray a bunch of them with a short burst, then we'll leap out again."

Sasha frowned. "Brief beam weapon fire won't do much damage."

"I know. We're not trying to cause damage; we're trying to scare them into *thinking* we're attacking the fuel convoy?"

Sasha grinned. "Gotcha."

"We'll go in and out fast, not let any defensive ships get a weapons lock. Stand by to leap out at least ten light-seconds, pause, and let's watch them redirect on our long-range sensors. Then, you find the chink in the flagship's armor."

Tony muttered to himself, then said, "If this works, you're the greatest captain in history. Right, sir?" He glanced at Raj.

Raj said only, "Hope you don't get your team killed, Lieutenant."

Cal managed a grin. "So do I. Opi, am I crazy?"

Opi had been following Cal's thinking in shock. "We'll either get blown to hell or we'll pull off the greatest coup in competition history. Right, sir?"

Raj said, "I guess we're about to find out."

After a moment, Cal said, "Sir, in our original study and sleep indoctrination on The Horde navy, we were told the minimum time that it takes The Horde to respond to an attack, due to their rigid procedures, is about two to three seconds. I've got a lot of simulator experience now, and it looks to me like nearer to five seconds. Can you comment?"

"Good guess, Captain." Raj did something astounding, at least to Opi. "Tony, you can safely give him three and a half seconds. Guaranteed."

The team goggled. Raj had never to their knowledge given them a hint.

"It's no secret," Raj said with a shrug. "You could have asked me any time and I'd have told you."

"Fair enough. Ready, Tony?"

"Sir," Sasha requested, "a one-second burst on the Gatling cannon?"

Cal started to shake his head, and Opi wondered if Cal thought of himself as a patient parent with a child begging for a new toy. He stopped the shake in mid-motion. "Very well, one second. But full beam weapons also."

"Yes, sir."

"Ready, Tony?" Cal asked.

Another "Yes, sir."

Cal called out, "Leap in three, two, one, *now*."

There were ships all around them, most within five to ten kilometers. Several ships lay directly ahead, all fuelers. The cannon rumbled and the beam weapons sang.

"Leaping!" Cal called again.

They leaped again. At ten light-seconds, they had to hold in place, awaiting the light waves that would reveal their attack to reach them. Tony set the main display to visual, max magnification. They watched as a ship embedded in the convoy flashed into a spout of flame, while another began to smoke.

As they watched the double-globe shield form, per Opi's prediction, Tony converted the display to tactical. He highlighted the flagship, and Opi began to study its remaining attack ships. She spotted the chink even before Cal or Tony, or even Letty.

"There!" Opi used the cursor on the display to highlight one area, just as Tony and Letty both pinpointed another.

This time Cal deferred to Opi. "What do you think?"

"Letty's. Nice spot, guys. There at the south end of the display with relation to the screen. An opening, and most of the ships in that area are moving and rearranging."

"Got it," Tony announced. "I can put us in there, sir, and we'll have ten seconds free from any other ship. 'Course, the flagship has its own armament."

"That it does. But at that angle we're behind most of the big stuff. They'll have to bring it around." He highlighted the point. "Coming in from the stern, right?"

"Dead astern, slightly off-axis. You might have five seconds before they return fire."

"You put me right at that point and that'll be more than I need," Sasha assured him.

"Take us in, Tony," Cal said.

Blink. The Horde flagship flashed directly ahead on the display.

The rumble of the cannon announced that Sasha was emptying his ammunition store. The flashes of exhaust tracked the rocket-propelled bombs, following the volley of fire. Their ship had no supernukes for this mission, but the four heavy bombs, a full load, penetrated the hull.

At Cal's order, Tony had plotted another ten light-second micro-leap. Cal triggered the leap and arced their ship around to survey the fleet.

A spot of light erupted on the screen, large even at a distance of more than two million kilometers. Then the display went off and the lights came up.

"Horde flagship destroyed, one hundred attack ships eliminated in the blast, six scout ships destroyed or seriously disabled. Exercise complete."

In a single motion they all turned to Raj.

"No," Raj said. "No team has ever stopped a thousand-ship fleet singlehandedly. You won."

He watched, with a wide smile, as they all hugged each other.

Raj stopped by their table as they wolfed down food. "Three hours until the next match. Meet at the assembly point as usual."

Opi and Tony ate for a full three minutes before they fled to the library, followed shortly by Sasha, who took an outrageous six minutes to satisfy his own appetite.

Cal decided that he couldn't contribute to their frenzy in any useful way, so he sat at the mess hall table with Letty, admiring her dark eyes and enjoying a leisurely meal.

As he munched an apple and contemplated a second plate of what purported to be chicken and noodles, he asked, "What do you miss most since you got here? Other than your parents."

Letty nibbled on cheese and crackers. "Funny, I haven't missed Mom and Dad a lot. Probably because every time I thought of them, I got a sour stomach remembering the fights. Not that I don't love them in my own way, but I don't miss thinking about them."

She scowled. "Or maybe I'd rather think about them in the abstract. They're parents, and they're mine, and they're out there somewhere, and in theory I love them. But bringing up pictures of them just evokes bad memories."

"Okay, what do you miss the most? Other than pizza."

"How do you know I like pizza?"

"Everybody likes pizza."

"True. Okay, I hate to admit this, because I like to think that I'm an independent, strong female without any of the so-called feminine weaknesses. I don't want to have to ask any man to get me something off the top shelf, or lift something for me, or defend my honor, for God's sake. But ... I really miss perfume and eye liner."

Realizing his mouth was open, Cal shut it. "You don't say."

She wrinkled her nose. "Yeah. Disgusting, isn't it? Me, the girl who aspires to be an Amazon. But hell, I'm still a *girl*. Every once in a great while I'd like to wear something frilly and put on a nice fragrance, preferably citrus or rose, but never damask. Mom always overused it. I'd like to go out and wiggle my ass and have some guy stare at me and say, 'Wow, what a hottie!'"

Cal shook his head, feeling that he had just had revealed to him a deep, fundamental truth about the opposite sex. After a moment he ventured, "You've always been a hottie to me."

Letty's sassy, irreverent smile returned. "What, you're hitting on me now?"

"No. Not, that is ... Well, maybe a little. I've always thought you were beautiful."

"Compared to sexpot Ophelia? Little waist, big breasts, creamy skin, beautiful, dark hair that I would kill for. Especially with this mop on my head!"

Cal let the corners of his lips turn up. "Opi's a doll. And I don't think of her as some sweet little thing that's just too feminine for her own good anymore. But you're what every guy wants. Smart, pretty, your own person. I'll bet you had dozens of guys chasing you back home."

"Not really—at least, not that many. Things were so screwed up with my folks that I generally stayed away from guys. I didn't wear much makeup, although I do like to pretty myself up sometimes. But if you stay away from lipstick and stuff, it keeps interest down. I did have one boyfriend, but things got so bad at home that I finally broke it off."

Cal reached across and put his hand on hers. "Hasn't worked in my case."

She withdrew her hand. "Oh, quit it! We haven't got time for romance, and we'll probably end up getting ourselves killed out there if we get into the elite corps."

He regarded her for a moment, realizing that his pulse had accelerated, the hand that had touched hers now damp with perspiration. "But if we weren't here, if we were home, going to the same school, what if I asked you out? You know, go to some new rock group's concert, out for a bite afterward?"

She almost smiled. "Maybe. But don't get your hopes up, Sir. I don't fool around with my commanding officer."

"Geez, I never meant to imply that ..." He stopped, as a grin finally slipped onto her face. "Then if we actually do get home, you might ..."

"We're in different cities back home, you know. But what the hey, if we get back, call me up."

Before he could reply, in rushed the rest of the team.

"Victory!" Opi cried, loud enough to make the few other team members at early lunch turn in surprise. Sasha and Tony both beamed.

"Surely you're not finished," Cal said.

Sasha shook his head. "Of course not." But his tone sounded superior. "We just got to a good stopping place."

"It'll identify Horde tactics ninety percent of the time," Opi crowed. "It's nearly as accurate as me, and a lot faster."

"It's the programming tool," Sasha told Letty and Cal.

"Simple once you learn it. There are rules to follow, like most programming languages, and some structural definitions you have to understand, but once you get the hang of it, things go pretty fast."

"What else do you need to do?"

Opi answered that. "It's not going to be good at defining strategies for complex fleet movements or large numbers of ships. But for most of our test scenarios it should work well."

"And what if we get another thousand-ship test?" Cal had to know the limitations, even though he knew it drove Letty and Opi crazy.

Opi shrugged. "The results will be fuzzier, and I'll have more to do on my own, but I've been doing that anyway. As we continue to work on it, it'll get better."

Tony grinned. "I'll tell you this, Cap'n. This'll help Opi make the right plan. You give me the right plan, and I'll get you close enough to those bastards to shove a rocket bomb right up their—"

"—Nose," Opi interjected.

They all laughed, and Sasha and Tony got trays for their second lunch.

The last exercise, with the new software, Opi's growing experience, and Letty and Cal's improving battle skills, was absurdly simple. They won easily.

And were declared one of the new Shadow Warrior fighting crews.

61 LETTY

The team stood at attention in Lieutenant Raj's office. *He's going to tell us that we need to spend ten hours a day doing exercises until the day we ship out,* Letty thought. Raj had told them that there was no formal graduation celebration. They would just ship out soon to begin flight training.

He interrupted her musing. "Congratulations on your achievement, Genghis Khan. You went undefeated, and achieved the best score ever. Your group of thirty teams will be transported shortly to the carrier training operations, where you will learn to pilot an actual ship. That won't take long, as you already have most of the skills you need."

"Sir," Sasha said. "How soon do we deploy to the fight?"

"You could be on a mission a few weeks after you arrive," Raj said. "You just need to sharpen your skills on a real ship, and then run a few practice missions. After that you will get right into the action."

"When do we ship out, sir?" Cal asked.

"In about seven days. In the meantime, you have six days of

leave at the Sheraton Waikiki on Oahu. Enjoy your stay."

"You're kidding," Letty said without thinking.

"No, Co-pilot Washington. You have two large rooms, one for the young men and one for the ladies, plus clothing for the beach. Enjoy yourselves."

"How're you gonna get us to Hawaii, sir?" Tony's skeptical expression evolved to hopeful. "Never been there."

Raj said, amused. "Surely by now you've realized that we have operatives in any number of places on Earth. How do you think we get familiar food for all our trainees? How do you think we get uniforms? We can't fly back to Molethan for everything while we orbit Earth."

Letty understood for the first time something that she had never even considered until that moment. The training staff had to feed, clothe, and maintain the health of hundreds of teenagers. They had to get all their supplies *somewhere*. It made sense that the Molethians had established settlements on Earth and maintained surreptitious trade channels to obtain needed supplies, including those for their own personnel.

But it just seemed *weird*. Weird to think that this alien race had been living among the inhabitants of Earth for a while, maybe decades. Weird to think that they had monitored, watched, registered, tested, selected. Then she thought, *It shouldn't sound so strange. Some agent, essentially invisible, kidnapped me out from under my parent's noses.*

In a way, Letty still felt uneasy, violated, betrayed. At least she understood the purpose now, and she trusted Raj enough to believe that The Horde posed a real and mortal threat to Earth. Still, for just a moment, she wondered if it would be possible to escape, to get away from Molethian authority.

Then she thought, *And go back to what?* To the same old life, the constant uproar, the petty bickering, the anger and frustration she had felt for the last two years? She laughed out loud, and her teammates looked at her in surprise. Their captors had well and truly snared them. Considering her former life, she knew with stark clarity that she would never go home.

"What's that about?" Cal asked.

Her gaze took them all in. She knew the answer before she asked the question.

"We'll be back on Earth. Any of you want to escape and get away from our 'kidnappers'?"

"Not me!" came from Tony. "Why would I go back?"

"Me neither!" from Sasha.

"And all Daddy's money, what good did it do him?" Opi said. "For all I know, it got him murdered. Here, for the first time in my life, I feel useful. I'm not just a helpless girl that can be pushed around by her stepmother."

"Same for me," Letty told them. "I'm here to stay."

Everyone looked at Cal. Looking flustered, he stuck his hands in his pockets. "I'll stay, at least for now. I've come to realize that nothing I did could have helped my father."

Raj said, "Glad you're not going to run off. But then, we wouldn't send you if we thought that was a problem."

"You have an hour to pack," he said, and told Opi, "No, you can't take a computer or tab. Sometimes you just need to relax."

An hour later, they boarded a small shuttlecraft. Destination: Hawaii.

———

MORNING. Letty took in the ocean and Honolulu beachfront from a tenth-floor balcony, munching fresh pineapple and mango slices, as Cal stepped onto the next-door platform.

"Good morning, Captain. I hope you had a good night."

"Would you knock off that 'captain' crap? I know you're kidding, but I don't want to hear that word for the duration."

"Aye, aye, sir."

Cal threw a piece of pineapple at her. "Don't make me come over there and hurt you."

She thumbed her nose at him. "Ha. Like you could catch me."

He changed the subject. "Want to go swimming?"

Letty considered. "Maybe. But I want to go on a sightseeing tour, see the island. I've never been to Hawaii, and I want to do it right."

"Do we even have any money to pay for a tour?"

"I'll see."

A call to the hotel concierge revealed that they could charge anything to their rooms but alcoholic drinks. Evidently Raj had remembered their ages and wasn't about to allow any funny stuff. Letty had no problem with that, after her experiences with her parents, and she felt sure Cal had the same sentiment.

Two more calls netted the name of a good tour agency, and shortly she and Cal were booked with a private tour guide. Tony and Opi weren't interested, saying they preferred the beach, and Sasha said he'd probably do some swimming as well.

Letty and Cal took in every sight on Oahu that their guide could schedule. An older man, native Hawaiian, dark-skinned and short, in a bright red-and-blue flowered Hawaiian shirt, he had an easy smile.

Later, Letty remembered the day as a series of flash vignettes accompanied by memorable smells and sounds. The roaring surf along the Banzai Pipeline on the North Shore. The fragrance of the tuberose lei that their guide presented to her. The magnificent statue of King Kamehameha at the city center, and the hallowed majesty of the Arizona Memorial at Pearl Harbor.

She liked Pearl Harbor best, especially the Arizona's memorial, a glistening ark floating above the sunken ship, more like a church than a monument to the dead. She stood with Cal in its center, watching small bubbles of oil drift up from the still partially filled tanks of the mammoth, sunken ship. She could make out the circular base of a fourteen-inch cannon turret, although a brisk wind roiled the bay. Like many others, she bought flowers to toss out onto the water. Then she abruptly grabbed Cal's hand and squeezed it.

"What's this?" he asked with a smile.

"Don't take it to mean anything. You just need to hold someone's hand here."

"I'm available."

She squeezed again. "Good."

Blue sky overhead, the sun bright on their heads, and the air cool. Letty felt that she had experienced few such wonderful days before.

When the ferry returned them to shore late in the afternoon, their guide drove them toward the beach hotels of Honolulu.

Turning to Cal, Letty said, "Most of those men died frightful deaths, but at least they're memorialized forever. If we die out there, wherever *there* is, will there be a memorial for us? Will anyone ever know how we trained, what we risked, and how we died?"

Letty could sense the sudden dampening of his good humor when he said, "I doubt it. But perhaps someday, those back here on Earth will be told."

She mentally punched herself. *You dunce. We've had such a great day, and now you cleverly killed the mood.*

Determined to lift his spirits, Letty forced a grin and punched him in the side. "Of course, we have to do something first! Between Opi's smarts, Tony's nav instincts, Sasha's programming and artillery skill, and your aggressive leadership, I'll bet we win some real battles this time."

"Maybe so. With Opi and Tony and Sasha and me being so great, what the hell use are you?" Cal gave her a sly grin.

Mission accomplished. Cal had perked up again. She whacked him smartly on the back of the head. "I'm there to see you don't get too conceited, smartass."

Cal grinned and this time, he grabbed her hand. He held onto it as they strolled back to the hotel.

62 CAL

The phone ringing on his bedside table woke Cal on their fifth day in paradise. He scooped it up reflexively with his right hand, as he rubbed sleep from eyes with his left. "Cal."

"Cal, this is Lieutenant Raj. How're you doing?"

Cal sat bolt upright. "Uh, I'm fine, sir. What's up?"

"The activity we discussed is starting. All I can say over this line. I need you and your co-pilot back here right away. Sorry to cut your leave short by a couple of days."

"No problem, sir."

"How quick can you get dressed and packed?"

"If I shower, half an hour. Ten minutes if you want me to cut it short."

"Shower. Be on the roof helipad in thirty. Don't disturb your teammates. We'll call the others back tomorrow, but you and your co-pilot need to start getting things in place."

"Yes, sir. Letty?"

"I've already called her." The line went dead.

Cal headed to the bathroom, noting that the broad windows

onto the patio revealed Honolulu still cloaked in darkness, bright lights of nearby hotels the only light, as their room faced the Pacific Ocean.

Returning from the bath, a glance at the room clock showed 3:30 AM. Only four hours of sleep. *Oh, well, I slept twelve hours yesterday.* He scratched a brief note to his roommates, leaving them blessedly asleep. "Raj called. We're going back now. You get one more day of leave—enjoy!"

Cal didn't bother to shave. In twenty-five minutes he opened the roof access door and joined Letty, who stood in the middle of a flat, open area away from an equipment house.

"Boy, you're slow," she greeted him. Dressed in shorts and a tight top, with no makeup, her bushy head of hair blew wildly in a stiff breeze that sailed across the roof. Hair askew and with no makeup at all, even in the dim light of the rooftop, she looked absolutely beautiful.

"He called you first, he told me."

Abruptly, Cal crossed to her, wrapped her in his arms, and kissed her firmly on the mouth, a soft, sweet, dizzying moment. When he lifted his head away, she clung to him briefly before she finally stepped back.

"And what the hell was *that* about?" Her eyes had widened and she was breathing hard.

"Because we're going to war, and I wanted to. On the ship we have to be all business, so it was my last chance ... Just so you know, I care about you, and if we ever get a moment away from the war in the future, if we survive, I'm planning to ask you out. Will you go?"

She didn't hesitate. "Yes."

His heart skipped a beat, but he managed to cover it. "Good. Now let's see what Raj wants."

Almost on cue, a black shape silent as death flitted out of the dark sky and settled lightly to the deck. As a door on the side slid open, they crossed to it, threw in their travel bags, and climbed aboard.

If they had expected to see Raj, they were disappointed. A droid pilot greeted them with a vague nod and said brusquely, "Please fasten your restraining devices," in Molethian. As they did so, the ship swooped up with breathtaking acceleration, and shortly they were boarding their training ship.

In Raj's office, he beckoned them to sit in the two chairs before his desk and sized them up. "The vacation has helped. You needed the rest."

"I could have used another four hours' sleep today," Cal said with a grin.

"You can catch up tonight. I needed you here today, and if I was going to have you, I had to collect you before dawn."

With that, he became all business. "The Horde armada invading this arm of our galaxy is one of the largest we have seen on a single mission, and it's begun to move with much greater speed.

"They are less than ten thousand light-years from Earth. At their current speed it will take several months to reach this star system, but they are picking up velocity.

"They are also beginning to bypass suitable worlds for colonization, as though they are searching for established civilizations. Intelligence assesses it is because our harassment and constant sniping have begun to register with their strategic planning functions. They appear to have realized that several races are allying to thwart their advance, and we believe that this realization has irritated them extremely. Thus, they are coming for us."

Letty's face pinched in alarm. "What can we do, Sir? You told us yourself that we can't outgun them! How many ships does the entire Molethian fleet possess?"

Raj grinned. "That's a military secret, of course, but I can say that our entire fleet represents less than ten percent of the oncoming armada. That in itself is probably only a few percent of the total Horde fleet.

"I agree, we cannot win directly. I want to believe they can be slowed or diverted by tactics similar to what we have used in the past. Some of our approaches will have to change, however, as The Horde is finally responding to our strategies.

"Tomorrow we will return your teammates. Combat crews will ship out shortly after that.

"The good news is that I am coming with you. I will be a unit commander in the new fleet. However, by the regulations pertaining to our training, I will not be your commander. I have no idea who that will be. However, I anticipate fighting beside you, as I will be a member of your Shadow Warrior Squadron."

Raj coming with us! Cal couldn't hide a smile. "Great, sir! I would be proud to eventually fight under your command."

Letty looked excited as well.

"Not right away," Raj said. "Now I need your team to gather tomorrow to continue your study of attack strategies.

"Understand, there is a great deal of difference between planning training exercises and doing the same for an actual attack on a Horde task force. However, I hope to talk to your new commander and inform him that Opi and your other teammates have talents that will be of great value to our efforts.

"By the way, your commissions as officers are official. As I'm sure you know, all flight crews are Shadow Warrior officers. Crew members start as under-lieutenants, except for the pilot, who is a lieutenant. Your unit commander is an upper lieutenant, the squadron commander a captain. Any questions?"

Cal and Letty exchanged glances, then Cal said, "No, sir."

"Good. Get situated and recall your crew tomorrow."

"Thank you, sir," they said in unison.

When Opi, Tony, and Sasha returned and learned of their

new rank, they celebrated for a full two minutes. Then they began an exhaustive effort to complete Opi's database and Sasha's planning tool.

Less than forty-eight hours after resuming their duties, they boarded a shuttle for their first duty station.

63 OPI

Inside the cavernous Red Squadron hangar, the ship mechanic, a droid, showed them to their Shadow Warrior ship, a small silver torpedo lined up in a row of ten similar vessels. He told them to call him "Four." He happily gave them a quick look inside the cockpit.

Inside, the cabin closely resembled the simulator in which they had trained. Tony, at the nav station, said, "Cool, just like the one we learned in. Captain, I'm ready to launch."

Cal, at the pilot's station, grinned back. "Me, too. Opi, we need to download your knowledge base and the planning tool. How quick can we get that done?"

Opi almost laughed. Even her teammates had no idea how fast her abilities were growing. "Downloaded when we arrived, sir. Correct, Four?"

The droid nodded. "That is correct, Under Lieutenant Prefontaine. The ship is fully prepared, ready to launch. You are required to check all ship systems and instrumentation, and perform all operational tests that can be completed while docked."

At the gunner station, Sasha asked, "And what's your function, Four? We haven't seen many droids, or IRs before, so what do you do?"

The droid smiled. At least, the lips moved up. Shorter even than Tony, and clad in a Molethian uniform, its features were vaguely Molethian as well. It spoke good English and seemed to be pleased to use the team's language when asked.

"I am your engineer," Four said. "You also have a Seven robot, which is a high-level technician, to assist me in keeping your ship in top running order. Each ship has two droids in the crew.

"With your implants, it has been determined that you can outperform droid personnel in battle. However, for normal, everyday operational maintenance and repair, we are quite capable."

Letty surveyed the cabin. "So, where is this Seven?"

Four gestured to a cabinet beside Tony's console. It was identical to the one inside which Tony had hidden when the team and Raj were trying to catch the cheating Rebel team. So that's what they were for! Opi had always wondered. "In there, until needed. Once you take the ship out, I will join him until you need my services. Hopefully not in combat."

Cal thanked him. "When can we start shakedown?"

"After team meetings. You will meet your new squadron commander today, Captain Nhan."

"Odd Molethian name."

"He's human. Vietnamese, I believe."

Opi's curiosity got the better of her. "Who's our unit commander?"

"That determination has not been made. Only two new sub-commanders have been identified, Lieutenant Rajasekaran and Lieutenant Grall, who is Molethian. Command assignments will be made in the next twenty-four-hour period."

Four obligingly showed them items of interest in the cabin.

There was no trainer's seat, of course, and the cabin was a meter or more deeper. At the rear were a series of cabinets and storage compartments, containing everything from blankets to first-aid supplies, to stimulants for long duty assignments to basic medicines such as headache remedies and disinfectants. There was even a small cleaning mop, which Four indicate was his to use on his frequent cleanups of the ship interior. The rear space included a tiny toilet nook and a miniscule sleeping area, complete with mattress, for long missions.

Another bin held a water supply and some food rations that resembled the chocolate bars that Galigan had first handed out.

Finally, the droid addressed Cal. "Sir, unless you need me, I will retire to my holding area."

"Uh ... Sure. Dismissed."

The droid bowed, turned, and proceeded to a closet beside Tony's station. It stepped into the tight area beside another smaller droid and closed the door.

"Never met a smart machine before," Tony said, amused.

Cal shrugged. "We've seen lots of droids. We've just never had a formal introduction. But then again, I've never piloted a real spaceship before." He consulted Letty. "What's our duty schedule?"

"We have ten more minutes for familiarization, according to my tablet. Then an acting commander will take our unit out for the first time. We'll fly basic maneuvers and some practice sorties for about a week. Once we complete unit qualifications we'll be cleared to go into battle."

Opi had been listening with interest, which suddenly plummeted. "But with no real strategic exercises, there's really nothing for me to do!"

"Guess that's right. I hadn't thought about it." Letty's brow wrinkled. "Sorry, Opi, but we have to get familiar with the ship. None of us wants to go into our first mission without a good feel for how the ship performs, how the instruments and computers work."

"Listen, this mother ship is pretty big," Opi said. "It's bound to have some good computer resources. Is it okay if I skip some of the operational exercises? I can find a computer station and really get some additional work done."

Cal didn't appear enthusiastic. "I don't think so. You need to get used to the actual experience of being on a Shadow Warrior ship. Remember how the artificial G on that shuttle hiccupped and malfunctioned? Raj said Shadow Warrior ships are just fair compared to big ships like our trainer. He told Letty and me that it might take a few days for everyone to get their 'sea legs.'"

Opi couldn't help that her voice went up a few keys. "But there's so much to do! Give me a few days with Sasha's planning tool and I guarantee I'll be five times the planner I am now. If I can get library time, my performance could go up even more."

"Opi, this carrier is a combat ship, not our trainer. I doubt if it even has a library. And you do need time aboard, to get the feel of working with Tony for real."

Opi huffed an exasperated breath. "Okay, okay. I'll make a deal. I'll go on the first five or ten live flights, and if things are going well, let me stay back on the carrier, at least once in a while."

Cal hesitated, but after a moment, Letty said, "That's reasonable. Any improvement on Opi's part gives us an edge on a mission. Right?"

By the end of two intense days of training, the entire team seemed ready to stay back on the ship with Opi. For those first and second days, Raj acted as their unit commander, which made the acclimation exercises more pleasant. But he worked them mercilessly for about sixteen hours at a time.

By the end of the first day they had launched from the warship at least two dozen times, used all thrusters, and Sasha had fired the Gatling gun and blast cannons at several targets. Tony had navigated several leaps, up to a dozen light-years, along with the other nine ships in their unit.

After the second long day, they were familiar with the ship, although the spotty artificial gravity had caused some problems, and Opi felt nauseated until late into the second day.

Both Opi and Sasha lost their lunches during one weightless period the first morning. Four, undisturbed, said that such incidents were not unusual, and cleaned and sanitized the cabin. Four also continued to make adjustments in the artificial gravity generator, and by the end of the second day, he had eliminated the worst of the fluctuations.

Their first launches revealed the enormity of the attack ship carrier that based the Shadow Warrior squadrons. Having arrived on a shuttle with limited viewports, and being too busy to do much but alternate between their quarters and the launch bay, they had no concept of the vessel's size. Seeing it for the first time through the forward viewer, Tony whistled, and the rest joined in a chorus of "Oohs!"

Opi decided that it had to be a kilometer long, and perhaps two hundred meters in diameter. Bays stationed along its cigar-shaped length provided for simultaneous launches of ships from all five squadrons. Each squadron lived in quarters near its own hangar.

Bubble-like turrets scattered along its length containing Gatling guns and blaster cannons. Although it was well-armed, Raj pointed out that the Shadow Warriors provided substantial defense.

If Opi and Letty had thought living conditions aboard the training ship were tough, they now discovered how lucky they had been. The sleeping room for their squadron—the "barracks"—consisted of one enormous bay with fifty beds and five adjacent bathrooms. Opi had read somewhere that naval ship bathrooms on Earth were called "heads," but the Molethian name translated something like "relief space." Whatever they were, they were microscopic sized, making the bath in their training quarters look as luxurious as the one in her room in Hawaii.

Hours were strict, due to the communal living. Lights out at about 1900 standard and back up at 0500 in the morning. The Molethian day was longer and divided into twenty hours, ten before and ten after noon, which was a little over twenty-five on Earth.

Letty didn't seem to let the living conditions bother her, at least not outwardly, but Opi thought she would die of embarrassment when she first stood in line to use the toilet.

Determinedly, Opi stuck it out working with the crew. But every minute she could spare from sleep she spent in the ship library.

64 OPI

The rudimentary library, mainly a series of files on Horde movements and battle scenarios, was freely available, Opi discovered. Carrying her portable memory unit/tablet, she left the barracks early and ate in one of the two mess halls that served the five squadrons. It appeared identical to the one on the training ship, except that there were some vegetable, meats, and odd baked goods that must be Molethian.

Shortly, she began her work at one of three stations in a ten-foot-square library space that was also referred to as the "Data Compartment." Its closeness stirred claustrophobic feelings, but she shook off her nervousness and set to work.

Using Sasha's planning tool, she began to codify the information she'd gathered.

Between the constantly enlarging personal database in her head and the one she had set up as a part of the tool, she recognized after four hours of intensive study that she had discovered no new information.

Further, she had dug back into the oldest records, which

covered many of the Molethians' initial skirmishes with their enemy. Within a day or two she would have reviewed all the available battle records with Horde adversaries from the first encounters more than fifty years ago.

For the first time she began to summarize the various Horde strategies more carefully, adding rules to the planning tool so that as trends showed she would be able to identify an attack strategy more easily.

She also added Horde trends in resupply, force replacement, and rotation. A number of particulars began to stand out, items that she had perhaps registered at some lower cognitive level but never consciously acknowledged. The entire Horde invasion/occupation rationale began to stand out in icy clarity.

First, Horde leap drive was astoundingly inferior to the drive of the Molethians and their allies. Records kept for more than fifty years showed that Horde technology had proven to be relatively static, and leap drive technology, in particular, had not changed over the decades at all. Their leap drive could apparently not travel much more than about ten light-years at a time. Although ships could perform several leaps a day, their engines were very energy inefficient, so that traveling as much as a thousand light-years took days.

Horde armadas moved slowly, swallowing systems and establishing settlement centers in an orderly, but lethargically paced manner. They could afford to move deliberately, scouring a small volume of the galaxy, destroying all civilized races, and securing an area totally before moving on.

In addition, their weapons were quite primitive. They rarely used any sort of explosive material except in bombarding a target planet, and their beam weapons, though relatively high-powered, were simply incapable of penetrating Shadow Warrior vessels except under intense, multiple-ship attacks. Further, they had never responded to the fact that Shadow Warrior ships had projectile weapons that penetrated any sort of force field armor, and most physical armor, with relative ease.

She began to suspect that Horde armies were set in their ways and inflexible simply because they didn't care that some opponents had superior technology. So what if an invasion force suffered 50% casualties in subduing an especially difficult opponent? With their enormous populations and manufacturing facilities, they could quickly replace the losses. And if, as most authorities estimated, total Horde forces were north of five million warships, with a proportional number of supply ships and maintenance hubs, they could easily supply more ships, even with the exaggerated transit time. Galigan had mentioned some of this information early-on, but it had not soaked in to a young girl still struggling over understanding her abduction.

Musing on the reams of data, she had begun to have an inkling of how Shadow Warrior attacks might do more damage in the future. She couldn't say exactly how at present, but the answer bubbled just beneath the surface, and she wouldn't give up until it popped up into the front of her mind.

SHE HAD DONE about all she could do with the available records on her third day in the data room when the door opened briskly and an upper lieutenant stepped inside. Opi gave him a glance, and continued with some last comments in her final file until he said sharply, "Under Lieutenant, you are supposed to come to attention when a superior officer enters a room."

Shocked, she bounced out of her chair. Raj had never demanded this except in more formal situations. "Sorry, sir! I thought you were coming to utilize the data room. I meant no disrespect."

"Hmmph. Your crew has been allowed to relax discipline far too much," he said.

Tall, human, his skin tan and his expression superior, the officer had craggy features, deep blue eyes, blond hair, and ears very close to his head. Quite handsome, actually. He had everything going for him but humility.

"No matter. I will see that you soon are back in the routine of more rigorous discipline. I am Morton Valin, your new unit commander. Now, why aren't you with your crew?"

Her surprise must have shown in her face because his sneering smile widened. "Did you think I wouldn't notice?"

"I'm very sorry, sir." Opi tried to sound contrite, not too successfully. "Lieutenant Rajasekaran gave me explicit permission to be here, as my services were not immediately required. I have been compiling Horde battle data, and with my teammate Sasha, devising a planning tool that will help us develop tactics against The Horde."

His mouth twisted. "Oh, yes, I heard about your little toy. Forget it. You are no longer devising exercise scenarios. My extensive experience will be all we need."

Opi wondered if her head would explode. "Sir, this could give us a real advantage in combat. I would be glad to discuss—"

He cut her off. "Under Lieutenant, I am not interested in your infantile plaything. Now, get to quarters and be ready for your next sortie this afternoon. Is that clear?"

Opi tried valiantly to keep her glower from showing by dipping her head. "Yes sir." Maybe he would take the bowed head for passive compliance. Gathering her personal tablet, she passed by him, head still bowed, and returned to quarters.

J ust relax," Cal said. "It wasn't personal, and after all, you know you're supposed to stand when an officer enters a room."

Opi's face burned apple-cheeked red, and the pupils of her dark eyes had grown so wide that the irises seemed not to exist. "Shh. Keep your voice down," he said. "Do you want word to get back to His Highness that you're critical of him?"

"He's an idiot!" At least Opi lowered her volume enough that it probably wouldn't carry to the nearest crews in their quarters. "He told me that he wasn't interested in my 'toy!' That's what he called it, a *toy!*"

Cal felt his brows rising, but he had to control both himself and Opi. Back when Dad had been sober he had talked about his own military service and the "spit and polish" officers, those interested more in outward appearance than in the performance of their unit.

"Yeah, I met him," Cal said. "Raj took me to meet him. He's just been promoted. Word is that he's a fine fighter, more by gut and guess than plan, and Raj had already warned me about him.

Sorry, I forgot to tell you last night. He's apparently a very competent warrior, but personally something of a jerk."

Letty patted her on the shoulder and pulled her down onto a bunk. "He's the boss and we have to work with him. Maybe when we get to know him, he won't be so bad."

"Remember, nobody believed your planning ability at first," Cal reminded her. "We had to prove it by winning exercises. We just have to prove ourselves to him.

"Someone with as much battle experience as he has probably thinks that's all that counts. We'll have to perform so well that he'll have to admit we know our stuff. Then maybe he'll give us a chance to help in planning." He grabbed Opi's shoulder. "Come on. Not much time for lunch, and then we have a training sortie and briefing this evening."

Opi grumbled, but finally left the barracks with Cal, his arm still around her shoulder. Opi wasn't the flighty butterfly that she had once been, by any means, but she had worked hard to earn respect, and Cal knew it hurt to be marginalized the way that Valin had tossed aside her offer of help.

The exercise turned out to be so simple that Opi wasn't needed at all which, Cal could tell, didn't make Opi feel any better. They leaped to a pre-determined point, turned Sasha loose on a pair of targets with both the projectile gun and blast cannons, jumped to another point and did the same, then proceeded through another six small leaps for gunnery practice.

Cal followed a set leap menu which Tony, obviously bored to tears, had simply copied into their console system. Opi jittered so much that Cal feared she would jump out of her chair.

After the rote sortie, they proceeded to a briefing room for their meeting. Cal had expected a squadron meeting, but there were exactly fifty people, ten teams, in the room. Cal didn't know all the new team members, but he could tell by the fresh faces—

like his own—on a few teams that only a few of the crews were recently graduated.

A number of teams were older, clearly with combat experience, and two teams were another race that Cal and his teammates hadn't seen before. Their short, stocky bodies and almost-albino skin appeared pixie-like compared to the humans. From what Cal overheard, they spoke fluent Molethian.

The teams were talking among each other, and several members made it a point to welcome them. Cal and his teammates made several acquaintances, most of the warriors being quite friendly. One group of grizzled human veterans, looking thirty or more, came over immediately and introduced themselves, shaking hands all round. Cal had to remind himself not to gape as he met these combat veterans. What stories they could tell! He made a vow to try to meet with them and talk to them about what it took to live through what must be dozens of Horde battles.

He tried to get over the shock of not being exclusively with his graduating class, but he understood. Though he had assumed that his class would go into battle together, it made sense to mix untried teams with those that had been through conflict. He assumed that the thirty new teams were distributed among the five squadrons and fifteen units that the carrier ship based—or perhaps were distributed to other carriers as well.

When Valin entered, one crew member called them to attention, but he said after a few seconds, "As you were." Immediately, several of the teams went to welcome him happily, so they must have fought with him and considered him a good leader. *One mark for Upper Lieutenant Valin*, Cal thought.

Quickly the group seated itself, and Valin ascended a podium at the front of the room.

"Greetings to old colleagues and our newer teams," he said, maintaining a formal manner. "I am happy to bring you good news. With the advance of The Horde flotilla, Command has decided to probe their forces. Only our squadron is involved, and Captain Nhan has decided that our unit will make the first contact.

"Only ten ships, but our purpose, as usual, is not to win a victory. We are to simply observe their forces, take an inventory of the size and strength, and report back to command. Understood?"

"Yes, sir!" the experienced teams shouted firmly. Cal and his crew followed suit.

"Very good. Battle plans will be sent to you shortly. Be prepared to leave at zero-five-five-zero, Molethian standard hours. I look forward to fighting with you as we continue our resistance against the invaders. Dismissed."

He stepped from the stand and quickly left the room, stopping only to shake hands with a few of the older warriors.

Cal turned to his team. "You heard him. Let's grab some zees and get up early. I want to be the first team on the launch deck."

66 LETTY

L etty still had trouble sleeping in the open bay quarters. Finally, at Molethan 0400 standard, she rose, showered, and wakened Cal and the others.

Sure enough, they were early to the launch deck, although not first. Two of the experienced teams had arrived just ahead of them.

The launch deck, a cavernous space, reminded her of the storage and maintenance deck of the aircraft carrier they had visited at Pearl Harbor. Except this was white, neat, and crammed with ships, not dusty, vacant and timeworn like the carrier.

The ships, shiny and polished, sat in a long row, each with a separate launch door. Their silver bullet-shapes were fitted with small stabilizing fins on the tail, used for atmospheric maneuvering. Their painted noses gleamed bright red in the light of a thousand large floodlights in the distant overhead.

Deck crews, mostly droids identical to Four accompanied by smaller droids that must be Seven-techs, clustered about the ten ships in launching position, readying them for the first sortie.

The carrier held five squadrons, each identified by a color, and theirs was red. Each unit had a numerical designation, as did each ship, so that each ship was designated by the squadron color, unit number, and ship number. Letty had already memorized the designation of their ship, Ship Seven of Red Squadron Unit One: Red-17, "Red Seventeen," in ship jargon.

The pilot of one team had introduced himself last evening, so Letty made it a point to greet him.

Tall, black, grizzled, age thirty or more, he had introduced himself as Regan. "Up early, I see. Good habit."

Noticing that their unit commander was not in the area, she said, "How do you rate Upper Lieutenant Valin? I know very little about him, but I know he is experienced."

"That he is. He's a gut-hunch commander who gets a feel for the battle and reacts as appropriate. I haven't fought with him, but those who have respect him." His eyes narrowed. "Any problem with him on your part?"

"No, no," she said hastily. "I just saw him for the first time in our briefing. Our trainer, Lieutenant Raj, feels that he's capable. Lieutenant Raj was our trainer for all our training period, so it just seems weird to have a new commander."

"I understand," Regan said. "The familiar is always better. I have fought with Raj, and he is quite a pilot. I think that this is his first unit command, just as it is for Upper Lieutenant Valin."

Just then Valin entered, and Letty impulsively strode over to introduce herself. Dressed in the combat uniform of dark slacks and jacket, he appeared slightly distracted, but replied politely enough. Then he hurried to a position before the flight crews gathered near his ship, the first one in line.

By this time, the last few crewmembers were hurriedly entering, so he motioned them to sit in groups around him and stared pointedly at the latecomers. When all were seated, he began.

"Good morning," Valin said. "We are to scout The Horde

fleet's current position and determine the overall footprint of its force. In other words, we're to nose around and gather data.

"Following our mission, other units in our squadron as well as other squadrons will continue to explore and probe. We may also be assigned missions to explore the composition of the armada, including fighters, escorts, heavy fighter-bomber bombardment ships, fuel and supply boats, and so forth."

Letty knew her surprise showed on her face. All their exercises in training had included only one warship type, capable of bombardment and inter-ship combat as well.

Their unit commander smiled. "I see surprise even among some of our veterans. We know that The Horde is slow to change, but we have discovered that this fleet consists not only of the normal single-purpose ships but also a new model. That's disturbing news.

"Their standard fighting-and-bombardment ship has always performed sluggishly in ship-to-ship conflict with our Shadow Warrior attack units, and they have finally taken steps to improve their defenses, introducing a new fighter that is small, fast, maneuverable, and has larger beam cannons. The good news is that few of the new ships appear to be operational at present, but we must expect more in future encounters.

"Any questions about today's mission?"

On the far side of the seated group, a crew member raised his hand and Valin nodded.

"Sir, when do we get to go kick some Horde butt?"

Clearly pleased at the attitude, Valin said, "Not long, Michael."

It surprised Letty that he knew the crewman's name. Did he know all the crews by name already, or had he known the young man previously?

Valin went on. "We need to know what we're facing. Then we can engage in earnest. In three to five days we will be on full battle footing." Into the following silence, he said, "Okay, get to your ships. When you've cleared the carrier, gather at the first leap point, according to the mission scenario. When we are in range of Horde ships, I will assign specific recon tasks."

The crews jumped, scrambling to their ships. Letty and her crew had the eighth ship in line.

"All stations report in," Cal requested.

They sounded off:

"Nav ready."

"Weapons ready."

"Planning ready."

"Co-pilot ready."

Each Shadow Warrior ship launched directly from its individual bay. At a signal from carrier control, Cal activated the launch bay's door. A mild force field retained atmosphere while they launched. They felt the increasingly familiar hiccup in artificial G as they left the carrier and their own grav unit cut in.

"Ready to leap," Tony said, and Cal triggered the initial jump to the gathering point.

Letty watched Cal, knowing he had experienced discomfort in their first flights, but now he seemed quite at home at the helm.

Over the comm, Valin said, "For our newer crews, Horde ships move slowly, traveling through distinct leap locations, so that an entire fleet is rarely in the same local area in space. However, The Horde fleet occasionally stops completely. Scouts sent out earlier discovered their current location, where the fleet probably exchanges information with their reconnaissance ships and coordinates the next gathering point. While they're stationary, we can survey the column and its composition."

In a few crisp commands, he distributed their observation orders. Leaping to a point light-seconds from the oncoming armada, they made continuous micro-leaps around the massive column of ships, remaining the same distance. As they were never closer than fifty thousand kilometers from The Horde forces, and as their ships were highly stealth-protected, Letty felt confident that the Shadow Warrior ships were never detected. Letty didn't know the details of the stealth cover, but the mechanics were simple. In action, the silver torpedo-shape changed to a black matte, which faded into the background of stars, making each ship quite hard to detect from even kilometers away.

The true numbers of their foe quickly got Letty's attention. Even scanning a small portion of The Horde column, she began to grasp the staggering size of the invasion force approaching Earth. Assuming ships were distributed uniformly down the column, Letty swiftly estimated the total ship count.

"Thousands," she muttered.

"What?" came from Cal.

"The Horde is bringing thousands of ships toward Earth." She repeated the number almost reverently.

"Are you sure?" Tony asked.

"Yes. Conservatively. Maybe tens of thousands."

Back at the initial leap point, Upper Lieutenant Valin's sharp words came over the comm. "Red Unit, Red Lead here. Good work. Recon complete, good data for Command.

"Red Twelve reports four ships heading toward Horde-desirable planet four light-years away. Possible they sent scout ships while they refuel.

"Have informed Command of intent to eliminate enemy scouts. Red Unit, form up and stand by to leap on my order. Acknowledge receipt of leap coordinates."

Letty heard each pilot call in.

With a nod from Tony to confirm he'd received the coordinates, Cal echoed in his turn, "Red Seventeen standing by."

As the last ship reported in, Valin ordered, "Leap now!" and Cal initiated.

Red Seventeen lay half a kilometer from Valin's ship, even closer than Red Twelve. The leap had put them a hundred thousand kilometers from a pale, green planet with only scattered pockets of water large enough to be visible on its surface.

Valin directed them to use telescopic sensors to scan the vicinity of the planet.

Tony activated comms almost instantly. "Lead, Red Seventeen. Visual on all four, transmitting positions."

"Copy," Valin's voice crackled over the radio. Tiny red triangles denoted each Shadow Warrior target on tactical.

There was a moment's silence as the other ships verified acquisition. *Holy crap*, Letty thought. *Our first real mission and we get into a battle.* Cal was hanging on every word from the comm, so she twisted toward Tony and grinned.

Tony, she could see, was so excited that he was literally bounding up and down in his seat, straining the security belts as he moved.

Turning the other way, she could see Sasha equally focused on the weapons console. Only Opi noticed her look, and shot her a brief thumb's up.

Valin's transmission brought her back to her console as he said, "Transmitting target information to unit. All ships, attack per the assigned target. Ships Twelve, Seventeen, Eleven, Ten take the lead."

Letty could see the assignments. All ten craft were involved. The two experienced crews, Ten and Twelve, had a single wingman. Being rookies, their ship, Red Seventeen, and also Red Eleven, each got two backups. *Probably to clean up the mess if we screw up*, Letty thought.

"On my order, leap to within firing range."

"Yes, sir," Cal snapped.

Letty's heart pounded out three seconds before Valin ordered, "Leap."

The order had barely cleared the speaker when Cal triggered the leap engines. Their target lay dead ahead only a few dozen kilometers, and they closed fast.

Cal said, "Fire at will, Sasha."

The Horde vessel probably had detected them, but it had no time to react.

Sasha triggered the projectile cannons. The vibration and noise sounded much more intense than in simulation, and the result shocked Letty. The horde ship shattered, its fuel tanks exploding as they passed within half a kilometer.

They grinned at each other. Their first kill.

Letty tried to feel at least a little sorry for The Horde crew. Intelligent beings who were, like Red Seventeen's crew, simply doing their job. But she couldn't. Those creatures would destroy their ship and Earth without regret.

Good riddance, she thought, wishing it had been a thousand ships rather than just one.

"Good shooting, Red Unit." Valin's call poured like chocolate syrup over the ice cream of their encounter.

"A good day's work. Let's head for home."

67 SASHA

The next two days dragged by for Sasha. He knew that all squadrons had to log hours in space, and Warrior Command needed to analyze every detail about The Horde fleet for coming attacks. Other than a little time in the gym, however, there was not much else to do. He couldn't wait to experience the sheer joy of combat again. Finally, he begged Cal to request more targeting exercise, and Cal, probably as stir-crazy as Sasha, seemed happy to comply.

Sasha thought Valin was a bit pompous, especially for his total lack of understanding of Opi's ability and Sasha's own software creation. However, he was gratified that Valin readily granted the Genghis Khan crew unlimited flight time, and complimented them on their diligence.

Pleased beyond words, Sasha followed his crew to their craft and spent most of the third day in combat scenarios, as Tony navigated them all over the training sector.

Finally even Cal had to give up. "There is such a thing," he told Sasha, "as being over-trained. Let's relax a little."

Sasha had to admit that two eight-hour shifts in their ship might be pushing it a little. "And do what?"

They were all sitting in the mess hall. Opi spoke up. "Maybe we can tour the ship?"

Cal jumped on the idea. "Sounds good. But we probably need permission of Upper Lieutenant Valin."

He left the table to inquire and returned to tell them Valin had no problem with their tour. Together, they left Red Squadron's section of the ship. Wandering along passages and through the other squadron hangars, they began to gain an appreciation for Molethian technology.

The carrier resembled one of the old-fashioned German dirigibles he had seen in a history book, Sasha thought, only ten times as long. Fully a kilometer in length, it was divided into eight sections. At the very front were Red Squadron's hangar and quarters. All squadron sections on the ship were identical, with living and hangar facilities, which included maintenance and repair for the ships with the requisite staff, mainly droids. There were two mess halls, one forward not far from Red Hangar, and another one, they were told, farther aft.

Next came Green Squadron, with identical facilities, then command headquarters and support, including logistics, administrative, and medical, which took perhaps a tenth of the overall length. A very nice Molethian non-commissioned officer welcomed them to the command area and showed them around. Unfortunately, the ship's captain, an upper commander, the young NCO told them, had been in meetings all day, so they didn't get to meet him (nor, thought Sasha, had they expected to).

Blue Squadron followed, then arms and ammunition. Toward the stern of the mighty ship, Brown and Orange Squadrons followed in sequence, the second mess hall between them, and finally, power, engineering, and propulsion.

Touring the ship took half a day, and they lunched that day in the aft mess hall. In the forward mess hall that evening, with their meals finished, they had begun a lively conversation with Regan and the Red Twelve crew when they were joined by Valin. As he approached, he motioned them to keep their seats.

"Recon is completed," he said. "The first attacks begin in the morning with one ten-ship unit from each squadron participating, fifty ships in all. Red One will represent our Squadron. We launch at Molethan six hundred standard. Questions?"

There were none.

When Valin left, they continued their conversation.

Red Twelve had only one woman, a quiet, dark-haired girl named Marta. Sasha thought she was extremely pretty. The men didn't include her in their conversation, so Sasha started talking to her as Cal, Letty, and Regan discussed what to expect tomorrow.

"What's your position?" he asked.

"Navigator. I'm new—the guys have been together for twenty missions or so, and a couple of them have hundreds of sorties, but I'm the rookie. They've been nice about it, but I feel like a little kid around them."

Sasha registered that she indeed looked like a child compared to the rest. She couldn't be more than seventeen, and she looked younger.

"I'm the gunner," he said. "We're all new, so I know how you feel."

Her lips curled in a timid smile. "You may be new, but you got a kill the first day we went out. Nice work."

Sasha felt as though he were in the act of blushing. Marta was slim, with dark hair, hazel eyes, and a mouth that was just plain sexy. Opi was beautiful and a friend, but he had always regarded her—once they became friends—as almost a sister. As he looked into Marta's inquisitive eyes, he discovered that his feelings were distinctly *not* brotherly.

They talked about their duties for a while, but Sasha had a hard time keeping his pulse down and his attention on their assignments. Marta wasn't Opi-beautiful, but she was lithe, athletic-looking, and quite pretty. In half an hour, he had decided firmly that he wanted to spend more time with Marta.

As the crews rose, Sasha suddenly blurted, "After the missions tomorrow, if there's time, can we meet for lunch?"

She had said little, but her expression resolved into a soft smile. "Yes, yes. Thank you, Sasha."

GK's crew was silent as they turned toward their quarters, but Red Twelve's crew sang out, "Marta's got a boyfriend!"

Cal, Tony, Letty, and Opi laughed all the way back to their bay, and even Sasha wore a silly, satisfied grin.

THE NEXT MORNING, at their ship, Cal told the team he had mentioned her planning software and abilities to Valin again, with no response.

Opi remained surprisingly upbeat. "Maybe he'll come around. After all, my experience and our analysis tool are based on simulation. His experience is based on real battles."

Cal still looked upset. "Your experience is with simulators, but your studies were of real battles. He shouldn't discount it so cavalierly."

"Maybe if we have problems tomorrow, he'll be more interested in talking to me later on."

Sasha wasn't sure, and Cal shook his head as well. Sasha headed toward the Red hangar.

The further their commander got into the mission scenario, the faster Sasha's pulse raced. Finally—going to war!

A hundred Horde ships had been sent ahead to scout a planetary system, and they were to destroy the entire sortie if possible.

Valin could certainly orate, giving an energetic speech, but to Sasha, the mission itself was exciting, and he could have done without all the rah-rah. Valin tried to pump everyone up, reminding them that this was the first major encounter with the advancing fleet, and declaring loudly that it was time to send a message to the invaders. Finally, he shooed them to their ships.

As they assumed their stations, Sasha asked Letty, "Are you all inspired now?"

She rolled her eyes. "I miss Raj."

Before he could reply, Cal called for status and they all shouted "Ready!" in turn.

Cal checked comms. "Awaiting signal to launch."

Sasha felt his insides tighten. Their first big test. He took a deep breath and turned to the gunnery console.

68 CAL

"Ships away," came over the comms.

Cal applied thrusters, and they surged toward the leap point.

Opi tapped Cal on the shoulder, her face a study. Her appearance bothered him; she had to be chewing on something.

He tapped her arm. "What's the problem?"

She jumped. "I don't like it."

Letty and Sasha turned to her in unison, Tony still busy setting up coordinates for the jump. "What is it?" Letty asked.

"I've only seen a Horde invasion fleet send out a hundred-ship scouting sortie when they suspect an ambush. Twice they had five hundred more ships in reserve to counter our side's attack, both times with terrible results."

"A real engagement, right?" Cal said. "Not some exercise?"

"Of course. Both battles were decades ago, but they were real, not simulations."

"When we get to the leap point, I'll signal the commander," Cal said.

Opi nodded, still distracted. She returned to her portable,

searching battle scenarios with the fervor that might once have brought a smile to Cal's face. Now it brought a concerned frown. Opi had accrued such vast knowledge about The Horde that if she worried, Cal worried. Period. Eventually Upper Lieutenant Valin would appreciate Opi's value. At least, Cal hoped so.

He asked, "Tony, Raj is unit commander of Green Two, right?"

"Yes, sir."

"Could you contact him on our comms, ship-to-ship, without a general broadcast?"

"Yes, sir," Tony said, seeming surprised. "You can reach any ship directly on narrow comm. It really isn't proper protocol, though."

Cal grinned. "Since when has propriety concerned you?"

"I don't know what that means, but I'll call him."

"Not now. But be prepared."

At the leap point, the five units gathered in groups. Fifty ships ready to attack, fully a quarter of the crews "rookies" like Red Seventeen's.

Valin came on their comms, issuing specific orders. Red One would attack from aft of The Horde group, which totaled more than the one hundred ships Command had anticipated. He directed a standard attack formation. Even Cal, much less knowledgeable than Opi about such things, recognized the deployment structure.

As they made the usual initial leap to a point a few light-seconds from their target, Cal saw Opi frantically analyzing. She didn't look just concentrated; she looked worried.

As they got their bearings, Tony sang out, "Formation sighted, sir. They are about to enter the system where we blasted the four ships last week." He scratched his head. "They are very widely dispersed. It's an unusual spread, approaching the planet.

It stretches back in a cone-shaped formation nearly a thousand kilometers long."

"Makes them harder to engage," Cal observed. "They're also probably looking for their four scouts. Opi?"

She raised her head from the portable. "We're headed into an ambush, sir. They used this exact formation ten years ago and caught two dozen Warrior ships off guard. Only one survived. We're about to be trapped like foxes by the hounds."

Cal got the point. They were preparing to attack; he had to move fast. He called out, "Red Seventeen to unit leader."

A moment later, Valin's voice snapped through their speakers, "Seventeen, Lead here."

"Sir," Cal said, "Our planner's spotted a potential ambush."

They could hear the sneer in Valin's reply. "Seventeen, this is *real war*. Follow my lead, that's an order."

Cal almost screamed in frustration. "Lead, requesting permission to leap with engines hot."

It took precious seconds to generate sufficient leap power. Going in "hot" would mean keeping leap power at maximum.

"Negative, Seventeen," Valin said. "Form up for attack. Lead out." The comms snapped off.

Cal swore under his breath. "Get Raj."

In a few seconds Raj came on line. "Red Seventeen, Green Lead here."

"Sir," Cal almost shouted, "Opi's spotted a trap. Heads up!"

A long silence followed. "Copy, Seventeen."

"Go in engines hot, sir!" Cal persisted. "Warn your ships!"

Another long pause left Cal sweating. Then Raj said, "Roger that, Seventeen. Green Lead out."

Cal blew out a sharp breath. "Everybody hold your breath."

"I hope we're wrong," Opi muttered, "but I don't think so."

They waited in silence, Cal shifting uncomfortably in the pilot's seat as though this were their first training exercise.

Shortly, Valin transmitted the signal to advance. Cal triggered Tony's plotted leap, and a stretch of deep space lay before them. Silver dots scattered across their long-range displays.

They would micro-leap again to begin the attack.

Surveying their targets, the trailing section of the scout column, Cal identified about twenty ships. He and Red Eleven were closest, with the rest of the Red ships spread along the rear of the column.

As the Shadow Warrior ships appeared, Cal counted down, marking their attack points and exchanging target data with his fellow pilots. In seconds, Valin's voice came through their comms, "On my mark. Three, two, one, leap."

Cal initiated.

Directly ahead lay a Horde ship, with two more to port a few kilometers farther away.

Cal said, "Fire at will."

Sasha opened up, and the Gatling cannon rumbled.

Under cover of its racket, Tony said softly, "Jump engines still hot, sir."

The ship ahead disintegrated as they swept past. The other two moved directly ahead as Cal fired thrusters. He could see their blast cannons sparkling to life as Sasha fired again.

One ship exploded as the other fired at them, its weapons a combination of particle beam and laser blast, sparkling red as it crossed the gap to their ship. Their shields glowed red, absorbing the blast, and Sasha continued to fire. Sasha felt no contact from the beam, but the lights dimmed momentarily as the shield generator sucked power to absorb the energy of the blast.

Red Seventeen's projectiles penetrated the skin of the enemy vessel, and the energy beam lit it up. Sasha had already targeted several other more distant ships.

Concentrating on tactical, Letty gasped. "Cal, ships coming

in from six directions! Lot and lots of ships, maybe hundreds! Must have been hidden behind the planet."

Watching the long-range display, Tony yelled, "Holy crap! She's right, sir. Coming in from all over the place."

Cal toggled his comm line. "Red Unit, Red Seventeen! It's an ambush! We're in a trap!"

Valin's angry voice came back. "What trap? What—?" He strangled into sudden silence.

Cal could identify at least twenty ships, the new type, small, fast, and sleek, zeroing in on his own.

"Bringing her about!" he warned the others, and leaned on the directional controls. "Sasha, you've got a straight shot."

Thrusters flared and roared, and the ship swung toward the attackers. Sasha opened up, spraying bullets ahead as the ships came in. This time, Sasha felt buffeting from all the energy blasts as multiple ships began firing.

"Captain, we can't take this beating long!" Sasha yelled. "Our shields are not going to last at this rate."

To port on the forward display, Red Eleven exploded.

Cal knew he was overmanned, and they were within seconds of losing the shields. Abruptly, he decided—and triggered the leap.

Two things happened simultaneously. They leaped, and the ship's shield and power readouts on the status display dropped to zero.

"Where are we?" Cal yelled at Tony. His display showed no ships, only random stars.

"No idea," Tony replied, brow creased. "But we're dead in the water. We're lost, Cal."

69 TONY

Four turned from the leap-engine status display to Cal and Tony. His left hand dangled and an auxiliary plug protruded from the disconnected joint, tying him into the ship network.

"Sir, diagnostics indicate that the shield generator power drain overloaded the fusion reactor. Circuit breakers shut leap power as the leap initiated, before reactor damage could occur."

"How far did we leap?"

"I am not sure, sir, but it couldn't have been very far."

Tony had been listening with one ear as he directed the nav computer to take sightings, and personally analyzed the star fields on the visual display. "Hah!" His voice rang with his satisfaction as he turned to Cal.

"Good news, I hope," Cal said.

"I have our position pinpointed. We're only about three light-seconds, say eight hundred thousand klicks, from our attack point. Plotting a vector back to our carrier will be no sweat."

"Try to contact Red Squadron."

Tony gave him a look. "Are you kidding? Any of our ships

that survived got away—and it's fifty light-years back to the carrier. I wouldn't suggest an SOS call right now—The Horde is the most likely fleet to hear it. You know we don't share many comm frequencies, but they can still detect EM radiation."

"Com isn't available at present," Four told them. "Due to engine failure, only life support and sensors are currently active."

Cal turned back to Four. "What about it? Is there any leap-engine damage?"

"None evident, sir. It's the power generator. You understand that our power source is a small fusion reactor?"

Cal nodded. "We studied it briefly, but I'm not a nuclear engineer. Give me the nuclear-power-for-dummies version."

Four seemed a little confused, so Letty intervened. "Just give us the non-technical explanation."

"Ah. Very well. The power surges due to the simultaneous high levels of leap and shield power caused some automatic circuits to switch off. Those can be reset. However, the fusion reactor overheated even before shutdown.

"You see, the nav computer is programmed to avoid shutting down too soon, which would leave you vulnerable in battle. Thus, it delayed shutdown until just before the reactor would have become critical and destroyed itself. We must let the reactor cool for several hours, then I can send Seven to assess the situation and determine if repair is possible."

"Is there a radiation danger to Seven or to us?"

"Oh, no. Fusion reactors are not like fission reactors. There is very little residual radiation. A bit of secondary radiation is emitted from the container, but it is minimal, and we are well-shielded. Seven himself is completely immune. His circuits are radiation-shielded and his body, which is mainly composites, simply lets the radiation pass through."

Tony had continued to watch both tactical and wide-view optical displays, looking for any sign of surviving Shadow

Warriors. The Horde sortie had disappeared, and all he could see at that extreme range on his optical sensors were clumps of metal —debris. He was afraid that what he saw was the scattered remains of Shadow Warrior ships.

Nothing else showed for several minutes, then the view changed drastically. He knew Opi didn't like him to swear, but Tony couldn't help himself. "Holy Mother Mary!"

That got everyone's attention. "What?" Opi asked, just as Letty, who had also focused on the displays at her station, let out a considerably more colorful epithet.

"Horde ships! Thousands! They just started poppin' out of leap, right where we were fightin' an hour ago," Tony said.

They concentrated on the main display.

Not bothering to wait for an order, Tony started shutting off power circuits to sensor units, leaving on only the computer and display circuits, which utilized very little energy. As he finished, their craft ceased to radiate anything but a trickle of power.

"Good thinking," Cal said. "Will they see us?"

"No chance. At this distance, with all our stealth cover, we're okay." Tony held up a hand and crossed his fingers.

Cal turned back to Four. "As soon as the reactor is cool enough, get Seven in there. We need to get back to Command. Dear God, I hope a few of our ships got away."

Everyone else dipped their heads, either a nod of agreement or a brief prayer for their comrades. Tony wasn't sure which.

Four said, "We can examine the situation in three to six hours, sir."

"Good." Four returned to his closet, and Cal continued, "We can monitor Horde ships passing this leap point while we wait, maybe get an idea of how they operate."

Hours passed, as thousands upon thousands of Horde ships arrived, paused to refuel, and vanished to the next leap destination.

Tony and his crewmates continued to count, though Tony was soon seeing spots before his eyes. It seemed the parade of craft would never end, but eventually it did, and he relaxed a bit.

Shortly after the procession of Horde ships disappeared, more than five hours later, Four emerged from his closet and activated Seven. It was half Four's size and more monkey-like than human or Molethian, designed to explore small engine compartments. Seven didn't speak. It communicated with Four via radio, or with the humans via the ship computer.

After a minute's communication, Seven obediently went to the rear of the small cabin, unscrewed an access cover, and crawled into the innards of the engine space. Tony mentally crossed his fingers and went back to scanning.

Half an hour passed, and Four suddenly straightened and entered the crawlway. He was gone for some time.

Tony, for his part, was totaling up his count of The Horde invasion fleet to compare with Letty, assuming she would want to compare numbers to make sure that their account was as accurate as possible. He knew he had seen easily thousands of ships—far more than even the original survey of Red Unit One had revealed. Not just tens of thousands of ships, but many tens of thousands—perhaps as many as a hundred thousand ships. More than their probing sorties had estimated by a good deal.

Sometime later, flashes appeared on the screen. More ships.

"More traffic!" he yelled, and everyone swung back to the optical displays.

After a moment's scrutiny, Opi said, "Tony, give me max magnification."

He did so. The tiny dots resolved into oblongs. He still couldn't tell anything about the class of the ships, but Opi suddenly crowed, "Those are tankers!"

"Tankers? I don't understand. We've already seen a lot of tankers," Cal said.

Opi brightened. "Yeah, but those were interspersed in groups along the convoy. Don't you get it? These ships are *all* tankers!"

Her crewmates looked blank.

She exhaled an irritated breath. "Geez, you guys really don't get it. Okay, okay, I know I'm the data geek. Listen up: The Horde attack force has passed. Remember, they can only leap about ten light-years or so at a pop. Plus, they use lots of fuel. Our ship could leap half way across the galaxy on our current fuel load, and our carrier ship could hop, skip, and jump over to the Smaller Magellanic Cloud and back if it needed to without refueling.

"Horde ships can't. They have a serviceable leap drive, and it works well enough, so they don't bother to improve it. Since their drives are inefficient, they set up staging points along their deployment routes, where fuel ships gather. As empty supply ships return, full ships gathered there exchange supplies with the returning tankers, which then reverse course and proceed down-stream, to the next designated stop.

"I get it." Cal said. "They constantly shuttle tankers along their route. The shuttling probably goes way back to the nearest permanent Horde center, likely a thousand light-years or more distant."

"Right. More than likely, they establish a stop like this every five to ten leaps, fifty to a hundred light-years or so. I think it is referred to as a Horde 'waypoint'—Shadow Warrior probes have observed this behavior previously. As they progress, they estab-lish more waypoints. A constant flow of supply ships moves back and forth, exchanging fuel and ammo stores. We just spied their newest link."

"Man," Tony said with a grin. "If we were operational right now, we could cause them some serious grief!"

He had thrown Opi a glance; her expression caused him to swivel back. A grimace of concentration twisted her face.

"What?" Tony asked.

"Shut up, Tony let me think. What you just said, there are possibilities here."

He gaped in surprise. Opi almost never said anything rude. Something big must be percolating.

As she buried herself in her thoughts, Four emerged from the engine bay crawlspace, followed by Seven.

"Okay, how bad is it?" Cal asked.

Four looked almost apologetic.

"Not good," Four told him. "The leap engines are fine, no damage there. The fusion reactor shut down appropriately, and it has cooled enough to verify that it is undamaged."

Tony shrugged. "Sounds good so far. What's the problem?"

"The power cables, sir. Twenty-four of them route power from the fusion reactor to the leap engines, and to ship power distribution, life support, and weapons systems. Fifteen are intact, but the rest are damaged."

"What about spares?" Cal asked.

"I'll have to check the exact number, but certainly not fifteen."

"I need to take a gander," Cal said.

Tony stopped him. "Sir, you're the biggest of all of us. Let me go. I'm the smallest guy, and I know enough about the engines to give you a solid report."

Cal made an almost invisible shrug. "Makes sense, Tony, go ahead."

Tony stood and said to Four, "Lead the way."

With a left-handed salute to his crewmates, he grinned and followed Four into the tunnel.

T he crawlway, a narrow, rectangular, metal tunnel, had Tony shivering in short order. It brought back an awful memory, cowering inside a dumpster, as a gang of youths, one of whom he had roughed up in a fistfight, rampaged through his neighborhood, looking for him. He had almost died of fright.

Resolutely, he shoved those memories aside. They were in a fix, but even if he died here, it was better than dumpster diving.

The tunnel ended in an equally tight engine space. Tony barely found room to wriggle out of the crawlway, and he couldn't stand upright. The place where he and Four huddled, maybe a meter and a half square, sat adjacent to a cable tray. A large group of cables connected to the fusion reactor on the right and the leap engines on the left. More cables ran from the reactor up to overhead terminals that connected power to life support and the electrical power grid.

The titanium bulkheads held only a few gauges and controls such as switches and rheostats. Simple touch panels wouldn't work here. Each control had to handle way too much electrical power.

Tony agreed with Four's diagnosis. Several cables had melted in two, mostly the longer ones between the power unit and life support. Apparently, ship power distribution included power to the shields, and shield overload had melted the cables.

Tony counted. Twelve cables destroyed. "How many spares?"

"Ten, sir, all long. The problem is we can restore life support and shields, or engine power, but not both."

"What about restoring engine power and life support?"

"Does not work that way, sir. Ship power conduits go to a central power management unit, which distributes power to life support and shields. When the cables ruptured, power distribution shut down."

"How can that be? We have heat and oxygen."

"There is a battery backup, sir. It is more than half gone."

"Just wonderful. Things keep getting better and better. What about this? Connect life support, charge the batteries, then disconnect and hook up power to the leap engines. We can stay on life support with batteries until we get home."

"Will not work either, sir. Shields activate during a leap, to protect the ship for the fraction of a second we are in non-space. Everything has to be operational or we cannot leap."

Opi wasn't near, so Tony spewed a long and colorful series of profanities.

Four hung his head. "I am terribly sorry, sir."

"Damn it, I'm Tony, not 'sir.' I'm just pissed off that we're in this fix. You know, I had planned on livin' to a ripe old age."

"Dying of anoxia is not too bad," Four observed. "You simply go to sleep. And it will get cold, so that will make it easier."

"Well, thanks for those encouragin' words."

Four hung his head again.

Tony whacked his shoulder. "I'm not mad at you, Four, just pissed in general.

"Hmm. Let's think about living, not dying."

"Yes, sir. That is, yes, Tony."

After studying the situation, Tony said, "What about this? Disconnect the longer, damaged cables. They're so long that even half of one might be enough to reach the leap-engine. How are the terminals on the cables connected?"

"They are welded."

"Do we have a welder?"

"Seven's arm has a rudimentary one. It would probably serve. That's a good idea. It shows how intelligent life has mental abilities that we droids cannot yet mimic. I had not thought about that. Let us see."

Four set about measuring, using a metal tape that unrolled from a small door in his side.

"Tony, it might work," he said after the few minutes. "Four long cables could be shortened and used as connections to the engine. The rest are too damaged or brittle to use. Still, with the long spares, that should be enough.

"We will have to leave life support off a good deal longer as we do the repair and testing. It is going to be close."

"Then get Seven in here and get started."

"Already notified, Tony. Go back to the flight deck to make room for Seven."

Tony obliged. As he climbed out, Seven dived into the tunnel. Turning to his friends and seeing their expectant and worried faces, he said, "I have good news and bad news."

71 OPI

After Tony's explanation, Opi focused fiercely on her discovery of the new The Horde waypoint. *Otherwise, she reflected, she might die of fright. Better to die in a pitched battle,* she thought, *with death so swift the event never even registered.*

Everyone was quiet, trying to ignore the fact that cabin temperature continued to sink. Sasha and Tony, and Letty and Cal held low-voiced discussions, but Opi ignored them and worked on her portable, though its battery had also begun to die.

Finally she shut it off and announced, as bravely as she could, "We need a conference."

The rest looked up at her, surprised.

"I think we might be able to knock out the whole Horde invasion force with maybe a couple thousand ships."

"You're kidding!" Cal said in surprise. More quietly, he followed up, "Of course you're not kidding. Sorry."

"It's okay. Anyway, here goes.

"I start with the assumption that we can get home to our carrier."

"I like that assumption," Tony said brightly.

"Me too. Here's the deal: waypoints are probably scattered over a thousand light-years—maybe several times that—back to the nearest Horde center. The Molethians don't know for sure. In any case, the tanker chain, *all fuel and ammunition*, goes through each waypoint. *Every single bit.*

"You know how the waypoints work; they're like pearls on a string. The farther The Horde invasion fleet progresses, the more pearls, the longer the string. Apparently a new waypoint is established every ten leaps or so, say every hundred light-years. That means that there are dozens, if not hundreds, of these nodes in the chain, *and all the supplies go through every node.*"

"Further, The Horde communicates just like Molethians do, or we do on Earth, for that matter, via electromagnetic waves. That means if there is an ambush here, there is no way to warn the armada that is continuing forward. An ambush here could stop all incoming tankers with their full loads, and also destroy the empties coming back to refuel. Control this point, and we completely shut off their supplies of fuel and ammunition. We could strangle the whole armada. Eventually they would run out of fuel and be stranded."

Cal objected. "When tankers stop showing up, Horde Command will eventually figure something is up, and fighters will be sent back. They won't just sit there and run out of fuel."

"True." Opi smiled, satisfied that for once, nobody was ahead of her. "But they have another problem. Although there are tankers in the convoy, they're continuing forward. By the time they send ships back, they may have traveled so far that the small attack ships can't travel back on a single fuel load. They'll have to send the older, bigger ships, maybe even with a tanker or two. We'd outgun them badly if we kept fifty or more ships at this waypoint, and I'll bet we can handle any return attack. They'll already be short of fuel, so they probably won't send back a huge number of ships."

"Remember, a small number for them is hundreds," Cal said.

"Yeah, but the farther they travel, the harder it will be to reverse course. When they finally decide to retreat, they'll quickly exhaust what fuel they have, and they'll all be stranded. If we do it right, we can end this invasion right here."

"I think you're right," Tony agreed.

The others nodded slowly, as though finally getting the point.

She managed a smile, despite her core of fear. "Of course I'm right. Isn't that why you keep me around?"

Letty leaned over to hug her. "Damn right. Way to go, Opi. Maybe we can convince Command to go with this."

"We couldn't even convince Valin," Cal muttered.

Sasha spoke hesitantly. "That might not be a problem, Cal. He didn't go in hot. His ship is probably debris."

"Dear God, I hope not," Letty said softly. "He was an over-confident jerk, but he had a lot of experience, and even Opi will admit that this move by The Horde was unusual."

That quieted them all.

After a moment, Opi said, almost to herself, "I'm feeling lightheaded."

Sasha nodded. "And it's getting colder."

At that moment, Four came through the opening to the crawl-way. "We are working as fast as we can, but it will be some time before life support and general power distribution cables are reconnected. We will hurry."

"How long?" Cal asked.

"Perhaps forty minutes."

"And how long will we have any oxygen in the cabin?" he persisted.

"Perhaps thirty to thirty-five minutes, at your current rate of consumption."

"Then get back in there," Cal said sharply.

Four scrambled back down the tunnel.

Opi tried her best not to give way to total hysteria. She gulped. "Doesn't sound good."

"I think we can extend the oxygen," Letty declared.

Cal frowned. "How?"

"We're sky-high, worried, hearts pounding. Reduce our metabolism to a minimum, and we use up oh-two more slowly."

"How do we do that?" Sasha asked.

"Medical supplies!" Cal bounded to the supply cabinet. Pawing through vials and bottles, he found automatic syringes and bottles of sedative. Retrieving them, he said, "Here. If we put ourselves under, we lower our metabolism, stretch out the oxygen and prolong it for twice as long as if we were awake. And, if we don't make it, it's an easy way to check out."

The idea of being put under and not waking twisted Opi's insides. She said to Tony, "Tell me we'll wake up."

"Hell yes! And then we're going on a date."

She managed a timid smile. "A date?"

"Unless you say no."

"Yes."

Tony grinned. "Glad that's settled. Okay, let's do this."

Cal decided to administer the shots, using separate auto-injectors and filling each from the sedative bottles, following a printed instruction card. The sedatives were mainly intended for wounded crew members, but Cal figured they would do the job.

Sasha volunteered to go first.

Lying prone on the deck, he scowled as Cal adjusted the injector for the proper dose based on his approximate weight. "Geez, that looks like an awful big shot. Are you sure I'm supposed to get that much?"

Cal frowned as Opi shivered, in complete agreement with Sasha. "You weigh one sixty-five, right?" Cal prodded.

"Yeah, about that. I don't weigh every day—the last time I weighed was in gym back on Earth." His scowl deepened. "God, I hate needles."

Opi agreed a thousand percent.

"Not really a needle," Cal said. "Sort of a jet-injector."

Sasha frowned but finally said, "I guess that's a bit better."

Opi watched as Cal bent over. "Ready?" he asked.

"Hell yes, let's get it over."

Sasha grimaced as the injector was attached. Cal pressed the trigger.

"Odd," Sasha said. "Didn't feel a prick or ..." And he was out.

"I'm next," Opi announced. "Like Sasha, I want to get it over with."

"I'll go next," Tony said quickly.

She shook her head. "No, Tony, I want you holding my hand when I slip away."

Opi lay down beside Sasha, patting his side, smoothing his hair. Tony was the one that made her all tingly to be with, but Sasha had become very dear. "Good night, Sasha," she told the form. "Here's hoping we wake up soon."

As Cal attached the injector, Tony moved beside her, took her right hand in his, put his other hand on her shoulder. "See you in a couple hours. Then we can talk about that date."

She grinned at that. As consciousness faded, she thought, *I hope I get to help stop The Horde. It's one great thing I can do.*

Then darkness settled over her.

As Tony settled into sleep, Cal turned to Letty.

"I can myself give a shot," she told him.

"So can I. Don't worry, I can get the shot done before I pass out."

He prepared the injection as she lay down beside Opi. He bent over her with the syringe. Hesitating, he said, "Looks like Tony and Opi have a thing going."

"Yeah."

"And you know I'm falling in love with you."

She smiled up at him. "I figured."

He leaned down, letting his lips touch hers, lingering, putting his free hand on her shoulder.

After a moment, he leaned back and said, "With everybody else out, if it didn't use so much oxygen I'd suggest more than just kissing."

An impish look crossed her face. "And if we had that oh-two, I might say yes."

"So I have a chance with you?"

"You know you do. Now give me the damn shot before I can't help myself. And kiss me again, so it's the last thing I remember."

As he gave the shot, he bent over and they kissed. Cal could feel her reaction, a surge of emotion transmitted through her lips. Gradually her mouth relaxed, and when he sat up, she was asleep.

He prepared his own shot, swabbed his arm, found the most prominent vein. Lying down beside Letty, he held up his left arm, attached the injection unit with his right.

He barely had enough time to put down the injector and grab Letty's hand before consciousness fled.

Hurry," Four said to himself.

The humans, his charges, were now unconscious, and the ship grew incrementally colder. The temperature still lingered at about absolute (Molethian measure) four eighty-six. He calculated that it corresponded to approximately ten degrees Centigrade. Not dangerous to the humans over an hour or so, but already uncomfortable.

Leaving his cable-connection task for a moment as Seven welded terminals on the re-conditioned wires, he crawled into the cabin. He pulled two large blankets from the equipment storage bin, and spread them gently over the silent forms.

Back with Seven, he had to restrain himself from urging the other droid to increase his speed. After all, logic told him that each terminal weld had to be strong and carefully tested.

As Seven completed the shorter cables, Four connected the longer cables between the fusion generator and life support. Adroit as Four's actions were, it took a long time. He worked, feeling as frantic as a droid could. He had rudimentary emotions, but mainly he felt a strong sense of duty to his charges.

Finally, with the last cable connected to ship power and shields, he left the rest of the cable modification and connection to the leap engines for Seven to finish.

Crawling through the tunnel, he returned to the pilot console, activated the fusion reactor, and brought up life support and control systems. When the displays sprang to life, he transmitted boot signals to the main system.

He estimated that the temperature had fallen to below zero Centigrade. He checked each of his charges carefully, using built-in diagnostics. Their bodies were cold, but each heart still beat faintly, and he began to hear deeper breathing as the temperature slowly increased and the hiss of air flowing through ventilation ducts could be heard.

"Thank God they are all right." He had picked up the saying from humans, determined to sound as much like his organic counterparts as possible.

Four had no way to determine how long his crew would be unconscious, but he had infinite patience. Sitting in the pilot's chair, he waited, motionless, as the crew's color improved.

In an hour, Seven reported that the rest of the cables were repaired, and Four brought up leap power.

Four hours later, his charges began to stir.

The display pinged as Sasha and Opi both woke, still groggy.

Four saw three red objects highlighted on tactical. Turning to the pilot console, he activated visual. Three ships appeared on the main display approaching Red Seventeen, still a hundred thousand kilometers away.

"Oh, my," he said.

They were definitely Horde ships.

74 CAL

Consciousness flirted with Cal's brain. Light, darkness, light, darkness. Tony's face swam into view. As consciousness solidified, Tony jerked him into a sitting position. Four knelt beside Tony, a concerned look twisting his features.

"Do you understand me, Captain?"

"Barely." Cal shook his head. "So ... we made it?"

"Yeah. I know you'd like to take a nap. So would I. Trouble is, we got bad news approaching."

Cal struggled to his feet and stumbled to the pilot console, scanning the display.

Letty vacated it, giving him a serious, tired look. "How're you doing?" She looked as loopy as Cal felt.

"Feel like I've been on a bender, except I don't drink." Sinking gratefully into his chair, he slurred, "Stations."

At gunnery, Sasha said, "Get ready to attack, sir?"

Cal shook his head.

Four had retreated to a position near his cabinet. Seven wasn't in view, probably already secured.

"Good work, Four," Cal said. "I guarantee you'll get a commendation. Are we hot?"

"Four had engines primed when I came to," Tony told him.

"Have they detected us?"

"Don't know. Probably. They're headed in our direction. But they can't tell much yet. I think I could micro-leap within a klick and we could blast 'em. They're old-style ships, slow and unwieldy. With the element of surprise, I think we won't have any trouble."

"Or we can run," Letty suggested. "Let them be. We have a lot of knowledge and Command needs it. I say leap. They'll see a leap signature, but they're too far away to see us very clearly. Maybe they'll think it's one of their own."

"Doesn't matter," Opi said. "We have to get home. We urgently need to talk to the carrier commander."

Cal grinned. "Yes, we do. At least, you do." A knife of pain slid behind his eyeballs, replacing the grin with a grimace. "Tony, course locked in?" He rubbed at his eyes with one hand. "Dear God, does everybody have the mother of all headaches?"

"Yes, dear," Letty said, and patted his shoulder.

Cal wasn't sure she knew what she had just said. While he pondered this, Tony said, "Course set, sir."

His head hurt too badly even to nod acknowledgment. Cal simply triggered the leap.

TO THEIR SURPRISE, a rowdy crowd of warriors treated Red Seventeen's crew like conquering heroes when they set foot in the hangar. Only one other Red ship stood in the hangar, Red Twelve.

Raj greeted them as they disembarked, and Captain Nhan, their squadron commander, stood beside him. Their Red Twelve crewmates clustered around the commander, each coming forward to hug the girls, pounding on the guys' backs with a continuous series of whoops, while many other Red Squadron crews came forward as well. Marta was there to give Sasha a warm embrace.

Captain Nhan's aide conducted them to a special conference room near the squadron command office, but Upper Lieutenant Rajasekaran accompanied them. Captain Nhan took the chair at the head of the table.

The conference room was as bland and uncomfortable as those Cal remembered on the training ship, but at least a side table held coffee. Everyone, including Opi, took large cups.

"Pardon the goofiness, sir," Cal said. "We ran out of air while our droids repaired our power cables, so we sedated ourselves to save oxygen. We've been conscious less than an hour."

Nhan frowned. "Do you need more time to recuperate?"

"We can't spare it, sir. We believe we have information that can change the balance of power for us, perhaps let us defeat the entire Horde invasion fleet."

Cal wasn't surprised at the captain's raised brows. "First, sir, I need to report about our mission."

"Later, Lieutenant." The captain gestured toward Raj. "Your former training leader gave us the whole story. Allow me to fill you in on the parts you probably are not aware of.

"Because of your warning to Upper Lieutenant Rajasekaran, he and his unit also went in hot. As a result, they all survived. That's the good news.

"The bad news is that we lost thirty-eight of the fifty ships, the Orange, Blue, and Brown units, and all Red but you and Twelve. A terrible loss, including your commander. The units that survived only did so because of your message.

"Now, what happened after the attack and your separation from the battle scene?"

Cal recounted their actions up to their return, with frequent questions from a handful of intelligence personnel. The rest of his crew offered additional details along the way. Cal made certain to give Four a solid commendation.

"I'm sorry we weren't able to save more crews, sir," Cal concluded. "Confronted by twenty ships, with hundreds more approaching and several Red ships destroyed by then, it seemed smarter to save our crew."

Nhan didn't appear disappointed. "You did well, son. You came back with valuable information. Please proceed."

Cal put his hand on Opi's shoulder. "Sir, our mission planner must tell you the rest. But first, she needs to give you some very important background."

Opi began hesitantly, but she gathered speed. She described her research during training, the hours spent analyzing every Horde battle recorded in the library, making a database, Tony's support and assistance, Sasha's work putting together the planning software, Letty's extraordinary coordination, and finally Cal's encouragement and leadership.

Nhan commented, "Sounds like you're pretty proud of your crew, Under Lieutenant."

"I am, sir. They're the greatest." She looked, embarrassed, at Raj. "Sorry, sir. I know you have a fine unit, but our crew is just the best."

Raj smiled. "She may be right, sir. I have a top-notch group of warriors, but this team has been extraordinary from the beginning. They started as five individuals that didn't even like one another, but they quickly became a close family."

Opi beamed. "Absolutely. I love them all. We all love each other."

She returned to her narrative. By the time she finished, Captain Nhan had evolved from astounded to credulous acceptance. "Well done, Under Lieutenant. This information needs to be acted upon, and risking a substantial number of our ships may indeed be warranted." He swung toward Raj. "Any comments, Upper Lieutenant?"

Raj dipped his head. "Yes, sir. Listen to Lieutenant McGregor. He briefly described a plan to me on the way here."

Nhan shifted to Cal, and he began.

"Sir, the fuel and supply waypoint is an important discovery. We knew The Horde fleets stopped periodically, but so far as we know, no one has ever pinpointed the periodic stoppage they make to do whatever it is they do—refuel, maintenance, whatever. We suggest stationing two groups of ships near that point, one to intercept empty ships returning from downstream, and another to destroy incoming ships from upstream.

"It's important that we not let a single ship escape in either direction. If we keep intercepting them, we can destroy hundreds, perhaps thousands of tankers. By the time the invasion fleet figures out that supplies aren't arriving, our hope is that their fuel stores will be decreased quite a bit."

"But surely," Nhan said, "their mission leadership will soon send recon ships back to investigate. For them, a small recon might be anywhere from a dozen to a hundred ships."

"Yes, sir. But we believe they'll be running out of fuel by then, so perhaps their recon sorties will be small and manageable. We also may have a way to inflict even more damage."

Nhan frowned. "How so?"

"Sir, we know the direction they're traveling away from the waypoint, and the direction from which they're approaching the waypoint." Cal said, "What I recommend is to move the flagship near the waypoint, perhaps a quarter of a light-year away. Constantly rotate our attack ships to the waypoint, keeping fifty or so there at all times to inflict maximum damage.

"Then send one unit back along their travel vector. We know they jump about ten light-years at a time. Find the next upstream waypoint—it can be identified by The Horde ships waiting there —and station our ships there as well, to intercept arriving tankers. We may have to search as many as nine hundred trillion kilometers looking, but since we know how they travel, we may be able to cut the search time considerably.

"If The Horde sends back a substantial number of attack ships, you can move our carrier back to the next upstream waypoint. We keep intercepting tankers until at some point we know the invasion force is getting very low on fuel. Then we start sniping, hit-and-run attacks at the main fleet, targeting the supply ships at first, just what we do best. If we play it right, there'll be ninety thousand combat ships that we can pick off at our leisure.

"With our fuel and ammunition reserves," Cal summarized, "our carrier and remaining warrior ships can continue to move upstream, waypoint to waypoint. Eventually, we'll be upstream far enough that they can't follow because of their supply limitations. Once we have their invasion force isolated, our carrier ships and attack fleets can start to demolish the remaining ships in The Horde fleet. I think—Opi thinks, and I agree—that this is the chance we've been hunting, a chance to destroy them completely."

Nhan took a deep breath and included all of them with a sweeping gaze. "Upper Lieutenant Rajasekaran, your thoughts."

"The plan is typical of Under Lieutenant Prefontaine and her crew. I know you need to confer with Upper Commander T'Kell and her staff, but I recommend that we proceed as Lieutenant McGregor proposed. We have a chance to eliminate The Horde fleet. This could mean total victory."

Nhan gave a curt nod, rose from his chair. "Very well. Lieutenant," he addressed Cal, "you and your team will report to sick bay, get checked out, and get some food and rest."

"Raj." It was the first time Cal had heard a command officer use a nickname. He and Raj must be good friends. "We need a new commander for Red One. Any suggestions?" He smiled as he asked his question.

Raj returned it. "Yes, sir," he said. "I recommend Lieutenant McGregor for acting commander, moving into the Red Ten position. The Red Twelve pilot is experienced, but I think Cal deserves the shot. As for the Red Twelve team, I recommend that you offer them to Orange Squadron's commander for their vacant unit command."

"Yes," Nhan said, "except Brown Squadron has requested him as the Brown One leader. Either way, surviving Red crews get a chance at command."

Nhan came around his desk, offering his hand to Opi. "Congratulations, Under Lieutenant. Your work may well save your race." He turned to Cal for another handshake. "Lead well and carefully, Lieutenant. Now you have responsibility for nine more teams. Good luck."

Outside Captain Nhan's office, all of them exchanged hugs and handshakes with each other and Raj. Then Cal and his crew made their way to sickbay.

Before he drifted off in his hospital bed, Cal leaned over toward Letty's. "Back when I put you to sleep, I wasn't kidding," he whispered. "If we win this war, I'm proposing. Be ready."

"Are you nuts?" Her hoarse whisper sounded scandalized. "We've only had a couple of kisses. We've never made love. You might hate being married to me."

"No chance, Under Lieutenant. You're mine, unless you totally turn me down."

She turned her head toward him. The expression on her face wasn't her usual, sardonic smile. "Probably won't."

Cal went to sleep smiling as well.

Two days later, Cal stood by Red Ten, the rest of his crew beside him, as the crews of Red Eleven through Nineteen gathered around, a complete new set of crews for Red One. Several were experienced crews from other units, though there were three rookie teams as well.

Cal tried not to show his nervousness visibly, though his palms were damp and sweat trickled down his back. Addressing his new unit seemed distinctly harder than a firefight with The Horde.

He knew he had to inspire his group, but he also knew that Valin's rah-rah approach wasn't for him. As the crews quieted down, he simply began to tell them, in a very low-key way, about their assignment. Eventually, he raised his voice a bit.

"We have an opportunity like no other Shadow Warrior teams in history. Always before we've sniped, hit and retreated, trying to be like shadows as we attack The Horde forces.

"Not this time. Now we're going for the gut. Our aim is to destroy the entire Horde armada."

He went on to explain what they would be doing, how they

would be able, if successful, to render the majority of The Horde fleet vulnerable to attack.

Many of those before him nodded and grinned, buoyed to be in on such an amazing opportunity.

A few, however, were clearly skeptical. As he finished, one pilot, old enough to be experienced as a fighter and five or six years Cal's senior, challenged him.

"Upper Lieutenant McGregor—"

Cal cut him off. "Just lieutenant, Marco, same as you."

Cal had immediately memorized the names of all crewmembers reporting to him, as well as going through their service records thoroughly. He might not know them all personally yet, but he knew a bit about each one. He smiled. "And this is an informal briefing. Call me Cal."

Marco seemed taken aback, both that Cal knew his name and that he didn't stand on ceremony. A little of the sarcasm in his voice drained away.

"Okay, uh, Cal. I mean, the plan sounds fine, and it'll be great if it works, but why have you been made our unit leader? Aren't you a rookie? How many battles have you been in?"

Cal grinned. "Exactly two, Marco, and I got my ass kicked in the second one."

Everybody laughed, even Marco. He was the pilot of the new Red Sixteen team. "Okay, I still gotta ask," he said. "What makes Command think a rookie makes a good unit leader?"

"I'll tell you why, Marco. Because I not only want to win, but I want to bring every single ship in Red One back. If winning means we have to sacrifice a few ships and crews, I won't do it stupidly. It's like what General Patton said in World War II. I don't want you to give your life for Earth, I want you to make the dumb bastard in that Horde ship give his life instead. I'll take you out and I'll plan on bringing you back.

"Besides that, I have the best planner in the Alliance." He

pointed to Opi. "She's working with Ops Planning to give us mission plans that will make us victorious in every battle and give us the best odds of making it to the *next* battle. Is that a good enough reason?"

Marco grinned. Short and dark, with a round face and a jaunty manner, he said, "Yeah, that might work."

"Good. You have your individual missions and our orders within the overall attack scenario. We are only to attack Horde tankers in the upstream sector of the waypoint, that is, ships bringing fuel from The Horde main base. Other units will have a reception for empty tankers returning from the current Horde fleet location.

"Our unit is one of five tasked to destroy all incoming ships. The most important point is, you *cannot* let a single ship leap back toward The Horde hub. As long as we prevent any ship from getting away, we prevent any indication to The Horde base that they have a problem, at least, for a while.

"Any questions?"

This time the crews remained silent. Opi didn't know if Cal had convinced Marco completely, but she noticed some respectful glances cast Cal's way.

"Okay," he said, "see you at the waypoint."

He and the other crew members quickly boarded their ship. Before he could seat himself, Opi crushed him in a hug. "You're wonderful. Cal, I'm so proud."

"Good speech." Sasha shook his hand. "Want a hug from me too?"

Cal whacked his shoulder.

76 SASHA

Sasha yawned. Two days now on station and not an enemy sighted. Realistically, he knew that the wait was not yet unreasonable. The Horde supply chain was not a continuous link, but a periodic activity, as groups of ships met at way points and transferred supplies. And just as Red One at the upstream end of the waypoint had not reported an encounter, neither had Brown Two, at the downstream location. As a result, both units were, Sasha figured, getting wound up as tight as a coiled spring. In his two battles to date, the excitement, chaos, and fierce crossfire of war had not bothered him at all. The waiting, however, was enough to make him crazy.

"Come on," he grumbled, "Let's get it on! We know you're out there. How about showing up so I can exercise the guns?"

Letty, in the co-pilot chair, faced away from Sasha, but she said soothingly, "Patience, Grasshopper. Your time of combat will come."

His head whipped around. "Grasshopper? What the hell does that mean?"

She waved a hand behind her back vaguely. "Forget it. Old

TV show I saw in reruns. Cal, how much longer 'til Red One rotates back?"

Cal had been conferring with Tony on Opi's latest attack scenario. She was apparently concerned that fuel ship convoys might have some of the new Horde fighter craft as escorts. Cal had argued that the new ships seemed in such short supply that they wouldn't waste them on escort duty. Sasha didn't have an opinion, but he had to admit that he was itching to take on one of the new fighters one-on-one.

It was Letty's turn to monitor the tactical display. They weren't right at the waypoint, lying about half a million kilometers off, keeping watch with the rest of Red One. Just as the display flickered, Red Fourteen sang over the comm, "Red Fourteen to Lead. Activity spotted at target site."

Sasha swung to his console as Cal returned to his seat, checking the display and switching to long-range visual. "Roger, Fourteen." Cal replied. "All ships, prepare to leap on my mark."

As Sasha watched, more and more of the fuel ships came into view. The escort ships were smaller, but even at that range, they looked like the standard Horde fighter/bomber.

Cal didn't attack at once. They needed to warm leap engines, but Cal also wanted to get a substantial cluster of ships—a target-rich environment—before he gave the word. Sasha waited almost breathlessly as the count went on. In thirty seconds, more than forty ships had appeared, mere dots on the tactical screen.

Cal gave the word. "Three, two, one, leap!"

Blink. A display full of ships stretched before them. Cal aimed at the rear of the group, his self-assigned part of the column. Five fuelers and three escort ships lay almost in a line before them. Their residual velocity was substantial, but Cal accelerated anyway.

"Gunner, fire at will." Cal hadn't finished the words before the Gatling cannon began to growl and vibrate. Sasha aimed and fired beam weapons as well, shattering one escort, but concentrating mainly on fuel ships. As Cal used thrusters to bank away in a hard turn to starboard, Sasha saw one fuel ship dissolve in flame, but several escort ships angled toward them. Before they could fire, Cal leaped again, and turned as quickly as possible to view the battle, now some half million kilometers away.

Sasha checked his ammo and beam weapon energy, as he knew they would only hesitate a moment. Sure enough, Cal said, "Leaping again," and they were back in the fray. At least half the fuel ships were destroyed, the rest no doubt frantically trying to power up for a leap.

Cal came in hard and fast, giving Sasha two more easy fueler targets, and the Gatling cannons roared. Fewer of the fighters were left to confront them, and as one vectored in from above to hit Red Ten with a heavy beam weapon barrage, Cal pulled up and Sasha let him have it with a Gatling volley. It exploded, as lights dimmed and the console told them, "Beam weapon fire intercepted. Shield power below optimum by forty percent."

Sasha frowned. That was lower than he would have preferred, but at least they had some shield power in reserve. Checking ammo again, he saw that cannon shells were nearly gone, although beam weapons were more than seventy percent charged.

"Good going," Cal tossed the attaboy back as he slowly brought the ship in a half-circle. "Red Ten to all ships. Report status as soon as possible."

Some of their unit, Sasha could see from the display, were still heavily engaged. Near Red Ten, only debris remained.

Some of the ships began to report in. Near the center of the conflict, two Red ships appeared to be beset by a number of Horde fighters. Cal accelerated and they swept toward the heaviest battles, as Sasha could see several other Red ships from the far end of The Horde column, their targets pacified, turning as well.

Directly ahead, four fighters engaged a Shadow Warrior ship, but Sasha couldn't identify which one. "Let's help him out," Cal said, lining up one of the enemy ships.

Sasha emptied the Gatling cannon at the ship, which shortly ceased to exist. As Cal came around, Sasha let another ship have a full beam weapon blast. The Horde ship shield held until Sasha thought for sure that they would ram it. Just as Cal swerved to port, an engine began to smoke on The Horde vessel. Abruptly it exploded.

"Good going, Sasha," Cal said. "Weapons status?" *

"Nearly depleted," Sasha replied. "No cannon ammo, beam power down to thirty percent."

Opi had been monitoring on Tony's forward display. "Sasha got an engine, but the whole ship went up. That's odd."

"No," Letty said. "With that damaged engine, they could never leap. I think they self-destructed. You know they don't like to surrender."

True, Sasha though, searching tactical for additional targets. He didn't see any. "Looks like we cleaned 'em up, Captain."

"So it does. How many in the convoy?"

The console replied. "Thirty fuel ships encountered, an additional twenty escort fighters. All targets accounted for."

Sasha checked shield status and took another count on the forward visual. Yes, the console computer had said the targets were pacified, but he wanted to be sure. As he did that, Cal was already on the comms.

"Red ships report."

"Red Eleven aye. No damage."

"Red Twelve, aye ..."

All ships reported in. Red Eighteen had minimal damage,

and Red Nineteen reported a minor hull breach, repaired by automated sealer. All in all, a full success.

Cal dispatched Red Eleven immediately to request an early rotation. He didn't expect another Horde supply convoy to appear immediately, but clearly Red One couldn't fight another major battle without resupply.

Sasha glanced around at Opi, who was still watching the forward view. "Congratulation, Under Lieutenant Prefontaine. Everything went according to plan."

Letty turned and gave Opi a pat, smiling at Sasha. "Right. Opi, you covered yourself with glory on this one."

Opi didn't smile back. "I haven't done anything yet. Get back to me in a month. If The Horde is a hundred thousand ships short of a full tally, then I might brag a little."

Cal turned to join Letty. "Amen to that. Raj told me that they've started serving ice cream in the mess hall. Shakes are on me."

Over a thousand ships. Opi could scarcely believe it.

They had taken their turns on station for three standard weeks, and not a ship had managed to escape Red One and its fellows.

As the fuel ships had very little defensive capability, it had been like target practice. Enough Horde tankers had been destroyed that great clumps of debris were circulating in the area, and they were beginning to have to maneuver quite carefully to avoid damage to their own ships.

Another carrier had arrived nearby, and now more than four hundred Shadow Warrior fighters were engaged in battle. A separate cleanup crew, essentially tugboats piloted by droids, captured debris and vectored it toward the nearest solar system's sun.

Opi's strategy had worked beautifully, and she was so happy she glowed. Back at the carrier, she bubbled over with conversation, and she had hugged all four of her crew as they docked and left the ship.

The comms alert pinged, and Captain Nhan appeared on the display. "Red One, Two, and Three. Orange Two reports finding next waypoint. Have destroyed all enemy ships in vicinity. Prepare for leap to new coordinates. Acknowledge receipt."

Numeric groups began to flash onto Tony's data display. "Coordinates received, sir," he said.

"No Horde combat ships returned," Nhan continued. "Number of waypoints downstream to Horde position unknown. Expect opposition. Wait two hours, then rendezvous with Orange Two at waypoint. Carrier will follow. Nhan out."

"Do you realize what finding their next upstream waypoint means?" Opi crowed. "It's another hundred light-years of separation between The Horde invasion forces and their supplies. If we can find one or two more waypoints, we'll have them!"

"I think we have them now," Sasha said. "They still react too slowly, move too slowly, attack too slowly. Remember, they're continuing to move forward. Pretty soon, there will be too many waypoints between their invasion fleet and fuel."

"I hope you're right," Cal told him. Before he could say anything else, a text message came through on his comms console, and he stared at it. "Well. The third carrier has located the main Horde armada, still over a hundred thousand ships. They are starting hit and run attacks on supply ships. We're hitting them on both ends, which means we have a good chance of bottling them up once and for all."

They proceeded to the next waypoint, continuing to destroy fuel ships moving toward the current fleet position.

After another week, having eliminated more than four thousand tankers, they were recalled to their carrier as new Shadow Warrior units were deployed.

Opi had noticed that over the last two standard days, supply traffic had declined appreciably. Opi estimated that Horde invasion ships were now separated from their nearest fuel waypoint by several hundred light-years. At roughly ten light-years per leap, fuel supplies were nearing out-of-reach status.

They were in the mess hall, consuming their first decent meal of the day. Due to the late hour, the mess hall was relatively quiet and vacant.

Sasha asked, "You think we can get a few days off? I'd like to hit the sack for a day. Even in the barracks, I think I could sleep the whole time."

On their ship, they had sometimes taken turns sleeping on the deck during long periods of inactivity. They also smelled fairly rank as well, as during their rotation back to the carrier, they often had time only for one decent meal and a few hours in the rack.

"It would be nice to get a bit of leave," she agreed. "What about it, Commander, do we get time off?"

"I don't," Cal said sourly. "The responsibilities of command are sinking in. I have enough paperwork to keep me busy for a week. Do you know that I have to account for ammunition expended? Fuel used? Damage to ships? And we had two ships with minor damage from an exploding fuel ship. Want to trade jobs?"

"You kidding?" Sasha said, mouth full of sausage omelet. "All I do is aim and shoot—I'll leave that paper stuff to you."

Letty patted his shoulder. "I'll help, oh fearless unit commander. That's part of my job, when you get down to it. Hey, are we going to get promotions out of all this work?"

"You deserve it," Opi declared. "But who knows? If Valin could be an upper lieutenant, can we tell just how promotions get ponied out?"

"Frankly, I don't care," Cal said. "I don't plan on fighting in this navy forever. If we can destroy the invasion, I'm going home.

According to what Galigan told us, I should have enough money saved up to get Dad out of debt and start a new life." He grinned at Letty. "And maybe get married."

"That's right." Tony's face suddenly fell. "Crews will be splitting up, reforming, squadrons changing." He leaned back in his chair. "What now? If we split up, are any of you stayin'? 'Cause I am. Nothin' for me back on Earth. I've already proved I can help the Molethians. Why not stay?"

"I'm staying," Sasha said. "Same as you, Tony. Nothing back there. I'm here for life." He grinned. "That is, given what we're doing now, however long that may be."

Opi surprised the rest. "Same for me. I had a miserable life back home. My bitch stepmom planned to cheat me out of millions and maybe kill me. I discovered in the Shadow Warriors that I can make something of myself. I'm staying, as long as they'll have me."

Letty stood suddenly, turned toward their quarters. Over her shoulder, she said, "Sorry, Cal. I think I love you, too. But I'm staying. To hell with home! It made me sick every evening with the fights." She stopped ten steps away and turned. "Don't worry, Cal. We'll find somebody to take your place."

Opi's heart sank as she watched Cal stand suddenly and follow Letty's progress out of the mess hall. Finally, he turned angrily. "I'm not leaving as long as there's a fight to finish, dammit!"

Tony grinned at Sasha and Opi. "Didn't say you were, Cal. We're your team, right?"

Embarrassed, Cal resumed his seat.

Tony said casually to Sasha. "Love's hell, ain't it?"

Opi leaned forward to take his hand. "Sure hope not. I'd give you a kiss if you didn't smell so bad."

They left Cal at the table and went to clean up. Though sad

for Cal, Opi felt free and happy for the first time about her own life.

The hot shower felt wonderful.

Four days off. Time for relaxation, more research, and perhaps a little flirting with Tony. Opi felt exhilarated, released from months of bondage. Her steps were lighter, her eyes clear, her smiles at Tony as intimate as she dared in a barracks full of her fellow crewmen.

Breakfasted, clean, the first one up of her team up, she hit the library determined to scavenge any additional historical information. Although fairly certain that she had covered all the available records, she made herself do one last review.

Nobody bothered her. She suspected that Tony and Sasha were trying to set sleep records, while Letty and Cal struggled with his paperwork and, she suspected, their relationship.

After several hours study she sat back, fairly certain that every single Horde battle record had been codified and entered into her data structure. Now she had to plan a few test scenarios to be sure that Sasha's planning software worked properly. She had become increasingly confident in it, but when they returned to battle, she wanted to know that she could completely rely on it.

She commanded the computer to not only search for any

additional Horde battle data, but also historical data in general. No more battle records appeared, but after a moment a file title popped up: "History of Shadow Warrior Formation, Early Activities of the First Squadrons."

Intrigued, she opened the first of a series of files and began to read.

Shadow Warriors had existed as a military organization for more than fifty years. Prior to that, no single military organization targeting The Horde seemed to exist. Apparently Molethan and the rest of the planetary systems that formed their allies (which she saw referred to as the "Alliance") had all begun to develop specialized military services to fight The Horde at about the same time.

Puzzled, she dug deeper to check references in some Molethan historic files. She moved from chapter to chapter in pre-Shadow-Warrior history.

The more she dug, the bigger her eyes grew. Feverishly, she accessed more historical files, until a warning appeared on her monitor. Additional files were classified, and she needed clearances to access the information.

Frustrated, she finally ran to the squadron offices, knocking hesitantly on the door of the office of Captain Nhan's aide. A small sign on the jamb showed his name, Upper Lieutenant Prima.

He opened promptly. "Yes, Under Lieutenant ...?"

"I need your help to get some file permissions, sir. I am not familiar with the protocol for permission of classified material, it's just never come up. However, if possible, I need to access some files on Shadow Warrior history."

He didn't even ask why. "Captain Nhan made it clear that you were to have access to all historical battle files."

Opi hesitated. "These aren't really battle files; they're more historical documents pertaining to the formation of the Shadow

Warriors corps.

"Still no problem. Do you have the catalog names?"

She did. He stepped to his terminal and quickly input the identity of the records and a password.

"Done, Under Lieutenant. Anything else?"

"No, sir. Thank you for your help."

Quickly, Opi returned to the library. The now-open files were far more extensive than she had assumed, and she had to search for more than an hour to identify the thread that she had been following. Finally coming across the material she had been pursuing, she dug in, passing through file after file.

The further she progressed, the more rapt her attention. As she had first picked up the trail, just before she had gone to Upper Lieutenant Prima's office, she had been pretty sure that she was simply misinterpreting the history. But now deep into the narrative, she began to come to the reluctant conclusion that she understood all too well. At first puzzled and confused, her feelings went from uncertain to outraged to furious. Her mood began to sink, shifting from incredulous through depressed to demotivated. The powerful resolve for her new life began to drain away and the old Opi threatened to reassert herself.

She had nearly hit total emotional exhaustion when Cal steamed in at full speed. "Opi, we have to get to the ship ASAP!"

She hopped up, her mind rebounding into the routine of team discipline. "What, sir?"

"Your plan has worked. The entire Horde fleet is running out of fuel. They're losing discipline, reversing their direction and trying to flee for home. But they're effectively out of gas. Some can't even leap. The commanders of our three carrier ships in the area are mustering forces and calling for an all-out attack. We launch in one standard hour.

"Command has apparently put out a call for substantial additional forces. Captain Nhan said there might be as many as two thousand fighters on station in a day or two."

Gathering up her papers, the data tab, and her memory cubes, Opi headed for the barracks. As she changed from the shipboard working uniform into battle dress, she shoved the anger and depression that threatened her whole view of the war against The Horde into a deep niche in her mind.

She could brood later. Now they had to kill invaders.

79 CAL

Sasha emptied his guns, followed immediately by a micro-leap, as Cal moved them several light-seconds from the battle.

"Ammo expended, sir. Let's go get a refill."

"Tony, plot a course home."

The words had scarcely left Cal's mouth when Tony replied, "Course laid in, sir."

Cal hit comm and told his remaining fighters to return to carrier to refuel and reload. Then he leaped again, and the carrier ship came into view. Cal contacted Flight Deck Control, and their computer began to exchange information. Shortly, the behemoth ship swallowed Red Ten into its metal womb, and the remaining Red One warriors followed.

Red One had been reduced to six ships, units in all the squadrons experiencing serious losses. Like Cal's unit, all the fleet faced heavy odds as they challenged the entire Horde armada in head-on battle. Fleet losses were high, and the combined Shadow Warrior forces on the twelve carriers now supplying attack ships, originally nearly two thousand, now totaled only a bit over half that.

The new Horde attack fighters had become their biggest obstacle, fast and elusive, with heavier armament and better shields. True, Shadow Warrior forces destroyed half a dozen attack ships for every warrior ship destroyed, but though The Horde had only a limited number of the new ships, they still numbered a thousand or more.

Horde losses were extraordinary. The latest communique from their carrier commander indicated that more than 50,000 Horde ships had been destroyed, most of the rest stretched out in a disorganized retreat. The remaining ships had bolted en masse, frantically attempting to get back into Horde space. All of the fairly rare command ships had been destroyed.

Stranded ships now stretched out over forty light-years, as far toward The Horde home base as they could reach before fuel ran out.

Battles had been fierce at first, due to the overwhelming odds, and initial losses were the highest. Now, however, Shadow Warrior ships simply skipped light-minutes at a time, checking sensors, and tracking the remaining ships. With Horde ships now mostly stranded in that multi-light-year line, pitched battles had deteriorated into a search-and-destroy operation.

In hours, Red Ten was back in the forefront of the hunters, skipping along the line of retreat and destroying all the ships they encountered. The new, smaller attack ships were the most dangerous and effective, if they had fuel left. Fortunately, most had expended their reserves, and simply tried to return fire from stalled positions.

Cal had begun to think that he and his crews would never sleep again. Two days previously, they had snagged a couple hours' sack time, but now, command had decreed that every available ship should be assigned.

First, Cal knew, there was always a small danger of Horde reinforcements appearing, making their cleanup far more difficult. Secondly, they needed to make sure that not a single ship escaped. If the entire Horde force simply disappeared, Horde command would surely proceed slowly to respond, and perhaps decide to take a different direction entirely for their next invasion. Oh, there might be additional probing attacks, but The Horde planning function moved so glacially that certainly the Alliance would buy time with a total victory.

Even Tony had quit wisecracking. Cal couldn't remember when any of them had exchanged banter or a joke of any kind. Opi simply stared at the tactical display, face drawn and hair disarrayed. Sasha bent over the arms console, hands engulfed in the control gloves, and methodically emptied his ammunition stores. Letty conversed in low tones when necessary, reminding him at times of command protocol that he was still becoming accustomed to.

Cal lost track of time. They hunted, destroyed, ran out of ammunition, returned to the carrier base for replenishment, and returned to battle. Days passed, with only brief respites for sleep and showers, and they were back aboard Red Ten.

Then, twenty-three days into the campaign, their comms beeped for attention. "All forces stand down. Return to base at once. I say again, return to base at once."

Cal relayed the order.

Two hours later, Captain Nhan addressed his remaining warriors in the Red Squadron assembly area. Cal assumed the other squadrons were meeting as well.

Mounting the dais at the front of the conference room, Nhan managed a weary smile and told the gathered group, "Good news. Great news, in fact. The remaining Horde ships are stretched for light-years back toward their civilization center, a base we have not yet discovered, but we estimate to be at several thousand light-years away.

"Ships encountered in the last standard day have been stranded and adrift," he continued. "We destroyed them all, with no mercy. In fact, many chose self-destruct rather than death at our hands. Intelligence assesses that remaining ships are isolated and their crews will soon be dead."

Relieved murmurs rose from the assembled crews, and Nhan nodded acknowledgment.

"We are establishing a force of one hundred Shadow Warrior ships," he said, "comprised of units from a new command ship that has just been assigned to this mission. They will be positioned at the farthest waypoint we have discovered so far, to intercept any approaching ships. Intel believes we can strangle any aid they try to send out. Eventually, when none of their ships return, they will likely give up.

"Their planning is ponderous, so further actions by their civilization will probably be slow in emerging. As we believe at this time that no ships returned to their base, it is likely they will not attempt another invasion until they have analyzed the cause of their defeat. We believe we have put off another invasion for a year or more."

As he paused to a resounding cheer, he managed another smile and continued. "The three command ships that bore the bulk of this battle and decisive victory have completed our duty. We will return to Molethan, and another class of warrior trainees will soon be added. Those of you who fought in this historic battle are hereby released from your obligations."

This time the cheering and applause was thunderous. It went on for a long time, as Captain Nhan beamed. He finally gestured for quiet. As the din died away, he said. "I'm nearly done here, and then your warrior units can proceed to some very well-deserved R and R. There's just one more thing I wish to say.

"We have prevailed, the first decisive total victory in the history of the Shadow Warriors. But The Horde, though slow-moving and clumsy, will eventually recover. Our conflict is not over by any means. Though you are released from all obligations, we urge those of you who have interest to stay with the fleet, to help us build a new warrior class. We will need a bigger fleet to be ready for the next attack and new strategies and tactics to defeat an enemy that will always vastly outnumber us. Think it over. We'll call you in shortly to discuss your future.

"For now, our congratulations." Captain Nhan smiled once more. "Go enjoy your well-earned time off."

Another cheer rose, which eventually died as warriors began to slip away. As Nhan stepped down, many came forward to shake his hand.

Eventually, Red Ten made its way toward their quarters. As they strode through the passages, Opi caught up with Cal.

"We have to talk."

Cal arched his brows. "You and me, or the whole crew?"

She looked so desolate that he paused, searching her features. "Trouble with Tony? Not feeling well?"

"No. Something else." Opi's voice became a wail. "It's a sham! We've been lied to for months, for our whole tour of duty as Shadow Warriors! We're not fighting *with* the Molethians!

"We're fighting *for* them!"

80 LETTY

L etty had been appointed by Cal as spokesperson. He
wasn't sure he could hold his temper, and Opi remained
too upset to say more than a few words. Tony and Sasha
had displayed only the mildest reactions, but their faces showed
worry as well as weariness.

They had obtained a meeting with the carrier's commander
by virtue of their success and Opi's planning skills. Upper
Commander T'Kell, who headed up their carrier, no doubt
planned to shake their hands, issue compliments, and dismiss
them. The commander had no idea that he was about to be
blindsided.

Letty did something she never did. Well, almost never. She
shivered. She had volunteered to commit what amounted to
insubordination. She could only hope that Upper Commander
T'Kell wouldn't have them all thrown in the brig.

They assembled outside Raj's office, having invited him to go
with them, although Letty hadn't mentioned their concern. They
were to meet Captain Nhan in carrier headquarters.

Raj's expression showed his misgivings. "You aren't just

getting recognition here, something is up. You want to tell me what this is about?"

Cal shook his head. "Bear with us, sir. We have to do this our way."

Letty nodded, suppressing another shiver.

"Okay." Raj led the way, clearly unhappy.

A long walk, but by now Letty and her crew knew their way around most of the ship.

Stopping before a hatch not much different from the one at Squadron headquarters, Raj touched a button and the hatch cover slid aside. They entered a large, tan room with a relatively low overhead and a myriad of cubicles in which sat staff officers and workers attending to clerical tasks. A few of the workers were humans and droids, but most were Molethian.

This office area, Letty thought, *was no doubt the destination of all the electronic reports she and Cal had to produce.*

Raj led them down an aisle that bisected the area, toward a broad door leading into bigger and somewhat fancier offices. He turned down another aisle and stopped in front of a broad desk behind which sat an aide wearing the rank of Captain.

High-level stuff happens in here, Letty thought.

The aide smiled. "Go right in. Commander Nhan just arrived."

Raj led them through a door to the right of the reception desk. Cal brought up the rear.

Upper Commander T'Kell rose behind the desk as they entered, dressed in the amber-olive service-dress uniform they had rarely seen.

As the commander stepped from behind the massive desk to welcome them, Letty realized with a shock that Commander T'Kell was female. She had seen a few females on the training ship, but on reflection, she realized she had assumed there were no females in high-ranking command positions.

Commander T'Kell wore her rank, double pentagons, on small epaulets on her shoulders, the uniform tunic gleaming with gold buttons, although no decorations adorned its left breast. She stood quite tall, like Galigan, slender but not gaunt, with rather delicate features and skin of a lighter gray-tan Molethian shade.

She shook hands with all of them, reserving her warmest greetings for Cal and Opi. Letty had no problem with that.

Resuming her chair, the commander of the carrier beckoned them to several chairs arrayed before her desk. When everyone had seated themselves, she began.

"I wanted to personally thank you for your contribution to our historic victory. Never before have we attempted a pitched, head-on battle, nor have we ever fully defeated our adversaries. Thanks to Under Lieutenant Prefontaine's quite elegant strategy, I obtained support from seven additional carriers in Wings One and Eight. We went on to win an amazing and historic victory, learning important strategies that we had not considered before."

She singled out Cal with a smile. "Lieutenant, we owe you and your crew an enormous measure of thanks. There will be a ceremony later, and you will each be awarded the highest decoration we bestow, the Medal of Service.

"Upper Lieutenant Rajasekaran will also be awarded the Medal of Leadership, for his excellent training and for his early recognition that you were a particularly talented crew."

She let her gaze take in the rest of the crew. "As Captain Nhan has told you, you are released from your Shadow Warrior obligations. However, we earnestly request that you consider making a career for yourselves in our service. Your contributions to the Shadow Warriors can be significant, and with your help and leadership the Shadow Warriors can become an even more effective fighting organization."

T'Kell paused, surveying them each with large, inquisitive, dark eyes. "Do any of you have thoughts on this?"

As one, Raj and her crew swung toward Letty. *She asked for comments*, Letty thought. *Now or never.* She stood.

"Sir," she began, "we appreciate your kind words. However, we have some reservations about the organization itself and its leadership. We feel that we can go no further as participants in Shadow Warrior service until some key questions are answered.

"Let me make it clear that we are not being insubordinate. You have released us from service, and we expect that you will honor that release. We have served willingly and effectively. Several of us are inclined to continue as members of the Shadow Warriors, but we have a question that must be answered before we proceed. May I continue?"

T'Kell looked more curious than anything else. "Please do, Under Lieutenant." She smiled. "Of course, I do not guarantee that I can provide an answer."

Feeling freed, Letty launched into the kernel of her speech. "I understand. Sir, we have discovered in our research that Molethians do not participate in the fighting at all. When we were brought aboard our training ship, we were told we would fight alongside Molethians and other planetary civilizations against The Horde.

"We've discovered that is not true. We may in fact be fighting alongside other civilizations, though we've only seen one other race besides humans. But there are no Molethian Shadow Warriors in the fighting ranks. At least, not that we have seen.

"We want to know why, sir. Why don't you and your race fight along with us?"

"Holy cow!" Raj exploded. "Is that this big mystery you were worried about? I could have told you about that!" He came to a halt, embarrassed. "Sorry, Sir. May I speak?"

As he asked the question, Red Ten's crew regarded him in disbelief.

Before he could say anything else, Captain Nhan intervened.

"Raj, let me take this. I know it well." He glanced toward the ship captain.

"Go ahead," T'Kell told him. "If you have no objection, Upper Lieutenant?"

Raj nodded. "No, Sir."

When T'Kell dipped her head in agreement, Nhan spoke softly, as though he understood these were words T'Kell would not care to hear.

"Many millennia ago, the races of Molethan were as diverse as those on Earth. As on Earth, they were aggressive and combative, participating in war after war, desolating their planet and their societies."

"Just like all the countries on Earth!" Opi blurted, then blushed.

"Right you are, Opi. At last, in a planet-wide agreement, they decided to genetically alter their descendants to make conflict less likely.

"As time went on, new generations were predisposed to less conflict and greater harmony. Their races gradually melded into one, which retained the genetic predisposition to non-violence. Not that they absolutely cannot fight, but most find it difficult, distasteful, and personally staining to engage in any kind of conflict.

"Using the droids you have seen, they are able to maintain order, and their meetings with other worlds' races were friendly and productive. They joined many civilizations in a peaceful series of alliances.

"Then came The Horde."

"And they don't negotiate," Cal muttered. He glanced at Commander T'Kell. "Sorry, sir. But from what Captain Nhan says, encountering The Horde is about the worst thing that could happen to a race devoted to pacifism."

Her smile was more nearly a grimace. "And you would be right, Lieutenant." She glanced at Nhan, and he continued.

"The allied civilizations came together to form the Alliance, and at the same time, Molethan founded the Shadow Warriors, devoted to delaying or deflecting Horde incursions.

"What could Molethians do? Few were inclined to fight, and yet they must become involved, as their civilization was clearly at stake. They determined that their best role would be manufacturing war materiel, conducting training, and seeking out soldiers among threatened races. These tasks they undertook, and they have done them well.

"Let me be clear: some Molethians do in fact fight. That is not widely publicized, however, as many Molethians feel it is shameful. But we *do* have Warriors from Molethan, and Upper Commander T'Kell is one. She has flown over a hundred combat sorties, as has your training commander Alitan.

"The first Shadow Warrior forces were largely Molethian because they discovered robotic fighters to be inferior to those whose intellect was enhanced by their cleverly devised implants. The practice of 'borrowing' young fighters from threatened civilizations was developed later on. As the force has expanded, more of our combat-ready units are from the other civilizations in the Alliance.

"So Molethians have served as they could, while we of the other races and planets in peril have provided a majority of soldiers for actual combat. Shadow Warriors are regularly recruited from allied races which do not share the Molethians' antipathy toward violence.

"However, the decision was made, in regard to civilizations that do not yet possess leap drive but are in the path of invading Horde forces, to impress candidates into service. The Molethians always choose those who suffer particularly heavy oppression or discomfort in their native situations.

"Molethians do their part in this ongoing war by providing a majority of the combat ships and resources and performing all the training of Shadow Warrior cadets. Their dearest desire is that every soldier survive to benefit from the fruits of victory."

"So that's why!" Opi blurted, then showed embarrassment again.

"Explain," Nhan requested.

"Sir, when I first began to review the battle data in the library," Opi said, "I discovered excellent, detailed histories, a chronology that allowed me to study a great deal about Horde strategies, tactics, and favored formations. But nothing had ever been done with that wonderful information. No studies, no historical perspectives, no battle analyses.

"Now I know why. Because Molethians in general don't fight," she acknowledged the commander with a nod, "you didn't see the purpose in such a study. But we humans, we're aggressive, combative by nature. To me, it was an obvious thing to start building."

T'Kell's face brightened. "You are correct, Under-Lieutenant. That would be beyond most of my race. Nor did any of our allies consider it. We have you to thank for your compendium of strategies and the analytical tool.

"Let me say that we did not lie to you. We told you that you had been appropriated for temporary duty. We trained you exceptionally well, using a number of human trainers like the upper lieutenant here." She gestured at Raj. "We simply withheld one fact. At that time, you did not have a need to know our full history. Now you do.

"When Upper Lieutenant Rajasekaran received this information, which would have been provided to you upon your choice to stay in the Shadow Warrior force, he embraced our goals and our offered friendship. Now it is up to you, Under

Lieutenant. You have served well and proudly, and your contribution will make Shadow Warriors more effective in the future.

"If you choose to retire, to return to Earth with the payment you have earned, go with our blessing. If you choose to continue as a member of our proud forces, we will welcome you. I can assure you that you have a fine future in our military organization and a challenging and satisfying life here, if you wish to remain."

T'Kell arose, causing the rest to stand as well. "I hope our honesty in this instance will mitigate any concerns you have. I await your decisions." She passed her gaze over them all. "Once again, thank you for your contribution to our war effort. Now, you are dismissed."

81 CAL

W hat seemed to be a completely different house and front porch greeted Cal after more than six months away. Fresh paint adorned the walls, while a new roof sat atop the eaves. The lawn had been mowed, the bushes that stood alongside the front walls trimmed. The house presented a totally new appearance from the one Cal remembered on the day he had disappeared.

Dropped off before dawn in a deserted park nearby, Cal had walked the two miles to his home. Now, as the sun peered over the line of roofs to the east, he turned up the front walk.

Crepe myrtles to left and right still glowed with bright pink flowers, though fall had settled across the neighborhood. Likewise trimmed, they reflected the care and thoroughness which Cal's father had shown prior to his mother's death. When Cal had been taken in early spring, the house had seemed more like a deserted hulk than the fresh, neat dwelling that appeared as he turned into the front walk.

Does Dad still live here? The house looked for all the world as though his father were gone and someone else had taken possession, repainting and renewing the exterior and carefully bringing the yard back to robust health.

Climbing the four steps to the porch, he crossed it and rang the doorbell. Through the screen he saw a new coat of varnish on the door.

It opened to reveal his father, gray hair neatly combed and body well-dressed in slacks and a long-sleeved twill shirt.

"Yes, can I ... Cal?"

In a second Dad had flung open the door and they were embracing. No smell of stale beer or last night's vomit tainted him; the aroma in Cal's nostrils was a light, pleasant after-shave.

Finally, his father released him, face incredulous. "Son, where have you been?"

Cal's wry smile hid a thousand stories that he might someday tell his dad, but not quite yet. "Can't say much, Dad. I can tell you that I have joined a ... a classified governmental service, and that I have a very rewarding position."

"Government?" He beckoned Cal eagerly inside. "I didn't think they took anyone but college graduates. You're only sixteen."

"Seventeen now. And yes, it's a bit unusual. But I guarantee you that it's legitimate, and that it's important. They only recruit young, highly-qualified candidates."

Eventually they sat on the sofa. His father's story all came out in a rush. How he had discovered Cal was missing, how he had sobered up and searched frantically for days, assuming that his drunken behavior had driven Cal away, how he had resolved to make a home for Cal, should he ever return. And he had.

"I have a good job now, one that pays well, using my engineering abilities. And ... I even have a girlfriend. I hope you don't mind."

"Mind? Of course not! I'm so glad ..." Cal started to say,

"... you've gotten your life together." Instead, he said, "... you're okay, and that things are working out."

"Can you stay for a while?"

"Just a short time. Then duty calls, I'm afraid. But I'll be back as I have time."

He stayed three days, and it was like old times.

But then his new life beckoned, a life full of conflict, and danger, but one he could no longer resist. One that had not only a sense of belonging, but also a bushy-haired beauty with dark, penetrating eyes, someone with whom he longed to spend the rest of his life. One that included a team of friends that he could not let down.

And just as much, he wanted to continue the fight, to make certain that The Horde would never threaten Earth or the civilizations of the Alliance, including Molethan. He waited expectantly in his father's back yard the next evening as a shuttle from the carrier landed silently and softly on the lawn.

He hugged his father as the shuttle hatch opened, watching as his father looked on, goggle-eyed, at the small spaceship that would return him to friends and duty. No matter that Dad saw—Cal had a hunch that before long, everyone on Earth would be let in on the secret.

He climbed aboard and went back to his new life.

ABOUT THE AUTHOR

Educated in electrical engineering, Nathan worked as an engineer and engineering manager, primarily at Texas Instruments, before joining the University of Texas at Dallas as a teacher. He taught full-time for 16 years and continues to teach half-time.

He is married to Faye Lynn King, PhD, herself a long-time professor of Social Science in Dallas. She is Nathan's copy editor, specializing in grammar and preventing the author from his most frequent bad habit of using too many commas. He has three daughters, the youngest of which, Sharon, is also an author.

Nathan began writing seriously in 2012 and has attended seven Superstars Writing Seminars. He has a story in the *Purple Unicorn Anthology* with daughter Sharon, and a short story sale to Mike Resnick's *Galaxy's Edge*. *Shadow Warriors*, the first of a young adult science fiction series, is his first book sale. He and Sharon will soon release an anthology of SF stories, *To the Stars*.

Nathan's background is in computer engineering, and he still conducts a sophomore course in digital circuits, assembly language programming, and fundamentals of computer architecture. His teaching awards include two as Best Teacher in electrical and computer engineering and a top teaching citation from the university.

In his "spare" time, he loves weight lifting, hiking in Rocky Mountain National Park in Colorado, and solving crossword puzzles with Faye Lynn.

IF YOU LIKED ...

SHADOW WARRIORS, YOU MIGHT ALSO ENJOY:

Taylor's Ark
by Jody Lynn Nye

Solar Singularity
by Peter J. Wacks, Guy Anthony De Marco, Josh Vogt

Typhoon Time
by Ron Friedman

OTHER WORDFIRE PRESS TITLES BY NATHAN DODGE

One Horn to Rule Them All

Our list of other WordFire Press authors and titles is always growing. To find out more and to see our selection of titles, visit us at:
wordfirepress.com